"WE WILL FI[...]

Danielle's throat tightened.

"South," said Snow. "Charlotte fled south."

"We're on the northern edge of an island nation," Talia said. "Do you think you could narrow it down a tad?"

"I can't. She's hidden from the mirror, the same as Armand."

Danielle cleared her throat. "My father's house is south of here."

Talia shook her head. "Charlotte knows we'll be hunting her. To hide in such an obvious place would be the height of stupidity."

Danielle folded her arms. "Charlotte let her mother cut off part of her heel because she believed that would be enough to convince Armand she was me."

"Good point." Talia snorted. "Come on, Snow. Let's go visit the de Glas house."

"I'm going too," said Danielle.

"Charlotte already tried to murder you once today," said Talia.

"I lived with Charlotte and Stacia for most of my life," said Danielle. "I know them. I can help."

Talia turned to the queen. "Bea, I'll have my hands full keeping this one out of trouble." She jerked a thumb at Snow, who rolled her eyes. "I can't be a nursemaid to both."

Danielle folded her arms. "Forgive me, Your Majesty, but your son is also my husband. My own stepsister may have taken him. The question isn't whether or not I'm going after her, it's whether or not these two are coming with me. . . ."

THE STEPSISTER SCHEME

Jim C. Hines

DAW BOOKS, INC.
DONALD A. WOLLHEIM, FOUNDER
375 Hudson Street, New York, NY 10014

ELIZABETH R. WOLLHEIM
SHEILA E. GILBERT
PUBLISHERS
www.dawbooks.com

First Printing, January 2009
1 2 3 4 5 6 7 8 9

DAW TRADEMARK REGISTERED
U.S. PAT. AND TM. OFF. AND FOREIGN COUNTRIES
—MARCA REGISTRADA
HECHO EN U.S.A.

PRINTED IN THE U.S.A.

For Skylar

CHAPTER I

❄

DANIELLE WHITESHORE, FORMERLY Danielle de Glas, would never be a proper princess. Not if the title required her to actually remember so many trifling details. She hadn't even learned the proper forms of address for human politicians, and now her tutor expected her to memorize *The Mortal's Guide to Faerie Courtesy: Navigating the Eightfold Path of Fey Politics* by the end of the week?

True, it was mostly her own fault. After her wedding, the king's steward had presented her with a trunk full of scrolls and books, "To study during your tour of Lorindar."

For three months that trunk had gathered dust while she and Prince Armand traveled the kingdom. She had tried to study, but there was so much to see. The old Coastal Highway to Colwich, with the ocean to one side and snow-painted oaks on the other. The bridge to Emrildale, built centuries ago by dwarves without mortar of any sort. Only the weight of the intercut stones held the great arches aloft. Every day brought new wonders.

With Armand's help, Danielle had learned enough to avoid embarrassing herself as she was introduced to various lords and ladies. She still couldn't remember the difference between a viscount and a baron, but so long as her mistakes were minor, nobody dared to complain.

As for the nights . . . her cheeks grew warm. Suffice it to say, she had spent very little time studying *books*. The extra three days they spent snowed in at South Haven had been particularly educational.

Still smiling at the memory, Danielle picked up another book from the bedside table. She opened to a random page and read:

> *Indulge not overmuch*
> *in wine or beer.*
> *Pick not thy nose,*
> *scratch not thy rear,*
> *and all shall say*
> *"A lady sits here."*

Danielle slammed the book shut and tossed it after the first. Much more of this, and she would be ready to go back to cleaning floors and cooking meals for her stepsisters.

She stood and rubbed her eyes. The polished black-and-white tiles were cool beneath her feet. The breeze from the open window carried the damp, salty taste of the ocean.

Her nose wrinkled. The breeze also brought the faint smell of manure from the gardens below.

Danielle walked to the window and knelt on a padded bench which had been embroidered with some royal crest or another. This one had a blue unicorn and a green bird that looked like a bloated chicken.

She pushed open the window, running her fingers over the rippled panes of glass. Tiny specks marred the glass: iron filings scattered into the mix when the panes were first formed. Pixie glass was supposed to protect a room from fairy magic, but in truth, iron only affected the weakest of curses. Still, enough people wanted such protection to keep Danielle's father in business for a good many years.

She smiled, remembering one of her father's last pieces, a window he had done for Duke Rokan of Little Hill. Mere filings sprinkled like pepper in the glass weren't enough for Rokan. For two weeks Danielle's father had worked to align dozens of tiny iron crosses, each one spaced evenly over the glass. A second layer of glass was then baked over the first.

Danielle had been only eight years old, but she remembered the finished window so clearly she could almost reach out and touch it. Not a single bubble or ripple had marred the glass. At a casual glance, the crosses appeared to float in midair within the frame.

A loud cooing sound made her smile. She leaned out, twisting her head to see several pigeons and one old dove perched on the green copper gutters which ran the length of Whiteshore Castle. The dove fluttered down to land on the sill beside her arm.

Danielle laughed. "I'm sorry, I've nothing to give you. You've already feasted on leftover muffins, cookies, and that bit of jam sandwich I smuggled up yesterday. If I feed you any more, you'll be too fat to fly."

The dove opened his mouth and cooed again, clearly unconcerned by such eventualities.

"Your Highness?"

Danielle jumped, and the dove fluttered his wings in annoyance.

A servingwoman stood in the doorway, a wooden tray in one hand. A trencher of bread sat in the middle, filled with glazed cherries and strawberries. A bronze cup stood beside it.

"Good morning, Talia."

The morning sun shone on her brown skin. Her voice was clear and smooth, almost musical. Only the slightest accent, an emphasis on the longer vowel sounds, distinguished her words from a native Islander. Danielle guessed her to be from the Arathean Deserts to the south, but Talia had never responded to Danielle's overtures.

Danielle still couldn't remember half of the nobles who visited each day, but she knew the names of every servant in the palace. Some were uncomfortable with the princess' familiarity, while others had started to relax in her presence.

Talia fit neither category. Strong and slender, she appeared only a little older than Danielle's eighteen years, yet something in her bearing made Danielle feel like a child. She bowed her head slightly, every movement proper, but her dark eyes met Danielle's without flinching. "I thought you might appreciate a snack."

On the windowsill, the dove cooed and hopped closer. Danielle glared in mock annoyance. "Did you arrange this?"

"Highness?" Talia was staring at the dove, clearly skeptical of a princess who chatted with the birds.

"Thank you for the food," said Danielle. "I appreciate your thoughtfulness."

Talia nodded and brought the tray around the bed. With her free hand, she stacked Danielle's books to one side of the bedside table, then set down the tray, all so smoothly the wine in the cup barely even rippled.

The movement pulled back Talia's sleeves, revealing pale scars across her right forearm. Talia noticed Danielle's gaze, but didn't bother to adjust her shirt. Instead, she moved to the bed, straightening the covers and returning *The Mortal's Guide to Faerie Courtesy* to the stack on the table.

"Don't worry about that," Danielle said. "I can—"

"You are princess of Lorindar, Your Highness," said Talia. "Not some ash-covered slave girl from the city."

Danielle flushed and turned away. Everyone in the

palace knew of her past, though nobody would speak of it to her face. Within days of the winter ball, rumors had spread through the city, growing wilder with every retelling: she had snuck from her house to attend the ball—no, she had stolen a carriage—no, she had ridden within an enchanted pumpkin, drawn by giant mice!

Danielle had nearly choked when she heard that last variant.

She grabbed the bread and tore off a hunk of crust, which she tossed to the window. The dove fluttered to catch it before it hit the ground. Bread dangling from his beak, the dove flew up to perch upon a tapestry to the left of the window. Crumbs fell past the old weaving, a faded depiction of the Midsummer War. The tiny stitching showed fairies and their enchanted servants standing at the edge of a great crevasse as armored knights and human wizards drove them back.

An old wine stain made a skirmish between human cavalry and a pair of griffins appear even bloodier. Danielle ran a finger over the stain. White wine should bleach out the red, and would be far less noticeable. She turned to ask for a bottle of white wine, then bit her lip. Talia was right. She was no longer a servant. But old habits were hard to break.

"The birds, you train them?" asked Talia.

"Not exactly." Danielle grabbed another piece of bread for the dove, wondering how she could explain without convincing yet another servant that their new princess was mad. This was the first time Talia had spoken to her, beyond the requirements of her duties. "You usually tend to the queen."

A brief nod as Talia straightened the candleholders mounted to either side of the window. Each was hand-carved oak, shaped to resemble a dragon. The dragon's tail held the candles, while a mirror clutched in its claws reflected the light back into the room.

"Do you have family here at the palace?" Danielle asked, trying again.

"No."

Silence stretched between them, until a shout from the hallway made Danielle jump.

"I wish to see my stepsister at once!"

Danielle's throat tightened as Charlotte barged through the door, escorted by two guardsmen. It was nearly four months since the wedding, and the sight of her elder stepsister was still almost enough to make her bow her head. Almost.

"You can go," Danielle said to the guards.

They hesitated, then bowed and backed away.

"Are you sure, Highness?" Talia asked.

"She's still my sister." Danielle forced herself to meet Charlotte's angry glare. Small, mostly-healed scabs marred the beautiful porcelain of her cheeks. Charlotte was taller than Danielle, her limbs graceful and slender. She wore a heavy blue cloak with gold trim, which accented her brown curls. Ribbons of silver and gold were braided through her hair.

Charlotte's neck muscles tightened as she studied Danielle in turn, taking in the emerald gown, the silver comb in her hair, the simple ruby bracelet one of her ladies-in-waiting had insisted she wear, saying it highlighted her eyes. Danielle fought to keep from fidgeting. She was still uncomfortable with the luxury of palace life, but she wasn't about to let Charlotte see that discomfort.

This wasn't the first time Charlotte had visited the palace, using her relationship with the princess to try to ingratiate herself to various nobles. She had never before come to Danielle's chambers, though.

The months had been unkind to Danielle's stepsister. Charlotte's mother had groomed her for a life of luxury, leaving her woefully unprepared to run the household that had once belonged to Danielle's father.

Charlotte's face seemed paler than Danielle remembered, and her eyes were shadowed and bloodshot.

Talia stepped around the bed, putting herself between Danielle and Charlotte. "Would the lady like something to eat or drink?" she asked.

"I'm not here to dine," Charlotte snapped. "I'm here to—" Her voice rose to a squeak as she spotted the dove perched on the tapestry. She backed away until she bumped the door, her wide eyes never leaving the bird. "Get that foul beast from my sight at once!"

The dove puffed out his feathers and flapped his wings, dropping the remainder of the crust to the floor. Charlotte screamed. She raised her hands to protect her face, just as she had done at Danielle's wedding.

Danielle flinched at the memory. She remembered the hateful glares of her stepsisters, and the cool, calculating look in her stepmother's eyes as she watched Danielle and her new husband pass through the crowd of well-wishers. She had tightened her fingers on Armand's arm, telling herself she would not let them ruin this day. This was her day. Hers and Armand's. Finally, she was *free*.

Despite everything, her eyes had begun to water. It should have been her mother standing there, not her stepmother. Her father, not Charlotte and Stacia.

"It will never last," her stepmother had said, loud enough for Danielle to hear. "As if a prince could be happy with such a common girl."

Charlotte and Stacia had laughed, as did a few others in the crowd. The prince's arm tensed. But before he could speak, a group of doves swooped down, wings fluttering as they clawed and pecked at Danielle's stepmother. Charlotte and Stacia screamed. Stacia tried to club the birds with her hands, but her efforts only drew the birds' wrath to herself and her

sister. Only when Danielle begged the birds to stop
did they finally fly away, leaving her stepmother blind
and bloodied.

Given the events of that day, Danielle could understand Charlotte's reaction. She turned to address the
dove. "Go," she said. "I'll save some food for you
and your friends."

Obediently, the dove hopped from the tapestry and
swooped out the window. Charlotte shoved past Danielle, pulling the window shut so hard one of the panes
cracked. Her hands shook as she fastened the latch.

"He wouldn't have hurt you," Danielle said.

Charlotte whirled. Pointing to the scabs on her face,
she said, "Your filthy birds disfigured me for life. They
murdered my mother. They would have killed me as
well, if we hadn't fought them off."

"They didn't murder—"

"Shut up." Charlotte pulled her cloak tighter, like
a child trying to protect herself from the cold. "They
blinded her. For seven days she lay in bed as the
wounds spread through her blood." She laughed, a
high-pitched sound that bordered on madness. "Re-
leasing doves at a wedding is supposed to be a sign
of prosperity. Tell me, Princess, what does it portend
when the doves try to *eat the guests?*"

"They were confused and scared," Danielle said.

"They swarmed over us." Charlotte swiped the wine
cup Talia had brought and drained it in one motion.
"Nobody else received so much as a scratch."

Danielle shook her head. She was certain she hadn't
ordered the birds to attack her stepmother and stepsisters. Not once in all the years since her father's death
had she struck back at her tormenters. Whatever fluke
had caused the birds to attack, Danielle was positive
she hadn't been the cause.

Almost positive.

Charlotte tossed the cup to the floor and glared at

Talia. "Haven't you better things to do? I wish to speak to my stepsister about my inheritance, and I'll not have a servant lurking about, gathering bits of gossip like a dog snatching scraps from her master's table."

Charlotte used to speak to Danielle in that same, dismissive tone. But Danielle had never met that disdainful glare with such a cold, tight smile. Talia stooped to retrieve the cup, using the hem of her apron to blot up the spilled wine. Her eyes never left Charlotte's face.

"I would be happy to escort you to the chancellor's office," Talia said. "Father Isaac is highly knowledgeable about such matters, and he—"

"I see," Charlotte said. "Now that you've married into royalty, you hope to use your newfound friends to bully my sister and me, to rob us of everything we have left."

"That's absurd," said Danielle, already weary. "Thank you, Talia. I'll ring if we need anything further."

Talia hesitated, then turned to go.

The instant the door closed, Charlotte whirled on Danielle. "You murdered my mother, *Your Highness*." She still moved with a faint limp, courtesy of that night when Prince Armand had arrived at the house bearing Danielle's lost slipper.

Danielle took a deep breath. "Is that why you've come? To hurl your grief and anger at my feet like the soiled linens you used to fling on my floor? I'm sorry about your mother, Charlotte. I asked the king and queen to provide healers, but—"

"My sister and I want *nothing* from you," said Charlotte, stepping so close that spit sprayed Danielle's face. From the smell, Charlotte had imbibed far more than a single cup of wine today. "Unless you've the power to raise the dead?"

Danielle took a discreet step back. "Then why are you here? Your mother left everything to you and Stacia. My father's home, my mother's garden, all of it belongs to you now. What more do you want from me?"

Charlotte smiled. Her free hand unfastened the bronze clasp at her neck, and her cloak slid to the floor. Beneath, Charlotte wore peasant's garb: a loose shirt of white linen, and a rough brown skirt. Normally, strings of gold or jewels would have adorned her long neck. Today she wore only a leather necklace threaded through a smooth blue stone. A long hunting knife hung from a rope belt. Her feet were bare, aside from a soiled bandage on her right foot. Charlotte's own mother had cut away part of her heel in a deranged attempt to fit Charlotte's foot to Danielle's discarded slipper.

"I'm here to do what my mother should have done," Charlotte whispered. Eyes wide, she yanked the knife from its sheath.

Danielle backed toward the wall. The knife alone wasn't enough to frighten her. She couldn't count the number of times Charlotte had threatened to throw Danielle into the fireplace, or bury her in the garden, or drag her down to the canals and drown her like an unwanted kitten. But those clothes . . . Charlotte would have sooner died than be seen in such poor fashion. She had always been her mother's fancy doll, garbed in the most expensive dresses and jewelry, even as Danielle shivered in ash-stained rags.

"You like it?" Charlotte asked, stroking her necklace. She waved a hand at the door. The iron bolt slid into place.

"How did you do that?" Danielle asked.

The blade caught the sunlight as Charlotte approached. "You think you're the only one with secrets? I know all about you, little Cinderwench. How your dead mother enchanted the prince, making him choose you over me. How she showered you with silver and gold for the ball. How she helped you scar my face and murder my mother."

Danielle reached the bedside table. Never taking her eyes from Charlotte, she reached down until her fingers brushed the edge of the tray Talia had left.

"I tried to help you and Stacia," Danielle said. "Armand wanted you imprisoned for your deceptions. I'm the one who urged mercy. I allowed your mother's will to stand uncontested, rather than fighting you for my father's home. I gave you the chance to start your own lives."

"The life I wanted, the life I was promised, is the one you took from me," Charlotte said. "You should thank me, *Princess*. Soon you'll be with your beloved mother."

"At least I'll be safe from yours," Danielle snapped.

Charlotte's eyes widened.

Danielle swung the tray with both hands, scattering the remnants of her meal across the room. As a weapon, the wooden platter was slow and awkward. Charlotte twisted, catching the blow on her left shoulder. She grabbed the other side of the tray, then sliced her knife at Danielle's arm.

Danielle released the tray. The knife missed, and Charlotte stumbled back. She threw the tray to the floor and advanced again.

"Help me, friends," Danielle whispered. She picked up *The Tome of Noble Manners* and held it in front of her body. It was no shield, but given the wordiness of the author, the book should be able to stop a knife.

Charlotte lunged. Danielle moved the book, catching the knife near the corner. The steel barely penetrated the heavy cover, but the force behind the blow

was enough to knock Danielle into the desk. Other
books clattered to the floor. The inkwell fell and
shattered.

Perhaps it was madness, but as the book was torn
from Danielle's hand, her only thought was how difficult it would be to clean the ink from the tile grout.

The bedroom door rattled in its frame, but there
was no way to unlock the bolt from the outside.

Charlotte reached for Danielle's throat, and the
window exploded inward. Shards of glass tinkled to
the floor as the old dove led a pair of pigeons into the
room. Charlotte screamed and spun, slashing wildly.

Danielle ripped one of the pillows from the bed and
flung it over Charlotte's arm, tangling the knife. When
Charlotte turned, Danielle punched her in the nose.
Charlotte stumbled back. Danielle grabbed the stool
and raised it overhead.

Before Danielle could strike, Charlotte touched her
necklace and shouted, "No!"

The stool shattered. Charred wood and splinters
rained down around Danielle. Charlotte blinked, looking almost as shocked as Danielle felt.

A pigeon caught Charlotte's hair in his feet and
tugged. Another pecked her ear. She waved the knife
about so frantically she almost cut her own face, but
it was enough to drive the birds back.

Danielle raced toward the bed, but her foot slipped
on the books, and she fell hard. She rolled away from
Charlotte, broken glass and wood pricking at her back.
One of the pigeons dove for Charlotte's face, but a
lucky swing of the knife sent him tumbling against the
bed, blood dripping from his wing.

"Drop the knife." Talia's voice was cool and firm,
more commanding than any servant. She stood in the
doorway, holding one of the oversized crossbows normally carried by the palace guards. Made of polished

black wood with gleaming brass trim, it should have
been more than enough to compel obedience. Danielle
had no idea how Talia had gotten through the door,
but her timing was divine.

"Wait," Charlotte cried.

"No." Talia pulled the trigger. A steel-tipped bolt
buzzed through the air.

At the same time, the dove lurched toward Charlotte, as if an invisible hand had struck him from the
side. The bolt tore into the dove's chest. He slammed
into Charlotte, leaving a bloody smear on her shirt,
then dropped to the ground. Tiny legs twitched slowly.

Talia didn't hesitate. She threw the crossbow at
Charlotte's face, bloodying her nose and knocking her
into the wall. Talia slipped a toe under the tray Danielle had thrown. A flick of her foot brought the edge
of the tray into her hand. Talia spun, moving like a
dancer as she hurled the tray into Charlotte's forearm.
Charlotte's knife clattered away.

Talia strode across the room. "Stay down, Princess."

Charlotte backed toward the broken window. She
closed her eyes, and her lips moved as if in prayer.
An instant later, the window frame cracked and fell
away, taking the remains of the glass.

Talia leaped, but Charlotte was faster, pulling herself through the opening even as Talia's fingers
brushed her ankle.

"Damn." Talia drew back from the window. "She
didn't even sprain an ankle."

Danielle turned to check on the dove, who lay in a
pool of blood. One look was enough to tell her the
bird was dead. The tip of the crossbow bolt protruded
from the dove's back, propping him to one side. She
brushed a finger over the soft white feathers of his
head, blinking back tears.

One of the pigeons had also been injured. He

dragged his wing along the floor as he approached. Danielle scooped him gently into her hands. "He's still bleeding."

Halfway to the door, Talia stopped to stare. "He's a pigeon."

"They saved my life."

Talia shook her head. "I saved your life. They distracted your stepsister long enough for me to get here."

Danielle looked at the open door. "How did you—"

"No time. Stay here with your birds, Princess. The guards will be here very soon." She slammed the door behind her when she left.

Danielle fought to keep from shaking as she climbed to her feet and peered out the window. Far below, Charlotte sprinted across the courtyard. She had dropped three stories from Danielle's window, but she ran with only the slightest limp.

Danielle inspected the pigeon's wing. The bleeding didn't look too serious, but she still fought the urge to seek out the king's surgeon for help. Instead, she set him gently on the middle of the bed. For most of her life, her stepsisters and stepmother had kept her locked away. She refused to let Charlotte confine her now.

"Thank you, my friend," she whispered. "I'll be back as soon as I can." Wiping her face, she hurried out the door after Talia.

Beams of golden sunlight illuminated the corridor as Danielle raced toward the stairs. Startled guardsmen lurched out of her way. One called out to her, but she ignored him.

Up ahead, Talia had already disappeared down the staircase. Danielle grabbed the folds of her gown with her free hand and ran faster.

By the time she reached the courtyard, Danielle's

heart was pounding in her chest and she had begun to sweat. Far ahead, Talia whirled, one hand slipping up her sleeve. Her expression changed to annoyance when she recognized Danielle.

"I told you to wait, Princess," Talia said, in a tone nobody had dared use to Danielle's face since the wedding.

"She's my stepsister," said Danielle, still running. "And I won't have your death on my conscience. Go and tell the guards what's happened."

Talia ran alongside Danielle. "I sent the guards to watch *you*. Which they've obviously failed to do."

Neither woman slowed. Danielle could see Charlotte pulling herself up on to the roof of the chapel. How she had climbed the stone walls, Danielle had no idea. Probably the same way she had survived the drop from Danielle's bedchamber.

Talia pulled ahead of Danielle as she sprinted through the garden, stooping once or twice to snatch something from the soil and earning a curse from one of the gardeners. Danielle did her best to keep up.

The sun illuminated Charlotte's form as she climbed to the peak of the chapel roof. Arms outstretched for balance, Charlotte walked toward the steeple.

By now, several people had emerged from the chapel to point and stare. Two guardsmen rushed from the northwest tower.

At the top of the steeple, a wooden cross decorated with silver towered over the chapel. The inlaid metal still gleamed, despite being almost twenty years old. Charlotte stretched one hand toward the cross. Danielle wasn't sure what she hoped to accomplish. If she could pull herself up, she might be able to jump to the north wall of the castle, but the guards were already closing in. She would be trapped.

Talia drew back one arm and hurled a round, green object toward Charlotte. Danielle saw another in

Talia's left hand, and recognized it as an unripe tomato. The first tomato caught Charlotte on the side of the head.

Charlotte's hand slipped from the cross. Her arms whirled as she tried to regain her balance. She started to fall, then leaped.

"Charlotte!" Danielle shouted.

Crenellated stonework rose to shoulder height on either side of the walkway atop the wall, making the jump even more difficult. Charlotte started to fall, and then it was as if the air itself gathered to lift her. Wind whipped her hair as she drew up her legs to land neatly in one of the gaps between the stones. She hopped down onto the walkway and turned back and forth. To Danielle's eye, she appeared frightened.

"Easy there, girl," shouted one of the guards.

Charlotte turned away, staring out at the sea below.

Another guard approached from the northeast tower. "Nothing there but a long drop and a messy death on the rocks at the bottom of the cliff, lass."

Danielle reached Talia in time to hear her mutter, "Sounds good to me." Talia raised her second tomato.

"Wait." Raising her voice, Danielle called out, "Charlotte, they'll kill you if you try to fight."

Charlotte began to laugh. She wiped her face on her sleeve, then spread her arms. "Let them. It doesn't matter. Without your precious prince, you'll never be anything but a filthy little serving wench."

Danielle's skin tingled, the hair on her neck responding to the barely-concealed edge of gloating in Charlotte's voice. She glanced at Talia, who was watching Charlotte with the same intensity as a cat preparing to pounce.

"Order her taken alive," Talia whispered.

"What?" Danielle stared, confused.

"The guards won't take orders from a servant,"

Talia said through clenched teeth. "Do not let her escape."

"There's nowhere for her to . . ." Danielle trailed off as she remembered Charlotte's leap from the window, and the way she had practically flown from the chapel roof to the top of the wall. She raised her voice. "Guards, I need that woman taken alive!"

One of the guards raised his crossbow while the others closed in. Charlotte smiled and fingered her necklace.

"Be careful," Danielle yelled. She knew that smile. "That stone around her neck, it's magical!"

Talia swore and threw her last tomato. It flew straight and true, catching Charlotte on the ear and knocking her to the far side of the wall. Charlotte shrieked in rage, then pointed toward the approaching guards.

The guard with the crossbow stumbled. His weapon twisted in his hands, coming around to point at Danielle.

A sharp blow to the back of the knees knocked Danielle down. A heartbeat later, Talia's foot slammed into Danielle's shoulder, flattening her against the earth. The crossbow bolt thumped into the ground where Danielle had stood. She looked up, barely able to see Charlotte as she climbed onto the outer edge of the wall. The guards ran toward her. One nearly grabbed her arm, and then Charlotte leaped away.

Danielle got to her feet and ran for the nearest stairway, a sickening feeling in her gut. She wanted to throw up, but she forced herself to keep going. Up through the tower, through the guardroom, and out onto the wall.

Damp, salty wind made her stagger as she stepped onto the wall. The guards crowded around the point where Charlotte had jumped, all save the one who had fired his crossbow at Danielle. He was still staring at his weapon, his bearded face white.

He jerked to attention when he saw Danielle. "Your Highness, I . . ." He blinked, then flung the crossbow away like its touch burned his hands. "I'm sorry, I didn't—"

"I know," said Danielle. She patted him on the arm as she hurried past.

One of the other guards moved to block her way. "You shouldn't be up here, Your Highness. A single misstep—"

Danielle kept walking. He stepped aside at the last moment, so close she could smell the sweat in his uniform and the sharp, metallic scent of polish from his helmet. She moved to the outer edge of the wall, to the gap where Charlotte had jumped. Resting her hands on the thick, white stones, Danielle leaned out to stare at the sea.

Far below, waves broke against the rocks at the base of the cliff. Clouds of mist transformed to glittering silver fog where they met the sun.

"Where is she?" Danielle asked.

"We don't know," said the nearest guard, a boy no older than Danielle herself, to judge from his smooth face. "When she fell, the mist . . ."

"I saw it, too," said another, rubbing his gray-stubbled chin. The single white plume on his helmet marked him as a sergeant. "The fog drew back, all but disappeared, and the water became still as ice. Then, for the life of me, it was like she shrank away to nothing."

"There was no splash," said a third guard.

"You two get down to those rocks and see if you can find any trace of her," said the sergeant. "I'm going to go report this to the captain." He gave Danielle a tight smile. "Don't worry, Highness. We'll take care of this."

Danielle wiped her face and backed away, to the sergeant's clear relief. She doubted the guards would find anything. From the look on the sergeant's face, so did he.

Charlotte had escaped. She would never take her own life. She loved herself far too much.

"All right, enough gawking," snapped the sergeant. "One of you lot escort the princess back to her quarters."

"I can do that, sir," said Talia. Danielle hadn't even noticed her. "I know you'll want every man on the wall to help protect us in case that woman returns."

He nodded and turned away, staring down at the ocean below. Talia took Danielle's arm and tugged her back toward the tower. "Come, Princess," she whispered. "We must talk."

Danielle allowed Talia to lead her from the wall. She felt dizzy, her mind numb as she tried to understand what had happened. Charlotte had tried to murder her. And Armand . . . "What did she mean about my husband?"

Talia's fingers tightened painfully on her wrist. "Come," she said again.

As they hurried across the courtyard, Danielle glanced up at the iron cross and prayed for Armand.

CHAPTER 2

❄

TALIA INSISTED DANIELLE remain outside until she examined Danielle's chambers. Only after checking every blanket and tapestry did she wave for her to enter. The instant Danielle stepped inside, Talia shut and locked the door behind her.

The dead dove still lay on the floor. The blood had begun to dry, becoming a dark, syrupy puddle. A weak coo led her to the wounded pigeon, who was still crouched on the bed.

"You're a witch?" Talia said, her tone making it less a question than a statement of fact.

Danielle stared.

"The way you command those birds. They fight and die for you."

"They're my friends," Danielle said. "They came to me when my mother died. The birds and the mice, they helped me with my chores and kept me company through the long hours locked in the attic."

Talia raised an eyebrow. "Best not to mention that to too many people. They think the royal family is quirky enough already." She picked up Charlotte's hunting knife. "You fought better than I expected, but you made a very stupid mistake."

It was the first time since the wedding that anyone

had spoken to her so bluntly. Anyone but her stepsisters, of course. Danielle was both relieved and annoyed. "What mistake was that?"

"You were quiet. Lesson number one: when someone tries to assassinate you, you scream like a spoiled child." Talia peered out the window. "There are hundreds of guards and soldiers in this castle, all of whom are better trained than yourself."

"Guards like you?" Danielle asked, cradling the pigeon in her lap. The wing would need to be bandaged and splinted, from the look of it.

Talia grabbed a pillow from the bed and stuffed it into the window frame, blocking all but a slim crack of light. "Tell me about your stepsister. Has she always possessed such magic?"

"If she had, she would have turned me into a toad years ago." Danielle glanced at the splintered remains of the stool. "She destroyed the stool without touching it, but she seemed almost surprised when it worked."

Talia grabbed one leg of the stool, tucking it through her belt like a sword.

"What are you doing?"

Talia used her foot to sweep broken glass to one side. "Whatever magic your stepsister used, there might be traces of the spell we can use to learn more."

"Are *you* a witch?" Danielle asked. The pigeon tried to flap his good wing. Danielle stroked the gray feathers and hummed a lullaby until he grew calm once more. "You knew I was in trouble. You got through the door, even though it was bolted from the inside."

Talia knelt by the dove's body, gently prying a few feathers from the sticky blood. "I have a friend who knows a little magic. Don't call her a witch, though. She doesn't like that." She slipped the bloody feathers into the pocket of her apron. "Did Charlotte say anything else about the prince?"

"Not until the wall. I don't understand. Armand is supposed to be in Emrildale, negotiating with—"

"He's not." Talia studied the room one last time, then turned her full attention on Danielle. "I thought I told you to wait here while I went after your stepsister."

Danielle lifted her head. "Yes, you did."

The slightest hint of a smile tugged at Talia's lips. "Leave the pigeon here. He should be safe enough, and there's plenty of spilled food for him to eat."

"No. He needs help." Only then did it occur to her to ask, "Where are we going?"

Talia opened the door to the privy. "To visit my friend."

Danielle didn't move. "In the privy?"

"Yes." Talia stepped into the dark confines, then beckoned for Danielle to follow. When Danielle still refused, she rolled her eyes and said, "She's also a healer. She'll be able to help your pet."

"A healer who lives in the privy," Danielle said again. When Talia didn't answer, she shrugged and took a scarf from the trunk by the wall, using it to rig a simple sling. She set the pigeon inside.

"And you thought me strange for talking to birds," Danielle muttered.

The smell of blood gave way to fouler things as she followed Talia into the privy. She blanched at the stench. The gutters channeled rainwater through the privies on the outer walls, washing away their contents, but it had been almost a week since the last rainfall. The incense she had burned yesterday evening did little to hide the stench. She had been back for close to a month, but her body had yet to fully adjust to the richness of palace food.

"Close the door," said Talia.

Danielle obeyed. The only light came from two narrow, slitted windows at the top of the small chamber.

She could just make out Talia's slender form, sitting on the bench beside the leather-padded hole.

Talia patted the bench. "Reach inside."

"Why?" She had cleaned worse things for her step-mother and stepsisters, but this was absurd.

"There's nothing to fear," said Talia. "Anything you might have . . . deposited has fallen two stories, where it can't hurt you."

"Who *are* you?" Danielle demanded.

"I'm the one who saved your life."

That much was true. Holding the pigeon close to her chest, Danielle bent and stretched one hand into the hole. A ring of worn, padded leather cushioned the edge. She clenched her teeth, half expecting this to be some kind of trick, but nothing happened.

"Search the underside of the bench, the back left corner."

The shaft beneath was square, which left four irregular triangles of stone beneath the bench. Gingerly, Danielle probed the corner Talia had indicated. Near the back edge, her fingers touched cold metal. A lever the size of her thumb protruded from the stone.

"Pull it," said Talia.

The lever moved without a sound, and the wall behind them cracked open.

Danielle gasped, which was a mistake, given the foul air. She reached out to touch the wooden panel. The entire wall moved easily at her touch, swinging on oiled hinges concealed in the woodwork.

Talia chuckled and pulled the wall fully open, revealing a triangular pit. On the far side, Danielle could make out bronze rungs mounted to stone bricks.

"Does Armand know about this?" Danielle whispered, peering into the darkness.

"Only the queen and two others." Talia put a hand on Danielle's shoulder. "And if this were a trap, I would have tossed you down that pit, and nobody would ever know what had happened to Princess Danielle Whiteshore."

Danielle's shoulders tensed. She put one hand on the edge of the doorway and tried to spin around, but Talia caught her elbow. Talia's other hand bent Danielle's wrist, holding her immobile. She couldn't turn without snapping her own arm.

"You're helping Charlotte?" Danielle guessed.

"No. I'm helping you." Talia let go. "You're too trusting, Princess. You welcomed Charlotte into your bedroom. You barely survived one assassination attempt, and now you're following a strange servant into the darkness."

"You saved me," Danielle said.

"Just because someone saves you doesn't make them an ally." Talia squeezed past Danielle, grabbed one of the rungs, and stepped onto the ladder. "Fortunately, I really am trying to keep you alive. I'd appreciate it if you did the same."

With that, Talia began to sink into the darkness. "Pull the door closed behind you. You'll hear a click when the latch catches."

Danielle reached for the topmost rung. The metal was warmer than she had expected. She started to obey, then caught herself, remembering Talia's warning. "How do we get back out?"

"That's better," said Talia. "There's another lever inside the door."

Danielle felt around until she located it. Only then did she pull herself onto the ladder and tug the door shut, sealing them in blackness. She closed her eyes, opened them again. It made no difference whatsoever. A quick tug of the lever opened the door again. "Where does this lead?"

"Only one way to find out, Princess." Talia's feet rang softly on the rungs as she descended.

Gritting her teeth, Danielle closed the door and followed.

The ladder seemed to descend forever. Danielle lost count at the forty-second or forty-third rung. The pigeon stirred twice, both times making her heart pound from the fear that it would fall. Her gown kept snagging on the rough-cut stone, and her knuckles were bruised and raw. At one point, she swore she felt something scurry past her fingers.

"Watch your step." Talia's voice sounded more distant, no longer directly beneath her.

A few more rungs, and Danielle's feet touched hard-packed earth.

"Don't move."

There was no light. Danielle kept one hand on the ladder. "Where are we?"

"Far below the palace. Another twenty feet to the north, and you'd be swimming."

A crack of white split the darkness, widening into an arched doorway. Danielle covered her face. After so much time in this pit, the light was as bright as the afternoon sun. She blinked, trying to clear her vision. Surely the blurring of her eyes deceived her.

"Princess Danielle. Welcome." Beatrice Whiteshore, queen of Lorindar, gestured for Danielle to enter.

Danielle stared. "What are you doing at the bottom of my privy?"

"Waiting for you." The queen stepped aside, smiling as Danielle stepped from a damp, dark underworld into a realm of luxury equal to anything she had seen in the palace.

The room was as large as Danielle's own chamber. The walls were whitewashed wood, trimmed with gold. The floor was polished marble. But where her own room felt open and spacious, this place was . . . cluttered.

Black-lacquered bookshelves lined the wall to the left. Floor to ceiling, the shelves were packed with more books than Danielle had ever seen. On the opposite wall, weapons of every variety hung from velvet-padded hooks and pegs. There were swords, knives, bows and crossbows, spears and chains, sticks of every size, and many other items Danielle couldn't begin to identify.

Oil-burning lamps sat in tiny stone niches in the wall. Curved disks of polished silver reflected the light into the room, making the steel weapons gleam.

Danielle's attention was drawn to what looked like a flattened spindle which hung between an oversized ax and a chained, spiked club. The spindle resembled a wooden cross, with white cord wound around the long end. Talia picked it up and tested a loop of the cord. She gave a satisfied grunt, adjusted her grip on the handle, and flicked her wrist. A lead weight snapped out from the tip and thudded into the door, drawing the line behind it like a whip.

"What is that?" Danielle asked.

"Talia brought several unusual weapons with her when she arrived," the queen explained.

"It's an assassin's weapon, a zaraq whip," said Talia. She drew in a bit of the line, then thrust the bare wooden tip forward like a knife. "It's not sharp, but a strike to the throat will leave a man helpless or dead, depending on how hard you attack."

Danielle started to respond when a sparkle of color overhead caught her attention. A map of Lorindar covered the ceiling. The map was beautiful, a work of art to rival the mosaics in the throne room up above. Highways, rivers, and footpaths crisscrossed through woods and mountains. The palace was a clear crystal

on the northeast tip of the island. The ocean shone
like actual water.

When she looked closer, Danielle could make out
the individual tiles of lapis lazuli that made up the
seas. The blue tiles cut a line through the center of
the island, marking the great chasm. Flakes of ame-
thyst formed a wide ring across the chasm, outlining
the boundaries of Fairytown. The Colwich Swamps to
the south were a kind of dark jade. Lines of blood-
red pebbles marked the roads, from the Coastal Highway along the west shore to the King's Road leading
southeast, to Dragon's Port. She followed the roads,
mentally retracing the journey she and Armand had
taken.

A black shadow drifted away from the coast, near
the palace. At first, Danielle took it for a spider, but
closer examination showed it to be a tile of polished
slate cut in the shape of a ship. "It's moving!"

Talia finished winding the cord back around her
whip. "Probably the *Sparrowhawk*. They weren't
scheduled to depart for another hour, but Captain
Williamson has always been an early riser. Especially
when he's angered another local husband or brother."

"Talia spends a great deal of time reviewing the
state of the kingdom," said the queen. She took Danielle's arm and gently pulled her through the room.
"Come, let me show you the rest of our little home
beneath the castle."

Danielle held the pigeon with one hand as she followed the queen through an archway in the far wall.
The room beyond was even larger and more magnificent than the first. Danielle stumbled over a stone lip
in the floor, but the queen caught her, supporting her
weight with fingers far stronger than Danielle would
have guessed.

Wooden trunks and barrels, faded with age, lined

the wall to either side of the archway. Even more books filled the shelves above the trunks. The collection here was as vast as the royal library. The walls in this room were bare stone, and the air smelled of oil and preservatives. Thick blue-and-gold carpeting covered the floor, a luxury marred by numerous stains and burns.

On the wall to the left hung a mirror, taller than Danielle herself. Unlike the small hand mirrors she had seen around the palace, this one was liquid smooth.

The silvering was flawless. Not a single speck marred the surface to distinguish reality from reflection. Her father would have wept at such perfection.

The frame was cast of gleaming silver metal. Danielle saw no trace of tarnish, so it wasn't likely to be silver. She knew better than most how hard it was to polish every nook of such a work. White gold? Could it possibly be platinum? It had been cast in the form of flowering vines crawling around the glass. Danielle reached one hand toward the glass. "This is a masterpiece of glasswork. Where did it come from?"

"Please don't touch that!" The reflection showed another woman hurrying into the room behind the queen.

"I'm sorry," said Danielle. "I've never seen anything like it."

She could have said the same for this newcomer. Though she looked a few years older than Danielle, her smooth, pale face evoked the innocence of childhood. She wore men's trousers tucked into high boots. A blue shirt draped her shoulders and made a half-hearted attempt to conceal the curve of her chest . . . though it would have had a better chance had she bothered to do up the laces. A polished silver pendant in the shape of a snowflake hung between her breasts. Danielle did her best not to look at it, or rather, at *them*.

A delicate choker circled her neck. Fine braids of gold wire held a series of tiny oval mirrors in place.

"I'm sorry I'm late," the newcomer said, breathing hard. "I was with Squire Timothy, and we—" Circles of red flowered on her cheeks. "Well, it doesn't matter." She grabbed Danielle's shoulders and pulled her into a tight embrace. "You must be Danielle. I'm so glad to finally meet you. It's been dreadfully unpleasant with only Talia to talk to."

"Shove it, Snow," snapped Talia.

Snow stuck out her tongue. "Don't worry about Talia. She's not happy unless she's stealing something or beating people to a pulp."

"Want to cheer me up?" Talia asked.

Danielle ignored her. "You're Talia's friend. The one she told me about." She picked up the pigeon. "She said you could help him."

Snow stared. "It's a pigeon."

"He helped me. Please."

Talia stepped closer to the queen. "It was the stepsister. The pretty one, Charlotte. She tried to kill the princess. She used magic of some sort to escape."

"You let her escape?" Snow repeated, apparently oblivious to the annoyance on Talia's face.

The queen spoke up before Talia could respond. "Princess Danielle, allow me to present Princess Ermillina Curtana of Allesandria."

"Snow, please," said the girl, dropping into a curtsy. She carried the pigeon to a table, setting him in front of one of the oil lamps.

"Princess?" Danielle studied Snow's face, so different from the queen's long features. "Is she your—"

"No," said Beatrice. "King Theodore and I have no daughters, and Armand is our only son. Snow came to Lorindar four years ago, shortly before Talia . . . arrived."

Snow snickered as she wound a bandage around the

bird's wing. "Before the guards found her stowed away in a shipment of cloud silk, you mean."

The queen sighed. "Like Snow, Princess Talia wished to escape from a rather unpleasant situation."

"Princess?" Danielle said again. "Talia, too?"

"Princess Talia Malak-el-Dahshat," said the queen.

In the corner, Talia gave a quick bow, somehow managing to make the motion sarcastic.

"So . . . you collect princesses, then?" Danielle asked, trying to absorb it all. Princesses weren't supposed to run around foiling attempted assassinations, let alone serving drinks or taking abuse from enraged stepsisters.

"I took in three extraordinary girls," corrected the queen.

Her words took a moment to sink in. "Three?" Danielle glanced around, half expecting someone else to step out of the shadows.

Queen Beatrice smiled. "Who do you think told Armand's driver where to find you, after the ball?"

"Queen Bea *knows* things," said Snow. She had taken what looked like a knitting needle and was using it to splint the pigeon's wing.

Danielle turned to look at the queen. "Queen . . . Bea?"

The queen sighed, but Snow didn't notice. "That's how she found Talia on that ship," Snow said brightly. "And how she knew you'd be coming to the ball. She left orders with the guards not to stop you."

"The visions are rare, and often they're damned vague," said Beatrice.

Danielle stared, taken aback. Her stepmother would have slapped Danielle's face, then locked her in the attic for such unladylike language.

"They also tend to leave me with a nasty headache," the queen added. "I'm sorry, Danielle. I knew something was wrong when I awoke this morning, but

I didn't know what. I sent Talia to watch over you while Snow and I hunted for the source of the threat."

"I tried searching the mirror, but . . ." Snow shrugged.

A magic mirror. Danielle's mouth went dry. "Her face as white as snow," she whispered. The story had spread through Lorindar several years before, just as Danielle's own story had done this past month. The beautiful young girl and her evil mother. The dashing hunter who awakened the girl from her curse. The death of the witch. . . . "You're Snow White?"

Snow nodded so vigorously her hair slipped over her face. She pursed her lips and blew it back. "Snow White sounds so much better than Ermillina Curtana. I hated that name."

"Snow was the most beautiful girl in her kingdom," Beatrice said.

Snow gave a modest shrug, which caused her shirt to slip down from one shoulder. "It *was* a rather small kingdom."

"She was exiled after her mother's death," the queen went on. "Banished under pain of death should she return."

"Why?" Danielle asked.

"For killing my mother," Snow said. "She was beautiful but terribly jealous. She sent me to the woods and paid a hunter to cut out my heart. Instead, he fell in love with me, and we lived together until she tracked us down. She murdered him, and almost killed me as well."

Snow picked up the pigeon and handed him back to Danielle. "Here's your bird," she said brightly.

"The death of Snow's mother pushed Allesandria toward civil war," said the queen. "The king had long been under his wife's spell, and her death left him in no condition to rule. Snow was too young to rebuild her nation. The more power hungry of her kin saw her as an obstacle to the throne, and wanted her hanged for matricide."

Snow glanced down. Ebony hair hid her eyes as she fixed her shirt. "Queen Beatrice and King Theodore helped my cousin Laurence take the throne."

"He was a less bloodthirsty choice than the others," the queen said. "We did what we could to help his cause. But by the time he took control, Snow's guilt was too firmly established in the minds of her people. When we attended his coronation, Laurence disguised Snow as a servant and helped me sneak her out of the country when we departed."

"I always liked Laurence," Snow said.

"I'm sorry," Danielle said, not knowing what else to say. Her own stepmother, for all her flaws, had never tried to murder her. "I thought . . . I thought it was only a story."

"It is," Snow said. "That doesn't mean it's not true. Just ask Sleeping Beauty there."

Talia sighed. "You know how I hate that name."

"Yes, I do," Snow said, grinning.

"Sleeping Beauty?" Danielle turned to Talia. At first, all she could think to say was, "Aren't you married?"

"Hardly," said Talia.

"But the stories, your prince awakened you with a kiss, breaking the fairy curse and—"

"Sometimes the stories are wrong," Talia interrupted. "Snow, have you had any luck finding the prince?"

The amusement vanished from Snow's face. "No."

Danielle's stomach tightened. "What's happened to Armand?"

"He disappeared sometime last night," Beatrice said softly. She looked away, and in that moment, Danielle saw a tired aging woman, not a queen with the strength and confidence of royalty. Queen Beatrice was afraid. "By the time I knew he was in danger, it was too late."

"Nobody told me," Danielle whispered.

Back home, such an unspoken accusation would have landed her in the attic, locked away for the rest of the day. Beatrice looked . . . not angry, but sad.

"We needed to know you weren't involved," said Talia, her words striking like knives. "There have been other attempts on the royal family over the years. Beatrice trusted you, but—"

"I do trust you," the queen interrupted. "But where my son is concerned, it's hard for me to trust myself. With so much at stake, I took Talia's fears to the king, who agreed. I'm sorry for that, and you have every right to be angry."

"I'm not angry," Danielle said automatically.

"You should be." Beatrice stepped closer, her fingertips closing gently around Danielle's shoulders. "One day, I hope you'll feel safe enough here to express that anger."

"Just don't express it as much as Talia," Snow said. "Or as violently. I've already had to replace three shelves down here."

Talia stood with her arms folded, watching Danielle like a falcon waiting for its prey to make a move. "The odds were against you being involved, but we had to know. When your stepsister arrived today, I thought she had come either to conspire with you or to issue her demands for Armand's release."

She couldn't blame them. Danielle was still an outsider here, an upstart girl who had dared to marry a prince. How could they not suspect her? She clutched the wounded pigeon close, automatically stilling her face to keep the hurt from showing. "Snow was the one who helped you get back inside the room?"

"I can do a lot through my mirrors," Snow said.

"For which I'm in your debt." Beatrice gave a slight bow in Snow's direction, then turned her attention back to Danielle. "I knew as soon as I awoke that Armand was in trouble. Snow confirmed it with her mirror. Theodore has already dispatched scouts to search the port where he disappeared, but they won't arrive for another day."

"I tracked Armand's movements after he left the ship," Snow said. "He dined with his men, then retired to his room for the night. He never came out."

"What does that mean?" Danielle asked. She stepped away from the others and stared at her reflection in Snow's mirror, as if her will alone could force it to show where her husband had gone.

"It means whoever took Armand is powerful enough to block Snow's spell," Talia said. "Charlotte knew the prince was missing. She has to be involved." She handed the broken stool leg and the bloody feather to Snow. "She used her magic on both of these."

Snow grimaced as she took the feather. "Do I look like some sort of magical hunting hound?" She stepped past Danielle and brushed the feather across the mirror, painting a faint circle of blood. The circle dried and flaked away an instant later, leaving the surface as clean as before. "Someone else cast these spells. At least, it wasn't Charlotte alone."

"She had a necklace," Danielle said. "She touched it right before the stool shattered."

"So she had an accomplice," said Talia.

"Stacia?" Danielle frowned. "That doesn't make sense." Charlotte would hardly trust her sister with something as important as protecting Charlotte's life.

Snow seemed to agree. "I doubt either of your stepsisters are strong enough to do all of this by themselves. I watched them both at the ball, then later at your wedding. If they had this kind of power, I would have felt it."

"If they had that kind of power, Danielle never would have made it to the ball," Talia added.

"So who was it?" Danielle asked.

"Probably witches," said Snow.

At the same time, Talia said, "Fairies, I'd bet."

Snow shook her head. "If Charlotte brought fairy magic past the wards in the wall, I would have known. Besides, no fairy would dare work magic within the palace. Malindar's Treaty prohibits it."

"And where are you going to find a witch strong enough to hide the prince from that?" Talia pointed to the mirror. "Ten shillings says it's fairies."

"Done."

"Why didn't your wards sense Charlotte's neck-lace?" Danielle asked.

"Because until she activated it, it was just a rock. Witches do magic. Fairies *are* magic. That makes fairies a lot easier to detect."

"Snow, can you use these things to find Charlotte?" asked the queen. "If she does know about my son, it becomes even more urgent that we find her."

"I'll try," said Snow. She took the broken stool leg and turned back to the mirror.

Danielle stared at the gold wedding band on her finger. Simple and modest. Armand had wanted to give her a heavy, diamond-encrusted monstrosity as a memento of their love, but Danielle had insisted. This thin ring was a duplicate of the one she remembered seeing on her mother's finger.

Beatrice touched her shoulder. Danielle turned, and the fear and pain on the queen's face were a match for her own. "We will find Armand."

Danielle's throat tightened.

"South," said Snow. "Charlotte fled south."

"We're on the northern edge of an island nation," Talia said. "Do you think you could narrow it down a tad?"

"I can't. She's hidden from the mirror, the same as Armand."

Danielle cleared her throat. "My house . . . I mean, my father's house is south of here."

Talia shook her head. "Charlotte knows we'll be hunting her. To hide in such an obvious place would be the height of stupidity."

Danielle folded her arms. "Charlotte let her mother cut off part of her heel because she believed that would be enough to convince Armand she was me."

"Good point." Talia snorted. "Come on, Snow. Let's go visit the de Glas house."

"I'm going, too," said Danielle.

"Charlotte already tried to murder you once today," said Talia. "If we find her, she—"

"I lived with Charlotte and Stacia for most of my life," said Danielle. "I know them. I can help."

Talia turned to the queen. "Bea, I'll have my hands full keeping this one out of trouble." She jerked a thumb at Snow, who rolled her eyes. "I can't be a nursemaid to both."

Danielle folded her arms. "Forgive me, Your Majesty, but your son is also my husband. My own stepsister may have taken him. The question isn't whether or not I'm going after her, it's whether or not these two are coming with me."

The queen studied her for a long time, until Danielle began to think she had overstepped herself. "Three extraordinary girls," she whispered, with another of those soft, sad smiles. "I can see why Armand was drawn to you."

"Your Majesty—" Talia began.

Beatrice raised one hand. "My dear Talia, this is the girl who snuck from her house for three nights to attend the winter ball, under the very noses of her stepsisters and stepmother. When they discovered the truth, they locked her away. Yet when Armand appeared, she again escaped her prison to find him. Would you have me lock Princess Danielle in the dungeons to prevent her from doing what she believes is right? Do you think even that would stop her?"

"*I* could stop her," Talia muttered under her breath.

"That's enough." Beatrice leaned forward to kiss Danielle's forehead, then did the same to Talia and Snow. "Danielle must be a part of this. I feel it in my heart."

Talia shook her head. "I hope your heart doesn't get us knifed in ours." With a sigh, she turned back toward the doorway. "Come on, Princess. Let's get you ready."

"Find my son," Beatrice said, turning back to the mirror. "And stay safe."

CHAPTER 3

❄

CLIMBING UP FROM the secret chambers beneath the palace was less disconcerting than the
descent, but by the time they reached the top, Danielle's hands had cramped into claws. Years of servitude had given her strength, but climbing used
different muscles than cleaning. Beneath her, Talia
muttered impatiently as she waited for Danielle to
open the hidden panel.

Danielle started to step into her room, but Talia
moved past her. She searched the room, then dropped
to the floor to check beneath the bed.

"What now?" Danielle asked, once Talia waved for
her to follow. The pillow Talia had stuffed into the
window frame blocked the sunlight, giving the room
a cold, evening feel. She moved the pigeon to the
center of the bed, then bent to retrieve a chunk of
bread from the floor. Everything was as it had been,
from the scattered mess of her meal to the bloody
dove staring sightlessly at the ceiling.

Danielle picked up the dove, moving him to the
desk next to the books. She took off the scarf she had
used for the pigeon and wrapped it around the dove's
body to make a crude shroud. Once they returned,

she would see about giving the bird a decent burial, perhaps by the bakery, given how the dove had taken to swooping down to swipe whatever fresh-baked goods he could get his claws on.

"You'll need to change your clothes," Talia said, eyeing Danielle's dress.

Cobwebs had turned the blue velvet gown a dingy gray. The heavy skirt had probably dusted the entire height of the pit. Dirt and grass streaked the shoulder, where Talia had pushed her to the ground earlier. Dots of ink and blood stained the side. Danielle's hand traced the design on the bodice, a soaring gull outlined in tiny pearls. Armand had commissioned the design for her.

"Why do I always have to carry everything?" Snow asked as she stepped out of the privy. Two large sacks hung from her back, the straps crossing over her chest.

"Because you're the one who insists on bringing your entire wardrobe every time we leave the palace." Talia took one of the sacks and brought it to the foot of the bed. A rainbow of silk, satin, velvet, and linen began to pile onto the mattress as Talia dug through the clothes, until the pile threatened to topple onto the poor pigeon. Danielle squeezed past Talia and moved him to safety.

Eventually, Talia produced a faded pair of trousers and a loose-fitting yellow shirt. A matching cap followed. "Wear those, Princess."

Snow dumped the other sack at the foot of the bed. She watched the pigeon hop back, and smiled. "He's moving well. I doubt he'll be flying for at least a month, but he should recover."

"Let me know when the two of you are finished worrying about birds," Talia said. "Some of us would like to try to save the prince, too."

"Oh, hush," said Snow. To Danielle, she added,

"The body can recover from almost anything, given time and strength. You just have to help it along." She reached out and patted the pigeon's head.

"Thank you," said Danielle. She pulled up the trousers, then took the calf-high boots Talia had produced from the second sack. They smelled like rotting grass.

"Carry this as well," Talia said, handing her a slender, sheathed dagger. The hilt was gold and ivory. Leaping dolphins adorned the black leather hilt. "Dolphins are dangerous creatures. They look beautiful enough, but they can kill a shark." She arched an eyebrow. "Get the point?"

Danielle strapped the knife to her hip. A brown vest with a poorly mended seam hung low enough to hide the weapon from casual view.

"Good enough." Talia turned to Snow. "If you're finished with the bird?"

Snow clapped her hands and hurried to the bed. Danielle turned away as Snow began to strip, tossing her clothes to the floor. Talia did the same, though she at least moved around behind the curtained bed for modesty.

"How do I look?" asked Snow. She wore a low-cut gown the color of blood. She tossed a light riding cloak over her shoulders, pulling the rabbit fur trim to her cheeks. She smiled and curtsied. "The Lady Anneliese Elina O'Dette of Emrildale."

Talia shook her head. "That is . . . atrocious." To Danielle, she said, "Call her m'lady. Anne of Emrildale, if anyone asks. I trust you'll have no trouble pretending to be a servant?"

"I think I can manage," Danielle said, matching the dryness in Talia's voice.

Talia finished pulling on her own boots, then began to dig through the second sack. She donned a shoulder bag, inserting the spindle whip she had taken from below. She also produced a pair of slender, metal-topped sticks which she used to twist her hair into a tightly braided knot at the base of her neck.

"Let's get moving." Talia paused at the door. "I doubt we'll find anyone at the house, but if we do, you stay behind me, Princess. If I say run, you run. Understand?"

Snow clapped her hands. "Come along now. I'll have no bickering among my servants." She slipped past Talia and stepped into the hall.

As she followed, Danielle heard Talia muttering, "Next time, *I* get to be the spoiled wench."

Not a single guard appeared to notice as they walked through the palace. Several times as they passed servants or guards, Danielle thought she saw a flash of light from the mirrors on Snow's choker. Each time, whoever they were passing would stumble and blink before moving on.

The soldiers at the southern gate barely glanced at them. Apparently, the queen had warned them that Lady O'Dette would be going for a stroll this morning. As for Danielle and Talia, they were simply two more servants. They might as well have been invisible.

Danielle found herself slipping into old habits with disturbing ease. She kept her head down and her gaze fixed on her shadow, a shrunken doppelganger of darkness trudging along the worn cobblestones of the street. The sun warmed her back and side, drawing beads of sweat from her brow. She stepped closer to Talia. "My stepsisters' home is—"

"The Merchant's Quarter, on High Street," Talia said. She gave Danielle a small smile. "You don't think Prince Armand came looking for you with only a single carriage and a few guards to defend him, do you?"

Snow hummed as she led them down the street,

keeping to one side to avoid a mule-drawn wagon and other traffic. Young children scurried about, running errands or carrying messages for their masters. Servants hurried past with groceries for the day's meals. Danielle barely stopped herself from waving at a hunched woman selling fruit. Old Mira had been a friend of her father, long ago, and she always used to slip sweets into Danielle's basket when she was out running errands for her stepmother.

Snow's appearance drew more than a few appreciative stares. She wasn't helping matters, the way she smiled at everyone and deliberately wove about to splash through the puddles left from last night's rain.

"Dignity, m'lady," whispered Talia.

"Oh, save your stuffiness for the palace," said Snow. Raising her voice, she began to sing an old drinking song about a sailor and a four-armed mermaid.

"We're hunting a possible murderess," Talia said.

"And if anyone looks too closely, I can always distract them one way or another," Snow said, touching her choker.

"Finish singing the verse about the seaweed, and you'll be distracting half the town," Danielle said.

"I love that part." Snow drew a deep breath, glanced at Talia, and bit her lip.

As they turned east, a gust of wind carried the smell of bloody meat through the street. Most of the butchers and tanners and furriers all crowded together along the same stretch of road. Blood 'n Guts Lane, the people called it.

Danielle had grown up within sight of the palace, but on a bad day the smell could carry all the way up to the Merchant's Quarter. She smiled, remembering the first time Charlotte had left her window open after an especially hot summer day.

Up ahead, a black-furred mutt lapped at a puddle.

He glanced up as they approached, his teeth bared. Danielle smiled and reached out to scratch his neck.

"Careful, Princess," said Talia.

"Hunter wouldn't hurt me." Danielle rubbed the dog's neck so hard his ears began to flap. Hunter gave one last snarl at Talia and Snow for good measure, then rolled onto his back in a puddle so Danielle could scratch his belly.

Snow rubbed the dog's chin, giggling when he licked her wrist.

Talia cleared her throat. "Highborn ladies do not frolic. Especially with mangy dogs in the street."

"You could use a good frolic," Snow shot back. "So he's filthy and smells of squirrel. He's still better company than some of the nobles I've known."

Another few blocks brought them to High Street, and Danielle's heart began to pound faster. She was *home*. There was the house of Samuel the wine merchant, the windows still boarded to keep his eldest son from sneaking out at night to visit Matilda down the street. Beyond was the house where Mary Bloomfield lived with her granddaughters, telling fortunes and selling magical wards made with bits of glass and scrap iron.

Danielle smiled as she spotted her father's house, a tall, weatherworn building with faded shingles and blue shutters. The house was roughly the same as those to either side: three stories, with the lowest level serving as the workshop and storefront. The large shutters to either side of the door could be propped up to provide shade for the men and women inside, while at the same time giving her father a place to sell his wares.

This morning, the shutters were all closed. The house appeared to be sleeping. Sleeping or dead. The gleaming sign which had proclaimed this the home of

Charles de Glas, Master of Glassworks, was long gone. The empty bar where it once hung was rusted brown.

The highest window, just beneath the peak of the roof, was nailed shut. That had been Danielle's room.

Now that they were here, Snow sobered. Chin held high, she led them to the house next door, where Andrew the silversmith worked with his sons. Danielle and Talia waited a few steps behind as Snow examined a bracelet.

"My sister, the Lady Bethany Celeste O'Dette of Emrildale, once purchased the most elegant vase from a glassblower near here," said Snow. "Do you know where I might find him?"

Erik, Andrew's older son, pushed the bangs from his eyes. "That would be Master de Glas next door. He's been dead a little over ten years now."

"How unfortunate," Snow said. She held the bracelet to the light, sniffed, and set it down again. "What of his widow or children? Is there anyone from whom I might still purchase one of his pieces? Preferably something larger and more expensive than Bethany's vase."

"Sorry, m'lady," said Erik. "His family lived there for a while, but lately it's been as you see it, all locked up and empty."

"But what about—" Danielle bit her lip, remembering her place. Where were her stepsisters staying, if not here?

Erik peered more closely at her, but then Snow leaned down to grab a silver rose brooch and he found more interesting things to study.

"I'll take this one." Snow reached into her satchel and dug around until she pulled out a small gold coin. "I've always liked roses." She turned the coin over in her hand. "You're sure the family isn't here?"

Erik licked his lips. "They say Danielle married the prince, but I don't know if I believe that. Folks like to tell stories, you know," he added with all the wisdom of a thirteen-year-old boy. He hesitated. "It's a strange place, that house. My uncle Cowen says the stepmother's ghost is trapped up there in the attic, doomed to stay a year for every day of misery she put Danielle through. 'Course, Cowen also believes the fairies will steal his teeth if he sleeps with his mouth open."

He turned to scowl into the house. "Every night, he ties a bandage around his jaw before he goes to bed. The man isn't right in the head, I'm telling you."

Snow slipped the coin into his hand. "Thank you, young sir."

Danielle glanced over her shoulder as she followed Snow away from the shop. So strange to be back, to see Erik selling silver and ogling the female customers, the same as ever. "He didn't recognize me." Had she changed so much?

Talia cocked a thumb at Snow. "Don't go anywhere with her if you want people to notice you."

They stopped at the home of Margaret Weaver, on the other side of Danielle's old house. Margaret confirmed what Erik had said. The house was abandoned, and had been for at least a week, though she occasionally heard noises during the night. She assumed it was rats or other animals. "The younger girl, Stacia, tried to take care of the place for a while, but she knew nothing of housekeeping. Don't know where they've moved on to now."

Margaret stared at Danielle. Though Danielle had spent much of the past years locked away, her stepmother had sent her out at least once a day to buy food and other necessities. These were still her friends and neighbors, far more than the people at the palace. She longed to pull off her cap and talk to Margaret, to feel like a real person again instead of a false princess.

Margaret started to say something more, when

Snow piped up, "Thank you so much." Her mirrors flashed, and then Snow and Talia were hurrying Danielle away.

"Disguise is more than clothes," said Talia, her voice low. "You still move like a servant girl." She studied Danielle's old house. "Is there another way in?"

"The servant's entrance," said Danielle. "On the other side of the house."

The narrow alley between the house and Andrew's next door was damp and cool, and the fires of Andrew's forge gave the air an acrid smell. The yellow paint on the servant's door was dry and cracked. Yellow flakes floated on the puddle by the door.

Talia tested the handle. "Locked."

"I don't have a key," said Danielle. "My step-mother never let me—"

"Step aside." Talia dropped to one knee. Twined into the laces of her boot were several long, jagged rods and wires. She slid two of these into the lock and adjusted her grip. Taking both rods in one hand, she turned the knob with her other and pushed.

The door swung inward. Talia put the lockpicks away and drew a long, double-edged knife from her other boot. "Stay behind me."

The kitchen was a disaster. Bits of food littered the table and floor, unrecognizable from the mold. A line of ants scurried to and from the wall, bearing away stale crumbs. It was all Danielle could do to keep from grabbing a bucket and rags from the closet and scouring the filth from her home.

The rest of the house was the same. Danielle wanted to weep. How had they done such damage in so little time? Her former home was like a hollow tree, rotten and empty. She hurried into her father's workshop.

Gone were the fine tools that had hung along the

walls, no doubt sold off for a fraction of their worth. Gone were the enormous bellows and the stacks of wood. Only the great fireplace remained, the tin hood dark with old soot. Glass crunched as Talia crossed the workshop, moving toward the front of the house.

"Someone was here recently," she said. "Footprints in the dust and debris." She pointed her knife at the floor, where a fragment of green glass had been crushed into smaller pebbles. "Looks like both stepsisters."

"How do you know?" Danielle asked.

"From the limps," said Talia. "Charlotte maimed her heel. Stacia lost a toe. They walk differently."

Danielle knelt to pick up a curved shard of blue-and-white rippled glass. This had been one of her stepmother's favorite vases. One of Danielle's daily errands had been to run to the city wall and gather fresh wildflowers. She had hated this vase.

"Upstairs," said Talia. "Erik said the attic was haunted."

Danielle and Snow followed her up the stairs, past the second floor where Danielle's stepsisters and stepmother used to sleep. Danielle peeked into her stepmother's bedroom. Old bandages littered the floor, brown and yellow with dried blood and other fluids. She averted her eyes.

Talia was already climbing the ladder to the attic.

"Wait," said Snow. She gestured for Talia to move, then hopped up and placed her hand against the trapdoor. "Your stepsisters have been practicing," she said.

She shoved open the door and pulled herself inside. Her choker began to glow with a warm, orange light.

"What is it?" Talia asked.

"Nothing dangerous," said Snow. "Old magic."

Danielle followed, automatically ducking her head to avoid the rafters. Cracks of light from the shuttered window drew white lines across the floor. Over the years, Danielle had marked the floor to track the time of day. Twelve sets of lines tracked the time, one for each month. This was mid-May, and the uppermost light was a finger's width short of the lunchtime mark. Past time for her to be down in the kitchen, preparing the meal.

"Over here," said Snow. Blobs of black melted wax had seeped into the cracks between the floorboards. Snow drew her knife. The blade was short, straight, and sharp. The only decoration was an oval of gold, engraved with a snowflake, mounted in the center of the crossguard.

Snow used the tip to break a chunk of wax from the floor. "Plain beeswax works just as well, but they all want black candles. Or blood red. My mother was the same way. Fat black candles, cobwebs thick enough to catch a stag. I think she raised the spiders herself, just to make the place more scary."

"What were they doing?" asked Danielle.

Snow pointed the knife at the ceiling. Smoke had darkened the wood, except for a circular area above the candles, as if the smoke had been unable to pass into the ring. "Looks like a summoning. They trapped something here."

"Can you tell us what they summoned?" Talia asked.

"Sorry." Snow sheathed her knife. "They cleaned up pretty well."

Danielle stared. "My stepsisters . . . cleaned?"

Talia walked to the window. Old boards split apart as she wrenched the shutters open. For the first time since the death of Danielle's father, sunlight streamed into the attic.

"Thanks," said Snow.

Talia looked around the room, then shook her head. "There's nothing here. Let's check the bedrooms."

Danielle was already climbing down the ladder. She ignored her stepsisters' rooms, heading for the ground floor.

"Where are you going?" Talia asked.

"To find Charlotte and Stacia."

Snow cocked her head. "How?"

"I'm going to ask my mother."

Danielle rounded the back of the house when shock froze her in place. She had expected to find the garden in similar disarray to the rest of the house. Weeds overshadowed what crops her stepsisters had bothered to plant, and she could see slugs on some of the leaves from here. But where neglect had begun to reclaim most of the garden, the hazel tree in the corner—her mother's tree—had been deliberately assaulted.

Bent and broken branches dangled from the central cluster of the tree. What leaves remained were brittle and brown. Clumps of dirt bordered a deep hole at the base, as if an enormous dog had tried to dig the entire tree from the earth. The entire right side of the tree appeared burned, little more than a blackened skeleton.

Danielle remembered when this tree had been nothing but a single twig of hazel, which she had planted in memory of her mother. She had come here for weeks, weeping and praying and remembering her mother's final words.

Remain pious and good, and I shall watch over you from heaven.

The tree had grown swiftly, sending up a clump of thin trunks which were soon as thick as her waist. No doubt her stepmother would have chopped it down long ago had she known what it represented, but the garden, like so much else, had been Danielle's responsibility.

Danielle hopped over the low fence. "Mother?"

"What's wrong?" asked Snow.

Danielle ignored her. Months before, these branches had rustled in response to Danielle's prayers, clothing her in the magnificent gown she had worn to the ball.

"Charlotte knew," she whispered. She had said as much, back at the palace, but Danielle hadn't realized what that meant.

"There's something else in that tree," Snow said.

"My mother's spirit." Slowly, Snow's words sank in. The tree wasn't yet dead. Danielle rushed forward.

"Princess, wait!" Talia shouted.

The ground shifted. Danielle grabbed the tree for balance as her feet sank into the soil. The branches were hot. The bark felt like it would sear her skin.

Danielle tried to step back, but the earth had swallowed her feet to the ankles. The branch in her hand snapped away, and a wisp of smoke rose from the broken end.

Talia sped into the garden, drew her knife, then stopped. "Should have brought an ax." With an expression of disgust, she slammed the knife back into its sheath. "Burn this thing to the ground, Snow."

"No!" Danielle shouted. "You can't!"

Several branches swung about, twining around Danielle's wrist. She yanked back hard enough to pull free, but lost her balance and fell. Her head landed among the rhubarb even as the dirt sucked her feet deeper.

"Maybe you haven't noticed," Talia said, "but this tree is trying to kill you." She grabbed Danielle beneath the arms and pulled. "What are you doing, Snow?"

Snow was hurrying back from the well beyond the garden. Rope trailed from the bucket in her hands. She ran to Danielle's side and tossed the water at the base of the tree.

Steam hissed from the earth, and the grip on Dan-

ielle's legs loosened. Talia grunted and pulled. Snow
grabbed her other arm. Together, they wrenched Danielle from the ground, though her boots remained
behind.

"That's your mother?" Talia asked as she retrieved
her knife. "And I thought my family had problems."

"No," Snow said before Danielle could answer.
"That's got to be what Charlotte and Stacia summoned. Probably to destroy Danielle's mother. It's
trapped within the tree, along with her spirit. They're
still fighting, and judging from the look of those
branches, she's losing."

"Can you save her?" Danielle asked.

Snow grinned. "If I can't outcast a pair of stuck-up
novices, I'll—"

"Less boasting, more casting," Talia said.

Snow pointed to the bucket. "Gather as much water
as you can and soak the dirt around the tree. Don't
get too close."

"How close is too close?" Danielle asked.

"If the tree tries to eat you, you should probably
back up."

Danielle stood by the fence, clutching the knife Talia
had given her in both hands. She didn't know what
good the knife would be if things went wrong, but this
way she didn't feel quite so helpless. A full water
bucket sat on the ground beside her, along with several pots they had fetched from the house. Her bare
feet and trousers were dark with mud, as were Talia's.

Snow stood facing the sky, exposing her pale throat
to the sun. A thin beam of sunlight shone from the
central mirror of her choker. Her traveling cloak was
draped over the gate, the fur soaking up muddy water.

As Snow muttered, the sunbeam gouged strange,
sharply angled symbols into the dirt. White frost
crusted the characters, defying the heat of the sun.

"What are you doing?" Danielle whispered. Her vision blurred if she looked too closely at the words in the earth.

"This is similar to the summoning spell your stepsisters cast. If my magic is stronger, it should draw the creature from the tree." She frowned. "I think it's a demon of some sort. Ethereal, which means it probably came from one of the lower dimensions. Maybe a Myrakkhan, or possibly a Chirka, though they're not really in season. They usually hibernate through the spring and summer. Still, they—"

"The spell, Snow," said Talia.

By the time she finished, frost circled most of the garden. The words curved round and round, shrinking as they returned to the starting point by the tree.

Snow gave a sheepish shrug. "I always run out of room at the end. I start out writing too big, and then—"

"Will it work?" asked Danielle.

"Sure." Snow brought her hands together. "Your stepsisters did the hard work, bringing the demon into our dimension. Now that he's here, all I need to do is call him, and he'll be trapped within the bounds of the spell." She gave a short, sharp whistle. "Come here, boy. Come here, little fire demon."

Talia raised an eyebrow.

The branches of the hazel began to shake, and withered leaves floated to the ground, but nothing else happened.

"It's fighting me," Snow said. Her lower lip protruded slightly, hinting at a pout.

"I thought your summoning spell would force it out," Danielle said.

"Not the demon." Snow stopped to wipe sweat from her forehead. "The tree. Your mother is the one fighting me."

"Why would she fight us?" Talia asked.

Snow turned to study Danielle. "Your mother, did she know magic?"

"No." Her answer came out more sharply than she intended. "Why would you ask that?"

"Asks the girl whose mother lives in a tree," said Talia.

Snow rubbed her neck. "If she didn't study witchcraft, she might not know what we're doing. The last time someone performed magic here, they loosed a fire demon on her. Don't worry, I'll get it."

"She knows me," Danielle whispered. No matter what Charlotte and Stacia had done to her, she would know Danielle.

"Let me try," Talia said. To the tree, she shouted, "Get out of that tree, you hell-spawned bastard!"

"Neither Chirka nor Myrakkhans come from hell," Snow said. "And I didn't see any of the ingredients the stepsisters would have needed to summon a proper hellhound."

Danielle did her best to ignore them. Why wouldn't her mother let them help? She had to know Danielle was here, that they were trying to save her. "What is it I don't see?"

Smoke began to rise from the center of the tree. She could smell the wood smoldering. Soon the entire tree would be in flames. "Snow, stop! You're killing her."

"I can't," said Snow. "The spell is already cast."

With a cracking sound that made Danielle think of breaking bone, the base of the tree began to split. Those branches that remained bent away from the crack, as if they sought to rip the tree in half. Which may have been precisely what the demon intended.

"That's it," Snow said. "Into the circle, little demon."

"The circle," Danielle whispered. She dropped to all fours, studying the circle where it passed closest to the tree. "Snow, look!"

Snow stepped back. "Uh-oh."

One of the hazel's blackened roots had poked through the mud, destroying a portion of Snow's spell. Danielle and Talia both dragged Snow away from the tree as the branches exploded in fire. Claws and teeth splintered the wood as an enormous wolf dug itself free. Its fur was a dirty gray, like old ash. Orange-and-blue flames rippled along its body. They were brightest along the back, reminding Danielle of a dog with raised hackles.

"It *is* a Chirka," Snow said. "A big one, too. What did they sacrifice to bring one here at this time of year?"

Talia bounded toward the gate. She slid through the mud, arms outstretched for balance, then spun like a dancer. One hand snagged the bucket, flinging the water squarely into the wolf's face.

Clouds of steam burst from its fur. Talia whirled and threw the bucket itself, which shattered on the wolf's head. The wolf shook, spraying dirt and sparks in every direction.

"Bad Chirka," Snow snapped. Her choker flashed, slowly re-creating the broken symbol in the dirt. "I'm almost ready."

The wolf ignored her, slinking around the edge of the circle. Glowing orange eyes never left Danielle.

The second water pot smashed into the wolf. The water clearly annoyed the demon, but it didn't seem to cause any real harm. Neither did the knife which followed, sinking into the wolf's throat. The wolf nipped at the hilt, but its jaws wouldn't reach. With a snarl, it crouched and sprang at Danielle.

Talia was faster, grabbing Danielle's wrist and flinging her toward the tree. As Danielle fell, she saw Talia twist out of the demon's way, barely avoiding the burning jaws of the Chirka. It slid through the mud where Danielle had been standing. Mud sprayed everywhere as it fought to recover.

"A bit of magic would be nice right about now," Talia shouted.

"What, you finally met something you couldn't just bludgeon into submission?" Snow knelt at the edge of the circle. The hazel roots had receded back into the earth, and Danielle could see the frost creeping through the soil. "Danielle, the spell is ready. Lure the Chirka into the circle!"

"Won't I be trapped, too?" Danielle yelled.

"Oops!" Her mirrors brightened, hastily adjusting several of the glyphs. "Sorry."

The wolf snarled and crept toward the tree where Danielle stood. Strings of drool swung from its jaws. Several times it lunged and snapped, ripping branches with its jaws, but it always drew back before reaching Danielle.

Danielle pressed deeper against the tree. The burnt wood smell made her eyes water, and she cringed each time she heard another branch snap.

The wolf was between her and the circle, but as long as she stayed here, enveloped by her mother's branches, the wolf seemed reluctant to attack.

Instead, it went after Snow. It leaped past Talia, knocking her back into the fence before bounding around the circle. Snow yelped and stepped to the side, trying to keep the spell between her and the wolf.

The wolf was too fast. Another bound and it was close enough to catch her. Teeth bared, it pounced.

Talia slammed her shoulder into the wolf's midsection, driving it toward the circle. It landed at the edge, off-balance. Snow drew back one leg and kicked it hard in the nose.

Sharp teeth caught the edge of Snow's dress. With

a jerk of its head, the wolf tossed Snow into her own circle, then stumbled away.

"You wanted its attention," Talia said. Her shirt smoldered where she had hit the demon, but she didn't seem to notice. She drew another knife and pointed it at the wolf's throat. Not that it would do much good. Talia's other knife was still protruding from the wolf's neck.

"Mother, please. . . ." Danielle whispered. She didn't know what else to ask. A gown and glass slippers were one thing, but what could she do against a demon?

The wolf leaped again. Talia planted the second knife in its throat, but as before, it barely noticed. All four paws slammed into Talia, smashing her against the house like a doll. Then the wolf sprang away from Talia and raced toward Danielle, so fast she didn't have time to move. Danielle held her breath, turning her face away as that huge, flaming body filled her vision.

Heat seared her skin, but the wolf didn't reach her. Charred and broken, the remaining branches of the hazel tree had stretched past Danielle to seize the demon's struggling body, wrenching the jaws back from her face. She could smell its breath, like rotten eggs, as white-hot teeth snapped for her throat.

Danielle jabbed her knife into the wolf's mouth. It bit down, wrenching the knife from her hand and flinging it into the mud. The heat seared her fingers. Her sleeve smoked as she pulled back, trying to press deeper into the safety of the tree.

The wolf still struggled. Branches and leaves began to burn anew, and with every lurch, the wolf came closer to Danielle. Her mother was too weak to hold it for much longer.

Danielle flexed her hand. The skin was red, blisters

already beginning to form between her thumb and finger. "Let it go, Mother. Don't let it take you, too."

Something sparkled in the branches to her right. At first, it looked like a shard of ice. Desperately, she reached through the burning leaves, and her fingers closed around the hilt of a sword. The blade was as long as her arm, a thin, flat shard of crystal or glass.

The wolf caught one of the largest branches in its jaws and twisted, ripping it from the tree and freeing itself from her mother's grip.

Without thinking, Danielle brought the blade through the branches and shoved it into the wolf's side.

The wolf yelped and backed away. Danielle followed, pushing the sword deeper, driving the demon toward Snow's circle. Snow stood on the other side, clapping her hands and calling the demon.

It darted to one side, whining as the blade ripped free. Danielle swung the sword in a wide arc, slicing a clean gash along the side of the wolf's throat and forcing it into the circle.

The Chirka stumbled, then struggled to raise its head. It looked confused. The jaw hung open, as if it could no longer work the muscles to close it. It tried to step out of the circle, then fell back as if it had hit a stone wall. The demon's dark blood steamed as it hit the soil.

"Got you," Snow said triumphantly.

Danielle dropped the sword. Turning her back on the wolf, she hurried over to the smoldering ruin of her mother's tree. Most of the leaves were gone, and those branches that hadn't broken were black from the heat. Small flames still burned along the roots.

When Danielle reached out to touch the trunk, she felt nothing but lifeless wood.

CHAPTER 4

❄

SOFT HANDS GUIDED Danielle toward the well. Snow eased Danielle's blistered hand into a pot of cool water, one of the few pots that hadn't been destroyed in the fighting.

"No," said Danielle. She tried to grab the pot, to take it to her mother's tree, but Snow held fast. She was stronger than she looked.

"She's gone," said Snow. "I'm sorry. Leave your hand in the water while I tend to Talia. I have a salve that will help your burns, but I need to treat her wounds first."

"What's to tend?" Talia said, flexing her arm. The upper part of her sleeve was a tattered, blackened mess. Her arm was red, but the burns weren't as serious as the one on Danielle's hand. Lines of blood marked her chest and stomach where the demon's claws had cut her skin. "It's a fire demon. The wounds cauterize themselves. I'll be fine."

Snow folded her arms. "You've got mud and who knows what other filth in those cuts. Either I tend them today, or I wait until they turn septic and you're too delirious to protest. Which would you prefer?"

Talia grimaced and sat against the wall of the house. Snow was already rummaging through her satchel. She produced a curved silver needle and a length of glimmering white thread, which she set to one side.

"You have no idea how much I despise needles," Talia muttered.

Their words barely registered. Danielle averted her face from the remains of her mother's tree, but the acrid smell of smoke drove it home with every breath. She could still feel the embrace of the branches as the tree struggled to protect her.

This was her fault. She had retreated to the tree, drawing the demon after her. Her eyes blurred. "I'm sorry, Mother."

Motion at the corner of the house snapped Danielle from her thoughts. Erik stood staring from the shadows, his face pale. He started when he saw her watching him.

"Danielle?" he whispered. He looked back at the demon, who lay unmoving in the circle. The flames had died, and it almost appeared to be a normal wolf, albeit a thoroughly charred one. "I heard the noise. I thought Hunter was fighting with another stray. I came back here—"

"It's all right," Danielle said. "I think it's dead."

"How did a wolf get—" His eyes widened, and his fear seemed to disappear between one heartbeat and the next. "Wow. Is that a magic sword?"

Danielle rolled her eyes. "Erik, who's minding your father's shop?"

"Oh, bugger," Erik said. He turned to go, then hesitated. "You know, there have been a lot of stories since you left. I wanted to say . . . I mean, we didn't know how bad. . . . I'm glad you're free. From your stepmom, I mean. And, hey, are you really a princess now?"

Danielle nodded. "If you keep quiet about me being here, I'll bring you something from the palace the next time I visit."

"Really?" He grinned so hard it looked like his cheeks would split. "Your secret will never pass these lips. My word on it, Princess."

Once he was gone, Danielle reached down to retrieve the sword that was her mother's final gift. The blade was perfectly smooth, sloping to a razor-sharp edge on either side. Bits of charred fur and blood still coated the glass. She pulled her hand from the water and used her damp sleeve to wipe away the gore.

The simplicity of the slender blade made the design of the hilt more impressive. The glass of the grip was tinged green, cast in the rough bark pattern of the hazel tree. Thin lines of wood were inlaid in the glass, spiraling around the handle for a better grip.

The "roots" at the pommel wrapped around a sky-blue sphere of glass. Twin branches formed the cross-guard. The hilt fit her hand perfectly, and the touch of the wood seemed to soothe her burns.

She raised the sword to the sun. Deep inside, just above the guard, she thought she could make out the shape of a hazel leaf, as if it had been etched within the glass.

The sword was just as beautiful as the gown and slippers her mother had provided. She wiped her face with her free hand, then rested the sword across her legs.

"Now do you understand why I didn't want you along?" Talia asked.

Snow made a *tsk* sound as she swabbed ointment over Talia's wounds. "She did kill the Chirka."

"She would have died if we hadn't been here to save her." Talia looked away as Snow threaded her needle. "No disrespect, Your Highness, but you don't know how to protect yourself. Snow and I can find your husband. Go back to the— Dammit, that stings!"

Danielle gently tapped the sword against a small rock in the mud. It chimed like crystal, but not a scratch marred the blade. The glass was so much lighter than steel.

"My mother knew how much I loved my father's work," she said. "He could make magic with nothing but a blob of molten glass, a blow tube, and a hot fire." She smiled, remembering. "When I was little, I used to gather up the splatters of glass after they cooled. They were like glass pebbles, smooth as water on the top, but rough beneath where they captured the imprint of the hearth. I'm sure he let the glass drip on purpose, just for me."

She flexed her fingers and winced. The skin felt raw and tight. She raised the sword into a guard position, smiling at the way the glass caught the sun.

"Hold the tip lower and fix your elbow," said Talia, her jaw clenched. "Your arm looks like a chicken wing."

"You don't want to have to protect me? Teach me how to protect myself."

"The best way to protect yourself is to go home," Talia muttered.

Danielle ignored her. To Snow, she said, "My stepsisters knew nothing of magic before the wedding. Someone had to guide them."

"Fairies," Talia said. "They've got a real thing for wolves. Always sending them out to stalk humans through the woods or sneak into houses or—" She hissed in pain as Snow tied off the final stitch.

"The spell was cast using witchcraft," Snow said firmly. "The signs in the attic were unmistakable. But the ingredients to summon and control a Chirka are rare. Most of them are illegal."

"Where would they go to get them?" Danielle asked.

Snow folded her needle and thread into a small bundle, then rummaged through her satchel until she found a brown jar. She dabbed greenish ointment over the cuts on Talia's stomach, rubbing it into the skin.

"There are only two places in Lorindar. We need to visit the troll."

Snow took Danielle's hand and began rubbing the ointment onto the burns. A cool, tingling feeling spread through her skin. The ointment smelled like fresh-cut hay.

Danielle flexed her hand. "You said there were two places to find those illegal ingredients. What's the second?"

"My room at the palace."

Danielle nibbled a seed cake, barely tasting the sweetness, as she followed the others through the Holy Crossroads toward the southern gates of the city. Church bells clamored to either side, signaling noontime worship. On the steps of Saint Thomas, a preacher in plain cotton robes shouted at the crowds, condemning the use of divine magic by mortal hands. "Magic is not meant for beings as fallible as ourselves," he shouted.

Normally, the preachers annoyed Danielle with their taunts and condemnations, but this time, she found herself in agreement.

On the other side of the street, a man wearing a blue cloak edged with gold symbols pointed and jeered. "Magic is a gift of the savior," he shouted. He drew a crucifix from inside his cloak. A winged fairy, cast from bronze, hung from the small cross. "The First Fairy, who lived and died as one of us."

"Idiots," Talia said. "The only reason the people haven't run the Followers of the Fey out of town is all the money the fairies send to push their farce of a church."

From the sound of things, the group gathered at the Church of the Iron Cross felt the same as Talia. Their taunts soon drowned out the cries of the Fey Church.

"Come on, while everyone is busy watching the

show." said Snow, threading her way through the crowds.

Talia pointed toward the small, gruesomely decorated Chapel of the Baptism of Blood, where a man and woman in crimson hurled epithets at the other churches. "It's nothing but an act to rile the crowds and put gold in their coffers, the same as any actor or tumbler."

"You don't believe?" Danielle asked.

"In them?" She snorted. "By the end of the night, most of these priests will gather at one of the churches and drink together like brothers."

"So what do you believe?"

Talia shrugged. "My teachers told me magic was brought to our world by Pravesh, Giver of Light. His sister Shiev was angry, wanting to keep that magic for the gods. She tore him into eight pieces and scattered the parts across the world. The fey rose from his spilled blood and spread throughout the world. They had Pravesh's magic, but were forever tainted by the violence and betrayal of their birth."

"Is that why you don't like the fairies?" Danielle asked. Talia said nothing.

Danielle finished her seed cake as she followed. She kept her head bowed, but it didn't seem to matter. Few people paid them any attention, and those who did would be unlikely to recognize her. Even Snow passed with little notice.

Snow had left her fancy gown and jewelry at the house, donning one of Danielle's old outfits instead. Charlotte and Stacia hadn't touched Danielle's things, probably deciding they were no good for anything but rags. The shirt and trousers were well worn, but clean. Snow was thinner than Danielle, so the clothes hung loosely on her slender frame, except in the chest and hips. An old apron provided a bit more modesty, and a moth-eaten scarf concealed her choker.

A yawning guardsman waved them through the open gates of the city. The hot, heavy air of the crowd gave way to a cool breeze, and the cobblestones beneath their feet changed to hard, dusty earth.

Danielle carried her sword under one arm, tied within a roll of blankets. Talia had bundled it so that Danielle could reach into the blankets and draw the sword without too much trouble, though they would have to unroll everything to get the sword back in.

She squeezed the blankets as she walked, feeling the crossguard press against her ribs. She wanted to take the sword and hold it in her hands, to feel the last gift her mother would ever give her.

"I should have come back sooner," she whispered. How long had that demon been trapped within the tree, weakening her mother's spirit?

Snow shook her head. "Your mother chose her death the moment she drew the Chirka into herself."

"This isn't how things were supposed to be."

"She died to save you," said Talia, her expression distant. "It's what any good mother would have done."

Tents and carts lined either side of the dirt road, spreading outward along the city wall. Prostitutes and lepers and actors, all those who found themselves less than welcome inside the city, gathered here around the gates.

"How long until we find the troll?" Danielle asked. Flies buzzed in annoyance as she stepped over a pile of horse dung.

"That depends on whether or not he wants to be found," said Snow.

It wasn't the most comforting of answers. "If he sells dark magic, why hasn't the queen done something about him?"

"It's hard to explain," Snow said, glancing at Talia. "He's exiled from Fairytown, but he's still of fey blood. And he doesn't actually perform any illegal magic himself. So the queen—"

"Abides by the treaty," Talia finished. She spat. "Letting him pollute our city with his foul magic."

Snow's face brightened. "But if he's the one who helped Charlotte and Stacia, that would be a clear violation of sections nine and twenty-two of Malindar's Treaty. Not only did he 'perform or otherwise facilitate the use of dark magic in a clear and deliberate attempt to cause harm to one of noble birth,' but Charlotte used magic when she tried to kill Danielle in her room, which means he 'aided in the use of dark magics on palace grounds.' "

Talia snorted. "Don't get her started. She'll recite the whole treaty from memory, then cite every case in the past century where humans or fairies were found guilty of violations."

"I like to read," said Snow, blushing. "There are so many books. I've read everything in the palace library at least once."

By now, scattered evergreens had taken the place of the makeshift town outside the walls, and the noise of the city was a distant whisper.

"And did any of those books tell you where to find the troll?" Talia asked.

"He's a troll, silly," said Snow. "We'll find him under a bridge!"

"I don't suppose there's another troll," Talia asked, her nose wrinkled. "One who lives beneath a less putrid bridge?"

Snow shook her head. "I check on him from time to time with my mirrors. He's there, halfway up Fisherman's Canal."

Fisherman's Canal ran along the inner edge of the wharf, a rocky strip of land at the base of the cliffs which had grown into a small town of shipbuilders, fishermen, and sailors. Seagulls filled the sky, occasionally diving toward one of the boats to try to swipe a meal. Others hovered over the canal, fighting the rats for the remains of those fish which had already been gutted. Their cries were a pleasant change from the shouts of the town.

Danielle cupped her hand over her eyes, grateful for the chance to rest. Palace life had spoiled her more than she realized, to be so out of breath.

Four footbridges crossed the canal, spread evenly between here and the end of the wharf. A short distance downstream, two rag-clad children had chased the birds away and were gathering bits of gut and meat from the water.

"What are they doing?" asked Snow.

"They use it for bait." Danielle grimaced. "At least, I hope that's what they're doing."

"They're standing right beside the troll's bridge." Talia muttered a word in a language Danielle didn't understand. "I'd rather not tell every kid in Lorindar what we're doing. Bad enough your neighbor saw you."

"Erik won't tell anyone," said Danielle. She glanced at a pair of gulls who were squabbling over a small black crab. Lowering her voice, she called out, "Come here, friends. I need your help."

"That's a neat trick," said Snow, as the birds swooped toward Danielle's head.

A few whispered instructions later, the gulls were flying past the bridge, the crab forgotten. They swooped low, their barking cries loud as they pretended to squabble over the gold coin Danielle had given the larger gull. The coin dropped into the water, and the gulls flew onward.

At first, Danielle wasn't sure the children had seen, but then the girl began wading away from the bridge. Danielle couldn't hear what she was saying, but the boy soon followed, shaking his head over what he probably thought was another childish fantasy. He yelped with surprise when the girl snatched the coin from the water, and then they were both running along the docks toward the road.

"Was that inconspicuous enough?" Danielle asked.

Talia rubbed her forehead. "It would be, if Snow would stop flirting with the sailors."

Snow stopped in mid-wave. She blushed as she clasped her hands together and turned away from the sweaty, shirtless men who were rolling barrels from one of the ships. "Sorry."

"Snow's not very good at 'subtle,' " Talia said.

Snow tugged her scarf off of her neck, earning a sharp whistle from the ship. She started to smile, then sighed when she spotted Talia's expression. "Fine. Subtle it is."

She brushed her fingertips over the front mirror of her choker. The whistling stopped, though the men continued to stare.

"That doesn't appear to have helped," Talia said.

"Wait for it." Snow smiled and waved again.

As one, the men turned away and went back to their work.

"What did you do?" Danielle asked.

"A small spell." She giggled. "They think we're men."

Not one of the dockworkers looked up as Snow walked down to the canal. Danielle grimaced as she followed Snow into the cold, slowly flowing water. The stones at the bottom were slick with dark green muck, and the buzz of insects was louder here as flies feasted on discarded bits of fish.

Cobwebs tickled her face as she stepped beneath the bridge. The air was cooler, the light dimmer than she expected. She kept her head and shoulders hunched to avoid disturbing the spiders. Dead insects filled huge triangular webs by the water and at the base of the bridge.

"Now what?" asked Talia.

Snow stepped to one side of the bridge. Weeds and spiderwebs hid the base of the archway, and black mildew covered much of the stone. "Now we search for the door."

She touched her choker. "Mirror, mirror . . ." Her voice trailed off.

"What's wrong?" Danielle asked.

"I need something that rhymes with door." Snow flushed and looked away. "A true master wouldn't need to speak at all, but the rhymes help me to focus the harder spells."

"Gore?" suggested Talia. She nudged a slimy mound downstream with her toe. "War? Whore?"

"I don't think we want that kind of spell," said Snow.

"Chore?" asked Danielle.

"Wait, I've got one," said Snow. "Mirror, mirror, small and round. Let the hidden door be found."

Nothing happened. All three of them leaned closer, peering at the stones.

"There," said Snow. She scraped one of the stones with her fingernail, dislodging a chunk of moss to reveal a thin hole the size of her little fingernail.

"Must be a very small troll," Danielle said.

Talia grabbed her lockpicks and knelt in the water. She used a straight steel rod to probe the hole, then drew out several more picks. A short time later, Danielle heard a clicking sound.

"Done," said Talia.

Snow's forehead wrinkled. "So where's the door?"

Danielle turned. "Behind us."

On the opposite side of the bridge, the damp, moldy stone had disappeared. A wooden door swung soundlessly inward. The hinges appeared to be made of some sort of silver rope. There was no latch or handle.

Dirty water darkened the dirt at the doorway. The tunnel beyond was dark and smelled of mud and dead fish.

"Lovely place," Talia said.

"He's a troll." Snow kept one hand to her throat as she stepped through the doorway.

Talia followed, her knife ready. Danielle shifted her bundle so she would be able to draw her sword at need. Not that she knew how to use it. She shivered as she stepped through the doorway.

A few steps in, she noticed the water trailing from her trousers and boots, streaming along the floor like raindrops dripping down a window. The same thing happened with Snow and Talia, leaving the floor within completely dry.

"Nice," said Snow. She ran her fingers over the hard-packed earth of the walls. "Witchcraft. Some kind of potion blended into the dirt to repel the water."

Shadows enveloped them as the door began to shut. Talia whirled, and her knife flew through the darkness. The blade buried itself in the dirt at the edge of the doorway. The door hit the hilt, pressed it to the doorway, and stopped, leaving only a thin crack of light.

"Trap?" Talia asked.

"Probably." Snow's choker began to glow.

Danielle walked onward, marveling at how fast Talia had moved. By the time Danielle had realized what was happening, Talia's knife was already there, blocking the door. "How do you do that?" she asked.

"Do what?"

"The way you move and react. When you fought the wolf, it was like you knew what was coming before it even attacked. And the way you threw that knife. I've never seen another human being move like that."

"Fairies," Talia said, her voice flat.

"I don't understand."

"My parents bribed the fairies to come to my naming ritual. Haven't you heard the story of Sleeping Beauty?" She grimaced at the name. "How they gifted me with extraordinary grace, the ability to dance like a goddess, beauty to make me the most desirable woman in the world. What's fighting but another kind of dance?"

"But you're not—" Danielle bit her lip, but it was too late.

"Beautiful?" Talia snorted.

"No, you're beautiful, it's just . . ."

"Not like her, I know." Talia cocked her thumb at Snow. "Well, beauty is a little different where I come from. Back there, people would think Snow too pale and skinny. And tastes change over a hundred years."

"If the fairies gave you beauty and strength and grace, why do you hate them?"

"Your stepmother gave you food and shelter and clothing. Why do you hate her?" Talia turned away without waiting for an answer, following the tunnel as it veered to the left.

Eventually, wooden floorboards replaced the dirt, and the tunnel took on more of a square shape. Danielle could still see roots penetrating through the ceiling, like tiny clusters of dirty white thread.

"Shouldn't we be in the ocean by now?" Danielle asked.

"Trolls are geniuses when it comes to tunneling," said Snow. "He could dig within a finger's width of the open sea, and we would be as safe as if we were in your room at the palace. Safer, really, considering what happened this morning."

The hallway stopped at another door, nearly identical to the first. The only difference was a glass sphere mounted in the center of the door. Talia searched for another keyhole, but she found nothing.

Snow pressed her eye to the glass sphere. "There's a curtain covering the far side."

"Do we knock?" Danielle asked.

"He'll be suspicious either way. Trolls hate the sun and the daytime," said Snow. "His customers would know better than to come before dark."

Talia pounded the door. When nothing happened, she drew back and gave it a good, solid kick.

"Tough door," Talia muttered, leaning against the wall to flex her knee and ankle.

Light appeared through the glass sphere. A hugely magnified yellow eye appeared, flitting this way and that. A gravelly voice said, "Come back at a respectable hour. Some of us are trying to sleep."

Snow peered through the sphere. "Very well," she said. "I just thought you'd want to know that Queen Beatrice will be sending letters to the king and queen of Fairytown, telling them how you violated Malindar's Treaty."

"What's that? Move out of the way, you. Let me see who else is with you."

Snow obeyed, and the yellow eye studied them all more closely. "Ah. So which one of you little treats is the one they call Cinderwench?"

"That would be me," Talia said, before Danielle could answer.

The troll chuckled. "I don't think so, my dark-skinned muffin."

Danielle kept one hand on her sword, more for comfort than anything else. "I am Princess Danielle. Are you the troll who helped my stepsisters?"

"Brahkop, at your service. As for that other matter, I'm afraid my transactions are confidential."

"Charlotte tried to murder me," Danielle said. "They killed my mother. If you know who I am, you know we can pay whatever you ask."

"She doesn't mean that!" Talia grabbed Danielle's wrist and yanked her back. "Are you mad?"

Danielle tried to pull free. "If he can help us find Armand, I'm sure the queen would—"

"No fairy bargain is as it seems," Talia said. "Nor do they often ask for money. Your soul, your joy, your future . . . whatever he wants, you don't want to pay it."

"Now that's plain unfair," Brahkop said. "To judge all those of fairy blood based on the nasty tales your kind spread about us. And what's all this about Malindar's Treaty? You can't prove I had anything to do with those girls. Even if I did, they're the ones who tried to kill the princess here."

"You called me Cinderwench," Danielle said. "Charlotte and Stacia are the only ones who call me by that name."

"Did I say Cinderwench? I meant . . . oh, dragon farts. You caught me."

Danielle stepped to the door and stared through the sphere. She could see nothing beyond Brahkop's eye and the distended bulge of an enormous nose.

Before she could speak, wisps of gray and white began to fall from the ceiling, drifting down around her head and arms. At first she thought they were more cobwebs, and she waved an arm over her head to brush them away.

The strands tightened, catching her arm and pinning the elbow by her head. She tried to duck beneath them, but bumped into Snow.

"It's a net of some sort," Snow said, her voice calm and curious. The strands were all but invisible. Danielle could see indentations in the skin of her arm as the net pulled the three of them closer together.

Talia dropped to the floor. Her legs glided to either side as she attempted to slip beneath the net, but the lower edge caught her chest and face, pressing her back against Snow's legs. She pulled out a knife and sliced back and forth at the strands. "Good net," she muttered. "Snow?"

"I'm working on it," Snow said.

"I promise a quick death, if it's any consolation," said Brahkop. "You'll barely feel the cuts as my net slices you into nice, bite-sized pieces. It will be quite a mess, but it's not the first time I've had to defend myself against trespassers."

Danielle twisted and hunched her shoulders. The net quickly tightened, but she was able to get her right hand to the hilt of her sword. That blade had killed the demon when normal steel failed; it might be able to cut Brahkop's net as well. She tried to pull the sword free, but she couldn't move her arm back far enough.

The mirrors on Snow's choker fogged over, and the strands slowed. Before, Danielle had barely noticed their touch. Now they grew cold, like blades of ice pressing into her skin.

"Not bad, my little morsel," said Brahkop.

Snow's elbows ground against Danielle's ribs as she fought Brahkop's net. Talia was still squirming on the floor, her head pressing hard against Danielle's knee.

"Talia, can you reach the blankets on my sword?" Danielle asked.

"Maybe." Talia's knife dropped to the floor. She squeezed her hand up the net, and her fingers closed around the end of the blanket. She pushed the blanket back, exposing the tip of the blade.

Danielle pushed the sword as hard as she could, trying to bring the edge into contact with the nearest strands of the net. The net dug into her fingers, drawing thin lines of blood. She gritted her teeth and pushed harder.

The blade touched one line, which snapped and curled away. A second broke a moment later. Danielle drew her hand back and twisted the sword to cut one of the crosswise strands.

"I'm not sure how much longer I can hold this," Snow said. She sounded mildly annoyed, like she was describing a stain on her blouse. "The spell is almost alive. It acts like one of those constrictor snakes. Every time I try to adjust my magic, it tightens a little more."

"I know you have stronger spells than this," Talia complained. "Can't you just destroy this thing?"

"Sure, but I thought you wanted to survive."

Danielle swiveled the sword back and forth, cutting a larger hole in the net. "Hold on," she said.

Talia snorted. "Like I've got anything better to do."

Danielle thrust out through the hole, then shook the sword until the blanket fell away. She cut downward, being careful to avoid Talia. She was halfway through a crosswise cut when the whole thing seemed to die. The net fell apart, leaving limp strands over the three of them. Danielle shuddered and brushed them away.

"Do you know how long it took me to make that net?" Brahkop complained. "All those tiny knots . . ."

"Move aside," said Talia. Danielle and Snow backed away. Talia rapped on the sphere.

"That's elven crystal," said Brahkop. "Cost me a good bit of change, but it's well worth the price. Completely unbreakable, unless you're an elf with the secrets to—"

"Who wants to break it?" Talia spun and smashed her heel into the glass. There was a popping sound as the sphere broke loose from the door. The force of Talia's kick drove it squarely into Brahkop's waiting eye.

The troll screamed.

Calmly but quickly, Talia shoved her arm through the hole. Her body pressed against the door, and there was a clicking sound from the other side. "There we go," she said. The door swung open.

Beyond was a great open room lined with shelves. Lanterns hung from gold hooks in the ceiling, casting a sickly green light over various pouches, bottles, books, and scrolls. Green and brown herbs hung drying on the far wall. Coils of glimmering rope filled an entire corner, stacked as high as Danielle's waist. Weavings made from the same shiny thread decorated the walls.

Doubled over near the back, both hands clutching his face, was Brahkop the troll.

Danielle stared. "Are all trolls so hairy?"

Brahkop straightened. At his full height, he was half again the size of a man, and twice as broad. Of the troll's face, only his nose was visible, a pale blue potato poking through waves of silver-white hair that hung to his ankles. Some of the hair had been braided, with beads and other trinkets clicking together at the ends each time he moved.

A great, meaty hand emerged from beneath the hair. Brahkop reached toward Talia. "So you plan to make me work for my meal, eh? Very well, let's see how—"

Talia scooped up the crystal sphere with both hands and smashed it against the troll's knuckles. He drew back, cursing, and Talia flung the sphere directly into his nose.

Brahkop staggered. Danielle hurried to join Talia, her sword ready. She tried to mimic the cold, determined expression on Talia's face.

Brahkop sniffed and held up his hands. "Enough."

"Are you sure?" Snow was browsing through the shelves. She pulled down a small vial of thick purple sludge. "I wanted a chance to try this. I've never seen what coagulated wyvern blood does to a troll."

Dark blue blood dripped from Brahkop's nose and slid down his hair. "I'm sure!"

Talia folded her arms. "In that case, I believe the Princess Danielle was asking for your help."

"I can't," said Brahkop. "I made a deal."

"Snow?" Talia said.

Snow smiled and began to work the stopper loose from the vial.

"No need to get violent, ladies," said Brahkop, wiping his nose.

Danielle stared. "You were going to eat us!"

"I was hungry." He shook his head, sending waves through his silver tresses. "Look, I'd like to help you. You beat me fair and square. But I can't. Your stepsisters drive a tight deal, and part of that deal was that I say nothing of where they went or what they planned to do."

Snow was carefully returning the vial to its place on the shelf. "Those of fairy blood can't break a contract," she said without looking up. "It's in their blood. You could cut him to pieces, and he wouldn't talk."

"Let's test that," Talia said, drawing her knife.

"You know, you're a very unpleasant human," said Brahkop.

"Are you the one who taught my stepsisters magic?" Danielle asked.

Brahkop shook his head. "Sorry, can't help you."

"What exactly was this deal?" Snow asked, picking up a mummified bat with a wingspan as wide as her outstretched arms.

"Can't say. It's all very secret."

Snow returned the bat to its shelf and picked up one of the weavings, an intricate pattern in a gold, octagonal frame. The strings formed the image of a leaping deer. "This is beautiful."

"Troll hair," said Brahkop. "All but unbreakable."

He fingered one of his braids. "My sister hit me with a curse, back when I got myself exiled. I could shave myself bald, and in an hour's time, I'd look like this again. Fortunately, I managed to make a name for myself selling troll hair ropes and weavings. I can knit you a set of mittens that will protect you from icy cold or the heat of dragon fire." He pointed to the door. "Nets like that sell for a pretty sum, I'll tell you."

"What about killing us?" Talia asked. "Was that part of the deal, or do you just like to murder royalty?"

"What royalty? I see three thieves who tried to break into my shop," Brahkop protested. "Royalty doesn't pick locks and wake hardworking trolls in the middle of the day and—"

"Sure we do," said Danielle. She lowered her sword and did her best to meet the troll's gaze. She wasn't entirely sure where the eyes were, beneath all that hair. "My stepsisters paid for your help. I'd like to do the same. I know you can't tell us where they went, but what can you sell me that would help us find my husband? If he happens to be with my stepsisters, that's certainly not your fault."

Brahkop cocked his head, making him look like an overgrown sheepdog. "Clever. You're sure you don't have fairy blood?"

"I'm sure." Danielle pointed to Snow. "She's a witch—"

"Sorceress," Snow corrected.

"—so she can use any magic you give us. Please."

"You're talking some mighty powerful magic," Brahkop said. "That sort of spellcasting doesn't come cheap."

"I warned you about bargaining with them," Talia said. "He's planning to trick you." She gave a disdainful sniff. "I doubt he even has the power to find your stepsisters."

"Oh, please." The beads in Brahkop's hair rattled as he chuckled. "Play that game on one of the beast caste, but don't expect to trick me into anything. I keep my bargains. You pay my price, I'll help you find your prince."

"What price?" Danielle asked.

"The child," said Brahkop.

Danielle glanced at her companions. "What child?"

"The one you carry in your womb, Princess."

Danielle felt like he had punched her in the stomach. She stepped back, nearly dropping her sword. "I'm not . . . How can you—"

"We're sensitive to this sort of thing," Brahkop said. He gently tapped the side of his nose. "It never lies. They say my great grandmother could tell you the baby's sex a week before you made it. I could smell it the moment you came through that door." He sniffed. "That's before your friend smashed me in the face, of course."

"No," Danielle whispered.

"Don't worry, I'll take good care of the little guy," said Brahkop. "Changelings are treasured, treated like royalty. Better than royalty, given the way you people treat your noble children."

"The little guy?" Danielle repeated. A son. Hers and Armand's.

"Why do the fairy folk always want human children?" Snow asked. "Do you know how many diapers you'd have to change? And what would you feed him?"

"Most of us are none too fertile, especially the higher castes," said Brahkop. "Then there are those who just like the taste. Not me, though. Not enough meat."

Snow put a hand on Danielle's arm. "If he's telling the truth—"

Danielle jerked away from Snow's touch. "You want my child?" she whispered.

"Afraid so," said Brahkop. "Hey, if it helps, I'd be happy to let you visit the lad, when he's older."

Danielle grabbed a handful of the troll's hair and yanked his head down to her level. The tip of her sword poked through the hair. "No," she whispered. "You helped my stepsisters destroy my mother. Now you're going to help us find Armand."

Brahkop started to shake his head. Danielle thrust her sword forward, eliciting a startled yelp.

"In exchange," she went on, "I'm going to let you live."

Her hands trembled with fear and rage. The troll was strong enough to snap her in two, but it wasn't Brahkop she feared. What frightened her was the realization that she meant every word of her threat. She had never wanted to kill anything before, but she would thrust her sword through his throat if she had to.

"We don't need him," Snow whispered.

Slowly, Danielle turned to face her.

"I can find Armand." There was no doubt in her voice.

"There you go," said Brahkop. He stepped back, gently tugging his hair from Danielle's grasp. "Problem solved. We can all relax and—"

"I want you gone from this place," Danielle said, keeping her sword pressed against his chest.

"What's that?" Brahkop asked.

"Are you forgetting how you tried to kill the princess of Lorindar with your net?" Danielle moved forward, driving the troll back a step. "Tomorrow morning, I'm sending a battalion of the king's guards down here with orders to rip apart every last stone of your little lair. This bridge will be broken one stone at a time. The tunnels will be collapsed. Anything left behind will be burned."

"You can't—"

"That includes yourself," Danielle finished. By now, Brahkop stood with his back to the wall.

"I'll protest to the queen!"

"Which one?" Snow asked, her voice sweet. "The fairy queen who exiled you, or Queen Beatrice, whose son you helped Charlotte and Stacia to kidnap?"

Brahkop didn't answer.

"Come on, Your Highness," Talia said, putting a hand on Danielle's arm. "Our troll friend has a lot of work to do if he's going to get everything packed up in a day. We should leave him to it. Unless you're planning to kill him?"

The calm, matter-of-fact tone of her question helped draw Danielle back from her anger. She could kill Brahkop if she chose, and nobody would stop her. A simple push would drive the blade into his heart.

Slowly, she shook her head. She refused to taint her mother's last gift by murdering an unarmed troll, no matter how much he might deserve it. She turned away, still shaken by the intensity of her reactions.

She had only taken a single step when Talia grabbed her by the arm and wrenched her off-balance. Talia twisted the sword from Danielle's hand and spun.

Danielle crashed to the floor. She rolled over to see Talia ducking to the side, avoiding Brahkop's huge fists. Talia swung the sword. The glass sword cut a deep, dark gash along the troll's arm, above the elbow.

Brahkop howled and stumbled back. Talia leaped after him, cutting his other arm at the wrist, then thrusting the sword at his face. Brahkop fell onto the floor, barely avoiding the attack.

"Wait! I won't try to stop you, I promise. I'll leave tonight. My word as a fairy!"

Talia pressed her heel against Brahkop's chest. The

sword rested against the side of his neck. The hair had fallen away to reveal the pale blue of his throat. Talia didn't appear to be putting any weight on the sword, but the edge was still sharp enough that blood beaded along the glass.

"You're the princess of Lorindar," said Talia. "It's your right to decide whether he lives or dies."

Danielle pushed herself up. Her elbow throbbed. She would have a nasty bruise from that fall. "He's bound to keep his word, right?"

"It's in their blood," said Snow.

Danielle's body was numb as she turned and walked through the doorway. Snow followed. Talia shut the door behind them, then handed the sword back to Danielle.

"Next time you turn your back on an angry troll, Highness, you're on your own." Talia walked away, shaking her head and muttering something about naive children trying to get themselves killed.

Danielle barely heard. She kept hearing Brahkop's voice in her mind, over and over.

She was going to have a son.

CHAPTER 5

❄

DANIELLE STOOD BEFORE Snow's great mirror, turning this way and that as she studied her reflection. Her cycle had been erratic since she moved to the palace. She touched her stomach with one hand as she counted the weeks. It could have happened at any time during the last month of her journey with Armand. Their stay in Emrildale was a likely guess. Snowed in for three days with so little to do. . . .

She had blamed the slight bulge of her stomach on her new diet. Of course she had gained weight now that she was eating full meals on a regular basis.

She wondered if her mother had known. If Brahkop could sense her unborn son, surely her mother's spirit had done the same. She wanted to believe. The idea that her mother endured long enough to learn of her grandson brought some small sense of comfort.

She flexed her hand, still tender from the demon's attack.

"Here," said Talia, coming into the room. She held a white leather scabbard. "It might be a little long for that blade, but at least you'll be able to carry it without hauling those blankets everywhere."

"Thank you." She picked up the sword and slid it into the scabbard, smiling faintly when she noticed the embossed snowflake worked into the leather. "Does Snow still need this?"

"Nope." Snow hurried into the room behind Talia. "The queen will be down shortly." To Danielle, she added, "That was from my training blade, back when Talia was trying to turn me into a warrior woman. I told her I preferred magic, but she insisted I learn to defend myself."

"What happened?" Danielle asked.

"She cheated," Talia grumbled.

Snow covered a giggle with her hand. "I cast a spell on my sword. I lunged, she parried, and the instant the blades touched, they both turned into giant daisies. Talia was so surprised, I managed to whack her on the head with mine. She had yellow specks of pollen in her hair for the rest of the day."

Danielle managed a weak smile. She raised her arms as Talia belted the sword around her waist. When she finished, Danielle ran her fingers over the hazel patterns in the crossguard.

"Danielle?" The queen's face was red, and she was breathing hard. Without a word, she crossed the room and pulled Danielle into a tight hug. "Snow told me about your mother, and about your son."

Danielle didn't move. A part of her wanted to bury her face in the queen's shoulder and weep, and another part wanted to pull away. She did neither, and after a moment, the queen stepped back. Beatrice's gaze went briefly to the sword. "I wish I could have known her. She seems a truly remarkable woman."

Danielle's throat tightened. She managed a tight nod.

Mercifully, the queen appeared to notice her discomfort and changed the subject. "Snow also tells me you threatened to loose my guardsmen on that horrible troll."

"I didn't mean to overstep myself," Danielle said. "He threatened—"

"I know what he threatened."

Danielle took a deep breath. "I've never been so angry. But I never thought he would take me seriously. I'm not—"

"You showed him a good deal more mercy than I would have," Beatrice said. A hint of a frown tugged her lips. "I've already ordered my men to carry out your orders. By this time tomorrow, Brahkop's home will be nothing but rubble."

Danielle managed a nod as she struggled to understand. The idea that she could command that Brahkop's house be destroyed, that she had the power to make that happen . . . it frightened her.

"You're princess of Lorindar, remember?" said Talia.

"And that child is my grandson," added the queen, her face softening. "The future heir to the throne." She hugged Danielle again, then smiled. "You should have seen Theodore's face when I told him it was a boy. He had been talking to Captain Grant about mounting a few more cannons on the north wall. He sent everyone away in the middle of the meeting. Apparently, it's not kingly to be teary-eyed in front of your men."

A harsh scraping sound interrupted them. Snow dragged a heavy stool across the room, setting it in front of the mirror. "I'm ready."

"Come," said the queen. She placed a gentle hand on Danielle's shoulder. "Let us find my son."

The hilt of Danielle's sword jabbed her beneath the ribs when she tried to obey. She wrenched the belt around and sat.

Snow leaned down, so close her breath tickled Danielle's ear. "Stare into the mirror. Think of your husband. Any memory will do, but the more vivid, the better."

The first thing that came to mind made her face burn. She shoved that memory aside, on the chance that Snow might be able to see her thoughts. Instead, she tried to remember the day after the ball, when Armand had come to her house. She remembered the feel of his hand on hers as he helped her into his coach. Her stepsisters had been screaming, her stepmother fuming, but Danielle barely heard.

Only when the door was shut and the horses' hooves began to clop as they drew her away had she started to believe this was real. Years of unshed tears slipped down her cheeks. She wiped her face and turned away, hoping Armand wouldn't see.

From the window, she saw Charlotte and Stacia standing in the road, blood pooling around their feet. Danielle shuddered. That her stepmother had been so horrid to Danielle all these years was bad enough, but that she would maim her own daughters. . . .

Armand reached past her, pulling the curtains closed and shutting out that part of her life. Danielle gasped when she saw the fresh blood on his sleeves. Drops of vivid crimson stained the white satin of his pants as well.

"I'm so sorry," Danielle whispered. "My stepmother, she . . ." She shook her head. "We must soak those in cold water before the stains set. We can stop at Helena's Apothecary Shop over on Garden Street. Watersnake venom will break down the blood and release the stains, and I can—"

Only then did she realize the prince was laughing. His shoulders shook, and he held his clean hand to his mouth. She drew back, confused.

"Please don't be offended, love," Armand said. He glanced down at his clothes. "This is nothing. I've never liked this outfit anyway. So much gold thread . . . I feel like a pirate's treasure." Another bout of laughter took him.

Slowly, Danielle's mood changed to confusion, then annoyance. "What's so funny?"

"I've spent my life surrounded by politics," Armand said, still chuckling. "My parents were always fiercely protective and loyal to their only son, but the same can't be said for the endless aunts, uncles, cousins, and other relatives scattered across Lorindar. Backstabbing and betrayal were as much a part of my diet as fish and venison."

An unprincelike snort escaped his nose. "On this day, I've finally met a family to make my own seem pleasant."

"That's good," said Snow, startling Danielle from her memory and drawing her back to the present. She wiped her eyes with her sleeve, still feeling Armand's touch, hearing his laughter. Was it the mirror's power that brought such vividness to the memories?

Danielle tensed her legs, bracing herself against the sensation that she was tumbling into the mirror. Her reflection seemed to grow, as if the glass were falling toward her.

Snow's voice was a delicate breeze across Danielle's cheek. "Mirror, mirror, old and great. Show me Princess Danielle's mate." She giggled. "Assuming you haven't mated with anyone else recently?"

Danielle shook her head, too disoriented to take offense.

"Concentrate, Snow," snapped Talia.

Like ripples on the water, dark rings spread across the center of the silvered glass. They rebounded from the edge of the frame, blurring Danielle's reflection. Colors and shapes flashed past between the rings.

The mirror went dark. Danielle leaned closer, and her stomach twisted. "What does that mean? Why can't I see anything? Is he dead?"

"No," said Snow. "If he was, we'd still see the bod—" She bit her lip and glanced at the queen. In a softer voice, she said, "We'd still see him."

"He's been hidden," Beatrice said. "Through magic.

The same thing happened when Snow used me to try to find him."

Danielle grabbed Snow's hand. "You said you could find him."

"Armand is twenty years old," Snow said. "The bond between parent and child weakens over time." She pulled her hand free and placed it on Danielle's stomach. "The babe in your womb is another matter. He's a blending of your essence with Armand's. Over time, as he grows into his own man, the bond will fade. But for now, that child is the most intimate connection we have to the prince. Even more intimate than your own, Princess."

The queen cleared her throat. "Please, Snow. A little less lecturing, and a little more magic, if you would be so kind."

"Sorry." Snow brushed her fingers along the platinum frame of the mirror. "Mirror, mirror, with power so wild. Show us the father of Danielle's child."

The mirror brightened. Clouds rushed past, so fast Danielle reflexively pulled back. She would have fallen right off the stool if Talia hadn't caught her shoulders and held her in place.

Danielle found herself looking down at a great chasm, as though she were a bird circling far overhead. A silver bridge spanned the gap, sparkling like a spider's web in the morning dew. Slowly, the mirror drew back, revealing elaborate palaces to either side of the bridge. Spires of ebony and gold stretched into the sky, reaching to touch the clouds themselves. She saw great, thick forests and cities of such color they looked like a rainbow had shattered and fallen to earth. A group of winged horses circled an empty field, carrying glowing men and women so small that six could ride on a single horse.

"I can't get any closer," Snow said. "There's too much magic."

"That's enough," said Talia. "I told you it was fairies."

Snow rolled her eyes. "Just because he's in Fairytown doesn't mean—"

Fairytown. Danielle squinted, trying to see through the whirling images in the mirror.

"Enough," interrupted Beatrice. "I'll talk to Ambassador Trittibar tonight. He will arrange for the two of you to enter Fairytown. You leave in the morning."

"I don't understand," said Danielle. "If we know where he is, why can't we go to the fairy king or queen and ask them to find Armand? Doesn't the treaty—"

"If we could prove that one of their subjects had taken a citizen of Lorindar to Fairytown, we could present evidence to the fairy court," Snow said. "The treaty requires them to respond to any request for such a hearing within seven days."

"But even if we had proof that one of their people was involved, we don't know which court to go to," Talia added. "The king and queen aren't on very good terms. We could spend days arguing our case to the queen, only to find it's the king's people who helped your stepsisters."

"So we go to both courts." Danielle looked from one to the other, then turned to the queen. "Ask them both to help find Armand."

"And they'll help us why?" Talia asked. "Out of the goodness of their hearts? They lost the war. Humans forced the treaty on them. They're not exactly our friends, Highness. If we want Armand back, Snow and I need to go get him."

"Then I'm going with you."

The queen was already shaking her head, as if she had anticipated Danielle's words. "No, Danielle. The demon in that tree nearly killed you. I've already lost my son. I won't risk losing my daughter-in-law and grandson as well."

"You haven't lost Armand," Talia said. She was already heading to the other room, gathering weapons from the wall. "We'll bring him back."

"I know my stepsisters," Danielle said. "I know how they think. I can help."

Beatrice touched Danielle's cheek. "I do understand how you feel. If it were up to me, I'd be on a horse to Fairytown this very moment. But we have other responsibilities, Princess. I trust Talia and Snow with my life. They will find Armand."

"Fairytown is a big place," Danielle said. "And what will they do if Charlotte and Stacia decide to move Armand elsewhere? Without me, they'll have no way to find him."

Talia returned, tucking small knives about her person. "They murdered your mother. They would have murdered you if I hadn't saved you. Twice. Come with us, and you're more likely to get yourself and your son killed than to save your husband."

"The first attack was in my own bedroom," Danielle said. "Do you truly think I'll be safer here than I would with the two of you to protect me?"

Both Snow and Talia watched the queen, waiting for her to choose. Deep down, Danielle could understand their protests. She was no warrior, and the thought of putting her unborn child in danger made her want to weep.

"My mother died when I was too young to know her." Danielle stepped down from the stool. "She stayed with me, but all my life I've been unable to touch her, to hear her voice or wrap my arms around her. Her loss broke something deep inside my father. I began to lose him the same day I lost her. When he died years later . . ."

"You're risking the prince of Lorindar," Talia said.

"I know that." Danielle shuddered, remembering the way Brahkop had reached for her. If it were her alone, she would have gone without a second thought. She closed her eyes and turned away. "I also know that if my father had been given the chance to save my mother, and he had refused that chance because of me, I would never have forgiven him."

"I could order you to stay," the queen said.

Danielle pointed to Talia and Snow. "You said you trusted them with your life. Do you trust them with mine? Mine and my son's?"

The queen's lips pursed. "I think I liked you better when you were the obedient servant girl." A smile softened her words. She turned to Talia. "I'm asking you to be responsible for Danielle's safety."

"I knew you were going to say that," Talia muttered.

Danielle wrapped her arms around herself. "Thank you, Your Majesty."

Talia ducked back through the doorway and studied the map on the ceiling. "We'll need a ship. The *Phillipa* is fastest, but they're halfway around Lorindar, escorting a silver merchant. Of the ships moored here, *Silver Wind* is probably the best choice. We should send a runner down to tell Captain James to prepare."

"Trittibar will send you on your way first thing in the morning," the queen said. "You should eat dinner and prepare for tomorrow."

Talia shook her head. "They took Armand to Fairytown. That means the fairies are involved. We can't go to their ambassador and expect him to help us over his own people."

"Trittibar has always been a friend to Armand," the queen interrupted. She stared into the mirror, her eyes unfocused. "The two of them used to sneak out of the palace together, visiting the taverns and gambling with the people. I'm told my son developed quite an arm for darts." She smiled, momentarily lost in the memory. "He needed time away from the palace. Time to see what the world was like. And every boy needs to believe he's pulled one over on his mother and father from time to time."

"You knew they were sneaking off?" Danielle asked.

The queen's smile grew. "My dear child, who do you think gave Trittibar the idea?"

Talia didn't say another word until they returned to Danielle's room. As before, she searched the room herself before gesturing for Danielle and Snow to follow. When she did speak, her words were curt. "I'll fetch something to eat from the kitchens. The two of you stay here. Remain quiet, and stay away from the window."

She opened the door, then stopped in mid-step. "Your Majesty."

"Talia, isn't it?" King Theodore stepped inside. Danielle saw two guards waiting in the hallway. His expression was almost playful. "Strange . . . I knocked a short time ago, but there was no answer."

Danielle started to respond, but he held up his hand. "No need. I came to congratulate you, not interrogate you."

The king was taller than his son, his brown hair dusted with gray. The padded shoulders of his jacket made him appear even more imposing, as did the heavy boots that clomped against the floor. His beard was neatly trimmed, framing a face which was longer and narrower than Armand's. But when he smiled, his cheeks dimpled in a way that left no doubt he was the prince's father.

"Beatrice said she would send you to see me, but I grew impatient." He stepped forward to give Danielle a gentle embrace, as if she were made of porcelain. When he backed away, his brows lowered. "You've had a busy day, I see."

Danielle looked down at her clothes, still stained from the filthy water of Fisherman's Canal, and covered in dust from the secret passage. "Very busy, Your Majesty."

"Don't tell me. My wife's secrets are her own." He glanced at Snow and Talia, and his voice turned somber. "Have you learned anything of my son?"

"The queen believes he might be in Fairytown," Snow said carefully.

"I see." He studied each of them in turn. When those hazel eyes met Danielle's, she felt as though he was peering into her mind, reading her thoughts as though she were one of the books from Snow's shelves. "I would lead my troops to Fairytown tonight if I thought it would get him back."

"It would only get him killed," said Talia.

"Yes." The king embraced Danielle again. "I'm sorry, Danielle. Today should have been a joyful day. Will you—" He jumped as the pigeon hopped across the floor, bandaged wing dragging beside it. He started to speak, then stared again.

"He fought Charlotte. He helped to save my life." Danielle picked up the bird and stroked its neck. "It will take time for his wing to heal. He'll need food and a place to rest. Could you . . . ?" Her voice trailed off as she remembered who she was talking to. She started to stammer an apology.

"Of course." The king reached out to take the pigeon, who began to struggle.

"It's all right," said Danielle. "He's going to take care of you." The pigeon settled warily into the king's arm.

"Will you be joining us for dinner?" he asked, still staring at his new companion.

"Perhaps it would be better if the princess dined here," Talia said, her words a careful balance between statement and request. "She has been feeling unwell."

"I haven't," Danielle protested. She had been a little queasy after leaving Brahkop, and she could do without traversing that ladder again, but she certainly wasn't ill.

They ignored her. "I understand," said the king. "In such cases, it's often best to rest. I'll let the staff know you may be indisposed for several days."

"Thank you," said Talia.

"I trust you to take good care of her in her . . . illness."

"Naturally."

He nodded, then used his free hand to take Danielle's, planting a quick kiss on her knuckles. "Be well, Princess."

Talia followed the king out of the room. In the hallway, she turned back to say, "Try not to get yourself killed before I get back, please."

The door slammed shut. Snow was already dumping her bags and moving to the fireplace. She blew on the embers to revive the flame. "I can't believe you asked the king to watch over your pigeon," she said. "The expression on his face was worth half the gold in the treasury. I wish Bea had seen it."

"Talia resents me," Danielle said.

"Talia resents everyone." Snow poked a stick into the fire. "Don't take it personally. She . . . she's not very good with people."

Danielle moved to the window, listening to the cries of the birds outside. "I should have known Charlotte would do something like this."

"Probably," said Snow.

Danielle blinked. "What?"

"You should have known. You lived with Charlotte and Stacia for years. But you wanted to think that everything would be fine. That your stepsisters would go off and have their own happy little lives, and you'd spend the rest of your days basking in the warmth of your love, while little birds sang songs of peace and joy." She tossed another stick into the fireplace. "I made the same mistake. The next thing I knew, an old woman was slipping me a poisoned apple."

Talia returned a short time later, carrying a platter of baked eel and asparagus, along with a dusty bottle of wine.

They ate in silence. Though the chefs had done a magnificent job as usual, Danielle's stomach rebelled at the smell of the eel. She made do with asparagus and bread, barely tasting either. She kept thinking about Armand, and what Snow had said.

Ever since her father remarried, Danielle had believed a day would come when she would be free, when her life would again be her own and she could be happy. She clung to that belief like a shield after her father died, protecting her from her stepmother's wrath and her stepsisters' cruel games. Just as she now clung to the belief that she would see Armand again, that her son would know his own father.

As she ate, she kept seeing her mother's tree, burned and dead. The smoke from the fireplace made her think of the Chirka wolf ripping its way from the broken hazel branches.

Talia didn't bother with a goblet, taking a long drink directly from the wine bottle before passing it to Snow. To Danielle, she said, "Are you sure you want to come with us, Princess? Lone demons or trolls are nothing compared to the dangers of Fairytown. We don't even know if we'll be able to find Armand once we get there."

"He found me," Danielle said.

"He didn't have to face a Chirka," said Snow.

"No, he had to face my stepmother. I'm going."

Talia walked to the bags Snow had carried up from below. She dug through one until she found a black lacquered pipe and a pouch of tobacco. She packed a bit of the brown leaf into the pipe, then used a branch from the fire to light it. "It's late. You should sleep, Princess. I don't know when you'll be able to rest again, and I'll wager you won't have such nice, clean sheets when you do."

"My husband is missing. My mother is gone. How am I supposed to rest?"

"You'd be amazed what people can sleep through," Talia said, her voice tinged with bitterness. She blew a stream of smoke toward the fireplace. "You, too, Snow."

"What about you?" Danielle asked.

The firelight danced red in Talia's eyes. "I've had enough sleep for four lifetimes."

Something in her expression stopped Danielle's protests cold. She grabbed a nightgown for herself and another for Snow, and changed in silence.

She didn't want to admit her exhaustion to Talia, but fatigue weighed her down with every step. She had fought a demon, then crossed half the city to fight a troll. Not to mention the long climb from the hidden rooms below the palace. Only stubbornness had kept her from collapsing on one of the benches down below.

"Don't worry," said Snow as she climbed into bed from the other side, taking the spot where Armand would normally sleep. "I don't snore."

Danielle swallowed a lump in her throat and forced a smile.

Snow was right: she didn't snore. But she was a blanket thief, and she tossed and kicked so much she nearly knocked Danielle out of bed.

Danielle yawned and looked around. No sunlight pierced the makeshift curtains over the window. She glanced over at Snow and shook her head. Snow wore her choker even to sleep. Orange light flickered in the oval mirrors.

Beyond the bed's silken canopy, the fire silhouetted Talia's form as she danced. She wore tight, knee-high trousers and a black vest. Her feet were bare. A long, sinuously curved blade flashed in her hand, too large for a knife, but not quite long enough to be a proper sword.

Talia spun and slashed the blade in a tight, flat arc. At the same time, her back leg shot upward, the heel snapping out at groin height. Danielle winced in sympathy for Talia's imaginary foe.

Already Talia had leaped away from the fireplace, somersaulting soundlessly across the floor and rising with her weapon held high, parrying a blow from above. She twisted, drawing the blade across her enemy's stomach and then pivoting again to strike with her bare hand.

Danielle listened to the hiss of the blade through the air as Talia made her way around the room. Every movement was graceful and efficient in its deadliness.

"What happened to you?" Danielle whispered.

Only the faintest hesitation gave any sign Talia had heard. And then she was turning away, catching a foe's arm with her free hand and flicking the tip of her sword across his throat.

Danielle studied Talia closely as they crossed the courtyard. She found no trace of weariness or fatigue. Snow still yawned and squinted against the rising sun, and the muscles in Danielle's shoulders and legs protested with every step she took, but Talia might as well have spent the previous day relaxing in the sun.

Danielle paused to tug her cloak back over her sword, glancing about to make sure nobody had seen.

It wouldn't do to have people asking why the princess was walking about armed. "Ambassador Trittibar lives here in the palace?"

She had seen the fairy ambassador twice in her time here. He was a tall, overly slender man with long white hair and a boyish face. His eyes had a purple hue, and they shone like fresh-blown glass.

"He has an apartment by the mews." Snow pointed to the tall stone enclosure which housed the royal family's hunting falcons.

"That's not common knowledge," Talia added, her voice firm. "The queen would prefer it remained such."

Danielle nodded without understanding. The mews were a narrow structure built against the wall, like a miniature home on stilts. From the size, she guessed at least a dozen birds could live comfortably inside.

Feathers and white fluff littered the grass. She could only assume there was another secret passage, like the one in her own chambers. She knew there had to be at least one other passageway, since the queen had never emerged through the hidden door in her privy. How many other secrets were hidden throughout the palace?

"King Theodore," she said softly. "What does he know about the two of you?" Danielle gestured to Talia and Snow. "Who you really are, and what you do for the queen?"

"Theo has his own spies scattered throughout Lorindar," said Snow. "He doesn't tell Bea about them. Why should she tell him about us?"

"*King* Theodore knows I'm one of the queen's personal servants," Talia said, scowling at Snow. "And he knows Queen Beatrice sometimes tends to matters best kept quiet. They have an understanding. She's saved his life at least twice that he knows of."

A young man in the green and silver of the Whiteshore family bowed as they neared the mews. He held a string of dead rabbits in one hand.

Danielle forced a smile. She had hoped they would go unnoticed, but even this early in the morning there were people about.

"Good morning, Peter." Peter was a third-year apprentice to the master falconer. Thick leather gauntlets protected his hands and forearms.

Peter straightened. "Are you leaving us, Your Highness?"

Danielle glanced at the bulging travel pack Talia wore over her shoulder and the rolled-up blanket Snow carried in the same way. Danielle had offered to help, but it would have been too suspicious for the princess to haul her own belongings around like a common servant.

"I was looking for . . . I thought I would go for a picnic," Danielle said. "Along the eastern beach." She flushed. "We just wanted to stop and see the birds before we went, that's all."

Peter waited, clearly unwilling to question the princess' word. "I was getting ready to feed them," he said slowly. "If you'd like to take one out for a hunt, I can—"

"No, you don't have to do that," said Danielle. She glanced around for help, but Talia appeared to be fighting a smirk.

Snow had plucked a handful of clover from the ground, and was brushing the leaves over her lips and chin. "You're not very good at this, are you?"

"Is everything all right, Highness?" Peter set the rabbits down. "I heard about the attack yesterday. Are you sure it's wise to leave the palace? If you'd like, I could fetch one of the guards to escort you."

Before he could move, Snow stepped closer and shoved her clover in Peter's face. "Do these smell funny to you?"

Peter sniffed. His eyes fluttered, and his body sagged. Talia caught his arm, spinning him around so that his head didn't strike the mews as he fell.

"You're the princess of Lorindar," Talia said. "He wouldn't dare question you like that if you didn't treat everyone as your friend. All you needed was to order him to leave, and he would have done it."

"Did you hurt him?" Danielle asked.

"Hardly." Snow grinned and picked up the clover. "He'll take a quick nap, though. If he remembers us at all, he'll think we were a part of his dream."

Talia was looking around to see if anyone else had noticed. "People sometimes talk about their dreams, you know."

"I can promise you he won't talk about this one." She tugged Danielle's hand, pulling her around Peter to the corner where the mews pressed up against the palace wall. Ivy coated the stone here, and the mews shaded the wall from the sun. Snow glanced around to make sure nobody was watching, then pressed her face to a gap in the stones where the mortar had crumbled away. "Want me to save a few clovers for you?"

A faint voice answered, too low for Danielle to make out the individual words. Snow giggled. "It's not Danielle's fault. She's too honest for her own good. Don't worry, Talia and I will teach her. She'll be lying like a politician in no time."

"Who are you talking to?" Danielle asked, trying not to take affront.

Snow stepped back. Moments later, a tiny man stepped out from a crack between the stones.

Danielle stared. "Ambassador Trittibar?"

"At your service, Princess." No taller than Danielle's finger, Trittibar held an ivy leaf for balance as he gave a quick bow. He looked the same as Danielle remembered, only smaller. His hair was pulled into a long white braid, as was his beard. He wore a billowy shirt of bright green, which clashed horribly with his rust-colored trousers. A silver sash and belt completed the disastrous ensemble.

"So the queen tells me you need to enter Fairytown?" He fumbled with a pouch at his belt. "Why don't you ladies step inside?

"Said the dragon to the virgin," Talia muttered.

Trittibar continued as if he hadn't heard. "Quickly now, before young Peter recovers. We wouldn't want to use another enchantment. Too many spells in one morning aren't healthy for a growing boy."

"How do we get in?" Danielle asked.

Snow was already reaching down to take something from Trittibar. She held out her hand to Danielle. A tiny brown speck, no larger than a flake of pepper, lay in the middle of her palm. "Eat this."

Talia caught Snow's wrist. "We don't even know what that is."

"You don't think you can fit through my doorway looking like that, do you?" Trittibar asked. "Even if you could, think what you'd do to my furniture!"

"The queen trusts him," Danielle said. She pressed the tip of her finger to Snow's palm. The speck stuck. She brought her finger to her mouth, touching the tip to her tongue. Whatever it was dissolved almost instantly, with a faint, bitter taste which reminded her a little of pickles.

A wicked grin spread over Snow's face as she took Danielle's hand. "Hold on, Princess."

Snow's fingers began to grow, her hand enveloping Danielle's. Soon, Snow's index finger looped around Danielle's wrist. The wall stretched upward, as did Snow and Talia. Danielle's shoulder twinged as her arm was pulled up, until she hung from Snow's grip. Her feet kicked the top of the grass. By now, Snow held Danielle's hand with only her finger and thumb.

Her other hand reached down to cup Danielle's back and legs like a doll.

"Isn't it fun?" Snow asked.

Danielle clutched the side of Snow's hand. She knew she was no higher than before, but if she were to fall, she would tumble many times her own height before she hit the earth.

Snow brought her hand to the wall, where Trittibar waited with his arms ready. He took Danielle's hands, guiding her down like a coachman leading his lady from a carriage. Her shoulders brushed the stones to either side.

"Welcome to my humble home, Your Highness. Do watch out for spiders."

"Spiders?" Danielle's hand went to her sword, which had shrunk along with her. Given her size, even the smallest spider would be as large as her head. She searched the shadows overhead for any sign of motion.

Trittibar chuckled. "Most ladies of your station would scream at my little jest. I hope you'll forgive me. You have my word, there are no spiders in my home. I deal with enough vermin in my position as ambassador."

He stepped back, motioning for Danielle to follow. The gap in the stone widened farther back, giving him room to squeeze past her. "Princess Talia." He extended his arms and waited as Talia shrank.

Talia ignored him. Without a word, she jumped from Snow's hand and joined Danielle in the darkness.

Outside, Snow touched her tongue to her hand. She seemed a giantess as she reached out to grab the ivy on the wall. Her grip tightened as she shrank. She brought her other hand up to catch a leaf directly above the crack. Switching both hands to the leaf, she swung her feet back and forth like a child, then jumped.

Trittibar tried valiantly to catch her, but only managed to break her fall. They tumbled to the ground together. Snow was giggling as she pushed herself off of the ambassador.

"Graceful as always, Princess Ermillina," said Trittibar. He accepted her hand, and Snow pulled him to his feet. Dusting himself off, he glanced out one last time to check on Peter. "If you'll come with me, ladies?"

The stones of the inner wall were as thick as Danielle's arm was long. At least, when she was her normal size. The wall itself was three stones thick. For someone Trittibar's size, an entire mansion could fit within this wall.

To her right, two white feathers hung suspended by the quills, covering a slender doorway. The feathers seemed to interlace, bound so tightly they appeared to be a single feather with two shafts. Trittibar clapped his hands, and the feathers parted to reveal a miniature apartment.

"Please leave your shoes at the entryway," Trittibar said, stepping past them.

Danielle kicked off her boots and followed him inside. Her feet sank into soft mole fur. "It's very . . . tall."

It was like standing inside a tower. Two stones had been left out of the middle of the wall, creating a tall hollow space. Danielle wondered if it had been built this way originally, or if this was a later addition.

Wooden steps spiraled up the rock. She knew they were within the palace walls, and that this entire space would be less than half her height, but at her current size it seemed to stretch up forever. Thin shafts of muted sunlight showed where other cracks led to the outside world. Wooden platforms jutted from the rock, suspended by golden threads and beams made of oak twigs.

The air smelled of maple syrup. Bookshelves lined

the far wall, though not nearly as many as the library beneath the palace. Velvet-cushioned chairs sat to one side. To the other, a blue flame heated a silver kettle.

"Fire is hard to maintain at this scale." Trittibar used a metal poker with a hook to retrieve the kettle. He smiled at Snow. "You've seen how fast twigs burn. Magically shrunken logs are little better than twigs. I used to use a normal-sized candle stub, but I like this better." He poured himself a cup of tea and sat down, still watching Snow.

"What does this have to do with Prince Armand?" Talia said.

Trittibar raised his hand, still watching Snow. "Well?"

"You slowed the flame," Snow said. She walked to the mantel and retrieved three more teacups. Clearly she had been here before. "It's hardly flickering at all."

"Very good." Trittibar poured the rest of the tea. "Speed it up again, if you can."

Snow handed the cups to Danielle and Talia, then knelt in front of the fire. She touched her choker and muttered to herself. Orange light rippled through the flame, then disappeared again. Snow took a deep breath and tried again.

"Remember, this isn't witchcraft," said Trittibar. "You're fighting fairy magic now."

"I thought the wards in the walls prevented fairy magic," Danielle said.

"They do." Trittibar grinned. "Fortunately, we're inside the wards. What good is mail to a warrior who stands within one of the links?"

"And the magic you used to shrink us?" Talia asked.

"Would have triggered the wards if Snow hadn't been here to muffle them." He turned to Snow. "The fire still burns."

Snow shook her head. "I can see the spell, but I can't break it."

"The trick isn't to break it," Trittibar said. He snapped his fingers, and the flame turned green. "Simply redirect the power."

"We don't have time for this," Talia said.

"Keep trying." Trittibar twirled the braid of his beard around one finger. "Beatrice tells me you believe Armand to be in Fairytown."

"And she told us you'd help," Talia snapped. "Are you going to tell us how to get into Fairytown, or are you going to waste our time with games?"

"Talia, please," Snow said. "Trittibar is—"

"No, my dear," said Trittibar. He sipped his tea. "I know the tale of Sleeping Beauty. She has earned her hatred. But before you loose your rage on me, tell me this. If your friend can't defeat my meager powers, how do you hope to overcome the magics of Fairytown?"

Talia didn't answer. The ambassador turned to Danielle. "The queen tells me there was an attempt on your life?"

"Three," said Talia.

"My stepsister tried to kill me in my bedroom," Danielle said. "They also summoned a demon, a Chirka, which attacked us when we went to my old house. And there was a troll who tried to kill us, too." She tasted the tea. It was too thick and sweet for her liking, and she set the cup on the table.

"An acquired taste," Trittibar admitted. "So they've taken Armand to Fairytown. But how would they gain entry?" He continued to twirl his beard as he muttered to himself. "Noble blood gives each of you the right, but your stepsisters would require special dispensation from a fairy of the pure caste."

"Charlotte leaped off of the north wall and flew

away to escape the guards," Danielle said. "How hard would it be to sneak into Fairytown?"

Trittibar pointed to Snow, who was talking to herself as she studied the fire. "Your friend is a moderately skilled witch, but she's yet to break my control of the flames."

"Maybe I would if you'd stop distracting me," Snow said.

Danielle rose without speaking. She picked up the teapot, nudged Snow to one side, and flung the contents into the fireplace. Sweet-smelling smoke burst from the wood as the flame fizzled and sparked. Turning back to Trittibar, she said, "Now will you help us?"

"I see why Beatrice likes you," Trittibar said. "But the walls of Fairytown are harder to break." He stood and walked toward the stairs. "How much do you ladies know of Malindar's Treaty?"

Talia cocked her head at Snow. "She could probably recite it."

"Fairytown hosts the only surviving fairy hill for hundreds of miles in any direction," Trittibar said. He grabbed a large, leather-bound book. The cover was inlaid with silver, engraved to resemble a swiftly moving river spilling down the book's spine. "Through that hill lies another world, and the source of our magic. As you can imagine, we guard our city well."

He tapped the spine of the book, and the silver river began to flow. Glittering water rushed from the book to splash upon the floor. The metal continued to fall, but the small puddle on the floor never grew, nor did the metal in the cover diminish. He opened the book and stepped back, leaving it balanced upon the rippling falls. "You know this image, I assume?"

The painting was similar to the tapestry in Danielle's quarters. An army of human knights and wizards faced the strongest of the fairy creatures: giants, trolls, and even a dragon or two. Dead from either side littered the trampled grass. There were more human corpses than fairy, but the humans still outnumbered their foes.

"Few of your kind realize how close we were to winning," said Trittibar. "Another day, and all of Lorindar would have belonged to us."

"How?" Talia asked. She pointed to the painting. "You were outflanked. Prince Reginald's Silverlance cavalry cut you off to the north. Your only retreat would drive you east, where Queen Celeste had a small force of witches waiting."

Trittibar pursed his lips. "Look closer."

Danielle didn't understand, but she did as she was told. Her head nearly touched Talia's and Snow's as they peered at the painting, which was far more detailed than any human work. Detailed and gruesome.

Danielle lacked the training to distinguish different units or interpret the military maneuvers like Talia did. To her eye, the fairies were both surrounded and outnumbered.

"I see them," Snow whispered. She pointed to an area of trampled earth behind the prince's cavalry, where armored corpses lay.

"Very good," said Trittibar.

Talia snorted. "There's nothing there."

"But there is." Snow touched a fallen archer. "A fairy hides behind his body. Three others crouch here, concealed by the horse. They're everywhere."

Danielle squinted at the page. "I don't see—"

"You don't see, because they were hidden," Trittibar said. "These are my ancestors. My line long ago learned the secret of shifting our size. By the time the Battle of Fairytown began, most of your forces unknowingly carried fairy warriors in their packs, their tents, sometimes even in their armor. Every one of them was ready to die before allowing you to take that hill."

"I don't understand," Danielle said. She pointed to the horse. "It's a painting. How do you paint something that's unseen?"

"*She* sees them," Trittibar said, nodding at Snow. He pursed his lips. "Unfortunately for us, so did Malindar. He was a clever one. Young and foolhardy, but clever. Exposing us would have forced us to attack before we were ready, but the result would have been the same. Instead, the bastard pretended to flee. He and a handful of your wizards and witches then snuck back around, to the river. With our forces rallied to meet your army, Malindar managed to slip past us and enter Fairytown. He used the magic of our own hill to sunder the island."

Trittibar shook his head. "He would have sent all of Lorindar to the bottom of the ocean. Every last human would have died, along with most of my people." He turned the page, and Danielle saw a young man accepting a curved, golden sword from a honey-skinned woman who wore armor of living wood. "We had underestimated the depth of your madness, the length to which you humans will go to stave off defeat. So the king and queen accepted your terms. Their only condition was that none of your kind ever again be permitted within the walls of Fairytown. We couldn't risk the loss of our hill, and this was the only way to make sure nobody tried to finish what Malindar started all those centuries ago.

"The one exception is for those of royal blood. Your rulers insisted. They wanted free reign of the entire island. All others require the dispensation of—"

He stopped in mid-sentence and began to chuckle. "Trittibar, you diminutive old fool."

"What is it?" Danielle asked.

"Your stepsisters kidnapped Prince Armand. *He* could take them through the walls of Fairytown."

Danielle shook her head. "Armand wouldn't—"

"If your stepsisters have magic enough to conjure a Chirka, they're strong enough to cloud a man's mind." He closed the book. The silver waterfall reversed direction, flowing back into the cover with a ringing splash. "The treaty protects your nobles. No fairy would dare aid your stepsisters. But if Armand thought he was acting of his own volition . . ."

"What about Brahkop?" Danielle asked. "He tried to murder us."

"Brahkop's an exile," Trittibar said. "Casteless, and cut off from the power of the hill. By our law, he's no more of fairy blood than you, Your Highness."

"So why take Armand to Fairytown?" Talia asked.

"That's something you'll have to ask his kidnappers," Trittibar said. Setting the book on his chair, he led them back toward the door. "Peter should have recovered and finished with the birds by now, I think."

Danielle glanced at Snow and Talia. "I don't understand. Will you help us or not?"

"I am Armand's friend, Highness," Trittibar said. "I would be yours as well. When you reach the wall of Fairytown, speak the word 'Diglet' three times."

"Diglet?" Talia rolled her eyes. "That's the password to get into Fairytown?"

Trittibar was already pushing through the feather curtain, into the stone hallway. "Come, ladies." He chuckled as he walked. "Your ride awaits."

Trittibar hadn't restored them to their normal size, as Danielle had expected. Instead, he had climbed up the ivy to the spot where the roof of the mews joined the wall. The roof sloped at an angle which made climbing difficult, but not impossible. Talia strode like a cat along the cedar shingles, but Danielle and Snow moved more cautiously. Danielle's muscles were still sore from yesterday's exertions, and this climb left her cringing and rubbing her arms.

Trittibar crawled to the peak of the roof and cupped one hand over his eyes as he scanned the courtyard. He nodded, then hopped down to the second row of shingles. He touched one, and it fell inward like a trapdoor. "There she is," he said. "Her name is Karina. She'll get you to Fairytown by late afternoon."

"This is madness," Talia said.

"Nonsense," laughed Trittibar. "She's far faster than any horse or ship, and she'll keep you as safe as a dozen of your guards."

"If she doesn't eat us first," Talia retorted.

Danielle stepped around Talia to peer through the hole in the roof. The smell of straw and bird droppings filled her nose. She knew at once which bird was Trittibar's.

Karina was smaller than the other falcons, though she was still large enough to snatch all three girls in her claws. Her feathers were white as newfallen snow, tipped with red along the wings. She shrieked excitedly at Trittibar, shifting on her perch and spreading her wings. Her chest was mottled with red, and as she hopped to a closer perch, Danielle could see an amber crest on the top of her head.

"The splash of red on her brow is called the fairy crown," Trittibar said proudly. "They say it's proof that Karina is a descendant of the first falcon brought here by the fairy king, back when this world was born."

Most of the other falcons were still on the floor, ripping apart the remains of their breakfast. Trittibar put his fingers to his mouth and gave a low, warbling whistle.

Karina leaped into the air, flying directly toward the

spot where Danielle and the others stood. Danielle flinched and stepped back. The hole was too small. The falcon would snap her wings if she didn't turn aside.

Trittibar hastily tapped a second shingle, which began to open outward.

Karina burst through the gap, knocking the shingle so it banged against the roof.

"Quiet, you," Trittibar scolded, but he was grinning as he spoke. Karina landed and ducked her head, tucking her beak beneath one wing. Trittibar reached up to scratch the feathers of her chest. She twisted her head still further, and the neck feathers poofed out so he could reach the skin.

In the open sunlight, Karina was even more impressive. Though smaller than the other hunting birds, something in those pearl-black eyes told Danielle that this was a bird who knew nothing of fear. Both the energy of a child and the wisdom of a grandparent spoke to her from those eyes. "You're beautiful."

Karina bobbed her head.

"I'm not riding a fairy bird across this island," Talia said.

"Of course not." Trittibar gave the falcon one last pat, then walked over to close the shingles. "You'll be harnessed to her chest."

He led them down the other side of the roof. There, a stone gutter drained rainwater into a barrel on the ground. Trittibar stopped at a cluster of ivy which grew near the end of the gutter. Shoving aside the leaves and vines, he pulled out a large leather harness and an enormous basket.

"Dried willow from the elven forests," he said, tapping the basket. "Light as air, and strong as steel." He set the basket to one side and began tossing the harness straps over Karina's back and wings.

Karina took a playful nip at Trittibar's beard. He

yanked it free and used the end to swat her on the beak. "None of that now," he said. "It's time to work."

He pulled the harness tight, buckling the straps so they crossed in the center of her chest. Then he lifted the basket. "Could you hold this, my dear?" he said to Snow.

Snow grabbed the basket, which was twice as tall as she was, and held it steady as Trittibar threaded more straps through the back of the basket. A heavy sheet of white leather covered the top, beneath Karina's chin.

"This can be buckled from the inside or out," he said, showing them the brass buckles along the top of the basket. "Make sure all of the buckles are pulled tight. Otherwise there's nothing to stop you from tumbling out if Karina goes into a dive."

"I'm walking," Talia said. "I'll meet you in Fairytown."

Danielle was already moving toward Karina. Trittibar smiled and laced his fingers together, providing a stirrup to boost her into the basket. He was stronger than he appeared, hoisting her over the edge as if she weighed no more than a feather. Which was close to the truth, really.

Cushions and blankets lined the bottom of the basket. Danielle scooted to one side to make room for the others. The basket hung at an odd angle. Resting with her back against the far side, she sat facing Karina's chest, which seemed the most comfortable. She tried to find a position where her sword wouldn't catch the holes of the basket, and finally ended up removing the sword and belt altogether.

Snow slid down beside her, giggling. As soon as her feet touched the bottom of the basket, Snow was twisting around and pulling herself back up to peer out at Talia. "Hurry up, fraidycat. It'll be fun."

Talia threw one of their bags into the basket, knocking Snow down. Danielle watched as Talia turned back to Trittibar and asked, "How do we get back to our normal size? I'm not hunting the prince like this."

Trittibar grabbed a large pouch from his sash. One side was white, the other black, and Danielle could see that it was divided in the middle, like two sacks sewn together as one. Trittibar retrieved three black objects the size and shape of walnuts. "These spores will change you back to your normal, oversized selves. I trust I don't have to tell you to wait until after you've landed?"

Talia tossed the rest of their belongings in with Danielle and Snow. Ignoring Trittibar's offer of assistance, she jumped to grab the upper edge of the basket. She swung one leg over the edge and dropped lightly down beside Snow.

With three people, even shrunken as they were, the basket was fairly crowded. Danielle tried to squirm toward one side to give the others room.

Talia stood and began tugging the buckles tight. Danielle did the same on her side, working the thick, stiff leather through loops woven into the basket.

"Are you ready?" Trittibar asked.

Talia lay back, closing her eyes and muttering, "I suppose it's too much to expect that this thing is just going to run really fast along the ground?"

Trittibar chuckled. He walked around to pat Karina's wing. "Take them to Fairytown, swiftly as you can. And, Princess?"

Danielle hesitated, not sure which princess he meant.

"Bring your husband home safe. And yourself."

Trittibar whistled, and the world fell away. The falcon turned sharply to the left, away from the mews. Danielle fell against Snow, who slid onto Talia. Wind rushed through the basket as Karina soared past the top of the wall. She circled over the palace, climbing higher and higher until the people below were little more than specks.

Danielle gasped as the ocean came into view. Sunlight sparkled on the water. Frost tipped the waves nearest the cliffs while, farther out, the sea appeared as rippled blue glass.

Talia groaned. "If we survive this, I'm taking a horse back from Fairytown."

That *if* stuck in Danielle's mind long after the palace shrank from view.

CHAPTER 6

❄

DANIELLE HAD NEVER realized how large the kingdom of Lorindar truly was. She lay on her stomach, hands folded beneath her chin as she stared through the cracks of the basket at the land below. Though the initial launch had been terrifying, now she barely noticed the faint tremor when Karina flapped her wings, or the shifting of the basket as she curved this way and that, following the whims of the wind.

Talia, on the other hand, sat with her knees to her chest, taking deep, slow breaths. Sweat dampened her skin.

"Don't worry," said Danielle. "I'm sure we'll be there soon."

Snow shook her head. "It's a two-day ride on horse-back. But see down there, where the King's Road splits off to the east? That heads to the Coastal Highway, and it means we're making much better time. We should reach Fairytown later today."

"Fairytown," Talia muttered. "What a stupid name."

"That's not the true name," Snow said. "The fairies' name means something like 'Home away from home, trapped between two big rocks and surrounded by tasty mushrooms that make you feel like you're turning into a puddle.' But 'Fairytown' is shorter."

Talia caught a tuft of down that had slipped into the basket. She used both hands to shove the feather through one of the cracks, then brushed her palms on her trousers. "I'm never going to get the smell of bird out of my clothes."

Danielle rolled onto her side. "What did they do to you, Talia?"

"Who?"

"The fairies." She had wanted to ask since they left the palace, but it had taken until now to work up the courage. "I've heard the tales, but there has to be more to it. You're the one who told me stories don't tell the whole truth."

"I don't like to talk about it," Talia said.

"I understand. But we're going to be in Fairytown. From what Trittibar said, we might be the only humans for miles. I thought—"

"I'm not going to go into a berserker rage and start ripping the wings from pixies or tossing dwarves into the chasm, if that's what you're worried about." Talia grabbed a skin of water and took several deep swallows. "Don't trust them. That's all you need to know."

"Trittibar helped us," Danielle said. "Most of the fairies in your story tried to help you. Even after you were cursed, the last fairy did her best to protect you. Or is that not how it really happened?"

Snow had been deliberately moving away from them, digging through a bundle Trittibar had thrown in at the last moment. She pulled out an irregular ball the size of her head. The skin was clear on one side, white on the other, and filled with a thick red fluid. Snow pulled her knife and poked a hole in the skin. "Pomegranate seed," she said, sucking out the juice. She wiped her chin on the back of her wrist. "You should tell her, Talia."

"You should stay out of this."

Snow reached over to put a juice-stained hand on

Talia's arm. " 'Knowledge ranks first among all weapons.' King Phillipe the Second said that. The more Danielle knows, the better prepared she'll be."

"Phillipe. Isn't he the one who took a cloth yard arrow to the throat?" Talia pulled away from Snow's touch. "Knowledge might make a good weapon, but it's lousy armor."

"I don't mean to upset you," Danielle said.

"Of course not. Everyone always has the best of intentions." Talia snorted and tucked a few sweaty strands of hair behind her ear. "Sure, the fairies gave me their 'gifts.' Some of them take great pleasure in 'improving' us lowly humans. They gave me grace, beauty, the voice of an angel . . . everything a princess needs to satisfy her future husband."

She reached into her bag and pulled out the spindle-shaped zaraq whip she had taken from the palace. "Then there was the curse, that I would die by my sixteenth birthday."

"But you didn't," Danielle said. "The last fairy saved you. You can't judge all of them from—"

"The last fairy destroyed me," Talia said. Her dark eyes were numb and empty. "She perverted the curse. Instead of death, the spell brought unending sleep. Not just to me, but to everyone in the palace. She raised a hedge of thorns around our home to shelter us from the world. For a century we slept."

"Until your prince came," Danielle said.

Talia slammed the whip's handle against the basket hard enough to elicit a squawk of protest from Karina.

"With our palace gone, my uncle claimed the throne. For years they hacked their way through the hedge until they broke through. My 'prince' was the great-great-grandson of the man who ordered the murder of my parents, my brothers and sisters, everyone who might one day awaken and challenge their rule. The only reason they allowed me to live is that they didn't know what my death would do to the fairy's spell."

Danielle wanted to reach over and offer some kind of support, feeble and worthless though the gesture might be. But she doubted Talia would appreciate it. "What happened next?"

"The prince awakened me," Talia said. "The tales got that much right, at least." She rubbed her hands together, like she was trying to clean them. "A hundred years I slept, and not once did those fairies return to see how my family fared. The one who cursed me did it out of spite. But it was her companions, through their blindness and apathy, who destroyed us."

Danielle turned toward Snow, who had set the pomegranate seed aside and was staring out the side of the basket.

"Is that how it was with you?" Danielle asked. "Your life sounds so awful in the stories, but they say you found happiness in the end."

"For close to a year, I lived with the hunter my mother had hired to kill me," Snow said. "But then she learned of his betrayal and tortured him to death. I destroyed her for that." Snow shrugged and reached for another bag. "Did we bring anything else to drink?"

"Are all of the tales like this?" Danielle asked. "Did Jack Giantslayer fall into despair and poverty? Was Red Riding Hood murdered by wolves seeking revenge for the death of their kin?"

Talia snorted. "No, Red survived. But that kind of thing changes a woman."

"Changes her how?"

"The Lady of the Red Hood is one of the most feared assassins this side of Adenkar," Snow said.

Danielle stared, trying to read their faces. "You're joking."

"It's true." Talia rolled up her sleeves and touched one of the scars on her forearm. "Bitch nearly killed the queen a few years back."

Danielle lay back, trying to absorb everything they had said. Look at how much her own story had grown and changed in the past months. The only common thread was how perfect life was supposed to be, once she had married Armand. Her hands went to her stomach.

Talia wiped her face. "I don't mean to argue with old King Phillipe, but in my experience, the best weapon is a good weapon." She grabbed Danielle's wrist and slapped a knife into her hand. "Normally I'd start with footwork, but this isn't exactly an ideal training circle. Your sword's almost as light as this knife, but you hold it like a drunken woodsman with an ax. You're too tense, and it slows you down."

Danielle tried to relax her grip.

"Not that loose," Talia said. She rapped the blade with her knuckles, and the knife spun out of Danielle's hand. The blade jabbed a hole in one of the blankets. "Use the thumb and forefinger to guide the tip. That's where your control comes from."

She demonstrated with the knife, then handed it back to Danielle, who tried to imitate Talia's movements. She flicked the tip of the blade back and forth.

"Small movements. You're not strong enough for a brute force, hack-and-slash approach. Fortunately, you don't need one with that sword. A light kiss with the tip in the right spot will kill a man as dead as a broadsword through the heart." Talia touched her throat. "Here's your best target, if you can hit it. A feint at the groin is good, too, if you're fighting a man. The sight of a blade coming for their jewels will make most men leap back and lower their guard."

"I don't want to kill anyone," Danielle said, staring at the knife.

"I'm sure your stepsisters will be delighted to hear

that." Talia caught Danielle's wrist and twisted the knife from her hand. "It means they'll have a much easier time killing you." She gestured for Danielle to draw her own knife. "This time when I lunge, bring the blade across your body to knock mine aside. Take it slowly. First learn the movements, then worry about speed."

For close to an hour they practiced. Danielle suspected it was as much for Talia's sake as for hers, something to distract Talia from her discomfort. By the time Karina began to circle, Danielle's hand was cramped and sweaty, and her shoulder ached from trying the different lunges and parries Talia had made her do again and again.

Danielle put the knife away and turned over, studying the ground below. Awe swept all other feelings aside as she gazed down at the chasm that split the island in two. Malindar's Triumph, some called it. The canyon ran the width of the island, an ugly gash that seemed to stretch on forever. Even so high in the air, she could see no sign of the ocean.

Grass and trees grew right up to the edges of the chasm, and in some places, the trees actually clung to the vertical stone, maintaining an impossibly precarious hold. As they flew over the crevasse, Danielle could see water at the bottom, a ribbon of sky-blue glass.

"There it is," Snow said, pointing.

Karina veered west, and Danielle saw it: Fairytown. A huge wall drew a rough circle on either side of the chasm. At the center, a silver bridge joined the two halves of the fairy city. From here, the bridge appeared to be made of silk and spiderweb. Two castles stood on either side of the bridge. The one to the north was a wonder of white spires and majestic curves. To the south was an equally magnificent structure of ebony roofs and golden buttresses.

In some places, the land seemed almost mundane: the crowded greenery of the woods, an open field where a herd of cattle grazed. Other parts of Fairytown were like images from a dream. A small lake of ice shone like a jewel in the sun. Pink trees crowded around a sparkling path leading to the ebony palace.

Karina flew lower, toward the northern wall.

"Can't we land inside?" Danielle asked.

"Look up," said Snow.

Danielle moved to the side, squeezing next to Snow and pressing her eye to the wall of the basket. Long wisps of cloud drifted past overhead, but she saw nothing more except—

Wait. Several of those wisps had turned, mirroring Karina's flight.

"Cloud striders," Snow explained. "They can conjure lightning powerful enough to turn away a dragon."

"Don't worry," Talia added. "They probably wouldn't bother to use lightning on a nuisance like us. They'd just eat us instead."

No doubt similar guardians protected Fairytown against those who tried to enter through the river below.

Danielle braced herself as Karina dove toward the wall. It wasn't *quite* like falling, but Danielle's stomach still made a valiant attempt to climb out of her chest. Beside her, Talia clasped her eyes shut and muttered in another tongue.

Wind whistled through the basket. The trees grew larger. A brown strip of beaten earth flashed past, then returned as Karina shifted direction. They followed the road, swooping lower and lower, so fast Danielle thought they would crash. The basket shook as Karina pumped her wings. Danielle held her breath.

Beside her, Talia's fingers gripped the basket, her body tense as steel.

They touched down so gently that Danielle only knew they had landed because Karina's wings stopped flapping.

Snow was already standing to unbuckle the straps at the top of the basket. Danielle climbed to her feet to help, grimacing at the cramps in her thighs. Soon, cool air rushed in.

Snow tossed the bags out, then scrambled after, tumbling to the ground in an undignified heap. Danielle's landing was no more graceful. She hit the earth hard, then stumbled toward a cluster of dandelions at the side of the road.

"What's wrong?" Talia called out. Moving slowly, but still with more grace than Danielle could achieve on her best day, Talia slipped out of the basket and somersaulted to her feet on the road.

"That hawk needs a chamber pot."

By the time Danielle returned, Snow and Talia had finished unpacking. "Where do we go now that we're here? Do we need to inform the fairy king and queen?"

"Not if we can avoid it," Talia said. "They'd make great proclamations of their innocence and accuse us of trying to smear their names. Knowing fairies, they'd probably suggest we had arranged the whole thing ourselves in order to ruin them."

Danielle adjusted her sword and fixed her belt. "That's madness."

"That's fairy politics," Snow said. "Don't worry, I have a friend who should be able to help us."

Danielle barely heard. Now that more urgent needs had been taken care of, she had finally turned her attention to the wall of Fairytown.

Even at her full height, Danielle would have found

the wall an imposing sight. It was easily twice as high as the palace wall back home. Only instead of stone and mortar, this was made of vines and thorns.

The largest of the vines were thick as trees, with rough bark giving them the brownish color Danielle had seen from the air. The thorns varied in color from dark purple to almost pure black. The smaller thorns shone like liquid. The largest were the length of full spears. These were duller in color, and had a tendency to flake near the base.

Danielle turned to Talia, whose jaw was tight. "Are you all right?"

"Fairies like to manipulate living things," Talia said. "People, animals, plants . . . they're easier to shape and control than cold rock. I'm told the hedge of thorns became quite popular after my imprisonment."

The skeleton of a dog or wolf hung a short distance in, suspended on two medium-sized thorns. A family of sparrows had built a nest in the rib cage.

"I've seen it before," Talia continued. "Snow and I were here a year or so back, chasing a spy from Silvershell Port. He had a magical belt that let him transform into a donkey. He'd been hiding out in the stables for close to a year before Snow caught on. We spent a day tracking him around Fairytown, less than a stone's throw from this wall." Under her breath, so low Danielle barely heard, she added, "Hated it then, too."

"Did you catch him?" Danielle asked.

"It was six months at the most before I discovered him," Snow said, walking over to join them. "He lured us to the chasm south of Fairytown, then changed into his donkey form and tried to kick us over the edge." She grinned. "Let's just say the ass-kicking didn't go quite the way he had hoped."

"If I'd known how many times you were going to make that joke, I'd have pushed you after him." Talia finished strapping her short sword to her belt, swiveling it around so the hilt rode in the center of her lower back. Her whip went into a small sheath on her hip.

"You're no fun." Snow pressed one of Trittibar's magical spores into Danielle's hand. "Eat up."

The spore felt like a thin-shelled seed. Snow was already chewing hers. Talia tossed hers into the air, catching it in her mouth.

Danielle followed suit. The shell crunched open as soon as it touched her tongue, spilling dry, rounded nodules that tasted bitter and sour, like mushrooms gone bad. She forced herself to swallow.

"You might want to sit down," Snow said. She ignored her own advice, spreading her arms as she began to grow. Her feet pressed into each other, and her arms whirled madly as she fought for balance. She staggered sideways. With a happy shriek, she tumbled into the grass, giggling madly.

Talia simply balanced on the toes of one foot. Her other foot rested lightly on her thigh. That would be the fairy gift of grace. She held their bags in her arms, and kept her eyes shut as Trittibar's magic restored her and their belongings to normal size.

Following Snow's advice, Danielle sat with her legs extended as the magic took effect. Even so, she had to wiggle and squirm as her body spread across the earth. She had the strangest sensation of falling *up*, and her fingers dug into the dirt for security. She held her breath and shifted her weight, trying to keep the dirt from staining her clothes as her limbs stretched.

By the time she stopped moving, Talia had already grabbed one of the waterskins. She rinsed and spat. "Fairy magic tastes *foul*."

Snow brushed dirt and grass from her clothes. Streaks of green stained her sleeve and back, but a little vinegar would take that right out.

Karina flew to the wall, landing lightly on one of the outer thorns. She spread her wings and cocked her head.

"Thank you," said Danielle. "You must be hungry after flying for so long." The little falcon had crossed half the island in less than a day. "I'm sure you'll be able to find food on the way home. Please thank Trittibar for his help."

With a soft screech, Karina launched into the air. Danielle watched her disappear into the fading sunlight, then turned back to the wall of thorns. "How do we get in?" she asked. "There's no gate, no guards or doors."

"It's safer this way," said Talia. "Doors can be broken. Fortunately, Trittibar gave us the password." She strode toward the wall, her spine straight as a spear. When she was close enough to touch the nearest thorns, she raised her voice and said, "Diglet. Diglet. Diglet."

"What do you want?"

Danielle jumped. Standing on the road beside Talia was a little blue man with oversized pointed ears and a tangled nest of black hair: a goblin. His skin was a much darker shade than Brahkop's had been. Yellow fangs curved up from his lower lip, giving him a permanent grin. He wore a vest of soft purple leather with crystal buttons. Matching purple ribbons decorated his black trousers. A single short knife hung at his hip.

"Who are you?" Danielle asked.

"I'm Diglet, of course." Oversized yellow eyes studied Danielle. "And who might you be?"

"We need to enter Fairytown," Talia said, before Danielle could answer. "That's all you need to know."

Diglet sniffed. "No need to be rude, Your Highness. I'm just doing my job."

"If you know she's a princess, why did you want to know who we were?" Danielle asked.

Diglet stepped closer, sniffing again as he neared Danielle. "Commoner by blood, but. . . ." His bulbous nose wrinkled. "You married a noble, I take it? Got yourself knocked up with a little princeling, from the smell of it."

Danielle folded her arms, trying to quell a rush of embarrassment. Would everyone in Fairytown be able to smell her condition?

Diglet was already moving on to Snow. "Nobles all. But that doesn't tell me who you are or why you need entry into Fairytown."

"I'm sorry," Snow said, feigning confusion. "I don't remember where in Malindar's Treaty it specifies that a member of the servant caste is entitled to question human nobles before allowing them entry into Fairytown. But I do remember on page nine, section four, where those fairies attempting to deny nobles rightful entry shall be subject to punishment up to and including being bound in chains and flung into the chasm by the Dark Man himself."

"Easy now," said Diglet, raising his hands. "Ain't nobody denying nothing to no one. I was curious, that's all. It's not every day we get three princesses showing up at our wall. I'll be happy to escort you through the thorns. You, too, Highness," he said to Danielle.

"Good." Talia folded her arms. "Shall we get on with it?"

Diglet took a small step back. "About that." He glanced around, looking like a cornered animal. "Your friends can enter. I'm afraid you'll have to wait here."

Talia reached behind her back, whipping her short sword free so fast the goblin yelped. "I am Princess Talia Malak-el-Dahshat. My blood is every bit as noble as my companions'. You have no reason to detain me, goblin.''

"Nobody's questioning your blood," Diglet said. His voice had jumped in pitch, and he kept backing away until one of the thorns jabbed his neck. "Trouble is, you've been fairy-cursed." He tapped the side of his nose. "Whatever was done to you, the stench of it still lingers in your blood. You offended someone with a fair lot of power, Talia Malak-el-Dahshat, and I'm not about to let you—"

"*I* offended?" Talia repeated, her voice barely a whisper. Her sword shone in the fading sunlight.

"I'm sure that's not what he meant," said Danielle.

"Not at all," said Diglet. He reached up and gave his ear a nervous twist. "I'm sure it was nothing but a misunderstanding. This sort of thing happens all the time. Human maidens seducing fairy princes or—"

Snow caught Talia's arm and pulled her away from the goblin. "Diglet has a point. There's a subsection of the treaty which gives them discretion in barring those who have been found guilty of crimes against fairy citizens."

"I've committed no crime," snapped Talia. She glared at Diglet. "Yet."

The goblin folded his arms. "I'm sorry, Your Highness. You've been cursed by a fairy far stronger than myself. I'll not be the one flung into the hedge for allowing a fairy foe to wander freely throughout our home."

"I'll vouch for her," said Danielle. She pointed at Snow. "We both will."

"That's nice and decent of you, but who are you to vouch for her?" Diglet smirked as he waved at Danielle's clothes. "Your blood says you're royal . . . barely. But your outfit says you spend more time playing in the dirt than sitting on any throne."

His words carried little sting. All her life, Danielle

had been subject to far worse. "I am Princess Danielle Whiteshore." The name still sounded strange on her tongue.

Diglet stared. "Who?"

With a sigh, Danielle said, "Cinderella."

"Oh, right. The one with the glass shoes." He cocked his head. "How did you manage to dance in shoes like that? Sounds horribly uncomfortable." With a leer, he added, "Or maybe there wasn't much dancing, eh? At least not the kind that needs shoes."

Danielle turned to Talia. Over the past month at the palace, she had listened to enough pompous, over-blown politicians to learn the pattern of their speech. "Princess Talia, do my ears deceive me, or did this goblin just cast a most denigrating insult upon the name of Whiteshore? To imply I am little more than a tavern whore, or that the prince's taste would run to such?"

"Now wait, that's not what I—"

"I believe he did, Princess Danielle." Talia's grin was feral.

"I heard it, too!" Snow piped up.

"A most grievous slight against my honor," Danielle said. "Just as you insulted the honor of my friend, Princess Talia." She shook her head. "Queen Beatrice will be most displeased. As will your own rulers, I suspect."

"You can't tell my queen anything if you can't reach her." Diglet twisted and hopped backward, past the outer vines. He almost seemed to dance as he slipped deeper into the hedge. "I'd warn you not to follow. The thorns don't like strangers. Sorry, Princesses. That one's fairy-cursed, no mistake about it, and the queen's had too much trouble with mortals in the past. We're under strict orders. You can circle around to the king's side, but I doubt his dwarves will give you a better welcome."

Danielle waved a hand at Talia, who lowered her sword. Diglet was right. He was only doing his job. A thankless job at that. A single goblin, sent to deny those who sought to enter Fairytown. Few would bother to thank such a creature, but how many, upon being denied, would take their frustrations out on him? "How did you become the guard of this hedge, Diglet?"

Diglet shrugged. "A group of bandits killed Pirrok when he wouldn't let them through. The rest of us drew sticks."

"You drew the short stick?" Danielle guessed.

"Nah. Grint did. Then he pummeled me and broke my stick so it was shortest."

Danielle smiled. "Grint sounds like he would have gotten along with my stepsisters." Well, no. Her stepsisters would sooner die than be seen with the likes of a goblin. Still, the bullying was the same. She wondered what other jobs Diglet had been forced to do. Cleaning up after the others? Preparing their meals? And he wouldn't have had a loving spirit to help him escape his fate. What noble would fall in love with a goblin, taking him away from this life? Most likely he would keep guarding the hedge until someone like Talia grew irritated enough to run him through.

"The treaty says you can refuse to let Talia enter," Danielle said. "It doesn't say you must. What could we do to change your mind?"

"You could tell your friend to put that sword away, for one thing," Diglet snapped.

Danielle waved a hand at Talia, who scowled, but obeyed. "What if we paid you?"

Diglet snorted, then wiped his nose on his sleeve. "Goblin guards don't take bribes," he said haughtily.

Danielle studied the goblin, the way his gaze kept shifting to the ground, the way his shoulders tended to slump. "No, of course you don't. Because Grint and the other goblins would take it away from you."

"Something like that." He fingered the buttons of his vest. "Grint would steal the clothes off my back if he thought they'd fit."

In a way, it was brilliant. Diglet couldn't be bribed. If they killed him, it wouldn't change anything. They would still be stuck outside the wall, and the other goblins would simply choose the next unfortunate soul to take Diglet's place.

"What if we were to give you something truly valuable?" Danielle asked. "Something the other goblins couldn't take away?"

Diglet stood at the edge of the hedge and reached toward Danielle. "Everyone lock hands, and don't let go, not unless you want to spend your final days spitted like a pig."

Danielle twined her fingers with the goblin's. His hand was cool to the touch, rough with calluses and warts. His black nails were bitten ragged and scratched her wrist. Snow took Danielle's other hand, and Talia came last, having thrown their bags over one shoulder.

"Come on," Diglet said. He ducked beneath the first vine and began walking through the hedge. "Mind your step. The thorns know me, so they won't go out of their way to skewer you. But if you step on one, it'll go right through your foot, and once those babies go in, they don't come out."

Danielle hunched and twisted, trying to watch every direction at once. Sharp thorns caught her sleeve, but they didn't break the skin. A thorn like a curved sword tangled her hair, then flexed back on itself, allowing her to slide free.

"Don't worry, that's just the hedge's way of reminding you who's boss," Diglet said. "So long as you're with me, you're safe. Probably."

Danielle clutched the goblin's hand more tightly, both for protection and for balance. The vines were thickest on the ground, and it would be easy to fall as she turned and twisted after Diglet.

The air was darker here, and it carried a foul smell, like spoiled meat. She saw a line of black ants crawling up a vine as thick as her wrist. A thorn had broken away, and the ants swarmed over a crust of dried sap that looked like an old scab. Occasionally she saw bones or scraps of metal, though there were fewer and fewer the farther they penetrated.

"That's Yamma the ogre," Diglet said, pointing to a huge skull hanging on an equally huge thorn. "He plotted against the fairy queen. When she found out, he tried to flee. She let him get halfway through the hedge, then turned it against him. Not an easy death, but old Yamma makes a good landmark. It's easy to get turned about in here, you know."

Behind her, Danielle could hear Snow whispering. She glanced back. Snow was talking to Talia, who had her eyes squeezed shut. Both of Talia's hands clamped around Snow's wrist.

"We're almost there," Snow murmured. "You're doing great." She pressed close to Talia. Danielle moved her hand to Snow's shoulder as Snow reached for the bags. "Stop for a moment, there's a thorn caught on one of the straps . . . there you go."

"Thank you." Talia's voice was so strained Danielle barely recognized it.

Snow squeezed her arm. "I'll burn this hedge to the ground before I let it have you."

Diglet was still pointing out various sights and landmarks: an oversized beehive suspended between two thorns, a vine that had broken under its own weight, with smaller vines coiling up from the exposed ends. . . . "Hey, look at that. A hedge cat!"

Danielle looked up to see a slender gray cat slinking along the upper vines. The cat's long tail twitched furiously with each step.

"They hunt the birds and squirrels who nest in the hedge," Diglet said. "Most cats stay near the edges, but the hunting is better the farther in you go."

"Has anyone else passed through here recently?" Danielle asked. "Two human women, probably accompanied by a man."

"Not through here," Diglet said. "Not since I took over for Pirrok, at any rate. They might have gone around to the king's side, but you'd have to ask the dwarves about that."

"And there's no other way in to Fairytown?"

"Not unless they want to climb up from the chasm." Diglet gave a mock shiver. "That way carries dangers to make the hedge look as cozy as your very own bed. Come up on the queen's side of the cliff, and likely as not you'll find yourself in the labyrinth. The king's side is even worse. The dragon's nest is on that side. More sun over there, you see."

The vines had begun to thin, and Danielle could see patches of orange sky overhead. How long had they walked through the hedge? The thorns grew shorter as Diglet pulled them along. Purple-and-red buds sprinkled the vines. A few more steps, and the buds were fully bloomed flowers, each one the size and shape of a teacup. They smelled like fresh honey.

"Mind your step," said Diglet. "It wouldn't do to get yourself impaled this close to the edge." He hopped over a fat vine as thick as his body, drawing Danielle and the others after him.

The tangle of vines beneath her feet gave way to hard stone. Danielle found herself on a road paved with cobblestones that shone blue-green like the sea. Flower petals littered the ground. Crude tents stood to either side of the road, many painted with scenes of battle and carnage. A group of goblins sat in the middle of the road, playing cards and eating the roast remains of some kind of bird.

"Diglet's back," said one.

Another laughed and waved a well-chewed drumstick. "Good thing, too. I'm still hungry."

"Aw, he doesn't have enough meat to be worth butchering," said a third.

"Hey, tell the runt to run and fetch me. . . ."

The goblins' taunts stopped abruptly as Danielle knelt, placed both hands on Diglet's cheeks, and kissed him square on the mouth. His breath was foul and fetid, and his lips were badly chapped, but she held the kiss long enough to make sure every last goblin had seen. Breaking away, she said, "Thank you, Diglet. We would have been lost without your help."

Snow was next, throwing herself into the role with such enthusiasm that she knocked Danielle to the ground. "The way you fought those horrid kidnappers . . . it was incredible!" Snow wrapped her fingers around Diglet's ears and pulled him close, kissing him so long the poor goblin gasped for breath when she finished. "I'll always remember the sight of you leaping forth from the hedge, like one of the warrior gods of old, wreaking vengeance upon those foul beasts who would have stolen our virtue."

"Stolen your . . ." Talia coughed and looked away.

Snow blushed, but continued to heap praise on the little goblin. Diglet's smile was strained, like a part of him wanted to flee, while another part clung to Snow's every word.

Danielle looked at Talia, who scowled. Danielle twitched her head at Diglet. Talia's eyes narrowed.

I promised, Danielle mouthed.

I didn't.

"What are these humans going on about, Diglet?" asked the first goblin. "You don't even know which end of a knife to hold, let alone—"

"He needed no knife," Talia said, with one last glare at Danielle. "Diglet leaped upon the first bandit, driving him back with tooth and claw. He stole the villain's sword and laid about until they fled like sheep. Not one of those filthy beasts escaped his wrath."

Diglet looked up at her, his eyes wide, his blue lips slightly puckered.

"Forgive me, brave goblin," Talia said, her jaw tight. "Much as I wish to give you a proper reward, in my mind I still see you as you were in battle, your fangs red with blood. The memory of such violence nearly makes me faint."

Now it was Snow's turn to cough.

Talia stooped to plant a quick kiss on the top of Diglet's head. "Fare thee well, brave goblin."

Danielle smiled and blew him a kiss. "Your courage has earned you the gratitude of a future queen."

"Thank *you*, ladies," said Diglet. He bowed and lowered his voice. "Be careful. You, in particular, Princess Whiteshore. That child you carry is a tasty prize in these parts. Well, not *tasty*. I mean, except for a few witches over eastside. Plus there's supposed to be an ogre living in the king's swamps who enjoys the taste of human young, but I think he spreads those rumors himself. He doesn't appreciate visitors. Most of us in Fairytown don't even like human flesh. Too stringy, and unless it's drenched in a good mushroom sauce, you humans leave a nasty aftertaste. So I wouldn't worry—"

"Thank you," Danielle said firmly. Leaving Diglet with his dumbfounded companions, she turned and led the others up the road into Fairytown.

CHAPTER 7

❄

DANIELLE SHIELDED her eyes and stared at the horizon. Maybe she had spent too much time in the darkness of the hedge. "I could be mistaken, but when I woke up this morning, there was only one sun."

She glanced at the other side of the road to confirm it. Twin shadows stretched out beside her. Both were fainter than she was used to, except where they merged at her feet.

Snow pointed to the lower of the two suns, which already touched the horizon. "The Queen's Sun always sets before the King's. She's ruler of the morning, but as night falls, the King's Sun dominates."

"Fairies," Talia muttered, shaking her head.

Danielle had taken one of their bags when they left the goblin camp. She set it on the road and studied the sky. "How can there be two suns? All we did was pass through the hedge."

"The king and queen don't get along," Snow said. "Fairy nobles tend to be passionate, jealous, petty, and slightly mad. They're also tremendously powerful. Centuries ago, a poet compared the king's might to the blazing sun, and the queen's beauty to the moon. The fairies began to talk about the King's Sun and the Queen's Moon. Naturally, both wanted what the other had. The illusion is a huge waste of magic if you ask me, but it kept them at peace."

"As peaceful as fairies ever get," Talia added.

"Wait until you see the moons rise," said Snow. "The Queen's Moon is silver, while the king's is gold. Have you ever seen our moon on a cloudy night, when the light forms a halo? Here, if the moons are close enough, the halos intersect to form a dark rainbow. There are pictures in one of my books."

"If they're close enough?" Danielle repeated. "They move?"

"They grow closer together every midsummer and midwinter. On those two nights, the crescent moons rise together, forming a single ring in the sky. It's supposed to be a time of great celebration and mischief."

"If we're still here come midsummer," Talia interrupted, "I'm throwing myself into the chasm."

The land beyond the goblin encampment was as alien as the sky. Fruit trees of every variety bordered the road. Some, such as the apples and pears, were familiar. Others she had never seen before. Yellowgreen globes the size of her fist, tiny black berries growing in thick shining clusters, brown-crusted melons so large the branches bowed from the weight. The too-sweet smell of spoiled fruit filled the air.

"The goblins used to have a thriving market," said Snow. "They sold fruit to passing humans, back before the treaty. These days, with so few people coming in to Fairytown, they just make really bad wine."

A loud crack from the side of the road made Danielle jump. One of the trees toppled toward the road. Before Danielle could move, Talia grabbed her by the wrist and yanked her back. They landed hard on the road as the tree crashed down . . .

. . . and disappeared. High-pitched jeers and giggles came from a patch of quivering black wildflowers.

"Brownies," Snow said. She hadn't reacted at all to the illusory tree. She pointed to a tiny manlike shape darting through the orchards. "Mischievous little things, but they won't hurt us. The road through Fairytown is protected. None can harm you unless you leave it."

"I knew that," Talia muttered. She helped Danielle to her feet.

For a time, they walked in silence. Danielle felt like she was walking downhill, but every time she looked back, the road was as level as the sea on a calm day. Perhaps it was the road itself urging them onward.

"So where are we going, anyway?" Danielle asked.

"Snow has a contact in Fairytown," Talia said. "Some gnome who's close to the fairy queen. She says he should be powerful enough to snatch the prince back from your stepsisters."

"His name is Arlorran," said Snow. "He's the queen's summoner. Arlorran told me once that he spends a lot of time with the goblins, so he should be around here somewhere."

"You never did tell me how you met this gnome," Talia said.

"I met him a few months ago, on my mirror. I was trying to see Allesandria, but I coughed near the end of the spell, and ended up with this confused little gnome staring out at me."

Talia stopped walking. "A few months? You've been talking to a fairy all this time, and you didn't tell me? What if he was a spy? What if he tried to enchant you through the mirror?"

"Through *my* mirror?" Snow laughed. "I'd like to see him try. Besides, he's cute for a gnome."

"Will he help us?" Danielle asked.

"I think so." Snow glanced around. "He told me I should come visit sometime. I just wish he'd told me where he lives."

Talia groaned. "You mean you didn't stop to ask before we left the palace?"

"I did!" Snow flushed. "I mean, I tried. I couldn't get through. We haven't talked much in the past few weeks. I'm a little worried about him. I think he's depressed."

"A depressed gnome," said Talia. "That's great, Snow."

A low wall of weathered stone crossed through the woods, stopping to either side of the road. The stones were barely a foot high, enough to stop Trittibar in his shrunken state perhaps, but little more. There was no cement or mortar. Blue-green moss filled in the gaps between the stones. But when Danielle nudged one of the stones with her foot, she found it rooted in place as firmly as the palace walls back home.

"A boundary wall," said Snow. "Most of the fairy races build them. They're very territorial. This marks the edge of goblin territory."

"Not much of a territory," said Talia. "We haven't been walking for very long."

Danielle glanced back at the road. "I wonder if we should go back. Diglet might know how to find Arlorran."

"I doubt it," said Snow. "Goblins don't really concern themselves with outsiders. Especially those of higher castes, like Arlorran."

Danielle stopped and switched her bag to the other shoulder. "What we need is—"

"No!" Talia shouted.

"—a guide," Danielle finished. She blinked. "I don't understand. What's wrong?"

Snow giggled. Talia rubbed her forehead and sighed.

Before Danielle could ask again, a bobbing white light caught her attention. The light zoomed up the road, bouncing like a child's toy. It moved faster than the swiftest horse.

At the same time, a tall, pale-skinned man in old-style traveling clothes stepped out of the trees to their left. His silken tunic was tucked in at the waist, while his pants ballooned out over knee-high black boots. He tucked a polished walking stick beneath one arm, doffed a purple hat with a plume as tall as himself, and bowed low.

On the other side of the road, a hunchbacked old woman sprang up from the grass. She brushed dirt and worms from her ragged clothing and smiled a toothless smile. Her left eye was rheumy and pointed off to one side.

"Never ask for a guide in Fairytown," Talia said.

There were more. A toad the size of a dinner plate hopped onto the side of the road. Its warty body sagged over its legs, completely hiding the feet.

A fox crept from between the trees close to the man. The fox studied the crowd, sniffed the air, and bared his teeth at the toad. As he started to creep across the road, the old woman swooped down and seized the scruff of his neck. The fox snarled and snapped, but she held him at arm's length. Her free hand stroked the fox's back and tail.

"I could use a new scarf," she said.

"Ladies, welcome to Fairytown," said the man. He bowed again. "My name is Timothy Stout, and I would be honored if you allowed me to lead you wherever—"

The glowing ball slammed into Timothy Stout's backside, sending him face first into the grass beside the road.

"I take back what I said about not calling for a guide," said Talia. "This is kind of fun."

Timothy rolled and smacked the end of his stick

into the glowing ball, which flashed bright red and dropped to the ground.

"You killed it," said Danielle.

"Not at all. I merely taught it a lesson." Timothy tapped the ball again.

Glowing feebly, the ball began to roll in a lopsided fashion, fleeing back down the road.

A furious shriek drew Danielle's attention back to the struggle between fox and hag. The fox had finally managed to twist around enough to sink his teeth into the old woman's thumb. She flung him away, but he landed lightly on his feet and stared up at her with what Danielle could only describe as a smug grin.

"Princesses, please forgive my companions." The deep, rusty voice came from the toad, who had hopped into the middle of the road. "As a noble myself, let me urge you not to trust these ruffians. Their behavior is ill-fit for such ladies as yourselves, and—"

Timothy tucked his stick beneath one arm and used both hands to grab the toad.

"You see?" screamed the toad. "Hooligans, all!"

Timothy raised the toad overhead.

"Wait," Danielle cried.

He hesitated, and in that time, the toad struck back. Urine spread across the sleeve of Timothy's finely tailored silk shirt. With a howl of outrage, Timothy flung the toad into the woods.

"Stop it, all of you," Danielle snapped.

Timothy, the fox, and the old woman glared at one another, but none made any aggressive moves.

"We're looking for Arlorran the gnome," Danielle said.

"And I would be delighted to escort you," Timothy said, extending his arm. The gesture would have been far more gallant if his cuff hadn't been dripping with toad piss.

The fox yipped, and when Danielle looked down, she would have sworn he winked at her.

"Forget them," said the old woman. She pointed to the fox. "This rascal will lead you to a trap and eat you, and as for this fellow here, he'll take your virtue as payment."

Talia touched the handle of her knife. "If that fop tries to take my virtue, I'm taking his manhood."

"I only take what's willingly given," said Timothy.

Snow looked Timothy up and down. "He's pretty, but I don't think he's my type," she said. "He's far too impressed with himself."

"Go on, you scoundrel," the old woman said. "These ladies aren't for you."

"And what would you want?" Danielle asked. She was starting to understand this place. Nobody did anything for free.

"Me?" The woman rubbed her knobby, hairy chin. "I'd like to play a game, my pretty."

"Not interested," said Talia. "We'll find Arlorran on our own."

"How?" Danielle asked. "How much time will we give Charlotte and Stacia to work their magic while we wander aimlessly about Fairytown?" She folded her arms and turned back to the woman. "What game is that?"

"You'll lose," Timothy said in a taunting, singsong voice.

"A short way from here, the road splits in three directions," said the old woman. "You guess which road will lead you to Arlorran. If you're correct, I'll be your willing servant throughout your journey. Your every wish will be my command, from the moment you answer until you leave Fairytown. You'll need allies here, and my power is nothing to sneer at."

The fox wrinkled his nose, proving her wrong.

"And if I guess wrong?" Danielle asked.

"If you're wrong, you give me the son you carry in your womb."

Danielle rolled her eyes. "It's all about the unborn children with you fairy folk, isn't it?" Turning to Talia and Snow, she asked, "Is she telling the truth? Will she serve me if I guess the right road?"

"You can't," Talia said. "That's the heir to the throne, Princess."

"She is of fairy blood," Snow said. "If she makes a bargain, she'll have no choice but to keep it. But Talia's right. The odds are two to one against you, and you can't risk—"

Danielle smiled. "I'll play your game." She saw Talia close her eyes in disgust, and even Snow looked nervous. But Danielle wasn't worried. Not this time.

"Excellent," said the woman, rubbing her hands together. "One road will take you south. Another curves to the west. The third will lead you to the north. Your friend awaits you on one of these paths."

Danielle turned to Timothy. "You know where Arlorran is."

He nodded.

"Tell me which road, and I'll order her to serve you. 'From the moment I answer, until we leave Fairytown.' "

"Hey," shouted the old woman. "You can't do that!"

The fox began to yip, a sound suspiciously like laughter. Slowly, Timothy smiled. Lifting his walking stick, he pointed down the road. "You want the southern path, which will lead you to the First Forest. Most evenings, you'll find Arlorran in a tavern called the Tipsy Oak. You can't miss it."

The Queen's Sun had all but disappeared when they reached the three branches the old woman had described.

"They did tell us the road split," Snow said.

Talia rolled her eyes. "They might have been a little more specific about it."

The central road continued straight ahead. The northern path disappeared into a stone-ringed hole in the earth. And the southern branch, the one Timothy had instructed them to follow, climbed into the trees.

Ancient oaks grew on either side of the road. Danielle could see the roots twining around the edges of the road at the point where it left the earth like a bridge. The road itself was thick as Danielle's hand. Farther on, the trees grew like pillars beneath the road, carrying it higher and higher until it was little more than an emerald thread among the leaves. Branches laced together on either side like a railing. Danielle could see the whole thing swaying slightly in the breeze.

"Two suns make for healthy plants," Snow commented.

Talia was already heading up the road. Danielle rested her left hand on her sword handle as she followed. The wood and glass were warm to the touch. A sword would do her little good against the dangers of Fairytown, but simply touching it brought her comfort. "Please watch over Armand," she whispered, wondering if her mother could still hear her. "Keep him safe until we arrive."

Already the road had taken them into the upper branches. Leaves surrounded them, so they walked through a tunnel of green. Despite the climb, Danielle still felt herself stumbling forward, as if she walked downhill. Her knees and thighs were beginning to ache.

Eventually, they broke through the upper branches, reaching the very tops of the trees. Danielle gasped. The leaves to either side were a rustling sea beneath the stars. Flickers of colored light danced through the trees in the distance. Here and there, a few rogue branches broke through the canopy, stretching even higher. Behind them, the dark shape of the hedge curved in a great arc in either direction. Orange campfires marked the goblin camp, where the fruit trees were but poor, shrunken shadows of the woods now surrounding her. On the other side, in the distance, she could just make out the lacelike spires of the queen's castle, as well as the dark shadows of the king's.

"How large is this place?" she whispered.

"The last official census had the fairy population at just over thirty thousand," said Snow. "Of course, their tallies are a bit peculiar. Intelligent animals are counted—that's the beast caste, like our friend the fox—but not the dumb. The unnamed caste won't show up on any census, but there are only a handful of them. Some of the bloodless, like that glowing ball, only count as a fraction. But the numbers still come out pretty close."

"Thirty thousand," Danielle repeated. Yet so much of Fairytown was wilderness. "Where do they all live?"

"Remember, fairies can spread through the land in any direction," Snow said. "Trolls and kobolds burrow into the earth, while griffins and elves spread upward, into the treetops and cliffs. And don't ask me how they count the cloud striders and their riders, who can touch the land only once each year."

"Do those numbers include mortals?" Talia asked. "Those who stumble into Fairytown and never make their way out again?"

Snow nodded. "Most of them end up slaves. They were included in Appendix B of the census."

"You have got to find some other hobbies," Talia said. She leaned against the branches as she dug through her bag, coming up with a paper-wrapped bundle. She unwrapped it and handed Danielle a thick strip of dried fish, wrapped in what appeared to be seaweed. "Trust me, it's better than eating fairy food."

Danielle nodded, grateful for the rest. She hadn't wanted to say anything, but she was having a hard time keeping up with the others. "Is it true that if you eat the fairies' food, you can never leave?"

"Not here," said Snow. "We're still in our world, changed as it might be by fairy magic. If you ever pass through the fairy hill, though, you'll want to be careful."

"Then why—" she started to ask.

"Because fairy cooking tastes like mud," said Talia.

Danielle tried a bite, then doubled over the railing, spitting and doing her best to keep from throwing up. The seaweed had a sharp, salty tang, and the fish tasted of hickory smoke and some kind of pepper. Her stomach convulsed again, then began to settle back down.

"Maybe she would have been better off with the mud," said Snow.

Talia pressed a wineskin into Danielle's hand. "I'm sorry, Princess. I should have realized nadif would be too much for you."

"It's not. The taste is actually quite good, but the fish and the spice, I just—" The memory alone was enough to send her back to the railing. Several gulps of wine later, Danielle wiped her eyes and asked, "What *is* that?"

"The spice is called nadif," Talia said. "It's a recipe from back home. The queen loves it, but it's an acquired taste." She took a huge bite of her own fish and grinned. "The food in Lorindar is so *bland*."

"But it doesn't burn holes in your lips," Snow said, snatching the wineskin from Danielle.

Talia grabbed a strip of smoked lamb and handed it to Danielle. "Here, this one's milder."

Danielle ate as she walked. "Mild" was still strong enough to clear her sinuses, but at least she didn't feel like her head was on fire.

"Look at that," Snow said, pointing.

Up ahead, a fallen tree leaned against the road. The branches had broken or been cut away, leaving only a great trunk. This was one of the giants among giants. By any logic, the tree should have smashed right through the road when it fell. While the road did tilt where the tree had fallen, it didn't appear damaged. Merely stretched a bit.

"Does that look like a tipsy oak to you?" Snow asked. She didn't wait for an answer, giggling as she ran toward the enormous tree. Starlight glittered from her mirrors.

"She acts like we're on a picnic," Talia muttered, but she began to jog after Snow.

Danielle gulped the last of her food, wishing Snow had handed over the wineskin before she started running. Her tongue was still tingling from the nadif spice. Hopefully, the Tipsy Oak would have something mild to drink.

Touching her sword for luck and comfort, she hurried after the others.

Up close, the tree was easily twice as wide as Danielle was tall. The top had been cut away a short distance past the road. Young twigs still sprouted from the bark, appearing comically small by comparison.

"So how do we get inside?" Danielle asked.

Talia pointed to a line of sap dripping down the side of the tree. She grabbed a broken branch and pulled, peeling a thick section of wood and bark away from the trunk to reveal a jagged hole. Talia poked her sword into the darkness, then peeked inside. "Hello? Any gnomes down there?"

Her voice echoed and faded to nothing.

"Are you sure your friend Timothy was telling the truth?" Talia asked as she pulled herself through the doorway.

"He had to," Snow said. "If he hadn't, the old woman would have taken Danielle's child, remember?"

Danielle stepped up to the tree. "Does anyone have a candle?"

Snow touched her choker, and the front mirror began to glow.

"Thanks," said Danielle. The interior of the tree wasn't high enough to walk upright, but she could crawl on her hands and knees with little trouble. To her surprise, bark covered the interior of the tree, the same as the outside. She even saw clusters of acorns hanging from the upper part of the tunnel. She set down her sack and climbed in after Talia.

The inside was cool, with a pleasant nutty scent. She crawled ahead to make room for the others. The tunnel sloped downward, and soon Danielle gave thanks for the rough bark that scraped her hands and knees. A smooth floor would make it too easy to slip.

"What's that?" Danielle asked, pointing to a round hole on the upper part of the left wall.

Snow squeezed past to direct the light from her choker into the hole. A smaller tunnel led up and away from them. "Looks like the tunnel branches off."

Talia grabbed an acorn and threw it at her.

They continued downward, passing other side tunnels as they went. The only way to investigate them would be to go back and take more of Trittibar's shrinking spores.

Danielle's head began to ache. Crawling downhill for so long had sent her blood pounding into her skull. "Why would anyone make a tavern so inaccessible?"

"It's Fairytown," Talia said, as if that explained everything.

High-pitched laughter was the first clue their destination was near. The air took on a smoky smell, and Danielle heard a low buzzing that reminded her of hummingbirds.

"We're here," Snow said. The light from her choker disappeared.

Up ahead, a wide hole in the floor pulsed with light of every color, changing from blue to pink to green in a single heartbeat.

"Let me go first," Talia said. She drew her sword and crawled to the edge of the hole. "Oh, wonderful."

"What is it?" Danielle asked.

Talia put her weapon away and shook her head. "It's a pixie bar."

"Why would Arlorran be at a pixie bar?" Snow asked.

Talia grabbed Snow's wrists. "Let's find out." Bracing one of her legs on the far side of the hole, Talia lowered Snow inside. She dropped their belongings down after, then looked at Danielle. "Your turn, Princess."

Danielle scooted carefully to the edge. A streak of blue raced beneath her feet and disappeared.

Talia locked her hands around Danielle's. "Looks like a bit of a drop. Bend your knees and let your legs absorb the impact, and you'll be fine."

Danielle nodded, trying to relax. She could see the floor below, littered with old flower petals and acorn shells. Snow was already moving to one side, brushing debris from her trousers.

Talia gave a quick tug, pulling Danielle off-balance. Her breath caught as she dropped into the hole, but Talia didn't let go. Her shoulders twinged as she dangled there, and then Talia relaxed her grip.

Danielle's legs gave out, and she rolled onto her

back hard enough to bruise. Talia followed, landing in a crouch and then turning to survey the bar. She sighed and helped Danielle to her feet.

So this was a pixie bar. There were no tables, no barmaids weaving through the crowds. The room was roughly cylindrical, about the size of her bedchamber back at the palace. Smaller openings were scattered across the walls. Benches jutted out at all heights. Others crisscrossed the room. The largest bench passed in front of Danielle's face, where a small man tapped his foot impatiently.

"You lost?" he asked. Gossamer wings quivered, giving off green light and shedding sparks that disappeared before they touched the ground. He was barefoot, clad in loose brown trousers and a top that made an X across his chest, then disappeared between his wings. Green hair poofed from his head like a dandelion.

Danielle looked around. Most of the pixies in the room were watching her. Their curious stares brought back memories of her first time in the palace. Despite her finery, she had been certain everyone at the ball would see through her disguise to the rag-wearing, filth-covered girl she truly was.

As she had done that night, Danielle grabbed those feelings of insecurity and choked them into silence. Meeting the pixie's gaze, she said, "That depends. Is this the Tipsy Oak?"

One caterpillar eyebrow rose slightly. "Sure is."

"Then we're not lost."

Talia cleared her throat. "Do you have anything to drink that doesn't come in a thimble?"

The pixie chuckled. "Girl, I've got a snapdragon mead that'll put wings on your back with a single swallow. Take two, and you'll think you're queen of the fairies. Assuming your human blood can handle a pixie drink, that is."

Talia matched his smile and began to respond, but Snow caught her arm and said, "The prince, remember?"

Talia sighed. "We're looking for a gnome named Arlorran. Is he here?"

Wordlessly, the pixie turned to point to one of the upper benches. Near the roof where the bar was darkest sat a gnome. He towered over the pixies, though he was at best half Danielle's height. He was dressed all in red, save for a flat blue cap that hung down over his right eye. His white beard was stained yellow around the lips, either from drink or the ivory pipe he was smoking. Two pixie women sat to either side, sipping their drinks.

"How do we get to . . . ?" Danielle's voice trailed off. Talia was already climbing toward the gnome, using the benches to pull herself up. Danielle did her best to follow. The benches were more than wide enough, but they crossed at such random angles that she had to bend and twist to get from one to the next. She did her best to ignore the pixies who were watching with obvious amusement.

One pixie, giving off a cheerful blue light, leaned to a friend and said, "Next round's on me if she makes it without taking a tumble."

Arlorran hadn't appeared to notice them. All of his attention was on the two pixie women. "I'm telling you, lass," he said to the one on his left, who glowed bright yellow. "Once you go gnome, you'll never go home."

He swayed slightly as he leaned toward the pixie, his lips puckered. The pixie's wings flashed, and flames shot up from the end of Arlorran's pipe, igniting his beard.

"Grabblethorn's buttocks!" he swore, pouring some of his drink over his chin to extinguish the flames. Both pixies slipped off of the bench and flew away, giggling. Arlorran stuck the end of his beard into his mouth and sucked it dry.

Talia stopped long enough to glance at Snow. "Tell me there's another gnome around here."

By now, Arlorran seemed to have recovered from the pixie's attack. Aside from a blackened spot on his beard, he looked no worse for wear.

"You're Arlorran?" Danielle asked.

He blinked. "For a nubile human lady like yourself, I'll be anyone you want."

"We want Arlorran," said Talia.

"Oh, and Arlorran wants you, my lovely." He patted the bench. "Why don't you plant that lovely behind right here, and we'll see what we can do for one another."

Snow giggled, though she stopped immediately when Talia glared at her. She pulled herself up and said, "Arlorran, it's me."

The gnome lifted his cap, and his expression brightened. "Snow? Is that you?" He laughed. "I thought you'd never take me up on my offer. And you brought friends!"

"Why did you stop talking to me?" Snow demanded.

Arlorran's smile faded. "Been busy. Nothing personal, lass."

"Can you worry about your hurt feelings later?" asked Talia.

"Fine. We need your help, Arlorran," Snow said. Before the gnome could answer, she twisted onto the bench beside him and said, "*Not* that kind of help."

Danielle sat down on his other side. She had to hold the edge to keep from slipping off, and the handle of her sword jabbed her ribs.

"Athletic, aren't you?" said Arlorran. He gave Talia an appreciative smile as she sat beside Snow. The bench creaked slightly under their combined weight, but the wood was stronger than it appeared. "My lucky day. Yours, too, and that's a fact."

"I'm married," Danielle said.

" 'S good. You'll know what you're doing, then. I've no time for amateurs."

"This is your contact in Fairytown?" Talia asked. "A drunken, crippled old gnome?"

Arlorran's brow furrowed. " 'M not crippled."

"Touch my leg again, and you will be."

"No need for that," Arlorran said. He downed the rest of his drink, then tossed the empty cup into the air. A streak of purple light shot through the bar, resolving into a pixie woman who caught the cup in both hands.

"Bring me another," Arlorran said. "My friends are buying."

Gritting her teeth, Talia reached into a pocket and tossed a silver coin to the pixie, who caught it in the cup and disappeared.

"You should have told me you were coming for a visit," Arlorran said. He picked at the burned patch on his beard.

"I tried!" Snow said. "You stopped answering, remember?"

"True enough, true enough. I've been preoccupied these past few weeks. I'm surprised you haven't forgotten all about old Arlorran."

Snow plucked his beard from his hands and curled it through her fingers. "Now how could I forget such a cute little gnome?"

Arlorran chuckled and turned to Danielle. "So you're the one." He bent to look at her boots, and might have fallen if Danielle hadn't grabbed him by the collar and pulled him back. "Don't look like glass to me."

Snow shrugged. "He wanted me to tell him about the wedding. He sounds like a lecherous old man, but he's really a romantic sap."

Arlorran shook his head. "Sorry, lass. I'm lecherous through and through. Happy to prove it to you."

"Snow said you could help us," Danielle said.

"Maybe. Who is it you're trying to find?"

Danielle glanced at Talia and Snow. "How did you know we were looking for someone?"

"I'm the Royal Summoner for Her Majesty the Queen." Arlorran straightened. "It's what I do. My gift from the gods, if you will. Most of the time, it's nothing more than enchanting a new goblin so folks can call him to lead them through the hedge."

The purple pixie returned with Arlorran's drink.

"Thanks, Fraxxle," said Arlorran. He took a deep swallow, then sighed. "I do special assignments for the queen herself, along with the occasional freelance job. When the price is right. Summoning a dryad across the chasm to frolic with the satyrs, for instance. Tragic, that chasm your people made. The dryads wound up on the king's side, while the queen kept the satyrs for herself. They sneak across the bridge sometimes, but my way's quicker and safer."

"Does that mean you'll help us?" Danielle asked.

"For such lovely women as yourselves, I might be able to assist you, for a small fee. Maybe something like—"

Talia reached around to pluck the cup from his hand. Ignoring his squawks, she took a quick sip, then said, "Think long and hard before you finish that sentence, gnome."

"Right." Arlorran snorted, and his gaze went to Danielle's stomach. His eyes lit up. "In that case, how about—"

This time it was Danielle who interrupted. "If you

ask me for my unborn child, I'll have Talia stuff you
into your own pipe."

"Humans," muttered the gnome. "Some of you
treat your kids like they're dragon's gold. Others trade
their offspring for a good drink, or even a mediocre
one. Speaking of which, I believe that's mine." He
leaned over to grab his cup back from Talia. "And
you still haven't told me who it is you're looking for."

"My husband," said Danielle. She lowered her
voice. The closest benches were empty, but who knew
how acute the pixies' hearing was. "Prince Armand."

Arlorran raised his cup. "A right bastard, leaving
you in such a state. Now a gnomish man, he's loyal
to his mate. None of this sneaking away in the night,
abandoning—"

"He was kidnapped," said Talia. "They brought him
to Fairytown."

Slowly, Arlorran lowered his drink. His voice soft,
he said, "That's a serious accusation. We're not in the
habit of allowing criminals through these walls. These
kidnappers, were they human?"

Danielle nodded.

"Then they'd need magic to get in." He sucked on
his pipe, but the embers had died. He harrumphed
and held it out to Snow. "Do you mind, hon?"

Snow touched her mirror, and a tiny flame appeared
on the tip of her finger. She poked the bowl of the
pipe until a thread of smoke began to rise.

"That's better. So tell me, who is it that took your
husband?"

"My stepsister," said Danielle.

"Witch?"

"Charlotte's the one who told me about it, but
Stacia was involved as well. I'm not sure—"

"No, no," Arlorran said, rolling his eyes. "I mean,
is she a witch?"

Danielle hesitated. "I guess so."

Arlorran sucked his pipe, then blew smoke toward a pink pixie on a higher bench. "Can't help you. Sorry."

"Why not?" asked Snow.

"Summoning is a temperamental magic," Arlorran said gently. "Goblins are easy. The blue runts have no real willpower to speak of. I can do most humans, too. Or I could if the treaty didn't forbid it. But witches are another matter. If they're strong enough to take your husband and get through the hedge, they're strong enough to bind him, too. I'd like to help you, but there's no way I'll be able to yank him away from your stepsisters."

Danielle turned to Snow, pleading without words for her to argue.

"I don't understand," said Snow. "You told me you were the most powerful summoner in history, that you could conjure the lice from a beggar on the far side of the world."

"Right, and I told those lovely pixie girls I was only a century old. What's your point?"

"You lied," Snow whispered.

"People do that," said Talia, shaking her head in disgust. "Come on. This is a waste of time. We'll find him ourselves."

"Hey now, don't be like that," said Arlorran. "You ladies wouldn't understand, looking the way you do. But for someone like me, all old and shrunken and wrinkly, how else am I supposed to hold the attention of such a lovely woman?"

Danielle saw Snow smile, though she raised a hand to hide it the moment Talia turned toward her.

"I'm the summoner for the queen, that much is true. But magic has limits. You know that." He took another puff from his pipe. The smoke made Danielle's eyes burn. "Sorry, lass. I wish I could help, I truly do."

"You haven't even tried," Danielle said. "Charlotte

and Stacia are new at this. They might not have thought to protect Armand from a summoning spell. Or maybe they made a mistake. You can't just give up."

"Actually, I can," said Arlorran. "It's my right as a bitter, half-drunk old gnome to give up any time I like." He grinned and finished the rest of his drink. "And once I'm fully drunk, it will be my right to go home and pass out until it's time to enchant the next filthy, foul-mouthed, rat-eating goblin."

Snow reached out to touch his arm. "Please try," she said. "For me? I've so wanted to see gnomish magic in person." She lowered her eyelashes. "There's so much you could teach me, and it seems the least you could do, after the way you deceived me."

"Not tonight, ladies." He hopped down, landing hard on another bench. "I hope you find your fellow, truly I do. But if things don't work out and you find yourselves in need of . . . comfort . . ." Eyebrows wagged as he slid down to the next bench. "Now, if you'll excuse me," he yelled.

"Where are you going?" Danielle asked.

Arlorran patted his stomach. "Water the trees. Too much pixie juice." He gave them a quick salute with his empty cup, then hurried along the bench toward a small, satin-curtained opening in the wall, where he disappeared.

Snow was already unclasping her choker. She held it in front of her and squinted at the center mirror. When nothing happened, she tapped the glass a few times with her nail.

A blur of movement swept through the tiny glass, and then Beatrice's face appeared. "You're in Fairytown?" Her voice carried a strange aftertone, like tiny chimes.

"Arlorran can't find the prince," Snow said. "Do you have any other contacts we could talk to?"

"Most of our communications with Fairytown are carried out strictly according to the treaty." Beatrice's face shifted, like she was trying to look through the mirror to see where they were. "Is Danielle all right?"

Danielle took the choker from Snow's hand. "As long as Talia doesn't try to feed me any more nadif."

The queen smiled. "I remember the first time I tried it. And the first time I snuck some onto Theodore's eggs." Her expression turned somber. "I will talk to Trittibar. In the meantime, Snow could try again to use your child to find Armand."

Her voice broke slightly when she spoke her son's name. She glanced away for a moment. "Be safe. All of you."

"We will." The mirror shivered, and soon Danielle saw only her reflection. She returned the choker to Snow, then slid to the edge of the bench. A pixie fluttered out of the way as she lowered herself to another bench.

"Where are you going?" Talia asked.

"To change his mind." Danielle hopped down to the platform Arlorran had taken, then hurried toward the passage where he had disappeared.

"He's been doing this for hundreds of years, Danielle," Snow said as she followed after her. "If he says he's not strong enough to break through your stepsisters' spells—"

"He's already lied once," Danielle countered. "Charlotte and Stacia tried to hide Armand from you, but they couldn't. Not completely. You tracked him to Fairytown, didn't you?" Deep down, she knew Snow was probably right. But she couldn't simply give up.

"I know my stepsisters, Snow. They're lazy. Especially Charlotte." Charlotte, who had never once lifted a finger around the house. When Danielle had been sick for a week as a child, unable to tend to the others,

Charlotte hadn't even bothered to comb her own hair. The tangles had been so bad, Danielle was forced to cut them out when she finally recovered.

Of course, Charlotte hadn't been too lazy to beat Danielle for that supposed insult. Nor had she shown any reluctance to bully Stacia into cooking the meals and cleaning the dishes until Danielle was well enough to take over again. That was one of the few times Stacia had shown Danielle any kindness, bringing her tea and medicine to speed her recovery.

Danielle pushed through the curtains into the cramped tunnel Arlorran had taken. A brisk wind chilled her hands and face. She crawled upward, the air growing colder until the darkness opened into a crude wooden platform jutting out from the tree. Overhead, she could see where a second tree had fallen onto the first. That must be the tree they had entered from the road. The two had grown together, branches and bark merging into a single mass where they intersected. She looked around, spotting several small wooden outhouses built against the trunk.

Arlorran hadn't bothered with the outhouses. He stood at the edge of the platform, one hand holding a rope railing as he relieved himself over the edge.

He glanced over his shoulder. "Crude, smelly things," he said, twitching his nose toward the outhouses. "The pixies built 'em for us unfortunate souls who can't flitter off to some private place to take care of business like the birds do. Those who aren't too drunk to fly, that is." He pointed to a puddle of glowing green liquid near the edge of the platform.

"What is that?" Danielle asked.

"Pixie piss." He finished his business and turned around, still tucking his shirt through his belt.

The platform vibrated slightly as Snow and Talia emerged. Snow was retying her choker around her neck. Neither woman spoke.

Danielle took a deep breath. "What will it take for you to try?"

"I told you," said Arlorran. "Against a pair of witches, there's nothing—"

"I'm not asking for promises," Danielle said. "I'm asking you to try. Gold, jewels." She glanced at his flushed face. "Wine. Surely there's more to your desires than women and unborn children. Name your price."

"No promises?" Arlorran stared at her. "No guarantees? I try, nothing happens, and you pay my price? No tricks, no complaints to your queen?"

"I love him," said Danielle.

Arlorran shook his head. "You think the laws of magic give one whit about love, girl? I'm telling you, any witch worth her salt will—"

"Then it doesn't work, you get what you want, and we leave you in peace," Danielle snapped. "Will you help me find my husband or not?"

"You're making a mistake," Talia muttered, but she made no move to stop Danielle.

Arlorran cast a speculative look at Snow, then sighed. "Wings."

"What?" Danielle looked from Snow to Arlorran and back. "I don't understand."

"Wings." He hooked his thumbs together and fluttered his fingers. "Just once, I'd like to buzz around like those little glowbugs. See the world like they do." He shrugged and turned away. "My magic is a one-trick deal, and the few witches in Fairytown aren't the kind of folks I'd ask for a favor. You give me wings so I can fly, and I'll do my best to help you."

"Snow?" Danielle asked.

Snow shook her head. "I've never tried transformation magic before."

Arlorran shrugged and started to step past them.

"My mirror has all of the magic my mother used,"

Snow continued. Her words rushed together as she spoke. "I don't look at those spells much, because some of them are . . . unpleasant. But she changed her shape when she came to poison me. That was no illusion. I would have seen right through it. That was true transformation, which means the spell should still be in the mirror. It might take me a little work to adapt it for your wings, but I'm almost sure I could do it."

She smiled. "Of course, you'd have to come to the palace for a while. We'd need to spend a lot of time together, so I could prepare the spell."

"That's a mighty tempting offer," said Arlorran. "But if you fail, I'm left with nothing."

Snow folded her arms. "Days or weeks with me, and you call it nothing?"

Arlorran backed away until he bumped the railing at the edge of the platform.

"How is your risk any different than mine?" Danielle asked.

The gnome stared, then chuckled. "True enough." He grabbed Danielle's hand, still keeping her between himself and Snow. "Stand close to me. It'll help with the summoning. You're the one who loves him, after all."

"I thought you said love didn't matter," said Danielle.

Arlorran grinned, but he didn't let go of Danielle's hand. He lifted his chin, closed his eyes, and said, "Armand Whiteshore."

Nothing happened.

"Sorry, lass," Arlorran said, patting Danielle's hand. "It's like I said, your stepsisters have him all tied up. Magically, that is."

"That's it?" Danielle stared at Arlorran. Her chest tightened. Despite everything Snow and Arlorran had told her, deep down she had been sure it would work.

"You want thunder and colored smoke, I can do that," said Arlorran. "But that kind of effect costs extra, and it won't make one bit of difference." He tugged her toward the tree. "Come on. I'll buy you a drink. The pixies make a mint-and-acorn drink that will—"

"Summon Charlotte," Danielle said. She yanked her hand away and turned to stare up at the leaves overhead. Lazy or not, Charlotte wouldn't risk losing Armand. Not after all she had done to steal him away. But would she remember to cast the same protections for herself? Stacia probably would, but Charlotte was another matter. "Please."

Arlorran sighed. "What's her full name?"

"Charlotte—" Danielle hesitated. Charlotte had been Charlotte de Glas for many years, but she had never accepted Danielle or her father. "Charlotte Moors."

Arlorran spat and rubbed his palms together. "I'd better get a nice, cushy bed when I come to the palace. And I want a room where I can see the ocean."

"I'll give you mine," Danielle said. "Just try."

He nodded and repeated the name. "Well, sharpen my ears and call me an elf."

Danielle's heart began to pound harder. "It worked?"

From behind them, Charlotte said, "It worked." Then a powerful wind flung Danielle toward the edge of the platform.

CHAPTER 8

❄

As DANIELLE STUMBLED forward, she saw Talia drawing her whip. Danielle's waist hit the railing. She tried to catch herself, but she was moving too quickly.

The line from Talia's whip hummed, then arced past Danielle's arm. The line hit her bicep, and the weight snapped around, looping three times before slamming into the muscle. Wind buffeted her body, and the whip dug cruelly into her arm as Talia pulled. Danielle grabbed the whip with one hand, clutching the railing with the other.

"No!" Charlotte screamed. She pulled a knife and grabbed the blade, raising it to throw.

"Charlotte Moors," said Arlorran.

Charlotte vanished, reappearing beside Arlorran, four feet to the left. The knife spun harmlessly off of the platform, ripping through leaves and branches as it fell.

The wind died down. Talia tugged Danielle away from the edge, then drew her sword.

Charlotte clutched her necklace in both hands, whispering an incantation, when something silver plunged into her forearm. Charlotte screamed and ripped out a

metal snowflake, slightly smaller than her palm. Blood
dripped from one of the sharpened points.

She tried again, taking the necklace in her other
hand, and then Talia's boot slammed into her stomach. Charlotte dropped to the ground. Before she
could move, Talia grabbed her hand and twisted, flipping her onto her stomach. Her screams died abruptly
as Talia's sword touched the back of her neck.

"Another attack, mundane or magical, and you'll
be dead before you feel me move."

Charlotte stopped squirming.

"Give me your arm," Snow said, kneeling beside
Charlotte. She tore away Charlotte's bloody sleeve
and wadded it into a ball. "Never rip the blade from
the wound," she muttered. "That only makes you
bleed worse." She pressed the makeshift bandage over
Charlotte's arm. "Danielle, I've got a bunch of long,
clean rags in my bag. Can you get me one?"

Danielle finished unwrapping the whip from her
arm. She would have a few rope burns, as well as a
nasty bruise, but it was far better than the alternative.
She glanced over the edge and shuddered.

Snow's bag was near the doorway into the bar, well
away from the edge. Danielle dug through the bag,
shoving past dresses and cloaks and bits of silk better
left unexamined until she found Snow's medical sup-
plies. "You have an awful lot of bandages in here."

"I travel with Talia a lot." Snow tied the bandage
into place on Charlotte's arm, then used the end to
clean the blood from the metal snowflake. "Aren't
they pretty? Talia made a set for me last year," she
said. When no blood remained, she slipped the steel
flake into a hidden pocket on the side of her trousers.
"They were a birthday present."

Snow used another bandage to bind Charlotte's
wrists. Only then did Talia step away and retrieve her
whip. Danielle followed her.

"Thank you," Danielle said. "If you hadn't caught me—"

"You should have expected something like this." Talia shook her head. "But I should have, too."

"You're very good with that." Danielle nodded toward the whip.

"A zaraq whip was the last thing I saw before I slept, and the first weapon I mastered after I awoke." A short, bitter laugh escaped Talia's lips. "It was an assassination attempt gone wrong. My parents did what they could to protect me. We had bodyguards and wizards, food tasters and trained guard dogs. Everyone in the family drank a cocktail of various antitoxins each morning, mixed into our cactus juice." She made a face. "The cactus juice tasted worse than the antidotes. Not that it mattered. The poison on the needle of that zaraq whip had a magical component. I was asleep before I hit the floor."

"Someone tried to kill you?" Danielle asked. "You were just a child."

"I was a princess." Talia wound the whip with quick, economical twitches of her wrist. "I'm told the tale of Sleeping Beauty first spread to your country in a book of stories. Nobody knew how to translate 'zaraq.' They just looked at the pictures and decided it was a spindle from one of your spinning wheels. I used to wonder what kind of spinning wheels you people used, that could kill with a mere prick of the finger."

Snow hauled Charlotte into a sitting position. "That's all very interesting, but don't you think Danielle would rather hear about Prince Armand?"

Talia rolled her eyes. "Well, Princess? What shall we do with your stepsister?"

Danielle stared at Charlotte. Ever since they'd left the palace, a part of Danielle had refused to believe. No matter how much her stepsisters hated her, she couldn't convince herself that they truly wanted her dead. She had made excuses for Charlotte's earlier attack: someone else was manipulating her; her new-found powers had gotten the best of her; she was only trying to scare Danielle.

Yet the very first thing she had done after Arlor-ran's summoning was try again to murder Danielle.

She knelt next to Charlotte, whose face was turned away so that only her scarred eye was visible.

"Careful," Talia said. She held her sword so that Charlotte could see the sinuous curve of steel.

"Why, Charlotte?" Danielle asked.

Tears began to drip down Charlotte's face. Danielle stared. Not once had she seen her stepsister cry, not even at her own mother's funeral.

"It's not fair," Charlotte whispered. "You had everything."

For several moments, Danielle was too stunned to answer. "*I* had everything. *I*, who cooked your meals and cleaned your home and tended your hair and—"

"I should have been Princess Whiteshore," said Charlotte. "I would have been, if you hadn't cheated me. You and your dead mother."

Danielle flinched. "My mother is gone. Destroyed by the Chirka you summoned."

"Gone?" Charlotte looked up, and for an instant, sympathy pushed the hate from her eyes. Then her expression hardened again. "It doesn't matter any-more. You've taken everything from me."

"Is that why you took Armand?" Talia asked. "To reclaim what you thought was yours?"

A yellow pixie flew out of the tunnel. His flight was erratic, looping and spinning in every direction. He nearly collided with Talia before flittering past. He muttered an apology, but the words were too fast for Danielle to make out. He sounded like a hiccuping sparrow.

"Perhaps this isn't the ideal place for your interrogation," Arlorran said gently.

Talia nodded. "So take us somewhere better."

The gnome rubbed his beard. "I already offered to take you back to my place. You said you weren't interested. Besides, shouldn't you be worrying about your witch there?"

"Arlorran, we need your help," said Danielle. "You made a deal."

"Aye, and I did my part. I summoned the girl."

Snow looked up, an innocent smile on her face. "Technically, that wasn't the deal. You said, 'You give me wings so I can fly, and I'll do my best to help you.' You never specified what kind of help."

Arlorran removed his cap and rubbed his scalp. "Did I say that? Well that hardly seems fair, taking advantage of a poor, drunken gnome. I meant—"

"How many fairies have done the same to poor, naïve mortals over the centuries?" Talia asked. "You made a promise. So long as we need your help, you're bound to provide it."

Arlorran scowled, and his little hands balled into fists, crumpling his cap. He looked like he wanted to run over and strangle Talia with his bare hands, though he was far too short to reach her throat. Still, he looked ready to give her kneecaps a good thrashing.

"Please," said Danielle.

Arlorran threw his cap on the ground. "Should have pushed you over the edge myself," he muttered. "As for you," he added, glaring at Snow. "That's the last time I stay up all night, telling you old gnomish romance tales." He stomped to the center of the platform. "Well, come on, then. I haven't got all year."

Danielle glanced at the others. Snow shrugged and hauled Charlotte to her feet.

"Not so hard, you stupid wench," Charlotte complained. How many times had Danielle heard that same curse?

Talia gathered up their belongings, never taking her eye from Charlotte.

"Take my hands," said Arlorran. "Everyone touching. A little closer, if you don't mind. Wouldn't want anyone to get left behind."

Danielle took one of the gnome's hands in hers, then put her other hand on Snow's arm. Talia did the same on Arlorran's other side, leaving Snow's hands free to hold Charlotte. Charlotte tried to tug away, but a quick yank of her bound wrists pulled her back, scowling and swearing under her breath.

"These had better be some wings," Arlorran muttered. He sighed, whispered something under his breath, and then they were falling.

Danielle had barely drawn breath when she found herself in darkness, standing on what felt like stone. She had already bent her legs, preparing for an impact that never came, and only Arlorran's grip kept her from losing her balance completely. The smell of stale fish filled her nostrils, knotting her stomach.

"Easy now, ladies," Arlorran said. "Just give me a moment or two to light a lantern."

Before he could, light blossomed from Snow's choker.

"Sure, that works, too," said Arlorran. "Sorry about the smell." He ducked through an arched doorway in the wall. Thick, lambskin carpeting covered the floor in the next room, muffling his footsteps. There was a clanking sound, and he returned moments later, brushing his hands together. "Cranked open the chimneys. Ought to get a little more air moving soon." He looked sheepish. "I broiled up some rice and kraken last night. Old undine recipe. Spicy enough to burn the tongue out of your head, but the smell gets into everything."

"Sounds like your kind of food," Snow said to Talia.
Talia ignored her. "Where are we?"

"Home. The bedroom, to be precise. Where else
would I go with four lovely ladies in tow?" He pointed
to Charlotte. "Just make sure that one stays tied up.
Too bloodthirsty for my taste."

"And you're too short and ugly for mine," said
Charlotte.

"Take her necklace," Danielle said. "I'm not sure
what it is, but it helps her cast her spells."

"Done." Talia yanked the stone from around Charlotte's neck and handed it to Snow. She gripped Charlotte above the elbow and turned back to Arlorran.
"I meant where in Fairytown."

"Ten, maybe fifteen miles west of the goblin check-
point," said Arlorran. "Right on the border between
gnomish land and the woods the satyrs claim as their
own." He winked at Snow. "They say I've got satyr
blood in me. Did I ever tell you that? Some say it
makes me hardheaded, but there are other traits, if
you know what I mean."

Charlotte wrinkled her nose and turned away. "This
is little better than a rathole."

Danielle looked around. Arlorran's home appeared
to be a small cave. They had arrived in the center of
the bedroom, where the domed ceiling was highest,
and even here Danielle's head almost brushed the
stone. Pink quartz lined the walls and ceiling, sparkling in the light of Snow's choker.

Danielle peered more closely at one patch of quartz.
What she had first taken to be jagged irregularities in
the rock were really carvings: dragons and horses and
fairies and castles, most no bigger than her thumb, all
carved with excruciating detail. "They're marvelous.
Did you do this?"

Arlorran nodded, grinning. "That one to your left
there shows me and the queen, the day she appointed

me Royal Summoner. There you go, the one with the gold wire around her head. Best I could do for a crown."

All the carvings were inverted, so they appeared to be standing on the ceiling. Danielle craned her head, studying the tiny figures. The smaller of the two resembled Arlorran with a shorter beard. The larger was a well-built woman with a long, flowing gown. A line of gold around her brow provided one of the only details not carved from the quartz.

"You need to lie down to see them properly," Arlorran said, pointing to the bed. He hopped onto the low mattress and patted the quilts. "Care to join me? I'll show you all kinds of marvels."

Snow giggled and jumped on to the bed beside him, landing so hard she bounced him to the floor. The light of her choker made her face even paler than normal, like a ghost. "Look, Talia. Griffins!" She pointed to the wall, where a flock of griffins appeared to fly in a V formation.

"Do you think we could question the would-be assassin before we admire the art?" Talia asked. "Have you figured out what that necklace is yet?"

"It's blood-bound to Charlotte and one other, I'm not sure who," Snow said.

"Stacia?" Danielle guessed.

"No." She held the stone to the light. "It's a teaching trick, a way to help a young witch learn. The stone is bound to whoever has been helping Charlotte with her magic."

"Did the troll give this to you?" Danielle asked. Charlotte pressed her lips together and turned away.

"Snow, can you use that rock to find whoever's been teaching her?" Talia asked.

Snow shook her head. "Not unless she's actually using it, and I don't think we want that." She tucked the necklace into her pocket and glanced at Arlorran. "Speaking of tricks, how did you bring us here?"

"Summoning magic." Arlorran brushed himself off and walked over to sit on a small trunk by the wall.

Snow frowned. "I thought you could only summon others, or enchant them to respond to a summons, like you did with Diglet."

Arlorran stared at the carvings on the far wall. "Aren't there places that *call* to you, Princess? Places you belong?"

"My library," said Snow.

Danielle thought of her father's house, the way it had been before he remarried. Full of color, the sunlight sparkling from vases and bottles and windowpanes of all shapes and sizes. The smell of the smoke, the way the air rippled when he stoked the fire to blow a new vase.

"Only a few places I can summon myself to and from. The Tipsy Oak's one. The queen's palace is another. And this old place." Arlorran patted the wall. "Built it myself, back when your grandparents were still learning to walk. No way in or out, aside from magic. So do what you have to do, but if anything happens to me, there's a good chance you'll breathe your last down here." He looked at Charlotte as he said that last.

"We're trapped here?" Charlotte stared at the ceiling, like she expected it to collapse at any moment. "Buried underground, like animals?"

"Tell us where Armand is," said Talia, "and maybe you'll see daylight again some day."

Charlotte shook her head. "I *can't*."

With a disgusted snort, Talia turned to Snow. "Make sure she doesn't have any more magical surprises waiting for us."

Snow knelt on the end of the bed and stared at

Charlotte. For a time, neither one moved. Then, with no trace of modesty or embarrassment, Snow reached out and yanked Charlotte's collar, tearing the shirt.

"Careful, you clumsy wench," Charlotte snapped. She tried to pull away, but Talia held her fast.

Snow pulled again, exposing Charlotte's left shoulder, where a strawberry-colored mark the size of a coin marred her skin.

"Fairy mark," Snow said. Her light seemed to brighten on the mark. "I've read about them, but I've never seen one. It's the human equivalent of a fairy contract. If she breaks it, bad things will happen."

"What kind of things?" asked Danielle.

"Depends on the fairy." Snow pressed a fingernail to Charlotte's shoulder. The skin around the mark whitened, but the mark itself didn't change. "Her hair could fall out. She could be transformed into a trout. Her blood could boil, or her boils could bleed. She could lose bladder control."

"Not in my bedroom, she doesn't," Arlorran snapped.

Charlotte glared at the gnome, her expression so full of hate that Arlorran actually took a step back. "Snow White lacks imagination," she said.

"Sounds like your friends don't trust you to keep your mouth shut," said Talia. "Snow, can you tell who cast the mark? This is our proof the fairies are involved."

Snow gave the skin a sharp pinch. "It will take time. And a human could have cast the mark, too, with training." She closed her eyes. "I don't sense any other magic on her. She's safe."

Talia sighed. "If it's not too much trouble, do you think you could take the knife strapped to her leg, too?"

Snow grabbed the knife. "You only said to search her for magic."

"Now, then," said Talia. "You're going to tell us where we can find the prince." She held up one finger when Charlotte started to protest. "You tried to assassinate the princess, and you kidnapped the prince. That gives me the right to execute you on the spot. Twice. Whatever curse that mark carries, Snow here will do her best to protect you. She won't protect you from me."

"What does it matter?" Charlotte turned toward Danielle. "He doesn't love you anymore."

Charlotte's tone was far too vicious for idle words. She was telling the truth. Danielle thought back to what Trittibar had said about using Armand to get Charlotte and Stacia into Fairytown.

Not once in her life had Danielle given Charlotte the satisfaction of showing how deeply her words cut. Rarely had it taken such effort to keep her voice steady. "Yes, we know about the love spell," she said, praying she was wrong but knowing deep down her guess was correct. "We found Brahkop. We know what you and Stacia did."

Charlotte's eyes widened, and she bit her lower lip. Unlike Danielle, Charlotte had never learned to hide her emotions. Until today, the only person Charlotte had ever feared was her mother. Danielle felt slightly ill to see that same fear directed at her.

She knelt beside the bed. "I understand why you wanted to take Armand, but why did you destroy my mother?"

"You destroyed mine."

Talia stepped closer. "The fact that your mother was a crazy, self-centered, power-grubbing madwoman is what destroyed her."

Slowly, Charlotte looked up at Talia. "That, too." She turned back to Danielle. "Would you like to know how Armand and I spent our first night together? He's quite the passionate lover. I never would have guessed. He's so polite and proper when he's out in public." She smiled. "Skilled, too. Clearly, he's sampled his share of women before *you.*"

Danielle didn't realize she had grabbed her sword until the hilt warmed in her fingers. She caught herself before she spoke. This was another game, a taunt to make her react. She opened her hand and backed away. "Snow, what about my son? Can you use him to find Armand, now that we're inside Fairytown?"

Snow shook her head. "I already tried. Wherever he is, it's well shielded."

"What about Stacia?" Danielle turned to the gnome. "Can you try to summon her? With Charlotte helpless, Stacia might be more willing to take us to Armand."

"Be careful," Charlotte said. "Your precious prince swore to kill you if he ever saw you again. He knows you'll try to take him from me, and he loves me too much to let that happen."

"He pities you," Danielle said. "It's only your enchantment that makes him pretend to love you."

"Love, pity, what does it matter? He'll still slit your throat if you try to rescue him."

Danielle shook her head. "Armand wouldn't hurt me."

"He might," said Snow. "A love spell like that is as much about possession and jealousy as true affection. The thought of losing Charlotte might be enough to drive him to murder."

"Ha!" said Charlotte.

"She's lying about sleeping with him, though," Snow added.

"How dare you—"

Arlorran chuckled. "You're right. Should have noticed that myself."

Danielle turned to the gnome. She had suspected

Charlotte was lying, but how had they known? "I don't understand."

"Your stepsister is a virgin," Snow said, sounding genuinely sympathetic. "Virginity can affect various spells, so you learn to spot the signs early on. Poor girl."

"It doesn't matter." Charlotte was a poor liar. Danielle could hear the pain beneath her venom. "You'll never see him again."

"We'll see." Danielle stood. "Arlorran, try to summon Stacia."

Arlorran stepped back. "Be ready. Charlotte arrived spitting mad. If Stacia shows up the same way, you'll want to grab her before she can do any harm." He shook his head, adding, "Any furniture gets smashed up in the process, I'm holding you responsible."

Danielle drew her sword. Talia stayed where she was, her own weapon pointed at Charlotte's throat. Snow moved to the opposite side of the room, close to Arlorran.

"Stacia Moors," Arlorran whispered. He scratched his head through his cap. "Well, blast. I almost had her, but she tightened up her shielding spell there at the end."

"We still have Charlotte," said Talia. "Tell us where to find Armand and your sister, or I'll turn you over to the fairy queen." She poked her sword at the fairy mark on Charlotte's shoulder. "I don't know how you convinced the troll to help you, but the queen is bound by the treaty. Once we tell her you've kidnapped a human prince and brought him to Fairytown, nothing in this world will protect you. Believe me, you don't want to be on the receiving end of a fairy curse."

Charlotte glared at Danielle. "You'd like that, wouldn't you?"

"I don't want you punished," Danielle said, surprised to realize it was the truth. "I just want you gone from my life."

"The fairies, on the other hand, tend to be much more interested in punishment," said Talia. "Snow, can you contact the fairy queen from here?"

Snow unclasped her choker and held the front mirror to her face. "Mirror, mirror, how you gleam. Show me now the fairy—"

"Wait," said Charlotte.

Snow closed her hand over the mirror and rolled her eyes. "I know, I know. Gleam and queen don't really rhyme. But it's a pretty basic spell, so it doesn't matter. It's the flow of the words that counts."

Charlotte rolled her eyes. "Idiot," she muttered. She reached for Danielle, who took her hand without thinking. Talia moved closer. She didn't speak, but the unwavering tip of her sword made her warning clear.

"Let him go," Charlotte said. Her fingers were thin, the skin damp with sweat. Her shoulders trembled, and she refused to look Danielle in the eyes. "You can't save him. If you try, you'll only make things worse."

"Worse for whom?" Talia asked.

Charlotte ignored her. "Danielle, I swear on my mother's grave I'm telling you the truth. Get out of Fairytown."

Talia sighed. "Call the queen, Snow."

"Wait," said Danielle. She tried to remember if Charlotte had ever called her by her proper name before. Maybe in the very beginning, before her father died, but that was a lifetime ago. "Charlotte, you know I can't leave my husband."

"He'll be happy," Charlotte snapped. "The potion guarantees that much. And isn't that what you want? For your true love to be happy? Please believe me. You have to flee."

"Why?" asked Talia. "You've already lied to us, and the fact that you tried to murder the princess doesn't do much for your credibility."

"Killing this farce of a princess is one thing," Charlotte snapped. She turned her attention back to Danielle. "But believe me, if you keep searching for Armand, you'll wish I'd finished the job."

Danielle pulled her hand from Charlotte's grasp. "What are you afraid of? Tell me."

"If I could, I would." Charlotte touched the mark on her shoulder. "You can't imagine—"

Charlotte's breath caught. She pushed herself to the back of the bed, her wide eyes fixed on the doorway, where two rats darted past Arlorran's feet.

"Off with you, you blasted pests," Arlorran shouted. He grabbed a candlestick from the dresser and flung it at the nearest rat, who scurried to one side. "Damned things sneak down the chimneys from time to time. I built a grate, but you'd be amazed at the spaces a rat can squeeze through. Most of the time they fall and break their flea-bitten necks, but every once in a while one makes it down, usually when I'm here with . . . company. Ruins the mood something awful."

The two rats ran toward the bed. Snow watched them run, a confused expression on her face. Her hand went to her knife. "Talia—the black rat. Kill it!"

Talia didn't hesitate. She whirled away from the bed and swung her sword. The blade whispered through the air, slamming onto the rat's back with a dull thump. The second rat scampered away.

Talia raised her sword. The black rat shook his head. The blow had flattened the middle of his body, but he appeared unharmed. His pink tail lashed once, and then he began to grow. His fur seemed to absorb the light, until he was little more than a shadow which gradually stretched into the shape of a young boy.

The other rat was doing the same. This one grew even larger, taking on the form of a human woman.

"Stacia." Danielle raised her sword. The glass blade shone as she aimed the tip at her stepsister.

"That little fox," Arlorran whispered. "She didn't block my summons. She rode it right to my doorstep, then hopped free. I thought you said your stepsisters were new to witchcraft."

"I thought they were," Danielle whispered. But the Stacia she remembered had little in common with the calm, confident woman standing before her.

Stacia wore a gown of blood-red velvet, trimmed with black leather. A silver belt circled her overlarge waist. A web of delicate gold chain and rubies decorated her shoulders and chest, with a ruby teardrop suspended between her breasts. Pink spirals had been tattooed onto her left cheek and around her eye, partially concealing the scars left by Danielle's birds at the wedding.

Danielle's stepmother would have died to see Stacia dressed so.

Behind Stacia, the boy remained covered in shadow. Danielle could see enough to know he wasn't human. The limbs were too long, and his movements too fluid, as if his bones were nothing but water.

"Sweet, merciful queen," whispered Arlorran as he spied the boy. "Sorry, ladies. Best of luck to you!" With that, he turned and scurried out of the bedroom.

Talia lunged at Stacia, but the shadow was faster. He jumped to interpose his body between them. The sword slammed into his torso. He seized the blade with both hands as he fell to the ground, nearly ripping the weapon from Talia's hand.

"That wasn't nice," Stacia said. She pointed to Talia. "Kill her."

The shadow hopped to his feet, shoved the sword aside, and leaped. Talia brought the ball of her foot up to kick where his jaw should have been. He fell, twisting like a cat and springing again before Talia's foot touched the ground.

"Back!" Snow shouted. The light from her choker grew almost blinding. The shadow raised his hands and scampered away. Danielle started to follow, hoping to help Talia, when Charlotte kicked her in the side.

Danielle fell against Snow, and the light dimmed. Instantly, the shadow attacked again.

Talia dove away, changing the movement into a somersault and drawing her knife as she rose. With a weapon in each hand, she turned and sliced at the shadow's face, momentarily driving him back.

Charlotte was mumbling and pointing one hand at Talia. Danielle twisted around and smashed the flat of her blade down on Charlotte's wrist. Charlotte screamed.

"It's your own fault for being so clumsy, you stupid cow," said Stacia.

"They took my necklace," Charlotte shot back. "I'm doing the best I can."

"I know. That's the sad part." Stacia pointed to the bed, and one of the blankets twisted itself into a rope and coiled around Danielle's waist. "That's an interesting toy," Stacia said. "One last gift from your dearly departed mother?"

She crooked her finger, and the ends of the blanket whipped around Danielle's arms. Danielle braced herself, twisting her wrists until the edge of the sword touched the blanket. The heavy material parted at the lightest touch, and the blanket dropped to the ground. She raised her sword to strike.

Stacia's eyes widened with fear, and Danielle hesitated.

The shadow tackled her from the side. Cold hands clamped around her sword arm. Danielle saw Snow touch her choker, but before she could use her magic, Charlotte reached out with her good hand and grabbed Snow by the hair. Then Charlotte disappeared.

"Stop summoning me, you stupid gnome!" Charlotte screamed from another room. Danielle could hear Arlorran giggling.

Snow's light drove the shadow off of Danielle. Her arm felt weak and heavy, but she wasn't bleeding. She rolled to her side and stabbed the tip of her sword into the shadow's leg.

He let out a childlike scream, the first sound Danielle had heard him make, and scurried back to Stacia's side. Stacia opened her mouth to cast another spell, then twisted away as Talia threw her knife. It ricocheted from the wall behind her.

Stacia tried again, but Talia had already snatched the fallen candlestick and thrown it after the knife. The base caught Stacia in the side of the head. She dropped to her knees, and a line of blood trickled down her face.

"So it's only your friend who's invulnerable," Talia said. "Good to know." She spun her sword and strode toward Stacia.

The shadow darted around Stacia, putting himself between her and Talia.

"Flank her," Talia snapped to Danielle. "She can't fight us both. Snow, get this half-grown wisp of darkness out of our way."

This time, though the shadow cowered from Snow's light, he didn't flee. He whimpered and looked up at Stacia, but refused to leave her side.

Stacia touched her head where the candlestick had struck. Blood dripped freely, a gruesome mirror to the tattoo on the other side of her face. She wobbled as she backed toward the doorway.

Danielle moved to intercept her. Black, oily blood

marred the tip of her sword where she had struck the shadow.

"Stacia, help me!" Charlotte shouted from the other room. "This stupid gnome keeps dancing about, summoning me this way and that. I'm going to be sick!"

"Idiot," Stacia mumbled. She brought her bloody fingers to her mouth and began to whisper.

Another blanket snarled around Danielle's legs. She swung her sword down, awkwardly trying to cut herself free. She succeeded, but nearly sliced her own foot in the process. Her arm was still weak from the shadow's attack.

Stacia had already turned to flee. Her body began to twist and shrivel back into its rat form. "Come!" she squeaked as she transformed. The shadow followed.

Talia snatched her knife from the floor and threw. The blade spun straight toward Stacia, but again the shadow saved her.

"Dammit," Talia said, hurrying after the rats.

Snow and Danielle followed Talia through the doorway, into a larger room with two iron-rimmed holes built into the walls. Danielle could see a pink tail disappearing into the closest hole. "Where's Charlotte?"

"Turned into a rat and scurried after the rest of 'em," said Arlorran.

"Can you seal the top of those chimneys from here?" Talia shouted.

Arlorran ran to grab a small wheel to the left of the holes. He yanked his hands back the instant he touched it. He jammed his fingers into his mouth. "Hot as new-forged steel," he shouted, his words muffled.

Danielle sheathed her sword and ran back to the bedroom. She grabbed the torn blanket and wrapped it around her hands as she hurried toward the chimneys. Smoke rose from the blanket, and the smell of

burning wool filled the room, but slowly the wheel
began to turn.

"It's too late," Arlorran said. "Only a short hop to
the surface. And even if we had closed them off faster,
I don't fancy being stuck down here with the likes of
them." He walked away, shaking his singed hand in
the air. "I need a drink."

"Can you summon Charlotte back?" Talia demanded.

Arlorran muttered Charlotte's name, then shook his
head. "Sorry. Either she or her sister finally remembered to shield her."

He ducked through a rounded door. Danielle caught
a glimpse of bare stone walls and wooden barrels. Arlorran reappeared a moment later with a bottle of pale
blue liquid, shutting the door behind him. He nudged
the blanket with his foot. "Genuine unicorn hair, that
was. At least, that's what the fellow who sold it to me
said." He sniffed the air. "Smells like lamb wool to
me, though."

Danielle looked around for somewhere to sit. This
room appeared to be some kind of study. Like the
bedroom, the ceiling was made of quartz. Here, the
crystal had been cut into flat facets that reflected the
candlelight back to the far side of the room, where a
worn, heavily padded rocking chair sat. Dust and
flakes of stone covered the floor. Danielle could see
tiny tracks where the rats had scurried back and forth.

A rack of stonecarving chisels and hammers hung
on one wall. "Planning to carve myself a proper
kitchen one of these days, but I never seem to get
around to it." Arlorran stepped toward the rocking
chair, but Snow was faster. She grabbed Danielle and
dragged her to the chair.

"Pull back your sleeve," Snow said. "Let me see
that arm."

"It's nothing." Danielle flexed her arm to demonstrate. "You drove him back before—"

"*I'm* the healer," Snow interrupted, with no trace of playfulness. She tugged the sword from Danielle's hand and set it on the floor. Then she unbuttoned Danielle's cuff and folded back the sleeve. "I get to say whether it's nothing."

"But it doesn't even hurt."

"Listen to your friend, lass," said Arlorran. "You don't fool around with wounds from one such as that."

Snow sucked air through her teeth, pulling Danielle's attention back to her arm.

"What did it do to me?" Danielle whispered.

The skin was unbroken, but Danielle could clearly see where the shadow had grabbed her. Pale, dry skin had already begun to flake away. She touched one of the dark freckles that hadn't been there before. They reminded her of age spots.

Snow gently pinched her arm, then let go. The skin was dry and wrinkled, and retained the impression of Snow's fingers for several heartbeats.

"What was that thing?" Danielle asked.

Arlorran shook his head. "Listen, Princesses. I vowed to help you, whether I like it or not." He took a swig from his bottle. "So I'll tell you this much. Your stepsister gave you some good advice. I'd get out of Fairytown if I were you. The sooner the better." He kept glancing behind, at the closed chimneys.

"Her skin looks like his," said Talia, pointing to Arlorran. "It looks *old*."

"Hey, now. None of that." Arlorran moved toward Snow. "She's right about the aging, though. If it were me, I'd cast that light trick of yours again. Might help destroy any leftover power in the wound. Might not, either. Who knows? You're just lucky he didn't hold on any longer."

Danielle turned her face away as the light flared. Warmth like sunlight spread over her arm, sending tingles through the old skin.

"The effects don't run deep," Snow said. She put one hand on Danielle's arm and closed her eyes. "It brushed the muscle. You may feel a little weak, but that should pass over the next few weeks, as the skin and muscle grow back."

"You still haven't told us what that was," Talia said.

Arlorran scowled and set his wine on the floor. " 'Twas a darkling," he said softly. "Offspring of the Dark Man himself."

"I've read of him," said Snow. "He's a servant of the fairy queen. They say his touch can cause a man to wither away between one breath and the next. If he's merciful, he simply shrivels a limb or turns your eyes to dust."

"Does this mean the queen is involved after all?" Danielle asked.

Arlorran gave a violent shake of his head. "The Dark Man serves the queen, and none other. But his children, they're another matter. Wild and evil, they are. Casteless, too."

"The Dark Man is the queen's assassin." Snow turned to Arlorran. "I've never heard of him having children."

"Lots of things humans don't know about fairies," Arlorran said.

"Why would a darkling serve Charlotte and Stacia?" Danielle asked, trying to assimilate it all. A mere four months earlier, she had been living at home, suffering only the mundane torments of her stepsisters. Ashes ground into her blankets, or old eggs tucked away at the bottom of her trunk until the smell infested every garment she owned. She looked at her arm and shuddered. What would have happened if

Snow hadn't driven the darkling from her arm? She yanked her sleeve down, covering the aged flesh.

"That's the meat of it, that is," said Arlorran. "Darklings serve neither king nor queen. Even the Dark Man can't control them. The queen gave orders that any of those shadow-loving bastards who set foot on her land are to be destroyed. Not that most folks are likely to take on a darkling."

"So who do they serve?" asked Talia.

Arlorran shook his head. "Looks like they serve the princess' stepsisters, don't it?" He began to pace back and forth, circling away from the chimneys. "I'm telling you, this is more than you bargained for. Charlotte might not be much to look at when it comes to magic, but Stacia was strong enough to manipulate my own summoning, and not one witch in a hundred could do that. If she's got darklings scurrying after her as well. . . ."

"You promised to help us," Danielle said. "I need to know where they've gone."

"I *am* helping you, Princess. You don't want to find those beasts."

Danielle picked up her sword. Darkling blood still clung to the glass. "We hurt him as much as he hurt me," she said. She walked to the chimney and grabbed the blanket, searching for an unburned patch, which she used to wipe the blade.

Arlorran shook his head, but didn't answer.

Behind him, Snow winked at Danielle. "This is where you used to talk to me," she said, putting a hand on Arlorran's shoulder and guiding him toward the rocking chair. The chair was wide enough for her to squeeze in beside him. She pointed toward the ceiling. "Your image always had a pink tinge to it. I hadn't realized you could enchant quartz as a scrying surface."

"Took years to get it polished fine enough to hold the spell," Arlorran said. He turned his head to one side and let out a quiet belch.

"So why did you stop talking to me?" Snow's lower lip jutted out slightly. "It's been almost a month. Do you know how lonely it gets down there in my library?"

Arlorran shook his head. "Lass, I'm well over two centuries old. Do you really think you can flirt the truth from me with those long eyelashes and big—"

"Let's find out," said Snow. She kissed the tip of his ear, then twirled his beard around her index finger. "I really did miss you, you know."

"It's been a rough time for me," Arlorran said, patting her hand.

Talia snorted. "Us, too. We're the ones fighting assassins and demons and darklings, remember?"

"Be nice." Snow stuck out her tongue.

"You're a nice girl," Arlorran said. "All of you are." He frowned at Talia. "Well, maybe not all of you. Point is, I don't want to see you get hurt."

Snow smiled and ran a fingernail along the edge of his ear. "Arlorran, do you really think my friends are just going to give up and go home? We're going after Charlotte and Stacia, and I'm the one who'll have to protect us against their magic. Don't you think I'm better off knowing what it is I'm fighting?"

"You're better off getting as far away from here—" He glanced at Danielle, then Talia. "By Mallenwar's third teat, you're all too stubborn for your own good, aren't you?"

Snow kissed his cheek. "Pretty much."

"Come with me." Arlorran led them back into the bedroom, where he spread his hands. "The one you're looking for is here, carved in quartz. I'll give you an hour. Choose the right carving, and I'll help you catch your stepsisters. If you don't find it, you go home and live to be crotchety old grandmothers."

"I hate fairies," Talia said.

Danielle stared at the sparkling quartz. There had to be hundreds, even thousands of carvings. They would need days to examine them all. "By the time we find the right one, my stepsisters will be long gone."

"Don't worry, Princess." Snow smiled and climbed onto the bed. "Mirror, mirror, shining bright. Mark the clue with morning's light."

"Hey, that's cheating, that is!" Arlorran hurried after Snow, but he was too late. A beam of warm sunlight cut through the air, and one figure on the ceiling began to glow.

Bits of metal gleamed among the quartz. Danielle held up her hand to block Snow's light, which was a little blinding. She craned her head, trying to see the inverted image.

A near-vertical crack in the quartz had been carefully etched to resemble a cliff. At the top of the cliff stood the fairy king and queen, crowned with gold. Tiny winged men and women surrounded them, while others floated in front of the cliff, their wings so thin Danielle could have snapped them with her fingers. Nearly invisible needles of quartz connected the flying fairies to the rest of the ceiling. Deep down, at the bottom of the crack, a layer of clear quartz had been bonded to the rock. Danielle could just make out the shapes of pink fish beneath the water. She wondered how Arlorran had managed such intricate layering. Her father would have been fascinated.

"Dewdrop's Dance," Arlorran said. He pointed to one of the winged figures. "Dewdrop was a pixie, one of the most gifted airdancers ever known. He led this performance to celebrate the hundredth anniversary of the queen's rule." He shook his head. "Later on, he started spying on the queen for the king. She found out and fed him to the griffins. But he could fly like a dragon in springtime, Dewdrop could."

"Snow's light wasn't shining on Dewdrop," Danielle said. She peered more closely. The light had sunk into the crack, near the bottom . . . there. The clear quartz was smokier here, but she could make out a face beneath the water. A woman with long hair peered up at the dance. A line of silver circled her brow. "Who is this?"

"Damn my artistic integrity," said Arlorran.

"This crack is supposed to be the chasm, Malindar's Triumph, isn't it?" Talia asked.

Snow dimmed her light as she crowded beside Danielle. "Why is she wearing a crown? I've never heard of another fairy royal."

"She's no royal," Arlorran said.

Danielle reached out to touch the "water." The quartz was cool and smooth as glass. This was no human city, spreading out across the land. This was Fairytown, and its inhabitants lived in all directions, from the pixies and their tavern in the treetops to Arlorran and his underground home. "How deep is the crevasse? What lies beneath the water?"

"The bones of those who go poking about where they shouldn't," snapped Arlorran. "Dark creatures who'll tear you apart before you can say, 'I should have listened to old Arlorran.' "

"We found her," Danielle said, tapping the rock. "Tell us what we need to know."

Slowly, Arlorran nodded. "A deal's a deal." He stomped back into the study. "Come on, then. This will take time to explain, and if you mean to reach the chasm before your stepsisters, you'll need help."

"Thank you," said Danielle.

Arlorran hesitated. "Don't thank me, Princess. I'm doing you no favor."

With those words, he took their hands, and once again Danielle found herself falling into darkness.

Chapter 9

❄

THEY EMERGED AT the base of an enormous iron tower, beside a mud-slick road. The tower's twin stood on the opposite side of the road, with walkways and tubular passages connecting the two like an enormous ladder. A low mist turned the air cool and damp.

Glowing pixies darted around the walkways to cling to the sides. Most of them appeared to be polishing the walls.

Spikes of all sizes covered the towers. Close to the ground, they were the size of sword blades. They grew larger the higher one looked. The three enormous spears jutting out from the tip of each tower could have skewered a giant. Harsh and cruel as the towers appeared, they blended perfectly with the great hedge which passed behind them.

"Every one of those spikes can be adjusted from within. The higher ones can even be fired at intruders." Arlorran licked his lips. "Marvelous workmanship. Never been inside myself, but I'd pay a lot to see how they managed some of those tricks."

"Where are we?" Talia peered at the sky. Twin quarter moons faced each other over the horizon.

"This is the king's land," Arlorran said. "The dwarven towers."

"That's the opposite side of Fairytown," Danielle said. "We have to get to the chasm."

"Quit your whining," snapped Arlorran. "I told you, there are only a few places where the pull is strong enough for me to summon myself. If you want to reach the chasm before your stepsisters take their anger out on your prince, this is the place to start. Unless you'd rather take your chances on the road? Some of your race have been known to wander that road their whole lives, never finding their destination."

"I thought we were protected, as long as we stayed on the road," said Danielle.

"Protected, sure," said Arlorran. "That doesn't mean the road will take you where you want to go." He stuck his fingers in his mouth and gave two sharp whistles. One of the pixies whistled back, then disappeared through an unseen window above a spear.

"Damned dwarves," Arlorran muttered. "She'll be back just as soon as they give her permission to speak with us."

The pixie emerged again before Danielle could respond. She flew faster than any bird, a blur of yellow light that streaked down to hover before Arlorran. "What do you want, gnome?" she asked.

"Nice to see you too, Nexxle." Arlorran gestured at Danielle and the others. "My friends need transportation."

"Then it's fortunate they have feet," said Nexxle.

"They need something faster." He pointed to Danielle. "They need to rescue this one's husband. Nasty forces at work here, and they need all the speed and help they can get."

Nexxle's wings stilled, and she dropped lightly into the mud. "What kind of forces?"

Arlorran lowered his voice. "They set a darkling

loose in my home, Nexxle. Little bugger could have killed me!"

The pixie's scowl never changed, but her light brightened slightly. "Maybe he'll have better luck next time."

"Will you help us?" Danielle asked.

Nexxle spat. "Some husbands aren't worth rescuing."

"Do I have to call a meeting of the elders?" Arlorran asked.

Nexxle's light dimmed to almost nothing. "You would, wouldn't you? Never could take no for an answer. Stupid gnome." She leaped up, wings buzzing. "Stay there. I'll find someone to take you to the stables."

She returned to the same window and disappeared into the tower.

"What's she doing?" Danielle asked.

Arlorran rubbed his face with both hands. "Getting permission from the dwarves to come with us. The whole bloodline lost a bet with the dwarves, years ago. Had they won, they would have taken the towers and supplanted the dwarves as the king's guardians."

"What did they lose?" Danielle asked, watching the pixies work.

"One generation of servitude. One dwarf generation, lucky for them. Pixie generations are measured in centuries." Arlorran laughed, though there was little humor in the sound. "I have to hand it to them. These towers have stood for centuries, and I don't think they've ever looked so clean."

"Who is Nexxle, and why does she hate you so much?" asked Snow.

Arlorran pursed his lips. "She's . . . well, she's my mother-in-law."

Snow's body went still. "You're married?"

"Uh-oh," Talia muttered.

"I *was* married," Arlorran said hastily. "A long time ago. She died young, fifty years ago this month." He turned away from Snow and stared up at the tower. "A bit flighty, even for a pixie, but I loved her. You remind me of her, actually."

"I'm sorry," said Snow.

Arlorran shook his head. "Suffice it to say, pixies take family ties pretty seriously. I've still got rights here, though it pains them to admit it." He took a deep, tremulous breath. "Enough of my troubles. You need to know who's got your prince. Maybe the tale of the Duchess will drive some sense into you."

He took Danielle's hand and tugged. "Don't worry, Nexxle will catch up." He reached for Snow with his free hand, and soon he was walking along, swinging their arms like a child between his parents. "The Duchess' story is an old one. Goes back to when Fairytown was little more than a lump in the earth, surrounded by a ring of toadstools. The king and queen kept within the hill most of the time, coming out only once a year to hunt."

"To hunt what?" asked Snow.

"Humans, mostly." Arlorran gave an apologetic shrug. " 'Twas sport, little more. They'd capture their favorites, choosing the most handsome and beautiful of your race to be their playthings for the coming year. Others became slaves. Often the humans chose to remain with us, even when their year of slavery was up. It's not like we killed them, you understand."

"No," said Talia. "You fairies simply burst with kindness and compassion."

"We are what we are." Arlorran gave Danielle's hand a squeeze. "Now back then, there was one ambitious little sprite who hoped to take the queen's place. She was a gifted one. Illusions, enchantment, earth magic . . . they say she even knew a little summoning magic. She transformed herself into the most beautiful of men and slipped away before the hunt. She waited in the woods, and when the king and queen arrived—well, naturally the queen was struck by her perfection. His perfection, I mean. Blast it, how are you supposed to tell a story when the pronouns keep changing on you?

"Anyway, the queen claimed him for her own, which annoyed the king to no end. He couldn't concentrate on his magic, and the girl he tried to ensnare that night managed to slip away. Understand, the king had his share of dalliances, too. He and the queen always returned to one another in the end, but this fellow was a little too good-looking, if you know what I mean." He clucked his tongue. "I have the same problem when I visit the old gnomeland."

Danielle glanced at Talia, who rolled her eyes.

"So the queen takes her prize back to the palace, where he acts as overwhelmed and befuddled as any of you humans. She's about to bed the fellow when the king bursts in. Jealousy had gotten the best of him, as it often did. Fast as a dwarf can down a pint, the king throws his spear.

"Well, a spear in the back tends to be a bit distracting. The Duchess' spell unraveled then and there, leaving her naked and bleeding and still holding the silver knife she was planning to use to cut the queen's throat.

"The queen was quite miffed, as you can imagine. Nobody likes an assassin." He glanced up at Danielle. "I guess you can imagine, at that. But no creature in the world has a temper to match that of fairy royalty. The queen was all set to rip this sprite apart when the king intervened. He said he was impressed by the magical skill it took to fool the queen. Said he could use talented spellcasters like that. Personally, I think he just wanted to keep her alive to get back at the queen.

"The queen had already lost a good deal of face over the whole mess. Rather than risk an all-out fight with her husband, she backed down. But she swore that little would-be murderess would be tortured for a thousand years if the queen ever saw her again. The king agreed, promising to bind her to tasks that would keep her away from the queen."

"So what happened?" Snow asked.

Arlorran chuckled. "She played the same game with the king that she had with the queen. Seduced him into bed that very night, whispering sweet words into his ear to gain his sympathy. The king refused to release her, but he did allow her one wish. She said she wanted to see the sun rise one last time as a free woman. After that, she would serve him willingly. The instant he agreed, she fled. The king gave chase, but she was too quick. Dove into the earth and burrowed deep. She hasn't come up since. Until she comes out and sees a sunrise, she remains free."

"I've read everything in Lorindar about fairies, including most of Trittibar's books," said Snow. "I've never heard of the Duchess."

"Not many have, even in Fairytown. And I'd take it as a favor if you kept the story to yourselves. The king and queen don't appreciate looking like fools, and they've done what they can to keep the Duchess quiet. Harder to do, since the war. Once the chasm opened up, the Duchess made a home for herself at the base of the cliffs. Started luring some of the darker creatures of Fairytown to her."

"She still wants to overthrow the king and queen?" Talia asked.

"No doubt."

Danielle stared at the road, trying to imagine her stepsisters in league with a mythical usurper to the fairy throne. "How did you learn about the Duchess?"

"The queen told me," Arlorran said. "Back when

she made me summoner. First thing she told me to do was summon the Duchess. Every few years she has me try again, hoping the Duchess will drop her guard."

"Why would she want to summon the Duchess?" Danielle asked.

"Because then the queen would see her, which means she could carry out her threat," Talia said.

"Just so." Arlorran's shudder wasn't entirely theatrical. "I told you, nobody holds a grudge like fairy royals."

"They haven't exiled her?" Snow asked.

"Exile her, and she'd be free of all ties to Fairytown," said Arlorran. "Including her oath to the king."

Danielle rubbed her arms, fighting a chill. "So why would the Duchess kidnap Armand?"

"Oh, she wouldn't," Arlorran said quickly. "She's still a fairy, bound by the treaty like everyone else. But there's nothing in the treaty to prohibit her from harboring your stepsisters, so long as she's not actively harming any humans."

"What does she get out of it?" Danielle tried to imagine what her stepsisters might offer someone like the Duchess. Her stepmother had lost most of the family's money over the years, spending the last on preparations for the ball. Charlotte and Stacia had nothing left. And their magic wouldn't impress someone with power enough to defy the fairy king and queen.

The buzzing of wings announced Nexxle's return. She carried a burlap sack three times her size. Those shimmering wings were stronger than Danielle would have guessed.

Nexxle tossed the sack to Arlorran. He did his best to catch it, but the impact knocked him onto his backside. "Thanks." He yanked the drawstring and rummaged about, pulling out several reddish-yellow apples. "Here you go," he said, tossing one to Danielle. He threw another to Snow, but Talia snatched it out of the air.

"Got anything else?" Talia asked. "Snow's . . . allergic."

Danielle glanced at Snow, who was even paler than normal. Snow forced a smile. "The taste makes me gag."

Thinking of the stories, Danielle couldn't blame her. If her mother had tried to murder her with a poisoned apple, Danielle would probably avoid them, too.

"They're not for you," Nexxle said. She flew low, smacking Arlorran on the head and knocking his cap to the road. "Come on."

She led them beneath a cluster of pine trees with needles that gleamed like silver. Nexxle's yellow light sparkled in the branches as she passed.

Danielle touched one of the branches, half-expecting the needles to pierce her skin, but they were even softer than the pines she knew from back home. She followed Nexxle onto a narrow trail.

"Never used to be a path," Nexxle muttered. "Stupid dwarves and their big, heavy boots. Might as well plant signs to mark the way."

Danielle finished her apple as they walked, following Nexxle's light through the darkness. She hurried to catch up with Arlorran. "You never explained why she doesn't like you."

"She wanted her daughter to marry a nice pixie boy," Arlorran said. "She wanted little grandkids darting around like drunken fireflies. Instead, her little girl left the family to run off with a wrinkled old gnome." He chuckled, but not fast enough to hide the longing that passed over his face. "Even if we could have had children together, can you imagine me trying to father a flock of flying kids?"

"You could have always summoned them back," Danielle pointed out.

"Ha! True enough. I haven't the temperament for the job, though. You on the other hand, you'll make a good mother. Assuming you don't get yourself killed or enslaved to the Duchess first."

Danielle shook her head. "Everything I know about being a loving mother, I learned from a tree."

Arlorran grinned. "That sounds like a tale strange enough to come from a fairy."

"Hurry up," Nexxle snapped. "The dwarves want me to finish oiling the spears on the eighteenth level, and I mean to be done before sunrise."

The trees thinned as they climbed a broad hill. What Danielle saw when she reached the top was almost enough to drive all thoughts of her stepsisters, the Duchess, and even Armand from her mind.

Tree-covered hills spread out in a wide circle, creating a grassy bowl. Grazing on the far side, painted by the light of a handful of pixies, was a small herd of what appeared to be horses. But they were like no horses Danielle had ever seen.

Huge, feathered wings lay flat along their sides. Even folded back, those wings extended far beyond the horses' backsides, looking like huge, feathered tails.

Nexxle gave a quick double-whistle, and one of the other pixies streaked toward them. This was a blue pixie, a male, with rumpled clothes and sweat-slick hair. He dropped to the ground in front of Arlorran, then gave the three princesses a long, appraising look. He punched Arlorran's leg. "You're doing well for yourself these days, old gnome!"

"Shut up, Quink," said Nexxle. "These three need mounts. Take care of them."

"We're going to ride them?" Danielle whispered. Her heart pounded with a blend of fear and longing.

"Aviars will get you to the chasm faster than anything save a dragon," said Arlorran. He pulled an
apple from the sack and hurled it out over the grass.
Instantly, four of the aviars spread their wings and
leaped. Their whinnies were higher in pitch than Danielle was used to, sounding uncomfortably like human
screams. Unshod hooves lashed out as they fought to
reach the apple. A brown-and-white stallion gave one
last flap of his wings, knocking a gray mare toward
the ground. He caught the apple neatly in his jaws,
dropped down, and galloped away to enjoy his prize.

"We're going to *ride* them?" Danielle asked again,
in a very different tone.

"Have fun!" said Nexxle, grinning for the first time
since they had met. She actually giggled as she disappeared back into the woods.

Arlorran grabbed another apple. "Trust me. You
try to cross Fairytown on your own, you'll face all
manner of trouble and challenges. These beasts will
fly straight and true, and most importantly, they'll
keep you safe."

"Come on," said Quink. "Let's find you ladies
some mounts."

The aviars backed away as Danielle and the others
followed Quink down to the field. Some rustled their
wings. The brown-and-white stallion nickered and
reared. Wings spread, he balanced on his hind legs far
longer than any normal horse could have.

"How do you ride them?" Danielle asked.

"Us? We use carriages." Quink pointed to a spotted
aviar near the back of the herd. A long, basketlike
contraption was strapped to the aviar's back. Two pixies sat inside, their light clearly visible through triangular windows. A third pixie stood on the beast's neck,
his arms and hands wound in the long mane. A thin
riding crop, twice as long as his body, hung from his
belt. "These aren't pets, ladies. When pixies go to war,

we can pack five or six warriors into every one of
those carriages, firing arrows and casting spells in all
directions while the rider controls the animal. That
doesn't even cover the damage a well-trained aviar
can do in a fight."

"But you won't be riding one of the warbeasts,"
Arlorran said sternly. "Isn't that so, Quink?"

The pixie stuck out his tongue. "You're no fun anymore." He emitted a shrill series of chirps, and several
of the other pixies began to lead aviars their way.
Arlorran pressed an apple into Danielle's hand, then
did the same for Snow and Talia.

"No loud noises or sudden movements," said
Quink. "On the ground, these fellows spook even easier than your horses."

Danielle smiled and held out her apple. She could
see some of the other aviars snorting and stomping in
their direction, but the pixies held them at bay. She
stepped toward the leftmost aviar, a gray mare whose
wings and mane were black as the ocean at midnight.
Those wide blue eyes never blinked as she sniffed the
apple. Slowly, she drew back her lips and plucked the
apple from Danielle's hand.

The aviars smelled like fresh-cut hay, with a hint of
a sharper, nuttier smell. "Can I touch her?"

"Pretty hard to ride if you don't," Quink said.

Danielle reached up to pet the fur on the side of
the mare's neck. One ear flicked back.

"You're beautiful," Danielle whispered, stroking
the neck. The aviar's skin was warm, almost feverish,
and the fur was stiffer than it looked.

An orange pixie flew up beside the aviar's head. He
waited until she finished eating the apple, then slipped
a brass bit into her mouth. The aviar took a step back,
but the pixie was faster, darting around her head and
buckling a light halter into place. The reins appeared
normal, if longer than she was used to, but a third

line ran along the top of the aviar's nose. This line was knotted to the center of the reins, right between where the rider would hold on. Danielle stared. In the past month, she had barely gotten comfortable riding a normal horse. "How do I—?"

That was as far as she got. The mare shook her head sharply, then sneezed. Spit, snot, and bits of apple sprayed over Danielle's face and chest.

"They're not too fond of the bit," Quink said, stifling a grin.

Danielle wiped her face on her sleeve. To her left, Talia had already climbed onto a bay with black wings. Danielle brushed the worst of the mess from her shirt. "So how do I control her?"

Quink flew up to stand on the base of the mare's neck. "If you're a pixie, you use the braids in her mane. For you, I'd suggest the reins."

Danielle ran her hands through the mane, finding one of the knotted braids. It was little thicker than a string, far too small for her to get a proper grip.

"Don't worry. If those meat-fisted dwarves can ride them, you'll be fine." Quink took the reins in his hands, holding them so that most of the slack fell between his hands.

"Guiding them left or right is the same as your landbound horses." Quink tugged the reins to the left, walking the aviar in a tight circle. "Make sure you keep the flight line loose." He pointed to the third line.

"To fly higher, shift your grip like so." He slid his hands back, until they touched the knot of the flight line. The length of the reins meant the flight line pulled taut before the reins. "Control the head and you control the animal."

He tugged, pulling the aviar's head up. The mare took a few quick steps, then surged up into the air. The rush of wind from the aviar's wings pushed Danielle back a step. "Slide your hands forward on the reins and pull the head downward to bring her back to earth," Quink shouted, guiding the aviar down. "You're not a screamer, are you? They don't like that. And unless you've got wings, you don't want to annoy these beasts while you're up there."

He hopped off and handed the reins to Danielle. "Need a boost?"

There was no saddle, and the wings were too high for her to use to pull herself up. She was still studying the aviar when tiny hands seized her collar. Quink's wings blew her hair into her face, and then her feet left the ground. Her shirt dug into her arms as Quink carried her over the aviar. She could have been light as air for all the strain the pixie showed.

"Pixie wings are magical," Snow explained. She had already mounted her own aviar. "They can carry twenty times their own weight, just like insects."

"I beg your pardon?" Quink said. He gave a disdainful sniff, then turned his attention back to Danielle. "This is one of the older mares. Probably the most easygoing aviar we've got. They calm down once they're past childbearing age. Still a lot of strength in those wings, though." He stepped away, shaking his head and muttering, "Insects, indeed."

The aviar started to follow Quink. Danielle leaned forward, wrapping her arms around the aviar's neck to keep from falling. The great wings jutted into the back of her thighs, shoving her farther up on the back than on a normal horse. There was no room for a saddle, and the aviar's spine promised all manner of interesting bruises before the night was over.

Talia guided her aviar alongside Danielle. "What's the matter, Princess? You look like a marionette with half her strings cut."

Danielle flushed. Her hands were damp around the reins as she forced herself to straighten, trying to mimic Talia's relaxed pose. The aviar chose that moment to do a little hop to the side. Danielle clamped her legs beneath the aviar's wings to keep from tumbling off.

"Relax," said Arlorran. He held another apple over his head. The aviar's movements stopped as she snatched it from his hand. "Keep your knees bent like that, beneath the wings. *She* doesn't want you to fall either. The more comfortable and relaxed you are, the easier it is on her."

Quink flew up beside her, dodging an annoyed flick of the mare's tail. "Careful with that sword. Try to keep the scabbard from poking her beneath the wing." He grimaced as he watched Danielle fumble with the reins. Talia trotted alongside, looking like she had been born to ride aviars.

Danielle gave the reins an experimental tug. The aviar jumped to the side, nearly knocking Arlorran to the ground. Quink glanced at Arlorran, a skeptical expression on his face.

Danielle closed her eyes. This wasn't working. She could barely control a regular horse. She could practically feel the aviar's discomfort growing with every clumsy move Danielle made. She took a deep breath and turned to look at Quink. "What are their names?"

The pixie pointed to Snow. "Your pale friend is riding Midnight, and the sour-faced girl is on Socks."

Talia led her aviar toward Quink. "Socks?"

The pixie grinned. "One of the kids named him." He pointed to the white fur on the ends of the aviar's legs. "It was that or Bootsie."

His lips quirked slightly as he turned back to Danielle. "As for your aviar, her birth name was Zoë. One of the dwarves renamed her, though. These days we call her Zirdiclav."

Danielle did her best to imitate the chirping sounds of the name. "What does it mean?"

"Hard to translate into your tongue," Quink said, glancing away. "Roughly, it comes out to 'Storm-breaker.' "

Arlorran sniggered. "They might not understand dwarvish, but I've picked up a smattering." He shook his head. " 'Zir' means breaker all right, but 'clav' is a dwarf word for an unexpected gust of wind."

"So she's . . ." Danielle covered her mouth with her hand. "Breaker of Wind?"

"She'll be fine," Quink said. "Ah, your friends might not want to fly directly behind her, though."

"I'll call her Wind," Danielle said. She leaned forward, pressing her body to the aviar's neck. She had never tried to talk to any animal this large before. Would the aviar understand? Even if she did, there was no guarantee she would listen.

"Please," Danielle whispered. Wind's ear flicked back. "I need to get to the chasm. My stepsisters are there, and they've taken my husband. My mate."

The aviar snorted. Danielle couldn't tell if she understood or not.

"I know I'm clumsy. I'm doing the best I can. Could your foals run and fly so beautifully when they were born?"

Another flick of the ear, and a slight shake of the head. The reins tugged free of her grip.

"I understand," said Danielle, praying that she did. She reached down until she touched the metal buckle. A sharp tug loosened the strap, and then she was sliding the reins up and off of the aviar's head. Wind shook her head, spitting the bit from her mouth and tossing the whole halter toward Quink.

"What do you think you're doing, lass?" Arlorran asked, hurrying to her side. "She'll dump you to the ground like—"

The aviar leaped, wings slamming down with such force that Arlorran tumbled onto his back. Danielle hugged the aviar's neck, pressing her legs beneath the wings. Her weight was too high, and she felt like she would topple off the instant she relaxed at all.

"Well, all right, then," Arlorran said, brushing dirt from his backside. "What do I know about flying horses anyway?"

Wind nickered as she cleared the treetops, where she stilled her wings and began to glide in slow, wide circles. Her head turned slightly inward, and Danielle swore she saw amusement in that ocean-blue eye.

Gradually, Danielle loosened the muscles in her legs, letting them slide down Wind's side until the wings no longer beat the back of her thighs. She could feel the powerful muscles pumping as the aviar maintained her flight.

Quink flew after her, the discarded halter dangling from his hands. "And how will you control her, you addlebrained, wingless nit of a girl?"

"I won't." Danielle swallowed, hoping this wasn't a mistake. "I'll trust her." She lowered her voice, speaking to the aviar alone. "Can you take me back down to my friends?"

The aviar's wings spread wider, slowing their flight. Danielle tensed as they swooped down, but Wind landed as lightly as a sparrow.

"Better," said Talia. "But you're still stiff as a statue. Keep riding like that, and you'll end up feeling like an ogre pummeled your legs with his club."

"Oh, hush," said Snow. "You're just jealous because you have to use the reins." She clapped her hands and beamed at Danielle.

"Princess Danielle?"

She looked down at Arlorran. "You don't have to call me princess."

Arlorran turned to watch Snow and Talia as they bickered. He lured Wind away with another apple, until they were out of earshot. Lowering his voice, he said, "You've a dangerous path ahead of you. Keep them safe, lady."

Danielle stared. "Me keep *them* safe? Talia's the one who can kill a giant with nothing but a bootlace, and Snow's magic is powerful enough to—"

"A mastery of weapons and magic will help, no doubt about it," said Arlorran. "But I know Snow, and I've watched you and Talia." He reached up to pat her on the leg. "Trust old Arlorran. Take care of those two."

Before Danielle could respond, Talia guided her aviar around. "Come on. The sooner we get moving, the sooner I'll be back on solid earth."

"They'll return to us on their own," Quink called. "Just say 'Home' once you've reached your destination."

Danielle started to ask how she and her companions were supposed to get back, then realized it didn't matter. If they found Armand, they could contact Beatrice to arrange for help through the fairy court. If not. . . .

"Thank you," Danielle said. She turned to look at Arlorran. "And you," she added.

"Remember what I told you," Arlorran said. "And don't forget about my wings!"

As they climbed toward the clouds, Danielle found herself trembling. The pixies were little more than sparks, and a single strong wind could toss Danielle to the ground. Very soon, though, something within her surrendered to the inevitable. If she fell, she fell. There was nothing to do but trust Wind to keep her safe.

Fear faded, giving way to a dreamlike sense of excitement. The cold night air chilled Danielle's skin, even as Wind's skin grew warmer from her exertions. This was so much more vivid than the flight from the palace, when she had been tucked away in Karina's basket. The air buffeted her face, ruffling her shirt and flinging her hair back in tangled streamers.

"Look at the moons," Danielle shouted. The wind sucked her words away, but the aviar appeared to hear, banking left in order to give Danielle a better view of the twin crescents. The moons faced one another, twin disks of silver and gold, the edges nearly touching.

She twisted back, searching for the dark shapes of the dwarven towers. The hedge disappeared into the distance. She had never understood how huge Fairytown was. She glanced to the east, where enormous rooftops poked through the trees.

"Giants," Snow shouted. She grinned and steered her aviar closer to Danielle. "The elves are the only ones who can grow trees large enough for the giants to use to build their homes. In return, the giants don't eat the elves."

Talia and Socks flew past on Danielle's right. "Come on," Talia yelled. "You can have your fill of sightseeing once we've found Armand." Her aviar pulled ahead, wings pounding.

Danielle and Wind followed. Sudden exuberance made Danielle giggle as they flew, so high and swift and *free*. She lowered her body and breathed in the musky, nutty scent of the aviar. She could have ridden like this forever.

And then Wind began to sweat. She didn't notice until they caught up to Snow. Danielle pulled her hand away to wave. The instant her arm left the aviar's fur, the wind chilled her damp sleeve, making her shiver.

Soon, salty aviar sweat soaked her arms and the front of her shirt, and she could feel it seeping into her trousers. She pressed herself closer to Wind for warmth. The wiry fur was slick and damp, and the mane kept sticking to her face, but the air was too cold to draw away.

The land below crawled past, marked by specks of campfires and lanterns. But the wind on her skin told her they were moving faster than any horse.

Up ahead, a wisp of cloud moved against the wind, sparkling like the sea as it undulated toward them. Danielle's aviar let out a long, quavering scream. The other aviars did the same.

"Cloud strider," Talia shouted. She tugged her reins, steering Socks away. "Warning us away from the palace."

Danielle turned her head. The black towers of the fairy king's palace were harder to see in the darkness. The silver bridge lay beyond, and she could see the lights of the queen's palace on the far side. Her own aviar turned to follow Talia. Danielle saw a quick flicker of lightning from the cloud strider, illuminating the long, winged form from within, and then it was flying back to the mass of clouds overhead.

"Land on the queen's side," Talia yelled. "If your stepsisters are traveling on foot, we will have beaten them. We should be able to follow them down."

"How?" Down below, the chasm stretched away for miles in either direction. "They could be anywhere. We can't guard the whole width of Fairytown!"

"Says who?" Snow called, grinning like a child. She was already guiding Midnight over the chasm. Far below, the river reflected broken shards of moonlight.

Danielle shivered and leaned closer to Wind. Her thighs and lower legs were cramped and chapped, and her backside throbbed with every beat of the great wings.

The edge of the chasm was thick with a kind of flowering willow tree. From a distance, they seemed like toys, each one identical to the next, spreading out for at least a mile on either side of the queen's palace.

"This way," Talia said, steering Socks toward the trees.

Danielle sucked icy air through her teeth as she watched. There was no gap through which the aviar could fly. The branches hung to the ground, and many stretched even further, clinging like leeches to the rough face of the cliff.

Socks' wings were perfectly still as he carried Talia closer to the trees. At the last instant he tucked his head, and his wings snapped back with a noise like a giant beating a rug. The aviar ripped through the branches and disappeared, with only a few falling leaves to mark his passage.

Snow followed, ducking her head as her aviar burst through the branches, and then it was Danielle's turn. She dug her fingers into Wind's skin, pressing her face against the sweat-slick fur.

Thin, flexible branches whipped her arms and head, and then Wind was galloping along hard-packed dirt, wings half-stretched as she slowed. Danielle gritted her teeth as those final steps drummed new bruises into her backside, not to mention the jarring of her bladder. "That wasn't so bad," she said, her voice shaky. She clamped her jaw to keep from crying out as she hoisted one leg over Wind's back and jumped down. Her legs gave out immediately, leaving her sprawled in the dirt.

Wind chose that moment to pass gas.

Snow's choker was already alight, showing where the trees had been trimmed back to form a wide, arched hallway. Purple buds tipped the branches, filling the air with the smell of nectar. Slivers of moonlight penetrated through the leaves, transforming dust in the air to floating flecks of diamond. The trees formed a kind of tunnel, the branches to either side woven as tightly as any wall.

Talia had already slid down from Socks, giving no sign of discomfort. She tossed their bags to the ground, then reached up to help Snow from her aviar.

"Get to the edge," Talia said.

"I'm on it." Snow hurried past Danielle. She, at least, had the decency to show some stiffness in her legs.

"You tense up when you ride," Talia said as she helped Danielle to her feet. "You have to relax. Let your body move with the horse. Or the aviar, in this case."

"Thanks," said Danielle. She grabbed one of the trees for support. The branches were harder than she expected, and the leaves drew lines of blood along her hand.

She felt like a thousand pixies were driving tiny knives into her legs every time she moved. She gritted her teeth and forced herself to take a step, then two. By the time she found a vaguely private spot to relieve herself, she was shivering from the cold. Peeling the front of her sweat-soaked shirt from her skin sent a new wave of goose bumps down her flesh.

"We've got plenty of blankets in the bags," Talia said when she returned.

Danielle made it halfway to the bag before Talia took pity and tossed the blanket to her.

Wrapping the coarse material around her body, she hobbled back toward Snow, who knelt at the very edge of the chasm. The branches here at the edge were little more than a thin curtain, swaying with the breeze. "What are you doing?"

"Watching for your stepsisters," Snow said. She had taken off her choker. Her exposed throat appeared strangely vulnerable. She ran her fingers along the mirrors, stroking them like pets. She tapped the last mirror, and the gold wire holding it in place began to untwine.

The mirror dropped to the ground and crept toward the edge, four wires carrying it along like a glowing insect. Snow tapped it again, and the mirror returned to her palm. She blew a puff of air, extinguishing its light like a candle flame.

"Go," she whispered. The mirror hopped into the branches and disappeared into the chasm.

"Arlorran's sculpture showed the Duchess watching from beneath the bridge," Talia said. "Her home has to be around here somewhere."

Snow nodded as she freed a second mirror. This one scurried up the tree, disappearing through the leaves. "I'm sending three down to search for the Duchess. Three more will climb the trees to watch for the stepsisters. Even if I can't find the cave myself, we'll be able to follow Charlotte and Stacia down when they arrive."

Soon only a single mirror remained. Snow kept this one and reclasped the choker around her neck. The light was proportionally dimmer, but Danielle's eyes had long since adjusted to the darkness.

"What do we do until then?" Danielle asked.

"We eat, and then we sleep," said Talia. "Rather, *you* sleep." She walked away and began leading the aviars down the corridor.

"What is this place?" Danielle reached out to touch the velvety leaves.

"The queen's labyrinth," said Snow. "It surrounds her palace. She likes to blind intruders and turn them loose in the maze. She waits a short time, then sends the wolves in after them. Anyone who survives is set free."

Danielle swallowed and backed away from the edge. She could easily imagine a helpless prisoner fleeing the howls of hungry wolves, only to stumble through that thin curtain and plummet into the chasm.

Snow wrinkled her nose. "Come on," she said, tugging Danielle toward their bags. "I don't know about you, but I could use a change of clothes."

Up ahead, Talia snorted as she brushed down the

aviars. "Snow always overpacks. She could probably
dress every member of the fairy queen's court and still
have a week's worth of outfits."

"I like to be prepared, that's all," Snow said.

Talia dropped her brush and walked back to snatch
something blue and satiny from one of the bags. "Prepared for what? You think they're holding Armand
prisoner at a fancy dress ball?"

Snow snatched the blue garment away and stuck
out her tongue. She dug through the bags and tossed
Danielle a fresh shirt and trousers, along with clean
undergarments. The drawers were lacier than she
would have liked, and the chemise had frilly ribbons
at the neck, but at least they were clean and dry. On
Danielle, the clothes were tight at the waist and loose
in the chest, but they would do.

Snow glanced at Talia, who had gone back to brushing the aviars. Dragging Danielle away, she lowered
her voice and said, "I've got another undershirt that's
nothing but lace, if you want to borrow it for when
we save Armand. Men love that sort of thing."

Danielle's cheeks grew warm.

"So what was it like when the two of you first met?"
Snow grabbed a shell-inlaid comb and began to work
the tangles from her hair.

"Strange," Danielle admitted. She sat down and
stretched out her legs, biting her lip to keep from
crying out. The first night when she snuck away to
attend the ball, Danielle never dreamed of catching
the prince's eye. Simply escaping her stepmother's
home, losing herself in music and dancing and the
sheer, spoiled luxury of the ball had been all she ever
wanted. "I didn't even recognize him at first. He
seemed so young. I thought he was somebody's son,
a minor noble, maybe." Only when she saw everyone
else falling back to give them space had she figured
out who her dancing partner must have been.

"I stepped on his feet," she admitted. "Glass slippers are not meant for dancing."

Snow giggled and passed the comb to Danielle, who sighed. Once again, Snow looked absolutely perfect. The sweaty strands of hair hanging in front of her face only made her more attractive. Danielle ran a hand through her own hair. She would be lucky if she didn't rip half of it out trying to fix the snarls.

"I thought my Roland was so old when I first saw him," Snow said. "So old, and so hairy. His hair was thick as a sheepdog's, all black, except for a few strands of gray. The gray ones used to bother him so. He'd pluck them out when he noticed them, but we were always finding more scattered across his back and . . . other places."

"Who was Roland?" Danielle asked.

"The man my mother hired to cut out my heart," Snow said, still smiling wistfully.

"But he didn't?" Danielle knew the question was a particularly stupid one the instant it left her mouth.

Snow giggled again. "I was young, but already woman enough for him to notice. He took me away to the woods to protect me. I learned to hunt and cook for myself, and I practiced my magic when he was away. We practiced a different kind of magic when he returned."

Her smile faltered slightly. "It was almost a year later when my mother found us. She arrived disguised as an old woman. One bite of that poisoned apple and I knew, but it was too late. She was already casting her spell, trapping me in a crystal coffin. I couldn't move. I couldn't even breathe."

"I'm sorry." Not knowing what else to do, Danielle reached out and squeezed Snow's hand.

"I heard everything, though. She gave Roland a choice. Finish the job he'd been paid to do, or suffer the same fate. He tried to fight, but she was too strong.

Finally, he took his knife and opened my coffin. He could have saved himself, but instead he chose to free me. By the time I recovered enough to fight my mother, she had already killed him."

Snow pointed to the branches overhead. "This place reminds me of our cottage. Deep in the woods, away from the troubles of the world, safe from—"

"This is the fairy queen's labyrinth," Talia said. She pressed a muffin into Danielle's hand. "Safe is hardly the word I'd use."

"Don't be such a wet blanket." Snow swiped a muffin for herself, then tugged the waterskin from Talia's shoulder. "The fairy queen almost never sends prisoners into the maze at night, and the creatures who patrol this place stay close to the castle. We'll be fine."

Danielle took a bite of her muffin. It was dry, and the small raisins inside were hard as wood. Goat cheese had been melted over the top. Plain, simple fare, as were the strips of dried lamb meat Talia handed out next. But her stomach seemed to prefer bland these days, and it was far better than the scraps she used to receive from her stepmother. The taste reminded her of simpler times, back when her father was still alive. Back before balls and princes and stepsisters who practiced black magic.

"The aviars are tied around the bend, munching the queen's maze," Talia said. "Hopefully, she won't mind. We don't know when the stepsisters will show up, so you should rest now, while you can."

Snow handed her choker to Talia. "The mirror will flash when they approach." A few crumbs slipped down her chin as she spoke. "Wake me, and I'll be able to see exactly where they are."

"If they don't show up tonight, we'll start searching the chasm for the Duchess in the morning," said Talia. She drew her sword and brought Snow's choker close, using the light to check the edge of the blade.

"What happens if my stepsisters have more of those darklings?" Danielle asked.

"Then we'll probably die." Talia flipped her sword to study the other edge. She ran a fingernail along the edge and clucked her tongue. Grabbing a small whetstone from her pocket, she sat down and began to sharpen the blade. "Get some sleep, Princess."

Chapter 10

❄

PERHAPS IT WAS the magic of Fairytown that twisted Danielle's dreams into nightmares. Or it could have been the child in her womb, or the fear and anxiety of the past few days.

In her dreams, Danielle found herself on her cot back in the attic of her old house. Her stepsisters laughed and danced around her as the shadowy form of their darkling wrapped knotted, soiled rags around Danielle's limbs, binding her in place.

When he finished, the darkling scrambled onto her belly, which had swollen like the hills outside of town. Producing a silver shovel, the darkling rammed the blade into her stomach and turned up a spade full of muffin, which he tossed aside. Charlotte and Stacia scrambled to gobble up the discarded raisins. Danielle tried to scream, but the darkling placed a slimy hand over her mouth. Her lips and tongue turned dry, aging and shriveling like the raisins on the floor.

The darkling returned to her stomach, digging out more and more muffin until he stood shoulder-deep in Danielle's belly.

He clawed his way back out and disappeared into the darkness. Stacia and Charlotte walked around to either side of Danielle. Charlotte produced a handful of seeds, which she tossed into the hole in Danielle's stomach. Soon an enormous cornstalk began to grow, breaking through the low roof to let the moonlight in. More darklings climbed down the cornstalk, disappearing into Danielle's stomach as she squirmed and tried to scream, but all that emerged was a weak gasp.

A cold hand clamped down on her mouth. "I'd prefer we not announce ourselves to all of Fairytown, if it's all the same to you," Talia said.

Danielle wrenched free and scooted away until her back hit the branches. She touched her mouth, then her stomach. Her clothes were once again damp with sweat, but she was unharmed.

"You were dreaming," Talia said, her voice an odd mix of annoyance and envy. She wore Snow's choker, and the lone, glowing mirror gave her face a nightmarish quality.

Danielle looked over at Snow. Whatever noise Danielle might have made, Snow had slept right through it. She lay curled into a ball, her blanket clutched tightly around her.

Through the branches overhead, the sky remained dark. Danielle stifled a yawn. "How long was I asleep?"

"Several hours. Not long enough. You need your rest, Princess."

The thought of returning to that dream made her shudder. "What have you been doing while we slept?"

"I finished feeding the aviars, then brushed them down. All the while trying not to inhale." She wrinkled her nose. "Quink wasn't kidding about Windbreaker, there."

Danielle managed a weak smile.

"I also cleaned up the mess you two left." Talia pointed to their clothes, which hung drying from the branches a little way down the tunnel.

"I'm sorry. I should have—"

"You're not a slave anymore, remember?" Talia snapped. "Stop acting like one." She picked up Danielle's sword and handed it to her. "Come with me."

Danielle managed a small smile. "If you're trying to convince me I'm no longer a slave, shouldn't you stop ordering me around?"

"You're obviously too shaken to sleep." Talia smiled. "I can remedy that. Besides, it will be good to get your blood moving so that your body won't be as stiff."

Danielle gasped when she tried to stand. She used her sword like a cane, hobbling after Talia until she reached a place where the passage split in two directions. To her right, she could see the three aviars. They slept standing up, bodies pressed together so their wings blanketed one another.

"This way," Talia said, leading her down the left passage. "Sit down and spread your legs apart."

Danielle raised an eyebrow, imagining what Snow would say if she were here. But she did as she was told, clenching her teeth at the strain on her thighs.

"Good. Lean to one side. You need to loosen the muscles, or you'll be completely useless in the morning."

Talia worked Danielle through a series of exercises, demonstrating each one with an ease that made Danielle want to punch her. Which might have been the idea.

When they were finished, Talia bounced to her feet, drew her sword, and turned to face Danielle. Her free hand tapped the glowing mirror. "This is your target. I want to see what you can do."

"I can barely walk, let alone stab you."

"Oh, you're not going to stab me." Talia's grin widened. "But I want you to try anyway."

Slowly, Danielle pulled her sword from its scabbard. "What about the noise?"

"Snow can sleep through anything." Talia folded her left hand behind her back. Her sword angled up across her body. "Bend your knees, then lunge."

Danielle set the sheath on the ground and tried to match Talia's stance. The effort sent new pain tearing through her thighs, but she clenched her teeth and forced her legs to bend. She lowered the tip of her sword until it was level with the mirror, then took a broad step forward.

The pain in her thighs made her yelp, but she managed to shove her sword forward the way Talia had demonstrated.

She expected Talia to step back or beat her blade aside. Instead, Talia stepped forward, twisting easily out of the way. Her fingers clamped around Danielle's wrist. At the same time, Talia brought the tip of her own weapon up beneath Danielle's chin, so that Danielle's eyes crossed trying to focus.

"Try to relax," Talia said. She released Danielle and lowered her sword. "You're tensing before you attack, and you draw your arm back before you lunge. You might as well scream, 'Here I come!' "

Danielle tried again, a smaller lunge that didn't tear her legs as badly. This time Talia danced aside and used the flat of her blade to tap Danielle's elbow.

"You served food for your stepmother and stepsisters, right?" Talia asked.

"Since I was old enough to carry a platter," Danielle said.

"Ever spill anything?"

For a moment, she could hear her stepmother's furious screams, calling her a worthless, clumsy, ugly mess of a girl, while her stepsisters laughed from the doorway. "Not if I could help it."

"Good." Talia stepped back. "This is the same thing. Keep your upper body straight and still. Turn sideways, so you present less of a target. Use your hips and legs to move. Try to stay with me. And *relax!*"

"Relax, she says," Danielle muttered. Moving with slow, easy steps, Danielle did her best to keep up with Talia. Talia retreated faster, and Danielle matched her pace. The tip of her sword barely wavered.

"Better," Talia said again. "Now fall."

"What?"

"You're carrying the wine, and you start to stumble. Leap forward to recover your balance. And *don't spill that wine.*"

Danielle did her best to obey. She allowed her body to overbalance, then danced ahead, keeping her body straight as she thrust her sword toward Talia.

Talia's sword snapped against Danielle's hard enough to knock it from her hand. Flushing, Danielle knelt to retrieve her sword.

"Not bad," Talia said. "Move like you did just then, shoulders loose and level, and your opponent will have a harder time knowing what's coming next. You're not chopping wood here. Brute force can be effective, but it's clumsy and wasteful. That sword is keen as a razor. With practice, the lightest kiss of steel can be deadlier than brute, sweeping blows. Now let's see if you can parry."

Danielle braced herself. Talia's lunge was deceptively slow. Danielle swung her sword sideways, knocking Talia's blade aside.

"Right," said Talia. "Let me show you what would happen in a real fight."

Talia attacked again, as slowly and gracefully as before. Danielle tried to parry, and Talia's blade dipped beneath her own, twisted, and smacked Danielle lightly on the knuckles.

"Of course, a real enemy would have sliced off your hand," Talia said. "Block the upper part of my blade with the lower part of yours, and don't swing so wildly. You look like a child playing stickball, Princess. You only have to move my sword far enough to the side that I can't hit you."

Danielle's fist tightened around the hilt of her sword. What did Talia expect? Danielle had never even touched a sword until her mother gifted her with this one, and it wasn't like she had fairy magic to guide her hand. She tried to block another attack and missed, taking a slap on the elbow that nearly made her drop her sword.

"You're tensing up again," Talia said. She pointed her blade toward Danielle's fist. "Your knuckles are white, Princess."

"Maybe that's because you keep hitting me."

"Better me than one of your stepsisters," said Talia. "A tight grip costs you speed and control both." She swung her sword overhead, bringing it down slowly toward Danielle's throat.

Danielle raised her sword to block, but caught Talia's attack too high on her blade. Talia pressed down, twisting both weapons around and wrenching Danielle's sword from her hand. The glass rang against the base of a tree.

"Pick it up and try again," Talia said.

Danielle straightened. She was beginning to understand why Snow had given up on weapons training with Talia. That imperious tone made Danielle's teeth grate. It was like being back home with her stepsisters. Danielle was just about to follow Snow's lead and tell Talia what she could do with her own sword when she noticed something strange.

Talia was smiling. It wasn't a huge grin. She didn't even look particularly happy. But the tension around her eyes had softened. As she stood there, absently twirling her sword through the air, she seemed *content*.

Slowly, Danielle retrieved her sword and did her

best to match Talia's stance. She was rewarded with another brief smile.

"Normally we'd go through all twelve of the basic offensive and defensive moves, but given your condition, I think we'll take it easy and stick with the four primary strikes and parries." Talia flexed her arms, then sank into a guard position. "Once we're through, I guarantee you'll sleep the rest of the night."

When Snow shook her awake the next morning, Danielle's arms and shoulders were so stiff she could barely move them. Her legs were even worse. She sat down and tried to stretch out the muscles the way Talia had shown her. The exercises hurt, but they did seem to help her move.

Snow laughed. "I see Talia was working with you last night. Here, try to relax."

Danielle groaned. "Do you know how many times I heard that?"

Snow scooted around behind Danielle and began to knead her neck and shoulders.

Danielle closed her eyes again, then gasped as Snow began to work on a knot at the base of her neck.

"Any sign of my stepsisters?" Danielle asked.

"That's why we woke you," said Snow. She tapped her choker.

Turning, Danielle saw that all but two of the mirrors had returned. The front mirror flickered like it was catching the morning sun.

"They're a little ways south of here, flying fast," said Snow.

"Flying?" Danielle glanced around. "Shouldn't we be getting ready? We can catch them before—"

"Catch them and do what?" Talia tossed their bags onto the ground. "We still don't know where the Duchess lives. If we fight your stepsisters here, they might be able to summon reinforcements. Or they could escape again. No, we wait and let them lead us to the Duchess' front door. Then we follow them down and do a bit of snooping.''

"What were you thinking?" Snow asked. "Does Danielle look like she's up for your brand of torture?"

"She did better than you did your first time," Talia shot back. "If she's going to travel with us, she needs to be able to defend herself. Besides, I made sure to take it easy on her."

"I remember your idea of taking it easy," Snow said.

Talia ignored her, tossing a hunk of cheese and smoked herring into Danielle's lap. "Eat quickly, Princess."

Danielle tossed the herring right back for the sake of her stomach, but she devoured the cheese. She finished off a large hunk of bread dipped in honey as well, along with the lamb from last night. Then Snow offered her a leftover muffin, and memories of her nightmare nearly cost her everything she had eaten.

"I'll get the aviars ready," Talia said.

Snow began bundling up the blankets while Talia fed the remainder of the apples to the aviars. Danielle ate as fast as she could, but by the time she crammed the last of the cheese into her mouth, the others were already finished. "I'm sorry," Danielle said. "I didn't mean to oversleep. I would have—"

"Don't worry," Snow said. "I needed time to contact Queen Bea anyway. Besides, it's normal for pregnant women to sleep more. Especially when Talia spends the whole night working them to exhaustion."

"It wasn't the *whole* night," Talia said. "And the stretches should have helped her legs after all that riding."

Snow rolled her eyes. She took Midnight by the reins and led her to the edge of the maze. Danielle followed, her hand on Wind's neck for support.

The great beast was clearly restless, shifting back and forth and ruffling her wings. Whether she was eager to get back to the open air or simply picking up on Danielle's own tension was impossible to say.

"Here they come," Snow said. She closed her eyes. "They've transformed from rats to birds. Two hawks and a crow, skimming the treetops."

"Wait for them," said Talia.

Danielle nodded. A part of her wanted to fly out of the maze and swoop down on her stepsisters, driving them to the ground so she could force them to free Armand.

Between her own exhaustion and her poor riding skills, she would be lucky if she didn't fall off her aviar.

"They're flying hard," Snow said. "They must have rested during the night. There's no way they could have kept up that pace for so long."

Talia climbed onto Socks' back. Snow mounted Midnight, never opening her eyes.

Danielle put one hand on her aviar's wing, the other on the long neck. The last time, Quink had lifted her onto Wind. "I don't want to hurt you," she whispered.

Wind snorted and dropped carefully to her knees, holding perfectly still as Danielle dragged herself onto the aviar's back. She bit her lip as yesterday's bruises announced their presence.

"There they go," Snow said. "They're skimming down the cliff, toward the river. Looks like they're planning to dive right into the— Hey, that's neat."

"What is it?" asked Danielle.

"At the bottom of the cliff, there's a shallow cave. I think it's covered by some kind of seaweed or vines." She opened her eyes and beamed. "That's why they waited until morning. Even if they had gotten here last night, the river is really just a branch of the ocean, which means the tides would have covered the cave."

"Couldn't they transform into fish?" Talia asked.

"Stacia can't swim," Danielle said. "She's terrified of water. Charlotte used to torment her about it. Once, before their mother married my father, Charlotte nearly drowned her in the bath. She said she was going to wash the ugly off of Stacia's face."

"Should have scrubbed harder," Talia said. Before Danielle could respond, Talia twitched her reins, nudging Socks forward. "Are they gone?"

Snow nodded. "They just flew into the cave."

"Keep an eye out," said Talia. "I can't imagine the Duchess appreciates guests, but there shouldn't be anything too nasty until we get to the cave. Not if she wants to keep her presence secret."

Midnight trotted through the branches and dropped away. Snow's delighted shriek quickly faded.

"Speaking of secrecy," Talia muttered. "Go on, Princess."

Danielle leaned forward. "Let's go."

Before, Wind had taken off from open ground, climbing slowly and smoothly toward the sky. Not this time, with the walls of the maze so close the aviars couldn't fully extend their wings. The branches rustled as Wind walked to the end of the path. Danielle could see the far side of the chasm through the gaps. Her throat clamped shut and her knuckles whitened on Wind's mane.

At the edge, Wind drew her rear feet up close to her front and hopped into the chasm.

Every muscle in Danielle's body tightened like steel as they dropped straight down. The aviar's wings spread slowly, steering them to the left, then slowly leveling out. Danielle could feel her breakfast battling its way up her throat. She gritted her teeth and forced it down.

The waves broke over the rocks, white spray splattering the base of the cliff. They flew close enough to the river that Danielle could feel the mist when Wind finally flapped her wings and began to climb up after Snow.

Wind twisted her neck and whinnied. Danielle had the distinct impression the beast was laughing at her.

"That wasn't very nice," Danielle said. She unclamped her aching hands.

Up ahead, Snow hovered over the water. She pointed to a spot on the base of the cliff. At first, Danielle couldn't see anything except wet rock and the spray of the river. Then two spots of sunlight sparkled on the water. Danielle realized they were Snow's last mirrors, bobbing up and down with the waves. Snow held out her hand, and one of the mirrors scurried across the surface like a water bug, then climbed the cliff. Snow flew closer, and the mirror jumped into her waiting palm.

"There," said Snow, pointing. Her other mirror swam toward the cliff.

"I see it," said Danielle. Matted vines hung down into the water, hiding the cave from view. Dirt and moss turned the weeds the same slick brown as the rest of the cliff. Tall weeds rose to twine with the vines. The cave was as tall as a man, but much wider than the passages of the labyrinth.

"I don't see any guards," said Talia. "Snow?"

Snow's forehead wrinkled as her last mirror reached the base of the cliff. It slipped past the weeds, and Danielle caught a final glimpse of the little mirror scaling the wall inside the cave.

"First rule of being sneaky," Snow said. "Guards rarely look up."

Talia tugged the reins of her aviar, turning him toward the cliff. They flew a short distance above the cave, close enough to the cliff that anyone inside would need to peek out through the weeds in order to see them. Danielle wondered how long the aviars could stay here without tiring. Most of the time, the aviars simply glided through the air. Hovering in one place had to require more effort. "Just a little longer," she said, rubbing Wind's neck.

"I don't see anyone," Snow said. "The stepsisters flew in unchallenged. There may not be any guards. Or they could be farther back. Some of the fairy races don't like to get this close to the sun."

"How far back does the cave go?" asked Talia.

Snow closed her eyes. "Maybe twenty paces. Then it climbs up and to the left."

Talia nodded. "If this were my subterranean fortress, I'd keep my guards back, out of sight. Sound carries awfully well in a cave. They'll hear us coming, and that gives them plenty of time to either shoot us or run for help."

"Plus, if they were closer, their feet would get wet when the tides rise," Snow added.

"I'm sure the Duchess is very concerned about the dryness of her guards' boots," Talia said. She led Socks to one side of the cave, then swung her right leg over the aviar's neck. She had to contort her body to avoid the pounding wings as she prepared to jump down. "The water's shallow here. Keep your eyes open for anything unusual. We'll send your mirror farther along to find whatever's hiding up the tunnel, and then we can—"

The instant Talia's toes touched the water, the river seemed to explode. Vines shot out, wrapping around Talia and her aviar. One caught Socks' wing. He screamed as he fell into the river, his other wing beating furiously.

"I see something unusual!" Snow shouted, yanking the reins as another cluster of vines reached for her. Others lashed up at Danielle. Wind flew back so hard that Danielle started to fall. She locked her legs beneath the aviar's wings, clinging with all her strength, but it wasn't enough. Her leg slipped.

Wind lurched sideways, slowing long enough for Danielle to recover. In that moment, one of the vines caught Wind's foreleg. Another snaked toward her neck. The aviar screamed and flapped harder.

"Don't fight it!" Danielle shouted, praying Wind would listen. "You'll break your leg. Hold still and let me help you." She twined her left hand in the thick mane. With her right, she drew her sword, trying to keep the blade away from Wind. She pulled herself higher until her face was at Wind's ears, then swung. Despite the awkwardness of the angle, the blade easily severed the vine around the aviar's foot.

Wind leaped skyward as Danielle knocked the second vine away. Once they were safely out of reach, Danielle looked back down. Snow was in the water, swimming away from her trapped aviar as vines and weeds reached for her. Talia's aviar was barely keeping his head above the surface. Talia crouched on Socks' back, slicing at the vines with her sword, but her attacks had little effect. She could shove the vines aside, but she couldn't cut them. Another group of vines shot out, and Talia dove into the water, swimming away from the cave.

"Go," Danielle said. Wind flew toward Talia, the tips of her wings skimming the water as Danielle stretched her sword toward the vines.

Talia surfaced a short distance from the cave. "What are you doing? Fly *away* from the trap!"

Danielle ignored her, waving her arm in ever wilder slashes as they neared Socks. She leaned down, her fingers clutching Wind's mane as she tried to cut the panicked aviar free without hitting his wings. Wind whinnied, and her blue eyes were huge with fear, but she flew even lower. More vines reached out, but Danielle was able to cut them away before they grabbed Wind.

"Got it." Danielle leaned out, and the tip of her sword sliced through weeds and vines. Socks splashed to the surface. His wings were bloody, and many of his feathers had been torn loose, but he was free. Danielle guided Wind away, then turned to see Snow clutching one of the vines in her hand. She sat by the cliff on a slowly spreading patch of ice. The tips of the weeds poked through the ice. They quivered and bent toward Snow, but couldn't break free to seize her.

Talia clung to the edge of the ice with one hand as she waved Danielle away. Midnight splashed through the water, swimming away from the cave.

"Get back to Arlorran," Talia yelled. "Have him contact Queen Bea."

Danielle was already guiding Wind toward Snow and Talia. Given the aviar's enormous wings, there was barely room for one to ride upon Wind's back, let alone three. But if Danielle could reach her friends, they might be able to cling to her legs, and she could pull them through the water to safety.

Several more of the vines snapped out. They appeared to be growing longer. Danielle cut one. Another wrapped around Snow's forearm and immediately began to freeze.

"There's troll hair wound through these vines," Snow said, sounding irritated. Puffs of white breath marked her words. She twisted her arm, and a new layer of frost spread up the vine. "Another purchase from Brahkop's former shop. That's what makes them so strong."

"Talia! Catch!" Danielle tossed her sword.

Talia dropped her own weapon on the ice and reached up, snagging the sword by the crossguard. She bobbed beneath the water, then launched herself even higher. A single swing freed Snow's arm. Another severed two more vines as they reached toward Talia.

Fog had begun to rise around Snow. Danielle could see her teeth chattering, but Snow didn't move. The spray of the waves transformed to flakes of snow. Talia grabbed one of the frozen vines and pulled herself up onto the ice.

"Get Snow out of here," Talia said.

"What about you?" Danielle asked.

"Your mount is exhausted, Princess. You can't take all three of us. Snow's as skinny as a child, and you're not much heavier."

"Hey," Snow protested. "I'm not *all* childlike." She glanced down at her clothes. Soaked to the skin, they more than proved her point.

Danielle shook her head. "I'm not leaving you alone."

"Dammit, Princess, I can take care of myself," Talia said. She tossed the sword back to Danielle, who barely managed to catch hold of the blade. It was a miracle she didn't slice off her own hand.

Talia picked up her own weapon and pointed. "I'll swim after the other aviars, and you can come get me once Snow's safe."

Snow kept looking back and forth between the two of them. By now, most of the vines were cut or frozen. "Could you two argue a little more quickly?" she asked. "This water is freezing, and the Duchess' guards should be showing up any moment now."

"Oh, no, the Duchess prefers not to involve herself in our little family squabble." The sneer in Stacia's voice was identical to the one Danielle had heard from her stepmother all those years. The vines had parted to reveal Stacia, Charlotte, and their darkling companion. "You arrived faster than I expected, Cinderwench."

Talia had already drawn her knife. She threw, but the darkling was faster, springing into the air to protect Stacia. The knife bounced off of his shoulder and disappeared with a splash. The darkling scrambled on the damp, frosty stone, trying to climb back to his mistress.

Stacia started to laugh. "Don't you realize you can't—"

Before the darkling could recover, Snow threw one of her silver snowflakes. Stacia screamed as the points embedded themselves in her thigh.

"Hurts, doesn't it?" Charlotte said. A bloody bandage covered her forearm from their fight at Arlorran's home.

"You always aim low, Snow," Talia said.

With a grim smile, Snow touched her choker and began to mutter a spell. A beam of white light shot down from inside the cave, piercing the darkling. His snarls changed to squeals of pain, and smoke rose from his skin. Danielle didn't understand where it was coming from at first, and then she remembered the lone mirror Snow had sent into the cave. But why hadn't that mirror shown Stacia and Charlotte coming through the cave?

Stacia clapped her hands, and the light disappeared. Danielle heard glass shatter an instant later.

"She broke my mirror!" Snow stared. "She shouldn't be able to do that."

Talia dove into the water, surfacing at the edge of the cave. She pulled herself up, swinging her sword so quickly that both Stacia and Charlotte stumbled back. The darkling shook himself like a dog. White smoke still rose from his body. Talia kicked him in the head, slamming him into the cave wall.

Danielle leaned forward and patted her aviar's neck. "Into the cave, girl."

Wind soared past the ragged curtain of vines. The

darkling spun and leaped to intercept her. Black fingers reached toward Danielle's throat.

Danielle swung her sword. The darkling somehow managed to change directions in midair, but the blade still sliced the tips from his toes. He landed hard and rolled into a ball, clutching his foot with both hands.

Danielle climbed down from her aviar, who retreated toward the light. She spotted Talia, still driving Stacia deeper into the cave. Charlotte lunged at Talia from the side. Talia kicked her in the face, then followed up with an elbow to the throat.

As Charlotte fell, Talia glanced back at Danielle long enough to shout, "Get out of here, you idiot!"

"She's so bossy," said Snow, coming up behind Danielle. "What does she think she is, some kind of princess?" She smiled and stepped toward the darkling. Thin beams of light stabbed the rock, surrounding him. Snow started to say something more, when her mirrors flickered. She touched her choker, and the light stabilized. "What's wrong with these things?"

Whether they were working properly or not, Snow's mirrors appeared to have caged the darkling. Danielle turned to help Talia. Before she could move, the rock wall behind Talia shivered. Flakes of stone fell away, turning to dust that vanished before hitting the ground.

"Talia, behind you!" Danielle shouted.

Talia sidestepped, bringing her sword around to defend against this new threat, but for once she wasn't fast enough.

Brahkop the troll jumped down from the rock, ropes of hair twining around Talia's sword and arm. His hair had tripled in length since Danielle last saw him. Long, silver braids wrenched Talia into the air, pinning her to the ceiling. Her sword clattered to the ground.

"Thank you, love," said Stacia. She limped toward Brahkop and slipped one hand through the masses of hair, stroking the troll's arm.

Danielle and Snow looked at one another.

"Your stepsister has strange taste in men," Snow said.

Talia tried to shout, but another length of hair wrapped around her face, muffling the sound.

"Let her go," said Danielle. She kept her sword pointed at Brahkop.

"Or maybe I should rip her apart instead," Brahkop said. "I still owe her for the cut she gave me."

Danielle hesitated. Charlotte hadn't gotten up from the floor, and Snow had the darkling trapped. Stacia looked battered and exhausted, but she might still have a spell or two in reserve. "I thought you were banished from Fairytown," she said, stalling for time.

Somewhere beneath all that hair, Brahkop shrugged. "I am. But marriage transcends all, here in Fairytown. My wife is a guest of the Duchess, and that means I'm welcome here. A good thing, considering what you did to my home."

"You're married?" Danielle looked back at Stacia. Ridiculous as it was, a part of her felt hurt that Stacia hadn't told her about the wedding.

"We can't all win princes," Stacia said, her voice raspy with pain and hate. "Brahkop is a better husband than you or Charlotte will ever have. Strong, loyal, powerful . . . he loves me more than life itself."

Stacia glanced at Charlotte. "Witchcraft was *her* idea, but Brahkop knew at once which of us was stronger."

With that, Stacia took a deep breath and blew, like she was trying to extinguish a candle. The light in the cave faded, and the darkling scrambled free.

"That's a nice blade, dear stepsister," Stacia said. Her voice grew deeper. *"Give it to me."*

To her horror, Danielle found herself obeying. She could hear Snow and the darkling fighting behind her, but when she tried to turn and help, her body wouldn't cooperate. She could do nothing but reach out, passing the glass sword to her stepsister, who grinned as she yanked it from Danielle's hand.

"I think I'll start with your feet," Stacia said, swishing the blade through the air. "That seems only fitting, given what Charlotte and I endured."

Danielle tried to back away. Now that she had complied with Stacia's command, she seemed to be back in control of herself. She had only taken one step when a length of Brahkop's hair slipped around her ankles, and she fell.

"After the feet will come the eyes. Just as your cursed birds blinded our mother, you will lose your sight as well." She touched the blade to the tip of Danielle's boot. "Soon you'll wish you'd never—"

With a curse, she dropped the sword and yanked her hand away. Droplets of blood covered her palm. Danielle stretched out, reaching for the falling sword. Brahkop yanked her back, nearly snapping her ankles, but she managed to catch the sword's crossguard. One awkward swing, and she was free.

Stacia's face was almost as red as her tattoo. "*Drop that—*"

A ball of shadows crashed into her stomach, knocking the wind from her. Snow brushed her hands together as she strode after the darkling. "Thought you were going to put those filthy claws on *me?*" she muttered. "I'll throw you to the desert and lay you out until the sun burns you to ash."

"Stay back," Brahkop shouted. He lifted the still-struggling Talia, his hair forming a noose around her neck. "Surrender, or I'll—"

Danielle lunged and swung, just as Talia had taught her. Her blade cut cleanly through the troll's hair.

"Aw, crap," said Brahkop.

Talia rolled away, snatching her sword from the ground. She came to her knees and dodged to avoid another strike from Brahkop. She landed next to Stacia, the point of her blade resting beneath Stacia's chin.

"Wait!" Brahkop raised his huge hands. "You win. Don't hurt my wife."

Talia licked blood from her bruised lip. "Snow, get over here. Find out where they've got Armand."

Snow hurried to join her. Talia glanced at Danielle. "You keep an eye on Charlotte. She may look broken, but I don't trust her."

Danielle moved toward Charlotte, leveling the sword at her chest. "Please don't move," she said.

Charlotte laughed, a sound so hoarse and bitter Danielle almost pitied her. Blood dripped from her nose, courtesy of Talia's kick.

"Look at you," Danielle whispered. Bloodstains soaked Charlotte's shirt. She hated to wear anything with the faintest stains. "What have you done to yourself, Charlotte?"

From the corner of her eye, she saw Snow bending over Stacia. Snow had taken one of the mirrors from her choker and was whispering a spell.

"Hurry," said Talia. "We're trespassers in the Duchess' home. I'm amazed we're not hip-deep in darklings."

"It's not the Duchess you need to worry about," Charlotte whispered.

Danielle dropped to one knee. "What do you mean?"

"You should have listened to me." Charlotte pressed her lips together.

Behind her, Brahkop shifted nervously. "What are you doing to her, witch?"

"Sorceress," Snow said. She kissed the mirror, then

placed the glass against Stacia's forehead. "I won't hurt her. I'm calming her, and erecting a ward that should stop her from using any more magic against us."

Talia moved back, keeping her sword ready.

Charlotte turned her head, staring at Stacia. "I went to Brahkop after Mother died. I hoped he would give us a way to contact her. We tried, but—"

"Be silent!" Stacia yelled. Charlotte's jaw clamped shut.

"Stop that," said Snow, thumping Stacia on the nose. "The sooner you stop fighting me, the easier—"

"You dare use mirror magic on *me*?" Stacia started to laugh, but it was a laugh Danielle had never heard from her stepsister. Angry and slightly mad.

Danielle rose, turning to face Stacia "What happened to her?" But Charlotte merely closed her eyes and shook her head.

Snow's forehead wrinkled. "How are you doing that?"

The mirror in her hand shattered. Shards of glass cut Stacia's face as they fell, but she didn't appear to notice. She reached up with one hand to touch Snow's choker. One by one, the other mirrors fell away. All but one broke into pieces on the rock. That last mirror landed squarely in Stacia's hand.

Talia raised her sword.

"Back!" Stacia shouted. Talia flew across the cave like she had been thrown. She landed hard near the entrance. Her weapon clattered to the ground beside her.

"What's happening?" Danielle shouted. "Charlotte, tell me."

Charlotte didn't answer. Whether fear or the magic of Stacia's command held her mute, Danielle couldn't have guessed.

Snow's hand closed over Stacia's. Neither spoke.

They seemed to be fighting for control of the one remaining mirror.

"Pitiful," whispered Stacia. She sat up and twisted her wrist, pushing Snow to the floor.

"Drop the mirror," Talia said. She had drawn another knife, and held it ready to throw.

"Or you'll do what?" Stacia asked. "All that fairy magic pumping through your blood makes you arrogant. What would you do, I wonder, if you were deprived of those gifts?"

Talia threw. The knife spun through the air . . . and missed. Talia stared at her hands. She took a single step and nearly fell, grabbing the side of the cave for balance.

Stacia began to laugh.

"You can't be here," Snow whispered. "You're dead."

"And you're a fool." Stacia cupped the mirror in her palm and brought her hands together, just as Snow reached for her own knife.

Stacia's magic was faster.

With her fingers still curled around the hilt of her weapon, Snow collapsed to the ground. The broken shards of her mirrors slid along the ground, surrounding her. Slowly, the shards began to multiply. The sound they made reminded Danielle of a thousand stones being drawn across panes of glass. They grew higher, taking on the shape of a glittering coffin.

Danielle moved sideways, never taking her eyes from Stacia. "Talia, are you all right?"

Talia's voice was that of a frightened child. "I can't walk."

Danielle spared a brief glance, long enough to see Talia standing with both hands pressed to the wall.

Stacia reached into the open coffin to poke Snow's arm. "Like poor Snow White here, your friend Talia carries the remnants of a potent curse. It should be simple enough to revive that magic, plunging you into another century of sleep." She smiled. "I'll have my own matching set of princesses."

"Who are you?" Danielle whispered.

"Don't worry, my dear Cinderwench," said Stacia. "We have plans for you. Plans which, unfortunately, preclude me from burning you where you stand."

"Get out of here, Princess," Talia snapped. She lurched away from the wall, walking like a toddler. Her arms were outstretched for balance. With every step she seemed on the verge of falling. Her appearance had changed as well. Her hair had lost its shine, and her skin appeared rough and leathery. Acne scars covered her cheeks and forehead.

"What do you want?" Danielle asked. She raised her sword and moved toward Talia. Stacia's eyes narrowed as she eyed the sword. Good. That meant Danielle wasn't completely powerless.

"Poor Charlotte," said Stacia. "Without her dear mother to look after her, the poor wretch was a complete disaster. Lost and desperate. Time and again she and Stacia tried and failed to summon the old bat. Fortunately, I was nearby." She scowled at Charlotte. "Took them four attempts before they got the spell right. Charlotte is an idiot, but Stacia turned out to be nearly as gifted a student as my own daughter."

"Your own . . ." Danielle glanced at the glass coffin where Snow lay. "You're Snow's mother."

"Queen Rose Curtana of Allesandria. And I disowned that wretched girl years ago," Stacia snapped. "I tried to teach her, to raise her to follow in my own footsteps, and she turned her back on my teachings. She fled, choosing instead to live with that filthy peasant."

"Maybe that's because you ordered her heart cut

out of her chest," Talia said as she reached the edge
of the cave. The light from outside turned her into
a shadow.

"I suppose that's true." Stacia lifted the mirror she
had taken from Snow and studied her reflection. "A
shame the pretty one wasn't strong enough to summon me."

Stacia rolled her eyes. "The pretty one would have
gotten herself killed the first time she went after Cinderwench, if I hadn't helped." A faint change in inflection told Danielle this was truly Stacia speaking
now, not Rose. They were both there, though Rose
appeared to be the stronger of the two.

The darkling tried to scurry toward Talia. Danielle
stepped to the side, waving her sword to keep it back.

"You said you were nearby," Danielle said. The
longer she stalled, the more time Talia had to adjust
to a body untouched by fairy grace. "I thought Snow
killed you."

"Ermillina destroyed my body, but she lacked the
strength to finish the job. I followed her over the
years, hoping to catch her unaware and claim her body
for my own. A fitting vengeance, don't you think?"
She drummed her fingers on the edge of the coffin.
"Unfortunately, the protective spells she wove with
my mirror were too tight to pierce."

"Why did you take Armand?"

Stacia laughed again.

"To get you," said Talia. "This whole thing was a
trap to lure you to Fairytown." She grabbed one of
the broken vines for balance. "I told you that you'd
be better off staying behind."

"Why would I care about a filthy servant girl, even
one who married into royalty?" asked Stacia. No, not
Stacia. This was Rose. "In the beginning, Armand
really was the only one we wanted.

"Without a body, most of my power was stripped

from me." The tilt of her head was different, more regal, and she spoke with a faint accent. "Age will soon take my daughter's beauty, and in this land she's little better than a peasant anyway. So I thought, what better host than the heir to the kingdom? Armand would father a child on this body, and I would grow up to claim this land for my own. Neither Brahkop nor Stacia were thrilled by the idea, but I was able to . . . persuade them."

Danielle turned to Charlotte. "You said Armand was enchanted to love you, not Stacia."

Charlotte turned away, but not before Danielle saw the tears in her eyes.

"Her?" Stacia laughed again. "Why would I choose such a weak mother? Stacia's gift would flow through my child's blood, making me that much stronger. Charlotte tried to prove herself by killing you. Fortunately for us all, Charlotte's attempt on your life was a miserable failure. And then my dear husband was kind enough to tell us of your news." She smiled and stepped toward Danielle, one hand reaching for her stomach. "You have no idea how delightful it was to learn I was going to be an aunt."

Danielle raised her sword. She didn't know what she would do if Stacia kept coming, but something on her face must have convinced her not to try. Stacia backed down.

She walked to Brahkop and ran her fingers through his hair. "Why settle for a royal bastard when I can take the true scion of Prince Armand and Princess Danielle? Everybody wins. I have the rightful heir, and Brahkop doesn't have to endure the thought of your husband having his way with this body."

Danielle shook her head. "Beatrice will—"

"She will do what?" Stacia asked. "Declare war on Fairytown? The Duchess' home is well-protected, child. Imagine poor Beatrice . . . her son and daughter-in-law taken from her. Then, months from now, her grandson is miraculously saved by some benevolent fairy. Think of her gratitude. Queen Beatrice will embrace the one tie she has to her dead son, and I will have a lifetime to take back what my traitorous daughter stole from me."

Danielle looked over her shoulder. Even if she made it out of the cave, Rose could still cast a spell on her. Look at how easily she had taken Snow and disabled Talia. Or she could simply send Brahkop or the darkling to catch her.

Stacia cast a disgusted look at Charlotte. "Get up.

Charlotte pulled herself to her feet, her head bowed.

Danielle stared at Charlotte, unable to feel anything but pity. She had tried twice to murder Danielle, to prove herself so that she could have Armand to herself. "It wouldn't have been real. He never would have loved you."

Charlotte didn't look up. "It would have been real enough."

"Enough of this," said Stacia. "Drop your blade, and I'll let your friend Talia live."

"So I can sleep for another hundred years?" Talia asked.

"Give or take," said Stacia. "These things really aren't that precise. You'll sleep, untouched by the years, until some dashing hero arrives to awaken you."

"No thank you, Your Majesty." Talia's voice shook. "I've been 'rescued' once before." She glanced at the river, and in that moment, Danielle knew what she was about to do.

"Talia, wait!" Danielle started to move toward Talia. As soon as she turned, the darkling raced forward. Danielle spun around, swinging her sword to drive him back.

Talia could barely walk. There was no way she

would be able to swim. "Beatrice will send someone to revive you," Danielle shouted. "Don't—"

"Sorry, Princess," said Talia. She had moved past the vines, so the sun illuminated the now-plain features of her face. She looked so exposed and vulnerable, like a frightened child. "I can't do it."

Before Danielle could move, Talia stepped into the water. Danielle ran after her. The scrape of claws on rock made her turn.

The darkling leaped.

Danielle swung with all her strength, severing the darkling's arm. His body crashed into Danielle, knocking her down, but he didn't attack. Shrieking in pain, he raced back to Stacia.

"Brahkop, take her!" shouted Stacia.

Danielle backed toward the water as the troll approached. She had to get to Talia before—

"Stop running," Stacia commanded. *"Drop the sword."*

Though she fought with all her strength, Danielle could only watch as her fingers relaxed and the sword dropped to the ground.

In a heartbeat, Brahkop was there. Ropes of hair looped around Danielle's limbs, hoisting her into the air.

It felt like Brahkop would crush her bones. Danielle closed her eyes and did her best to ignore the pain.

Help me, Wind, she whispered silently. On rare occasions, birds and other creatures had obeyed her even before she asked for their help. Like her wedding day, when she pleaded for them to break off their attack on her stepmother and stepsisters. Some of the doves had turned away the instant Danielle realized what they had done, before she had spoken a single word out loud. *Please.*

Of the three aviars, only Danielle's was still in any condition to help. If she hadn't already fled back to the pixies. If she was willing to risk herself to come to Danielle's aid. If she could hear Danielle's plea at all.

Stacia drew a knife from behind her back. The long, triangular blade was made of a dark metal, almost as black as the darklings. *"Don't move,"* she said. Danielle fought, but she couldn't even blink as Stacia stepped closer.

A high-pitched scream filled the cave. Hooves rattled against the stone as Wind burst through the vines.

Brahkop dropped Danielle and advanced toward the aviar. His hair spread out like a bizarre, oversized spiderweb, while other tendrils reached for Wind. Had he attacked like that back at his shop, Danielle and the others never would have beaten him. He had been holding back, deliberately letting them escape so they would come to Fairytown.

Go, Danielle said silently. *Help Talia. Quickly, before she drowns. Take her to Arlorran.*

Wind danced from side to side, seeking a path through Brahkop's web.

She'll die, Danielle said. *Please go.*

The aviar galloped away. Danielle heard her splashing through the water, and then there was nothing but the sound of the waves. She prayed Wind had been fast enough.

"Charlotte, go and tell the Duchess we've dealt with the trespassers," said Stacia. "But do not—"

"—say who you've captured," Charlotte muttered. "I know, I know."

Danielle watched her go. Of course they couldn't tell the Duchess they had imprisoned the prince and princess of Lorindar. The Duchess would have no choice but to act, or else risk violating Malindar's Treaty. But so long as nobody mentioned their names, the Duchess could enjoy the benefits of ignorance.

Sunlight flashed off Stacia's knife, focusing Dan-

ielle's attention. She held her breath, waiting for the
first cut. But instead, Stacia rolled back her sleeve and
sliced her own arm. Her stare seared Danielle's skin
as she walked in a slow circle, dripping a ring of blood
around Danielle's feet.

"Did you truly think you were meant to be a princess?" Stacia asked, and now it was undeniably her
stepsister's voice. "That destiny would set you upon
the throne of Lorindar? 'Queen Cinderwench.' What
a laughable idea."

She leaned closer, until her cheek touched Danielle's. "I know how uncomfortable you've been these
past months, a clumsy duck trying to live among
swans. Don't worry, my dear stepsister. With the
magic I've learned from Queen Rose, I'll be more
than happy to return you to your proper station."

CHAPTER II

❄

DANIELLE HUMMED AS she rubbed a soapy rag over the wooden floor of Stacia's bedroom. The humming bothered her far more than the actual cleaning. Her mind was her own, but thanks to the curse Stacia had cast, her body now obeyed her stepsisters. And Stacia preferred her slave cheerful.

Danielle couldn't even turn away as the harsh, caustic fumes of lye soap began to rise from the floor. The Duchess mixed her soaps with various flowers to soften the scent, but for Danielle, the smell of rose and honeysuckle mixed with lye was worse than the soap, triggering the nausea which had plagued her for . . . however long it had been.

She clenched her jaw and tried to breathe as little as possible. It didn't help. She could only watch as the meager contents of her stomach spilled onto the floor she had nearly finished cleaning.

With a groan, Danielle returned the rag to the bucket and stood. She stretched her back as she studied the mess.

A soft splash drew her attention to the corner of the bedroom, where a miniature waterfall trickled from the wall into a small, triangular pool. The water emitted a sparkling blue light as it splashed into the pool, so that the bedrooms were never truly dark.

A pair of pale, pink-eyed fish splashed again. Stacia rarely bothered to feed them, and since caring for Stacia's pets wasn't one of Danielle's duties, she was helpless to do anything herself. If not for the algae growing along the stones, the fish would have starved long ago.

The sight of the pool reminded her of the walk through the Duchess' cavern, following Stacia and Charlotte after their fight in the cave. She had kept her head bowed, already a slave to Stacia's magic. But she had glimpsed the great waterfall pouring down the side of the cavern into a wide lake, filling the air with soft blue light.

How long had it been? Her stomach was significantly larger than when she was captured. Trapped here in the tunnels of the Duchess' cavern, with the sun and the sky nothing but memories, she didn't know if weeks or even months had passed. If Talia had survived, she certainly would have reached Beatrice long ago. The fact that nothing had happened meant . . .

Danielle tried to wrench her mind to more pleasant things, but even her thoughts refused to obey her. Surely Beatrice wouldn't have given up. Snow had talked to her. She knew about the Duchess.

She knew, but they had no proof. No witnesses. Nothing that could force the fairy court to help. Ambassador Trittibar would do what he could, but . . .

Humming through her tears, she grabbed another rag and began sopping up the worst of the vomit. Once she finished the floors, she still needed to dust the common room and take care of the laundry. She tried to lose herself in the physical labor, to let her mind find peace the way it used to back in her father's home.

Her eyes ached. Not for the first time, she wished for enough freedom to at least light the oil lamps. A copper pipe ran along the front wall, about a foot from the ceiling. Bands of rusted metal secured the pipe to the wooden planks of the wall. The slow-burning oil came from a second pipe which disappeared into the wall above the door. Chains by the door opened and shut a tin hood, and the flint and steel built into the mechanism lit the wicks.

Crude windows were painted on every wall, as well as the ceiling. The angles of the walls were distorted, as if giant hands had squeezed the rectangular room from opposite corners. The walls themselves were clearly an afterthought, clumsily erected to hide the fact that they were living in caves. Gaps along the edges had been filled in with plaster. Every time someone bumped a wall, Danielle had to sweep up more plaster dust.

She grimaced and plucked a silver hair from her rag. On top of everything else, Brahkop the troll had a shedding problem. Every evening Danielle swept and scrubbed the floors of Stacia's room, and every morning, enough troll hair littered the floor and bed to weave a small rug.

Her lower back ached as she scrubbed harder, cleaning every last trace of vomit, then buffed the floor dry.

Good-bye. She didn't know if the fish could hear her. But after so long without a voice of her own, she would have been happy to talk to her own mop.

She crossed the hall and entered the large common room. As always, her eyes were drawn to the far end, where Snow's coffin sat upon a polished table that appeared to be made of stone. Stacia hadn't bothered to create a lid. Either she hadn't been strong enough, or she simply hadn't cared.

The table was deep brown, lined like wood, but

hard as rock. Embers still glowed in the fireplace at the end of the hall. When lit, the flames reflected from the mirrored coffin, sparkling over the walls.

Danielle fought to stop herself, to lock her muscles. Of all her duties, this was the most cruel. She would have happily mopped a thousand floors and swept an entire cave full of troll hair if she could have avoided this room.

Her struggles were useless. Grabbing a clean rag, she walked to Snow's coffin and began to dust her friend.

Snow looked exactly as she had in the cave. She never breathed, though her skin remained warm to the touch. The cuts on her hand were still fresh enough that Danielle's rag came away dabbed with blood.

A yellow spider had begun to spin a web between Snow's left ear and the edge of the coffin. A sudden fury overcame Danielle as she ripped the web. She tried to squash the spider, but it burrowed into Snow's hair and disappeared.

Danielle stared at the knife strapped to Snow's belt, even as she wiped the dust from the hilt. If only she could break free long enough to seize that knife and—

And what? She couldn't fight her way out of the Duchess' land, nor could she defeat Stacia. If she had the slightest control of her own destiny, she wouldn't be here, wiping dust from Snow's face.

Danielle's helplessness taunted her. Just as it did in Charlotte's room, where Danielle's sword was mounted over the bed. Every day, Danielle wiped the enchanted blade, wanting nothing more than to rip it down and fight. Every day, she failed.

She wiped her forehead on her sleeve, only then noticing the blood on her arm. The jagged edges of the coffin had cut the skin so cleanly she hadn't even felt it. She pressed her sleeve against the cut until the blood slowed, making sure none dripped onto her friend.

Once she had finished with the coffin, Danielle turned to the rest of the room. Several other tables sat in the middle, each one carved from the same stone as Snow's.

She had wiped two of the three tables when Charlotte came hurrying into the room. Charlotte had mostly recovered from the battle in the cave, though her nose still had a small lump near the bridge. "Stacia insists you return to her room once you've finished here. She says it smells like puke." She grinned, clearly enjoying her sister's misfortune.

"Of course, mistress," Danielle said. Even as she despised the words, the mere act of speaking brought a huge sense of relief. So rarely did she hear her own voice, she sometimes began to wonder if she truly existed at all. At least with her stepmother, her body had been her own.

Charlotte plopped herself down on one of the huge cushioned chairs in front of the fireplace. She clapped her hands, and a darkling emerged from the shadows. Had he been there the whole time? Even the curse couldn't stop Danielle's shiver of revulsion.

"You, fetch me wine to drink," Charlotte said. "Chilled. Something that doesn't taste like fish piss."

The darkling hopped onto the table and scurried toward Danielle. This was the same creature she had fought before. He moved like an animal, using his one remaining arm to help him run. He hissed, and for a moment, Danielle thought he was going to attack her. This wasn't the first time he had taunted her. He could wrap those black fingers around her throat, and Danielle would simply stand there as he choked her to death. How many times had she awoken to find him staring down at her, as though he wanted nothing more than to wither her flesh away to nothing? But somehow, either the Duchess or her stepsisters kept the darklings under control.

"Go now!" Charlotte snapped.

The darkling tilted his head. Even up close, Danielle could make out only the faintest hint of a mouth or nose. And then he was scampering away.

"Do you know where my sister is now?" Charlotte asked.

Danielle waited to see if the curse would compel her to answer. This was the first time in a month anyone had asked her a genuine question.

"Well?"

"I'm not sure," Danielle said. She spoke slowly, stretching out the words and savoring the brief control of her own mouth.

"After sending me to find you, she . . . *they* went traipsing off to meet with the Duchess."

Danielle tried to respond—but couldn't. Apparently, Charlotte had to ask a direct question.

"They're in the tower, working on a way hasten the growth of your child." Charlotte stood, stamping her foot and marching toward Danielle. "But did *I* rate an invitation to join them?"

That was a question. Danielle tried to set her fears aside as she searched for the right words to respond.

"I'm sorry, Charlotte. You don't deserve to be treated this way," Danielle said. What Charlotte *did* deserve, Danielle kept to herself.

Charlotte wandered over to Snow's coffin. "We were supposed to summon *our* mother, not hers." She poked Snow's cheek, then shivered and drew back her hand. "I understand why your friend murdered the old hag in the first place."

For once, Danielle was glad the spell stopped her from speaking her mind. Snow's mother had been a

selfish, controlling, cruel woman. It was easy to see
how her stepsisters' spell had mistaken Rose Curtana
for their real mother.

Danielle began to wipe the final table. The curse
was tugging her back to work, but she slowed herself
as much as she could, drawing out her time with Charlotte. After all, Charlotte wanted to talk, which meant
she had a *duty* to listen.

"Stacia spends all of her time with her lumbering
troll husband and that dead witch," Charlotte complained. "They leave me with a crippled darkling and
his friends for company. Do you have any idea how
degrading that is?"

Once again, the curse saved her. If not for Stacia's
magic, she would have laughed in Charlotte's face. For
years, her friends had been rats and pigeons. She kept
her words as sympathetic as she could. "They don't
appreciate you."

"They don't need me. They have you. You and that
brat in your womb."

The darkling returned, carrying a dusty green bottle.
Charlotte grabbed it from his hand, bit the cork free,
and spat it into the fireplace. "Now fetch me something to eat. Something *cooked!*"

As the darkling left, Charlotte shook her head.
"The first time I commanded that little snake to bring
me food, he left a pile of fish guts on my bed."

Danielle tried to speak, but her jaw refused to
move.

"Brahkop said the Duchess would take care of us.
He promised us a home worthy of royalty. I should
have known it would be little more than a hole in the
earth. He's a *troll*." Charlotte took a deep swig of
wine. "What does Stacia see in that hideous beast?"

The question gave Danielle the chance she needed
to speak again. She clenched her jaw, fighting for con-

trol of her voice. "He loves her." Then, quickly, she added, "How long until Rose takes my son?"

Charlotte rolled her eyes. "At the conjoined moons, a few weeks from now. When the two crescent moons come together on midsummer's night. Magic that powerful is bound to draw the attention of the king and queen, but they'll be . . . occupied." She drank more of the wine and turned away. "Stacia says it's the only time they set aside their differences and enjoy one another's company." She flushed. "You wouldn't believe the mischief the other fairies cause during the conjoined moons, when their rulers are too distracted to notice."

Charlotte laughed. "At least then I won't have to listen to Rose prattling on about her kingdom and her lost powers and her precious mirror. Stacia's bad enough, but both of them in one body is more than I can take."

She returned to her chair and took another drink. The bottle was half empty already. "Was the prince gentle?"

"I don't understand," Danielle said, still thinking about midsummer's night.

"In bed. When he . . ." She pointed to Danielle's stomach. "He was supposed to be mine, you know. Mother promised. I want to know what I missed. Was he kind?"

"He—" Danielle ground her teeth together. Charlotte had no right to those memories. "Tell me where he is."

"He has his own cell, somewhere in the tower. He thinks he's back home, and that Stacia is his wife. They're holding him in case something happens to your baby. He truly loves her, you know." There was no triumph in her words, only bitterness. "I thought if I could show them that I could control the magic, that I could kill you—"

Charlotte slammed the wine onto the floor so hard Danielle thought the bottle might break. "And then Brahkop learned you were pregnant! That's twice you've stolen him from me. I'm prettier than you or Stacia. Why am I the one who's alone?"

"Do you love him?"

Charlotte stopped moving. "What?"

"Armand. If you loved him, you wouldn't let Stacia and Rose keep him locked away like this. You have me. Let him go."

"So he can return home, find someone to break the curse, and lead the entire kingdom here to rescue you?" Her laughter had a hysterical note. "Really, Cinderwench. Do you think I'm stupid?"

Foolish, not stupid. Foolish and trapped and lonelier than you've been in your entire spoiled life.

"I think you've been horribly mistreated." Danielle was amazed she could get the words out without vomiting again. "But if you really care about Armand—"

"Even if I was his true love, I *can't* free him. I'm not allowed to see him, let alone kiss him. Not that he'd let me." She wiped her nose on her sleeve. "Stacia has a husband as well as a prince, and they both love her. How is that fair?"

Danielle's breath caught. So many curses were broken by something as minor as a kiss. "Is that the weakness in Stacia's spells?" Danielle asked. "If he kissed me—"

"He could kiss you all night long, and you'd still be cursed." She sneered. "He doesn't love you anymore, remember?"

"But I love him. If I kissed him, would it break Stacia's love spell?"

Charlotte shrugged. "Probably. Most of Rose's curses have that loophole. Something about leverage and possibility. An unbreakable spell takes too much power. True love is rare enough most spells are never broken. I don't really understand it all. Magic makes my head hurt."

Slowly, Danielle's hope gave way to despair. What good was knowing how to break the spell when she had no way of doing so? This was simply one more torment. To kiss Armand, she would have to be free. Armand could be standing right here, arms wide, and the curse would stop her.

Purple rivulets of wine dripped down Charlotte's chin as she took another drink. "You're not the one keeping him from me," she mumbled. "It's that baby."

The door slammed open. Stacia took one look at Charlotte, and her face twisted with disgust. "I told you to fetch Cinderwench, not to lounge about getting drunk."

Charlotte belched.

"How ladylike," Stacia said. She turned to Danielle. "Come with me. Before I set you to work, there's something I'd like to try."

Inside, Danielle recoiled from the gleam in Stacia's eyes. What were they going to do to her son? She could have killed Stacia in that moment, but her body obeyed her stepsister's will.

Two darklings waited in Stacia's room. Danielle recognized the one who clutched a platter of steamed fish in his single arm. Stacia must have intercepted him on his way back to Charlotte.

Both darklings crowded behind Danielle as Stacia led her around the bed to the small altar in the back corner. Stacia had forbidden Danielle to clean it, or even to touch it, and Danielle gave silent thanks every day for that small blessing.

The marble slab was stained with blood, along with the greenish residue of some old potion. Powdered ash covered the surface, and a halo of black wax showed where a candle once sat. Clots of wax had dripped down the side, black icicles that melted into the cracks between the floorboards.

"Please sit down," Stacia said, gesturing to the bed.

The false kindness in her voice made Danielle ill. She sat on the edge of the bed, as far from the altar as she could.

Stacia clucked her tongue, and the two darklings climbed onto the bed, one on either side of Danielle. The crippled darkling set Charlotte's meal on the blanket. He peered into Danielle's face, so close that his breath dried her skin.

"Wait," Stacia said. The darklings sat still. Their breathing was slow and congested, like that of an old man with a cough. One played with the cooked fish, dragging his fingers through the meat again and again until it was barely recognizable.

Stacia drew her knife and stepped over the altar. "I hate this part," she muttered. A quick cut to her arm opened an old wound, and blood dripped down to splash on the stone.

Stacia clenched her other hand over the cut. She set the knife on the altar and turned to Danielle.

She untied Danielle's apron and tossed it to the floor. Danielle held her breath as she approached, but the only thing Stacia did was press two bloody handprints onto Danielle's shirt, just beneath her ribs.

"Queen Rose is worried about your baby," Stacia said. "She feels he won't be far enough along to serve as a proper host when the time comes. Fortunately, I was able to suggest a remedy. Would you like to know what it is?"

"What are you going to do to me?" Danielle whispered.

"Not me. Them." She gestured to the two darklings.

Danielle glanced at her arm, where the darkling had grabbed her back in Arlorran's home. The skin and muscle had mostly recovered, but she still remembered the cold of the darkling's grip, the weakness of her arm as his touch aged her flesh.

"Oh, stop worrying. Do you think we would endanger Rose's future body?" asked Stacia. "Rose thinks we can protect you from the darklings' power. If all goes as planned, your child will age by days or even weeks, leaving you unaffected. You should be thankful, dear stepsister. Most women would pay dearly to bypass some of the pain and discomfort of pregnancy."

Stacia used a feather to brush more of her blood onto Danielle's shirt. "If you would be so kind as to hold still? For your own safety, as well as your son's." She turned to the darklings. "Touch only those places I've marked."

Mother, help me, Danielle prayed. She fought to get away from the bed, to evade those twisted shadows who even now reached for her stomach. Sweat turned her skin clammy. Her muscles tensed and her limbs trembled, but she couldn't even lift her fingers from the bedcovers.

The darklings pressed their hands to the bloody prints Stacia had left. Heat flared at their touch. Pain tore her skin. Her insides churned until she thought she would be sick. Stacia grunted and took a step back.

"Enough," Stacia said. Her face was drawn, and she held one hand to her forehead. *"Enough!"*

The darklings backed away so quickly that one landed in the pool with the fish. He scurried out and stood dripping in the corner.

"Rose's spell isn't as painless as she thought," Stacia muttered. "Still, you're starting to bulge a little more. That's something, at least." She wiped her hand on her skirt, leaving bloody streaks.

Danielle's whole body shook. Everything had happened so quickly. She looked down at herself, seeing the curve of her stomach. Her ribs felt like she had been pummeled from within, and her skin threatened to tear open. And then she felt a small blow against her rib cage. She gasped.

"What is it?" Stacia snapped.

"The baby," Danielle whispered. "He moved." The baby kicked again, and Danielle realized she was smiling.

"Good. That means he's still alive." Stacia massaged her forehead and stepped away. "Get back to work. This place still stinks."

She disappeared without another word.

Danielle did her best to carry out Stacia's orders. Her body was exhausted, whether from fear and tension or the darklings' touch, she didn't know. Sweat stung her eyes as she retrieved her apron and fumbled with the ties.

Don't worry, she whispered to the squirming baby in her womb. How much had the darklings aged him? Enough for him to twist about and stomp on her bladder, at any rate. All this time, she had hoped Talia or Beatrice would find her, but she couldn't afford to wait any longer. *I promise I won't let them take you.*

She pulled out a jar of honey-scented oil and poured it on a rag. The too-sweet smell made her queasy, but she clamped her jaw and began rubbing the oil into the floor where she had vomited earlier.

Can you hear me, friends? She looked toward the wall beside the fish pool. To one side, in the shadows where the pool touched the wall, a bit of wood and plaster had been gnawed away, opening a slender crack.

It had taken Danielle more than a week to duplicate her feat back at the cave, speaking to the animals without words. The first to respond had been a mangy black rat who was missing most of his tail.

Since then, she had managed to befriend four more

rats. They were timid creatures, terrified of the dark-lings who roamed the corridors, but Danielle had earned their trust. She told them when it was safe to sneak in and eat the crumbs from Charlotte's bed, or warned them about the arsenic-laced meats and cheese left in the corners.

It was Charlotte who did that duty, whining at great length every time she had to replace the poisoned bait. Despite the curse, Stacia was still too suspicious to trust Danielle with poisons.

Too suspicious, and yet not suspicious enough.

Two rats responded to Danielle's call, squeezing through the crack and darting into the relative dark-ness beneath the bed. One was her tailless friend. The other was younger, her black fur sleek and oily. Both were thin and hungry.

Go ahead, Danielle said, glancing at Charlotte's abandoned meal. The rats didn't hesitate, racing to the plate and using their front paws to pack their cheeks with smashed flakes of fish meat.

Danielle worked while they ate, waiting until they had devoured their fill. *It's time.*

As one, the rats disappeared again. Danielle scrubbed the floors while she waited. She prayed as she worked, asking for help and forgiveness both.

When the rats returned, Danielle's eyes watered with gratitude. They dragged a filthy handkerchief Danielle recognized as belonging to Stacia. They quickly opened the handkerchief to reveal hard, moldy nuggets of poisoned cheese. Until this moment, she hadn't been certain the rats were following her in-structions. Now all she needed was to find a way to return that poison to her stepsister.

Danielle stood, wincing at the pain in her back. She searched the room as she straightened the bedcovers. Perhaps the pillows? Would arsenic work through skin contact? Better for Stacia to consume it directly, but how could Danielle's rats slip the old cheese into her food without being noticed?

Stacia's knife. Day after day, Stacia drew her own blood to work her magic.

The rats were already moving. The younger one hopped onto the altar and braced the knife with her paws. The older one began rubbing his bit of cheese back and forth along the dark, bloody blade.

Be careful, Danielle said.

Soon the rats traded places, smearing more poison onto the edge. There was justice here. Stacia would be the one to use the poisoned blade on herself. It would be her own choice, her willingness to practice dark magic that killed her.

If the poison worked. If the rats had amassed enough to kill a grown woman.

Danielle gathered up the remains of the fish, then looked around for anything else to clean. With the exception of the altar, the room was spotless, which meant she had no excuse to remain.

The rats had already returned with more poison. *Wash yourselves in the pool when you've finished, especially your paws. Eat nothing until you've bathed.*

She hoped the water would dilute any remaining poison enough that it wouldn't hurt the fish.

As she left the room, she closed her eyes. *Forgive me, Mother.* All those years, she had tried to obey her mother's final words, to remain pious and good. Not once had she fought back against her tormentors. Now she would murder her own stepsister.

I have to protect my son. Surely her mother would understand.

Despite everything, guilt and doubt shadowed her as she headed toward Charlotte's room to finish cleaning. The baby kicked again as she shut the door, and then there was only guilt.

CHAPTER 12

❄

DANIELLE DUMPED THE LAST of the boiling water into a great pot, then began hauling Brahkop's clothes across the room. She only managed to fit three pair of trousers and one shirt into the pot before the water slopped over the edge. She glanced at the remaining pile and sighed. She'd be up all night trying to get everything clean.

She grabbed a paddle and began to stir, mixing the soap and the clothes together. Blue sparks in the water flickered as she stirred, the only source of light in the small room. Whatever magic caused the water to glow, boiling did nothing to stop it.

More water splashed onto her feet. *Wonderful. For the rest of the day I'll smell like troll pants soup.*

Footsteps in the hallway made her look up, though she dutifully continued to stir the laundry. The door opened to reveal Charlotte's none-too-steady silhouette. "Danielle?"

Danielle's breath caught. Only a day had passed since her rats poisoned Stacia's blade. Could the poison have worked so soon? "I'm here."

Charlotte crooked one finger, beckoning.

Danielle abandoned the laundry and stepped into the hall. Most of the oil lanterns were shuttered, but there was still enough light to see the way Charlotte stared at Danielle's stomach. Throughout the day, her apron had mostly concealed the effects of the darklings' touch, but Danielle had taken it off and rolled up her sleeves to do the laundry.

"Stacia really did it," Charlotte said. She reached out, brushing her fingers over the brown bloodstains on Danielle's shirt. Danielle shivered, remembering Stacia's touch, and that of the darklings. She had spent most of the day terrified that they would return to try again, but apparently Stacia hadn't yet recovered.

Charlotte turned and walked down the hallway. "Come with me."

Danielle followed. The two darklings played near Stacia's door. The door was open, the room beyond dark and empty.

The darklings had captured a small, yellow-striped snake. One had driven a nail through the snake's tail, pinning it to the floor. The other was chortling and jabbing the snake with a burning stick. When the fire on the stick died, he climbed the wall and stuck the end into one of the oil lamps to relight it.

Don't fight them, Danielle pleaded as she passed. *Don't let their torments arouse you. They're children. They'll grow bored and move on.* She doubted the snake would listen. Its pain and panic were too strong.

Charlotte led Danielle into her room, shutting the door behind them. "Sit down."

Danielle took a seat on the floor. Charlotte tugged the chain to open the lanterns. Danielle squinted as her eyes adjusted to the light.

As always, Danielle's gaze went to her sword, mounted over Charlotte's bed on two wooden pegs. She could still see spots of blood on the hilt where the wood had cut Stacia's palm, back in the cave.

"Do you know where your precious prince was to-night?" Charlotte asked.

Danielle shook her head. "Is Armand all right?"

Charlotte twisted her hands in the bedcovers, and for a moment Danielle thought she was going to scream. "We dined with the Duchess, and your prince could barely keep his hands off of her. Stacia and Brahkop were even worse. None of them even looked at me."

"I don't understand," said Danielle. "He loved *Stacia*. The spell she cast—"

"Stacia doesn't need him anymore," Charlotte snapped. "The filthy troll was more than happy to have his wife back again. He and Stacia mixed a new potion, turning the prince's affections toward the Duchess. He's to be a gift for her."

Leaving Charlotte alone and useless. The Duchess would take a human prince as her consort, payment for her hospitality. She wondered how long Stacia and Rose had planned this.

Charlotte bent down, retrieving a ~~small~~ clay pot from beneath the bed. She removed the lid and handed the pot to Danielle. "Drink."

Danielle brought the pot to her lips. The smell was foul, like a tea made from compost. She gagged.

Charlotte snatched the pot. "Don't spill it! Do you have any idea how hard I worked to brew this?"

"What is it?" Danielle asked.

"A brew of tansy and pennyroyal. I spent most of yesterday in the Duchess' library, reading one dusty old book after another. I had to send Lefty to steal the ingredients."

Danielle was still tired, and she didn't immediately recognize that "Lefty" had to be the one-armed dark-ling. Then her mind seized on the rest of Charlotte's words.

Her weariness vanished. She had once overheard a pair of women in the streets discussing herbs that could drive an unwanted child from the body. Tansy and pennyroyal were two of the most potent.

Her muscles tightened, and her hand shook as she reached out to take the pot from Charlotte's hand.

"Isn't this better than letting Rose have him?" Charlotte asked.

"Charlotte, why? There has to be another way," Danielle said, seizing the chance to speak. Every moment she could talk was another moment she kept the poison from her mouth.

"Did you know that once a love spell has been broken, it can't be redone?" Charlotte asked. "They severed Armand's ties to Stacia. They can't use magic to make him love her again. And they can't risk letting him love you, or else your curse might be broken. If you lose the baby, they'll have to give him to me. They'll have to! Don't you understand?"

"You don't need to take my son," Danielle said. "Can't you just let me go?"

"I'm sorry." Charlotte sniffed and turned away. "I truly am. But you've seen what Stacia's become. Do you know what Rose would do to me if I helped you escape?"

"We could both escape," Danielle said. "I'll protect you. Once we're back home—"

"There are worse things than darklings in the Duchess' cavern," Charlotte said. Her shoulders shook. "Drink."

"I'll tell Stacia," Danielle said through clenched teeth. She tried and failed to stop her arms from lifting the pot to her mouth.

"Then I'll cut out your tongue."

The pot touched her lower lip. The glazed clay was smooth as glass, and the smell seared her nostrils.

The smell. As her hands tilted the pot, she inhaled,

deliberately filling her lungs with the putrid smell. She felt ill, but it wasn't the stomach-knotting pains of nausea. She exhaled and breathed in again, willing herself to throw up. She began to weep. Even the smell of soap had been enough to trigger her vomiting. But that was before Stacia's darklings had aged her baby, rushing Danielle along in her pregnancy. Her body still ached as it tried to adjust, but the nausea had passed. In her impatience, Stacia might have doomed the baby.

Mother, please help me. Don't let this filth pass my lips.

"It's the only way," Charlotte said. "They'll have to give Armand back to me."

Danielle's hand twitched. A few drops spilled onto her tongue. The taste of mint and camphor filled her mouth.

"You're still fighting it," Charlotte said. She sounded impressed. She wiped tears from Danielle's face. "Maybe Stacia's curse isn't as strong as she thought." She reached for the cup, presumably to dump the contents down Danielle's throat. She was so close Danielle could see every scar on her face, every stain on her shirt where she must have splashed some of this very potion.

Those stains. Stacia had ordered Danielle to clean, to perform the same duties she had done for her stepmother. The longer those stains remained, the harder it would be to remove them. That shirt needed to be rinsed under cool water and washed as soon as possible. To ignore them would be to disobey Stacia's command.

Danielle's fingers moved. The pot slipped from her grip as she reached for Charlotte's shirt. Charlotte made a desperate grab, but missed. The pot shattered on the floor.

Charlotte slapped her, knocking her back. "What are you doing?"

"Your shirt was dirty," Danielle said.

"You stubborn, spiteful girl." Charlotte grabbed Danielle by the shirt. "Why do you have to ruin every single thing?"

Danielle could do nothing as Charlotte flung her against the wall. Her head hit hard enough to make her vision blur.

Rage turned Charlotte's expression monstrous. She had been pushed too far, and now she meant to finish what she had started back at the palace. She was going to murder Danielle. Stacia would kill her, but that no longer mattered. Charlotte was too far gone to reason with, even if Danielle had been free to speak.

As Danielle lay in the pool of spilled tea, she spotted movement by the door. The old, tailless rat stood on his hind legs and sniffed the air. Had he heard Danielle's silent pleas for help?

The oil lamp, Danielle begged. *Quickly.*

The rat raced up the wardrobe, then sprang through the air. Tiny paws clung to the chain hanging from the oil lamp. The links rattled, but Charlotte was too furious to notice.

Charlotte stepped away, reaching for the sword above her bed. "If you won't drink, I'll cut the damned child out of you myself. Don't move. This will be over quickly."

Please hurry. The rat was running along the edge of the pipe now. He stopped at one of the wicks. This one needed to be replaced. Only a faint spot of flame still burned. Heedless of his own safety, the rat patted out the flame with his paws, then tugged the wick as high as he could. When it would move no more, he began to gnaw at the base.

"I saw what this cursed sword did to my sister," Charlotte muttered. She grabbed one of the bedsheets and wrapped several layers over the handle. The rest of the sheet dragged behind her as she walked back to Danielle. "Let's see it stab me through *that*."

The rat yanked the wick free. He ran to the next flame and touched the end of the wick to the fire. The oil-soaked wick caught immediately, and the rat squealed in pain.

Charlotte spun just as the rat jumped. He landed on the top of Charlotte's head, shoved the wick into her hair, and tumbled to the floor.

The fire spread quickly. Charlotte swore and flung the sword away. The blade barely missed Danielle's face.

So close. All Danielle had to do was move her arm. She could take her sword and finish this. But the curse still held her prisoner. Charlotte had ordered her not to move. Until Charlotte or Stacia said otherwise—

"Help me!" Charlotte cried. Her brown locks shriveled and curled from the flames, and the putrid smell of burning hair filled the air.

Danielle smiled grimly as she climbed to her feet. She clamped one hand around Charlotte's arm and dragged her to the pool in the corner. Switching her grip to Charlotte's neck, she thrust her stepsister's flaming head into the water.

White fish cowered in the corner. Bubbles burst as Charlotte struggled, but Danielle held fast, pushing down until Charlotte's face pressed the algae-covered stone at the bottom. After all, the flames in her hair still smoldered, and Danielle had been commanded to help.

Charlotte squirmed, twisting her face and clawing Danielle's arm with her nails. Danielle braced herself. So long as Charlotte's mouth remained underwater, she couldn't issue any more commands.

Charlotte switched tactics. She grabbed the edge of the pool and pushed, trying to force Danielle back.

Danielle put her full weight onto her arms. Charlotte had never been strong. Danielle was the one who had spent her life at hard labor, beginning before her stepsisters awoke and continuing long after they retired for the night. Add Danielle's fury over what Charlotte had tried to do, and Danielle was easily strong enough to murder her stepsister.

Charlotte's struggles weakened. Her head twisted to one side. Her eyes were squeezed shut, like a child trying to block out a bad dream. A tiny column of bubbles rose from the corner of her mouth.

The rage began to drain from Danielle. Killing Charlotte wouldn't free her. It wouldn't save her baby. It wouldn't save anyone. Eventually, Stacia would find her here, standing over Charlotte's body. She would take Danielle's child, and then she would kill Danielle, the same as Danielle had done to Charlotte.

She twisted her fingers in Charlotte's hair and hauled her from the pool. Charlotte slumped to the ground, water darkening the floor around her head and torso. She coughed weakly, spitting water and blood. She must have bitten her tongue or cheek as she struggled.

Charlotte began to throw up. Once she finished, Danielle grabbed a blanket from the bed and tossed it over her shivering body.

"Good choice. If she's dead, she can't tell us what we need to know."

Danielle spun. Talia stood by the head of the bed, arms folded across her chest. A thousand questions raced through Danielle's mind. She would have sworn Talia hadn't been there a moment before, when she grabbed the blanket for Charlotte. Nor had Danielle heard the door open.

She tried to speak, but she couldn't. For some reason, a part of her found this terribly funny. She could murder her stepsister, but she still couldn't talk until someone asked her a question.

Charlotte groaned and reached for the sword. The glass blade slid along the floor. Charlotte lifted the blade, pointing it at Danielle. "I'll kill her." The words sent her into another coughing fit.

"Go ahead and try." Talia stepped toward Charlotte. She moved with none of the clumsiness Danielle remembered from the cave. Somehow Talia had found a way to throw off Stacia's curse. "You still don't understand what that sword is, do you? No matter how hard you swing, that blade will never hurt a hair on Danielle's head."

Talia glanced at Danielle. "Do you remember the fight outside the cave? I wasn't thinking when I threw the sword back to you. By rights, you should have lost the fingers on that hand when you caught the blade."

Talia watched as Charlotte pushed herself to her knees. "My guess is that blade will shatter before it will hurt Danielle," Talia said. "If I'm right, the sword will be none too happy about it either. Don't be surprised if one of the shards finds its way to your heart."

She sat down on the edge of the bed, waiting. She looked . . . tired. Her eyes were bloodshot. She smelled of sweat and mold, and her black clothes were worn and ripped. Her sword was gone, though she still carried a knife strapped to her waist. Two small sticks pinned back her hair, save for a few sweaty wisps that hung over her eyes.

"Your stepsister was kind enough to spare your life." Talia shook her head, making it clear that *kind* wasn't the word she really wanted to use. She smiled. "I'm not like your stepsister."

Charlotte shook her head and pointed the sword at Talia. "Maybe I can't kill *her*."

Talia shrugged and reached back to pull one of the metal-topped sticks from her hair. She held it by the tip, then flicked it forward. The stick spun through the air, and the blunt end struck Charlotte squarely in the eye.

Charlotte yelped and dropped the sword. Talia pushed off from the bed, catching the hilt in midair. The blade whooshed as Talia spun it around, bringing the edge to Charlotte's throat.

No question about it. Talia's fairy gifts were back.

"Now, then," said Talia. "Why don't we talk about the curse your sister placed on my princess?"

To her great annoyance, Danielle found herself compelled to step away from Talia and Charlotte so she could mop up the water that had splashed onto the floor. She used the blanket Charlotte had dropped to soak up the worst of it, twisting the blanket to squeeze the water back into the pool. Worst of all, she was humming again.

The humming caught Talia's attention. "Stop that."

If only it was that easy. Danielle used a dry corner of the blanket to scrub the grout at the juncture between the floor and the pool.

"Do you mind?" Talia said, jabbing the sword at Charlotte.

"Enough, Cinderwench." Charlotte's eye was bloodshot, but she still appeared able to see. Tears poured down her cheek, and she was constantly blinking and rubbing the eye.

Danielle dried her hands on her shirt and stood.

"Watch your manners," Talia said.

"What does it matter?" Charlotte grabbed a sheet and wrapped it around her shoulders. She was still shivering. "If you don't kill me, Stacia will."

"Lift the curse on Danielle, and maybe we'll keep you alive," said Talia.

"Stacia and Rose cast it, not me. Only a kiss of true love could break it now."

"So get Armand down here," said Talia.

Charlotte gave a tired, bitter laugh. "He doesn't love her."

Talia glared at Charlotte. "Princess Danielle obviously obeys you. So command her to obey her own wishes."

Charlotte shook her head. "I'd be commanding her to break the curse. I'm not strong enough to do that."

Talia studied Charlotte's bedraggled appearance. "Witchcraft and treachery aren't working out so well for you, are they?"

Charlotte glared, but said nothing.

Talia rested the blade of the sword on her shoulder. "What about you, Danielle? Do you know of any other way to break this spell?"

Danielle tried, but she couldn't speak. The questions had to come from Charlotte or Stacia. With a sigh, Talia jabbed the sword in Charlotte's direction and said, "Tell her to answer me."

Charlotte waved one hand. "Oh, go on."

"Only by killing Stacia," said Danielle. "If we break the curse on Armand, he could kiss me and end the spell. But he's with Stacia and the Duchess."

"So either we fight our way up the Duchess' tower to kill your stepsister and save your prince, or else we find someone else who truly loves you." Talia glanced at Charlotte and snorted. "I won't bother asking you to plant one on your stepsister's cheek. So I suppose there's only one thing left to do."

Before Charlotte could respond, Talia turned on her heel. The glass sword flicked out at Danielle's face.

At first, Danielle thought Talia had missed. Then her cheek began to sting. A line of blood trickled down the side of her face.

"You said the sword wouldn't hurt me!" Danielle

said indignantly. She froze, realizing what she had just done. She touched her cheek, marveling as her arm obeyed her will.

"So, are you free?" Talia asked.

Danielle went to the bed and reached beneath the pillow, pulling out a half-full bottle of wine.

"How did you know about that?" Charlotte demanded.

"I'm the one who spends hours working the wine stains from your clothes," Danielle said. "I fluff your pillows, change your sheets, and dust your room. I also polish the tin flask you keep hidden in the back of your trunk, and I clean the algae off the bottle in the back of the pool."

Danielle upended the bottle over Charlotte's bed, watching the crimson puddle soak into the sheets and mattress. She waited, but nothing compelled her to clean up the mess. Nothing more than her own need for tidiness, at any rate. "How—?"

"Don't you remember what I taught you, back in the queen's labyrinth?" Talia spun the sword, offering the hilt to Danielle. "The lightest kiss of steel is all you need. Or glass, in this case."

Danielle took the sword with both hands.

"That sword was a gift from your mother," Talia said. "When she first died, her spirit stayed behind in the hazel tree so she could watch over you. When your stepsisters summoned the Chirka demon, she trapped it within herself to protect you." Talia's voice was distant, almost sad. "Love doesn't get much truer than that."

"She's still here, isn't she?" Danielle whispered. "In the sword."

"A part of her." Talia nodded. "Otherwise you'd still be cursed, and likely missing some fingers from that clumsy catch outside the cave."

Danielle couldn't stop herself. She wrapped her arms around Talia and squeezed.

"Watch it," Talia said. "You're going to cut someone's arm off, waving that thing about."

"You really think I could hit you with a sword?" Danielle asked.

"In your dreams, Princess." Talia sighed and hugged Danielle back.

Movement near the door made Danielle break away. "Oh, no."

Danielle knelt and set the sword on the floor. The tailless rat raised his head and sniffed. Most of the fur around his head and front paws was burned away, and the skin was red and blistered.

Her eyes watered as she cupped the rat in her palm.

"What is it?" Talia asked.

"He saved me." Just like the dove back at the palace, the first time Charlotte had tried to kill her. And like the dove, the rat had paid with his life. He was old and dying, and there was nothing she could do.

"It's a rat," said Charlotte.

"Take her pillow," Danielle said. "We can at least make him comfortable."

"What?" Charlotte grabbed her pillow with both hands. "You're not putting that filthy thing on my—"

Talia grabbed Charlotte's arm and twisted. She plucked the pillow from Charlotte's fingers, then shoved. Charlotte staggered toward the wall, one foot splashing into the pool before she recovered her balance.

Danielle set the rat in the middle of the pillow. "I'm so sorry," she whispered. She wasn't sure he could even hear her anymore, as badly blistered as his face was. "Thank you for saving my son."

"What would you like to do about her?" Talia asked, pointing a thumb at Charlotte. "Want me to finish what you started?"

Charlotte's good eye widened. "Danielle, I tried to help you. I warned you not to come, remember? I warned you again, back in the cave, but you wouldn't listen. I tried—"

"You tried to keep me away so you could have Armand to yourself." Danielle picked up her sword. "You tried to murder me. You tried to murder my son."

Charlotte tried to back into the corner and nearly stepped on one of the fish. "Your life was so perfect. All I wanted was that same happiness."

"That's because you never learned to find your own," Danielle said. She turned to Talia. "Can you tie her up so she can't escape?"

Talia rubbed her hands together. "It would be a pleasure, Your Highness."

They used Danielle's sword to slice the sheets into strips, which Talia braided into ropes. By the time Talia finished, Charlotte could barely breathe, let alone escape. Charlotte lay on the bed, stretched diagonally across the mattress. Ropes bound her at the ankles, knees, wrists, and elbows. Another loop of rope secured her wrists to one bedpost, while her ankles were tied to the opposite post. Finally, Talia looped a gag around Charlotte's mouth.

"At least it's one of the wine-soaked scraps," Talia said. "Suck on that while you wait for someone to find you."

Danielle used the remaining rope to tie her sword on.

"What now?" asked Danielle. "There are darklings in the hallway. They'll be on us before we can go. . . ." Her voice trailed off, and she stared at Talia. "How did you get in here without anyone catching you? I never even heard the door open."

"Doors are too conspicuous." Talia reached into her shirt and pulled out a black and white leather pouch.

"That's Ambassador Trittibar's," Danielle said. "Trittibar is here? He's helping you?"

"Not exactly." Talia shrugged. "I thought that shrinking magic of his might come in handy, so I nicked his pouch before we left the palace. There are only a few spores left. Hopefully, it will be enough for us to reach Snow without being seen."

"You stole from the ambassador? After everything he did for us? Talia!"

Talia grabbed the wine bottle from the floor where it had fallen. Little more than a swallow remained in the bottom. Talia gulped it down, then grimaced. "Tastes like dirt." She tossed the bottle into the pool. "Would you like to yell at me, or would you rather save Snow?"

"Snow. But when we get home, you're apologizing to Trittibar." She studied Talia more closely. "I don't suppose you brought something we can use to wake Snow?"

Talia ignored the question and ran her hand along the wall. "The stone behind the wallboards is pretty rough. Plenty of room to squeeze about. Do you know where they're keeping her?"

"The common room near the end of the hall," said Danielle.

"Guarded?"

"Only the darklings in the hall. The common room is usually empty."

"Good." Talia leaned over Charlotte. "A strong, healthy woman could probably squirm free by the end of the night. For you, I imagine it will take at least a day."

She turned away. "Let's get going."

"Wait. What about—" Danielle looked at the rat and realized there was no point. The pillow around his head was a mix of soot and watery blood. The rough, spastic breathing had stopped. She swallowed a lump in her throat. "Never mind."

"Over here," Talia said, leading Danielle toward the rathole by the pool. She handed one of the spores to Danielle.

Danielle touched the spore to her tongue. Moments later, she and Talia were squeezing into the darkness past the pool. Talia glanced back and shook her head.

"What's wrong?" Danielle asked.

"Charlotte. When I was younger, I would have killed her to make sure she didn't follow." Talia sighed. "I think you're rubbing off on me, Princess."

The space between the wallboards and the rough-carved rock was cramped and filthy. Gravel and dust littered the ground, along with rat droppings, the empty shells of insects, and a healthy crop of mildew. The wooden planks of the wall were unsanded on this side. Splinters pricked at Danielle's clothes as she fought her way past a cobweb. "How did you find me?"

"Rode a rat," said Talia. "Nearly stabbed the thing in the eye before I realized it was there to help. I assume it's a friend of yours."

She reached back to help Danielle past a rock the size of a grown man's thumb. At their current size, it might as well have been a boulder.

"Even so, it took several days to sneak up here from the water. This is not an easy place to infiltrate. Whoever designed it knew what they were doing." Admiration warmed Talia's words. "I don't suppose you can call up anything more substantial than a rat? Maybe a team of manticores?"

"Sorry." From the sound of trickling water, they were directly beneath the pipe which circulated water into the fish pool. "Talia, what happened after you fell into the river? How did you break Stacia's spell?"

"Your aviar dragged me out. I assume I have you to thank for that. I finally managed to pull myself onto her back. I clung for dear life and told her to take me back to the pixies."

"They helped you?"

"Not exactly. Arlorran was gone, and the pixies were pretty mad when I told them what had happened to the other two aviars."

"Were they—?"

"Midnight and Socks were both alive the last I knew, but neither one was up for flying. The pixies sent a group back to get them. I don't know if they survived." Talia sighed. "I headed for the road, but it was all I could do to put one foot in front of the other. I'd have been lucky to make it a quarter of a mile without twisting my ankle or wrenching a knee. So . . . I asked for a guide."

Danielle grinned. "Don't you know you're never supposed to ask for a guide in Fairytown?"

Talia stopped walking. A tall wooden beam blocked their way. "Yeah, well, it worked. I met up with a strange little girl who had a duck's bill instead of a mouth. Don't ask. She removed the curse, and here I am." She rapped the beam. "This is where we'll need help, Princess. If you could call a few hearty rats, we'll be on our way."

"What aren't you telling me, Talia?"

"What do you mean?" Faint light penetrated the rathole behind them, but Talia was barely more than a shadow.

"You're the one who told me fairies never do anything for free," said Danielle. "What did you give that girl in exchange for her help?"

"Nothing important. Come on."

Her nonchalance only confirmed the worry in Danielle's gut. "Tell me."

"Princess, we don't have time for this."

"You can't reach Snow without my help." Danielle waited.

"Without your rats' help, you mean," Talia muttered.

Danielle didn't answer.

"She wanted what they all want," Talia snapped. "My unborn child."

Danielle felt like someone had reached into her chest and squeezed her lungs. "You didn't—"

"That's why I didn't want to tell you," said Talia. "I knew you'd overreact, especially given your current condition. Don't worry about it, Princess. Just conjure up some rats and let's get going."

"But you're not pregnant." Danielle's eyes widened. "Are you?"

"Not hardly. But fairies think about things in the long term. That's why they outbargain humans nine times out of ten."

"I'm sorry," Danielle whispered, touching her own stomach.

"Don't be. Now come on. The sooner we get Snow free, the sooner we can snatch Armand and go home."

She was too eager. Danielle reached out to touch Talia's arm. Talia jerked away.

"What else aren't you saying?" asked Danielle. There was no response. "Wind would have gotten you back to the pixies that same day. You hadn't gone far when you called for a guide. That was more than a month ago. What else did she ask of you?"

"Nothing." Talia's voice was so soft Danielle could barely hear.

"Was it the pixies? Did they punish you somehow?"

That earned a weak snort. "Those uptight glowbugs are lucky I didn't go back and shove them all into a jar."

"I thought you must have drowned," Danielle said. "I was afraid Wind hadn't reached you in time."

"No, she reached me. Saved my life." Her tone was an equal mix of anger and pain.

"Something else happened to you on the journey back," Danielle guessed. "Arlorran warned us it was dangerous to cross Fairytown without help. You were making your way to the crevasse, and—"

"I wasn't," Talia whispered. "I wasn't coming back."

"I don't understand."

"I left, dammit. I left Fairytown. I followed the road the other way, between the dwarven towers, out of the hedge, and away from this cursed place. I got as far as Little Hill."

Little Hill was a trading town about ten miles *south* of Fairytown. Danielle leaned against the stone, trying to understand. "You weren't going back to the palace."

"How could I? I had failed, Princess. Armand was still trapped. You and Snow were both lost."

"That wasn't your fault," said Danielle. "The queen would have understood. She—"

"Will you *please* stop being so damned nice?" Talia's voice had grown loud enough to make Danielle wince. She wondered if Charlotte could hear them through the walls. "I abandoned you."

Danielle started to reassure her, then bit her tongue. For whatever reason, it was clear Talia didn't want comfort right now. "Why?"

"Because of Rose." Talia drew a deep breath. "You saw what she did to Snow. How easily she stripped my 'gifts' from me. I . . . I couldn't take the chance of falling back into that never-ending sleep. I just couldn't."

"I understand," said Danielle.

"Do you?" Talia made a snorting sound, somewhere between a cough and a laugh.

"I know what it's like to be cursed," Danielle said.

Footsteps crunched in the dirt as Talia returned, until Danielle could feel her breath.

"Armand took you away from your stepmother's home," Talia whispered. "The kiss of your mother's blade freed you the second time. Do you know what broke *my* spell, Princess?"

"The stories—" Danielle stopped. If she had learned anything, it was the difference between stories and reality. "No, I don't."

"I was awakened by the agony of childbirth," Talia said, "as my twin children were expelled from my womb."

Danielle could see her shaking.

"My prince wasn't as kind as yours," Talia said. Her words were like knives. "I'm sure he began by planting a royal kiss on my cold lips. That's what you're supposed to do, right? But it didn't work. I didn't open my eyes and fall madly in love with him. So instead, he indulged another fantasy."

"Oh, Talia." Danielle reached out.

"Touch me right now and I swear I'll break your wrist. Princess or no."

Danielle drew back her hand.

"The thorns and vines died the day I awoke. The prince returned, ready to claim me for his bride. He found more than he bargained for."

"What happened?" Danielle asked.

"He brought me to his palace. And then I ran away."

The emptiness in those simple words made Danielle want to weep. "But your children—"

"They weren't my children," she whispered. "He sent them to be raised at one of the temples. I never learned which one." A bitter smile quirked her lips. "He said he would forgive me for being so crass as to bear children before we were married, but that it was better for everyone if the people never learned I was *impure*. That night, I killed him while he slept."

Talia shuddered, then wiped her face. When she spoke again, she sounded steadier. "To sleep is to be helpless," she said. "So when Rose threatened to revive my curse, I ran. Again. I couldn't do it. I couldn't let her—"

"She won't," Danielle said. "I promise. I won't let her."

"Don't make oaths you can't keep, Princess." Talia tilted her head to one side. "Is there anything more you'd like to pry from me? Shall I entertain you with further tales of my cowardice?"

"What made you return to Fairytown?" Danielle asked.

"The farther I went, the more I imagined you sitting here waiting for me to show up and save you. Right up to the moment they cut your throat, you'd still expect everything to work out, for me to rush in and help you rescue Armand. I kept seeing the disappointment in your eyes when you finally accepted the truth, and I couldn't stand it anymore. The world doesn't work like that, Princess."

"But you did come back," Danielle pointed out.

"Shut up."

Danielle searched for something more to say, something to let Talia know it would be all right. That Danielle didn't despise her for leaving. She could hear the pain in Talia's voice, and she would have taken back her questions if she could. "You're not weak," she said at last. "And I trust you."

"Idiot."

Danielle smiled. "Maybe."

That earned a short laugh. "If you're finished with the interrogation, Princess, would you mind terribly if we rescued Snow and Armand?"

CHAPTER 13

❄

DANIELLE WATCHED WITH ever-increasing skepticism as Talia unwound the line of her zaraq whip. She approached the gray rat who had responded to Danielle's call. Thanks to Trittibar's magic, the rat appeared roughly the size of a horse.

Talia reached out. The rat promptly snatched the weighted end of the whip and tried to chew it. "Would you mind?"

"Give that back, please," said Danielle. "She's not going to hurt you." She felt a twinge of guilt at that, remembering the last rat who had come to her aid. But like the others, this rat appeared to trust her. His eyes tracked Talia as she looped the line around his chest, tying a crude harness, but he didn't try to stop her. Talia tied a second length around her own waist.

"Don't worry." Talia leaned down, grabbing the harness in her hands so her body pressed flat against the rat's back. "The only thing you've really got to worry about is fleas. At this size, they can take a nice chunk out of you."

Before Danielle could answer, Talia and her rat were scrambling up the support beam. Danielle waited in the darkness, listening to the scritching sound of claws on wood. The rat climbed in fits and starts, pulling himself and Talia up, then stopping to sniff the air before continuing.

"Made it," Talia called out at last. "I'm out of the harness. Bring him back down."

Danielle nodded and summoned the rat. His descent was far less graceful. He climbed head down, one paw on the rough stone for balance, and his hindquarters seemed forever on the verge of flipping forward over his head. When he was halfway down, one of his paws slipped and he tumbled through the air, hitting the ground next to Danielle.

Danielle knelt to check on him. "Are you all right?"

The rat emitted a short squeak and began to clean his whiskers. He seemed unhurt, if a bit dusty.

"Hold still," Danielle said as she climbed onto the rat's back. She drew the extra loop over her waist as Talia had done, then grabbed the harness in front of the shoulders. The rat's back pressed uncomfortably against the bulge of her stomach. "I'm ready. Take me to Talia."

Riding a rat was very different from riding an aviar. Talia's makeshift harness held her securely to the rat's back, which was an improvement over the winged horses. But with Wind, Danielle had never worried that her mount would suddenly lose her grip on the sky. The rat had already fallen once. She kept herself as still as she could.

The worst point was when a millipede the size of her leg crawled onto one of the enormous bolts securing the beam to the stone. Fortunately, the rat let out a long, broken squeak, and the millipede backed down. Magic sword or no, Danielle wasn't ready to battle giant insects while mounted on ratback.

"Give me your hand," said Talia.

Danielle reached up, and Talia helped pull her and the rat onto a horizontal beam. Talia had taken out a glass bottle, which she shook vigorously. The water brightened into the same blue light Danielle had seen in the pool below.

"Handy stuff," Talia said. She handed the bottle to Danielle and began untying her whip from the rat. "The more you stir it up, the brighter it gets. I wouldn't want to drink it, though."

Like the walls, the space between the wooden ceiling and the stone above was full of cobwebs and dirt and dead bugs. Thick planks were nailed to the beams below. Dried plaster welled between the cracks like whitecapped waves frozen in winter.

Danielle hopped onto one of the planks. The ceiling held her weight easily. "The common room is this way."

They walked in silence, with Danielle occasionally giving the bottle another shake to renew the light. Her clothes were already damp with sweat, thanks to the warm, musty air. The extra weight of pregnancy didn't help either. Such a tiny thing, but her lower back already ached.

She kept one hand on her sword as they walked. Distance was impossible to judge, shrunken as they were with no landmarks. How far did they need to walk?

She turned back to the rat and whispered, "Take us to the common room."

The rat chittered and tilted his head. He turned around, obviously confused. Of course. He wouldn't know what the common room was.

"The sleeping girl in the glass box," Danielle said. "Take us to her."

The rat darted ahead, leading them through a narrow gap above the junction of three support beams. Danielle held her breath as she clawed her way past dusty cobwebs.

"Ah, the glamorous life of a princess," Talia said,

combing web from her hair. "I can see why your step-sisters were so envious."

Danielle grinned and hopped onto the ceiling boards on the other side.

"So how do we get down?" Talia asked. "I watched the rat climb down to get you, and I don't think I want to try that ride."

The rat was already scrambling over the next beam, running toward the far end of the room. A faint dripping echoed through the cramped space as they passed another pipe.

They climbed over four more beams before reaching the end of the room. The rat hurried ahead, stopping in front of a protrusion of square-cut stones. "The fireplace," Danielle said. "That must be the chimney."

She turned around, trying to orient herself. If the fireplace was there— She ran to the left, where the chimney disappeared into the rough rock of the cave, presumably carrying the smoke and heat to a nearby crack in the stone. "Snow should be right beneath us."

The rat squeaked and darted to a spot near the corner of the chimney. Danielle followed. As she approached, the planks grew grittier where bits of plaster had crumbled.

"It's probably been weakened from the heat of the fireplace." Talia drew her knife and jabbed it between the planks, gouging a chunk the size of her fist. "The plaster is dry and brittle all through here."

Danielle covered the glowing bottle. A thin crack of light shone from one side of the chimney, where some of the plaster had fallen away. The planks were poorly fitted to the chimney, resulting in a large space which was nothing but plaster. "We can get down over there."

Between Danielle's sword and Talia's knife, they

soon widened the hole enough for a person to pass through. Talia squeezed her head and shoulders through the hole. She drew back a moment later, her face tight. "Stay here. I'll see what I can do for Snow. I'll be able to help you down once I'm back to my normal size."

"What are you going to do?" Danielle asked.

Talia drew her whip. She untied the lead weight on the end of the line and tucked it into another pouch at her waist, digging around until she came up with a sharper, barbed weight. She tied a quick knot, gave it a tug, and grunted. She fished one of the spores out of Trittibar's sack and handed it to Danielle. "Just in case I have trouble getting back to you."

With that, Talia began sliding headfirst through the hole. A sharp thud vibrated the ceiling beneath Danielle's feet. Moments later, Talia's legs shot out of view.

"Talia!" Danielle lay flat and poked her head down. She nearly got kicked in the face as a reward.

Talia had embedded the end of her whip in the plaster, and now swung back and forth like a pendulum, kicking her legs to increase her speed. Once, twice . . .

On the third swing, Talia let go. Her tiny body compressed into a ball, turning in a slow, backward somersault as she flew toward Snow's coffin.

Danielle tensed. If Talia misjudged, she would smash into the side of the coffin, where the mirrored shards could cut her to shreds.

Talia twisted like a cat, bringing her hands and legs beneath her. She cleared the side of the coffin by a hair, landing squarely in the middle of Snow's ample bosom. She bounced down to Snow's belly as smoothly as any acrobat.

Danielle let out a sigh of relief. "She's a madwoman."

Behind her, the rat squeaked in agreement.

Talia climbed on all fours to the top of Snow's right breast, where she stood on her toes and peeked out over the edge of the coffin. She slid down, toward Snow's neck. There she stopped to look up at Danielle. She acted uncomfortable, almost nervous. She twined her fingers together, then wiped her palms on her trousers. She opened her mouth like she wanted to say something.

"What are you doing?" Danielle asked, trying to keep her voice quiet so it wouldn't carry.

Talia shook her head hard enough that her hair fell in front of her face. Planting one foot in Snow's right ear, she pulled herself up, grabbed a nostril for balance, and kissed Snow on the corner of her mouth.

Snow's eyelids began to flutter.

Danielle stared, so stunned she nearly fell out of the ceiling.

Talia was already making her way toward the edge of the coffin. She grabbed another spore from Trittibar's pouch and popped it into her mouth. "Get ready, Princess."

The door creaked open. In the faint light, Danielle could barely make out the shapes of the two darklings running through the door. She shuddered when she recognized the one-armed darkling who had helped to age her unborn son. They spread apart, searching the room.

Talia was already turning to face the darklings. She stood balanced on the edge of the coffin, arms outstretched as she continued to grow. When she was the size of an infant, she leaped soundlessly to the table behind the coffin. Another jump took her to the floor.

The spore in Danielle's hand was warm and damp from sweat. She could see the darklings making their way around the tables. Had they spotted Talia?

Talia crouched behind the table, nearly full-grown. She held out both hands and whispered, "Jump."

The darklings heard. As they ran toward Talia, Danielle closed her eyes, prayed, and pushed herself out of the ceiling.

Talia caught her in one hand and bounded onto the nearest table.

Huge fingers jarred Danielle to and fro as Talia dodged the darklings. Danielle wrenched her arm free of Talia's grip long enough to stuff the spore into her mouth.

She nearly choked on it as Talia dropped and rolled beneath the next table. Talia set Danielle on the floor beneath the bench and whispered, "Stay there." Then she was off and running, with both darklings in pursuit.

Danielle freed her sword as she waited for the magic to finish restoring her. Talia hadn't even drawn her knife. She was stalling, leading the darklings away from Danielle and Snow. She darted toward the door, and both darklings scrambled to cut her off. With a wild grin, Talia leaped and kicked off the wall with both feet, hard enough to launch herself over the darklings' heads.

The bench began to press against Danielle as she grew. She rolled out and stood. Snow still wasn't fully awake, and Talia could do nothing to hurt the darklings. Moving as quickly and silently as she could, Danielle circled around the table where Talia had turned to face her opponents.

Both darklings climbed onto the bench. Their limbs quivered as they prepared to leap. Talia smiled tightly as she spotted Danielle. Danielle raised her sword and nodded.

Talia stepped back and pretended to stumble.

They pounced. Talia rolled back, catching the first darkling with both feet, then launching him back through the air. He screamed and flailed, and Danielle swung with all her might.

He was dead by the time he landed on the ground. And the bench behind her. A bit also sprayed onto the wall. The mess would take hours to clean.

The second darkling was more fortunate. He landed higher, hands tangling Talia's hair. One arm snaked around her throat.

Talia sat up, then threw herself flat, crushing the darkling against the table with all of her weight. Her head snapped back, smashing the darkling's face. A normal foe would have been stunned, but the darkling clung hard, ripping Talia's shirt and biting her shoulder. Talia grabbed his wrist with both hands, trying to twist him away, but the black fingers simply dug into her skin.

Danielle ran toward the table, changing her grip on the sword. One hand held the hilt, while the other grabbed the blade for control. As before, the sword didn't even break her skin. "Talia!"

Talia rolled, and Danielle plunged the blade into the darkling's back. The darkling screamed and twisted. Hot blood splashed Danielle's arm as the darkling tore free and scrambled to the edge of the table. She swung again, wanting nothing more than to destroy this perversion.

"Fine control, remember?" Talia snapped. She rolled off of the table and staggered away, one hand touching her back. There was no blood, either from Danielle's sword or the darkling's attack. "You swing that thing like a farmer harvesting his crops!"

"I'm sorry," Danielle said, her voice tight. "Would you like me to put him back so I can try again?"

"Will you just kill the bastard already?"

Danielle tried, but the darkling twisted aside, going for Talia's throat. The darkling wasn't moving as fast as before, but he was still dangerous. Talia ducked again.

"Talia?" Snow stared bleary-eyed at Danielle and

Talia. Moving like she was still half asleep, she began to climb out of the coffin.

The darkling streaked past. His movement was erratic, like an injured cat, but he bounded across the tables too fast for Danielle or Talia to stop him.

"Snow, watch out!" Talia shouted, but Snow didn't seem to hear. She rubbed her eyes as the darkling sprang, fingers outstretched.

Snow smiled and tapped the edge of the coffin. A web of light shot up, spearing him in midair. It reminded Danielle of the light Snow had used back in the cave to drive the darklings back, burning their skin. Only back then, she had used only the small mirrors of her choker.

Her coffin was made up of hundreds of broken mirrors.

An instant later, nothing remained of the darkling but a puff of smoke and a smell that reminded Danielle of moldering leaves.

Snow smothered a yawn. "Got you!"

"About time you woke up," Talia said, rubbing her shoulder. "Do you know how long it took me to find a counterspell to that silly sleeping curse?"

Danielle blinked. Talia stepped closer and lowered her voice. "Breathe a word about what really happened, and I'll kill you myself."

Danielle looked at Snow, then back at Talia. There was a kind of weary resignation in Talia's dark eyes. Danielle thought back to what Talia had said about her bargain with the fairy girl, how Talia had promised her unborn child in exchange for the girl's help. Snow clearly had no idea how Talia felt. No wonder Talia had been so upset by Snow's flirtation with Arlorran.

"I promise," Danielle said.

"How long did I sleep?" Snow asked.

"A little over a month," said Talia.

Snow touched her bare neck and frowned. She

reached down to grab her knife. "Where's Prince Armand?"

"Charlotte said he was with Stacia and the Duchess." Somehow, Danielle kept her voice steady.

"And my mother." Snow reached out to touch the side of her coffin. "She's watching us, though these mirrors. She'll know I'm free."

"She must have sent the darklings to investigate when Talia broke the spell," Danielle guessed.

Snow's expression tightened, and the coffin shattered. Thousands of fragments fell onto the table and floor, a glittering explosion of broken glass. She looked at Danielle again. "You look more pregnant than you should."

Danielle put her hand over her stomach. "Stacia used those darklings to age my son," she said, pointing her sword toward the remains. "They want him ready by midsummer, so Rose can—" She clenched her jaw, fighting angry tears.

"The conjoined moons," Snow said. She rubbed her arms. "Clever. Wouldn't want the king or queen to notice what's going on."

"They've cast a new spell on Armand," Danielle said. "Your mother gets my child, and the Duchess takes my husband in payment."

"Talia, get Princess Danielle to Armand so she can break the spell." Snow's voice changed, becoming harder. Danielle had never seen Snow truly angry before. She still smiled, but her free hand was clenched tight around the handle of her knife. The air itself seemed cold as a winter wind. "I'll deal with my mother."

Talia grabbed Snow's arm. "What are you—"

"She cast me back into that damned box," Snow said, wrenching free. "She murdered Roland. I'm going to destroy her this time, Talia. I'm going to stop her."

"Snow, stop. There's a tower at the center of the cavern," Talia said. "Armand is probably somewhere inside. But the cavern walls are littered with caves and tunnels. There's no way for us to simply stroll into the tower and search for the prince. The Duchess has goblins and ogres and serpents guarding—"

"They aren't the ones we need to fight," said Snow. "The Duchess won't hurt us directly. She's still bound by Malindar's Treaty, remember? She'll let my mother fight, so she can proclaim her innocence if things go wrong."

"How are you going to stop her?" Danielle asked. "I know you're angry. Your mother cursed me, too, remember? But she beat you in the cave, and she's broken your mirrors."

Snow brushed her fingers over her neck, then shrugged. She strode toward the door. "I'll find Armand for you. If he's still enchanted, you'll have to overpower him without—"

"Stop," Talia snapped. "You can't fight her alone."

"I'm not going to." Snow smiled. "I'm going to summon the dwarves."

"What dwarves?" Danielle stared from one woman to the other. Talia's face was stone, and Snow's smile was the thing of nightmares. "I don't understand. The only dwarves we've encountered were at the king's gate."

"Not them, Danielle." Snow laughed and shook her head. "Haven't you heard the tale of Snow White and the Seven Dwarves?"

"You can't." Talia's voice was firm, the voice of command. "We don't need them. You've proven that you're strong enough to destroy the darklings. We'll return to Charlotte's room and steal a mirror there. You can use that to fight—"

"You expect me to face her with the feeble magic such a glass would produce?" Snow asked. "An impure thing of rippled glass and tarnished metal? You saw what she did to my choker, Talia. Even the enchanted mirror back at the palace might not be powerful enough. Not against her." She drew her knife and pressed the tip to her left palm. "The dwarves beat her before."

Danielle grabbed her wrist, thinking of her stepsister. Stacia had used blood for her own spells . . . spells she had learned from Rose. "What are you doing? How can dwarves fight your mother?"

"Let me go!" Snow wrenched away, but Talia caught her elbow and twisted the knife from her hand. "You don't understand," Snow said. She sounded close to tears. "I won't let her win again. I can't."

"Find another way," said Talia.

"There *is* none." Snow turned to Danielle. "The dwarves can help me find your husband. They can save him. They can save your son. You have to let me do this."

Talia folded her arms and stepped back. "Tell her the rest."

"We don't have time!" Snow said, her voice rising. "They know I've awakened. They're already preparing to enchant us both again. Do you want to protect your child or not?"

They were both watching Danielle, waiting for her answer. "There's always a cost," she said softly. "What happens to you if you summon these dwarves?"

"You're as stubborn as Queen Bea." Snow tossed her hair over her shoulder. "How old do you think I am?"

"I don't know." The question caught Danielle off guard. "Twenty-three? Twenty-four?"

Snow gave a quick bow. "I reached my eighteenth birthday earlier this year."

Danielle shook her head. "I don't understand."

"They're not dwarves, exactly," Snow admitted. "They're representations of the elemental powers of our world. But can you imagine a bard trying to tell the tale of Snow White and the Seven Anthropomorphic Incarnations of Elemental Magic? 'Dwarves' just sounds better, don't you think?"

"It was the seven dwarves who killed Rose," said Talia. "Each one will serve Snow White without question, but each demands a year of her life in return."

"Seven years?" Danielle stared at Snow, who smiled.

"That's why my mother never summoned them," she said. "Old age and ugliness frightened her even more than death."

"Talia is right," Danielle said. "There has to be another way."

"Then name it." Snow wiped her nose. "Choose quickly, Danielle. Unless you want to return to slavery."

Danielle racked her brain, desperately grasping at one idea after another. "Stacia's knife," she whispered. "I poisoned it. If we can force her to use her magic and draw her own blood, she might destroy herself." Quickly, she explained what she had done with the rats and the poison.

"I'm impressed," said Talia. "I didn't think you had it in you. But it probably won't kill her. The dosage isn't high enough. You might make her a little ill, but that's all."

"Are you sure?" Danielle asked.

"Trust me on this." Talia's smile was anything but pleasant.

"Fine." Danielle held out her arm. "Then give the dwarves seven years of *my* life. It's my husband we came to rescue. My child we're protecting. I'll pay the cost."

Snow's expression softened, and her eyes watered.

She covered her mouth with both hands. "You'd do that for me?" Without waiting for a response, she threw her arms around Danielle and squeezed so hard Danielle could barely breathe. Then, trembling, she pulled away. "I couldn't. You're already so old."

"I beg your pardon?" Danielle snapped. She pushed up her sleeve, but hesitated before offering the arm to Snow. "Just promise I'll be the only one to pay, not my son."

Snow nodded, still staring. "But—"

"I would die to save Armand and my son," Danielle said. "Seven years is a small price."

"Three and a half," Talia said, her voice strangely soft. She returned Snow's knife and extended her own arm. "We'll share the cost."

Snow bit her lip, then embraced them both, nearly stabbing Danielle's shoulder in the process.

"Do you think perhaps we should get on with it?" Talia asked. "Or is all of this hugging and merriment a part of the spell?"

Snow backed away, still smiling. "Don't be afraid," she said, her eyes sparkling.

Snow's fingers felt like ice water as she took Danielle's hand. Her knife dented the skin of her inner wrist. Danielle barely felt the cut. So keen was Snow's blade that only when Danielle flexed her arm did the skin separate and blood begin to flow toward her fingers.

Snow did the same to Talia, and then to her own forearm. She twined her fingers with Danielle's. Talia did the same, sandwiching Snow's hand between Danielle's and her own. Blood trickled over their hands and dripped to the floor.

Snow closed her eyes and whispered,

> *"Blood of life, blood of binding,*
> *hear me light and darkness blinding.*

Magic from the world's first turning,
Water flowing, fire burning.
Awaken earth with life so old.
Hear me, winds of winter cold.
Share my—"

Snow flushed. "I mean, share *our* blood, which I—, which *we* give freely, darn it." She wiped her face and shared a sheepish smile before finishing. "By this bond, we summon thee."

Snow relaxed her grip and stepped back, motioning the others to do the same. Danielle moved cautiously, glancing all about as she waited for something to happen. Her hand was stiff, and the cut had begun to sting. "When will we know if it worked?"

The oil lamps over the door brightened. The light of the small fires flowed together, growing into a tiny sun.

"What's happening?" Danielle asked, covering her eyes.

"They're coming." Snow's gaze was glassy, like she was watching from a great distance.

Crude limbs flailed from the light, moving with the awkwardness of a newborn. Soon those limbs gripped the pipe more firmly. A small, squat man formed entirely of light dropped gently to the floor. His features were vague and blurry. Pinpoints of shadow suggested eyes, while a darker spot might have been a mouth. Danielle had to squint to look at him.

Others followed. The fires of the oil lamp still burned, appearing weak and dim in comparison to the dwarf. Again the flames came together, and soon the lantern died as a second figure dropped down to join his companion. This one retained the strange yellow fires of the lamp. Flickers of blue swept across his extremities when he moved.

Water seeped out of the wall, congealing into a slender, feminine form. Her long hair was a miniature waterfall, ending in white mist around her waist. With every movement, she gave off a faint trickling sound, like a stream in springtime.

Snow's own shadow rose from the floor with reptilian smoothness. Soon it was the perfect twin to the man of light. He stepped away, leaving Snow without a shadow.

Floorboards splintered at Snow's feet. Danielle grabbed her sword and stumbled back. Even Talia drew her knife. Snow merely smiled and stepped away from the widening hole.

Dark green fingers of stone reached out. Moving as gracefully and easily as Talia herself, a statue climbed through the floor to join the others. Her skin was so finely polished Danielle could see the rest of the room reflected on her bare back.

A sudden breeze made the man of fire brighten, though Danielle saw nothing.

"What are they?" Danielle whispered.

"Wind, fire, water and stone," said Snow. "Light and darkness. The very elements of our world, summoned and made flesh."

Danielle kept her sword ready. "I thought there were seven."

Snow pointed, and the shattered remains of the coffin began to swirl about the floor. "The seventh is the embodiment of magic. She's too wild to be given her own form, so she will remain within me. She'll give me the power I need to find your husband and face my mother."

She stepped toward the cloud of glass, which began to re-form into a single mirror. Snow didn't bother with rhymes this time. Fragmented images flickered before her. Danielle caught a brief glimpse of Armand sitting at a table. It was too fast for her to follow, but Snow said, "I know where they are."

The contours of a woman's face began to emerge

in the cloud of glass. The features resembled Snow, aged twenty years. Knives of glass settled around the brow, a mirrored crown. The oversized eyes blinked, and the harsh lips pulled into a smile. "I expected you to flee."

"I know," said Snow. She clapped her hands, and the glass crushed together. Danielle saw the face flinch, and then glittering powder streamed to the floor.

"Your mother?" Danielle asked.

"She already knew I was awake," said Snow.

"You're taunting her?" Talia asked.

"She's impetuous when she loses her temper. I want to be sure she comes out to face me." Snow turned toward the door. The stone dwarf leaped like a jack-rabbit, driving her fingers into the wood and ripping it apart, just as she had done to the floor.

"You could have just opened it," Talia muttered. She drew her knife, then glanced at the ceiling, where her tiny spindle whip still swung over Snow's coffin. She hadn't been carrying it when she used Trittibar's magic to restore herself. "I don't suppose—"

Snow snapped her fingers, and the whip pulled free of the plaster. By the time it flew to Talia's hand, it had regained its full size.

"Nice." Talia's face was grim as she wound the line back around the spindle.

The hallway was empty. Snow followed her dwarves through the door, leaving Talia and Danielle to follow.

"What are they, really?" Danielle whispered.

"The dwarves? They're not good, if that's what you're asking. They tortured Snow's mother before they killed her," Talia said. "She told me about it once, after drinking way too much ale. Wind and magic held Rose in place while fire consumed her from the feet up."

Danielle glanced at Charlotte's door as they passed.

Thankfully, neither Snow nor the dwarves slowed their pace. Despite everything her stepsister had done, Danielle had no desire to see her tortured to death. If Charlotte did manage to work free, Danielle hoped she would be smart enough to stay hidden until this was over.

"Much of Snow's power came from her mother," Talia added. "She tries not to use the darker spells, but sometimes her magic ventures to the shadows." She shook her head. "I don't know what she fears more, having to face her mother again, or becoming her."

CHAPTER 14

❄

THE WIND RUSHED them along, pushing Danielle from behind so that every step felt like she was flying downhill, ever on the verge of toppling head over heels. Even Talia looked disconcerted.

Twice they were attacked by darklings, and both times Snow's dwarves made short work of their attackers. Danielle tried not to watch. The dwarves were fierce and gleeful in their destruction.

"There," said Snow, pointing to an irregularly shaped door at the end of the corridor. Unlike the other doors, this one appeared to be made of stone. There was no handle, and the hinges were mounted on the outside. A square of brass framed a tiny keyhole on the right side of the door.

"That will take us into the main cavern," said Talia.

Snow lowered her voice. "My mother is waiting. She'll try to destroy us the moment we emerge."

Talia knelt by the keyhole. "Hey, glowboy. Stick a finger in this lock so I can see what I'm dealing with." She peered into the hole as the dwarf of light squatted beside her, forcing Danielle to avert her eyes. "I should be able to get us past this. Looks like a typical fairy mechanism. Six tumblers on both sides. Tricky, but—"

Snow touched Talia's shoulder and gestured for her to move aside. The stone dwarf ran her fingers down the door. The screech of stone raised the hairs on Danielle's neck and arms.

This dwarf, like the rest, lacked any recognizable facial features. They were like unfinished dolls. Yet the bulge of her chest was clearly female, as was the roundness of her hips. Danielle wondered if that was a deliberate choice on Snow's part, or simply the nature of the dwarves.

"Be ready," Snow said.

Danielle nodded, trying to remember the things Talia had taught her about swordplay. She forced herself to relax, loosening her grip on her sword. "Small, precise movements," she whispered.

Stone fingers slipped into the crack on the side of the door. Rock crumbled, bringing a shower of dust and dirt.

Danielle tried not to think about the last time they had fought Rose and Stacia. "What will they do when we go through the door?"

"We may have more darklings to fight," Talia said. "The darklings don't seem to have much independence, and they obviously don't have any qualms about attacking humans. Or Rose may conjure up something new. Sometimes it's better if you don't try to guess what's coming. You'll prepare yourself for the familiar, and the unexpected will run you through before you realize you guessed wrong."

"Thanks. I feel so much better." She tried to think about Armand and their son. Whatever Stacia and Rose sent against them, she had to survive.

"Stay close to me," Talia said. "I'll do my best to protect you. Look for a way to reach the Duchess' tower. Hopefully, the dwarves will keep them busy while we sneak in to get your husband."

The stone dwarf stepped back and brushed her

hands together. Much of the rock had been gouged away from the left side of the door, exposing black hinges. The dwarf dropped to a crouch and surged forward, slamming her shoulder into the door. The sound was deafening. Even Snow winced and covered her ears.

After two more such assaults, the great door slowly toppled outward. The stone dwarf stepped through the doorway, followed by her companions.

"Subtlety was never Snow's strength," Talia said. Danielle could barely hear her over the ringing in her ears.

Snow was already hurrying through the doorway, with Talia close behind. Taking a deep breath, Danielle raised her sword and followed, climbing over the fallen door and hopping down onto the metal walkway outside.

The last time Danielle was here, she had been trapped by Stacia's curse. With her head bowed in obeisance, she hadn't fully absorbed the sheer size of the Duchess' cavern.

They stood more than halfway up the side of the cavern. From this height, the figures scurrying about at the base of the Duchess' tower were little more than insects. The tower itself made her gasp. It rose like a stalagmite from the center of the lake, nearly as broad as the castle back home. The tower narrowed somewhat near the middle, then expanded again to merge with the rock overhead. Railings and platforms circled the tower, along with several light, narrow bridges which stretched from the tower to the cavern walls. Other bridges had been raised like drawbridges, pressing flat against the tower. If the Duchess wanted, she could raise every bridge, leaving the tower inaccessible save from the lake below.

Danielle's sword reflected the blue sparks of the water running through the walkway beneath her feet.

The walkways were little more than wide gutters with open grates over the top. The light of the water illuminated the path as it flowed, spiraling down the walkways into the lake. Walkways and pipes and support beams lined the walls of the cavern, like the work of an enormous metal-spinning spider.

The huge door the dwarf had broken had smashed the railing and dented the walkway itself, so a stream of water now trickled over the side. Danielle could hear the metal straining under the weight of the other dwarves.

"Watch the enemy, not the scenery, Princess," Talia snapped. She pointed her knife past Danielle.

A short distance down the walkway, a handful of darklings fidgeted and danced. They appeared to be waiting.

"So, the brave Sleeping Beauty returns." Stacia stood farther up the walkway, near one of the few lowered bridges. "Shall we begin with you, Princess Talia? *Throw yourself over the—*"

Snow clapped her hands. A pounding sound echoed in Danielle's ears, blocking out the last of Stacia's words.

Talia rubbed her ears. "Is there a less obnoxious way to do that?"

Snow grinned and turned back to Stacia. A wave of her hand sent the dwarves of flame and light streaking ahead. Stacia fell back a step, her eyes wide. Perhaps the ghost of Rose was remembering the last time she had seen these creatures.

Stacia recovered quickly. An invisible blow knocked the dwarves back. The figure of light simply stopped, but the dwarf of fire landed on his back. Steam soon shrouded them from view.

"What's she waiting for?" Talia shouted. The darklings still hadn't moved.

"Rose knows I can protect us," said Snow. She

began to walk toward Stacia. "She won't waste any more power on attacks that would only fail."

As the steam began to dissipate, Snow's dwarves returned to her side.

Stacia backed away, moving to the foot of the bridge. "Tell me, Daughter, do you still hear your lover's screams when you sleep? Do you think the anguish of your friends will overpower that memory, as I sear the skin from their bodies?"

Snow took a step, but Talia caught her shoulder. "If you join her on that bridge, she gains a tactical advantage. She knows most of your dwarves can't fly. Neither can you, for that matter. She can. Go to her, and all she needs to do is shatter the bridge. She transforms into a bird, and you fall to your death."

"I could fly if I wanted to," Snow protested. "Probably." But she stopped walking.

Talia touched Danielle's arm. "Find another bridge."

Danielle stepped to the railing. Most of the bridges had already been retracted to the tower. She spotted one lower down, where a group of hunched dwarves led a mule-drawn wagon toward the tower, but it would take far too long to get there. Another, high overhead, was already swinging upward, chains clanking.

Several crowds had gathered to watch the confrontation. Danielle saw a group of goblins on one of the tower platforms, all pointing and staring. A handful of dwarves stood on the walkway below. Danielle couldn't hear them, but it looked like they were making wagers.

Once again, Snow sent the fire dwarf toward Stacia, and once again Stacia knocked him back.

"Stacia is afraid of water," Danielle shouted.

Snow grinned and pointed. The water dwarf began to disappear. When Danielle looked closer, she saw that the dwarf was melting through the metal grate, joining the water below. Snow's brow was wrinkled with concentration. "This would be easier if Stacia were standing *downstream*," she said.

Thin, scaled vines shot up from the grate. They wrapped around Snow's leg, yanking her to her knees. The vines looked like a cross between plant and animal. They moved with the speed of angry serpents, but sharp thorns protruded from beneath the scales.

"Snow!" Talia started to grab Snow, and then the darklings charged from behind.

"I'll slow them down," Danielle shouted. "You help Snow."

Danielle stepped away, raising her sword as the darklings ran toward her. She counted four, no, five of the foul creatures. What on earth had possessed her to face the darklings alone? Clearly, she had spent too much time with Talia.

The lead darkling crouched to attack. Danielle tensed.

Blinding light seared her eyes, and the darklings screamed. Snow's dwarf batted two of them over the railing before they could move. A glowing fist smashed a third against the stone wall. The remaining two fled, sprinting down the walkway like frightened rabbits.

Danielle turned back to Snow, who had already used her knife to cut most of the vines from her legs. The thorns had tattered her pants, but the white skin beneath was untouched.

Talia snorted and stepped back. "Maybe we'll just watch. Let us know if you need any help."

Snow pointed toward Stacia. Like the vines had done, the dwarf of water reached up from the walkway to seize Stacia's legs.

Stacia screamed. The dwarf climbed up, lifting Stacia over her head to throw her from the walkway.

"She can fly, remember?" Talia snapped. "That's not going to do us any good."

Snow barely even blinked. The dwarf turned around and walked to the end of the bridge, preparing to smash Stacia's body against the cavern wall.

Stacia plunged her hands into the dwarf's back.

Snow gasped and staggered backward. Talia dropped her knife and caught Snow's arms.

Danielle watched as the sparkling water of the dwarf grew cloudy and still. Frost spread across her body, and her movement slowed. Stacia twisted free and dropped to her feet, keeping one hand sunk into the dwarf's frozen back. The dwarf tried to reach her, but Stacia thrust her hand deeper. Soon even the dwarf's fingers had frozen stiff.

Stacia stepped back, pulling her hand free and clutching it against her chest. Another group of dark-lings swarmed forward, hoisting the dwarf up and pushing her over the railing. She tumbled down and shattered on the rocks by the lakeshore.

Snow jumped at the impact, then drew a deep breath. "That stung."

The dwarf of wind began to blow. Danielle's hair snapped back, and she grabbed the railing to keep from stumbling. Snow wasn't directing her wind at Stacia, but at the tower. "What are you doing?"

"The seventh dwarf has found Armand," Snow shouted. "Be ready."

Talia looked around. "Ready for what?"

The stone dwarf put one foot on the railing and leaped. The wind rushed with her, nearly sucking Dan-ielle over the edge in its wake. She stared open-mouthed as the flailing statue flew like an arrow to slam into the side of the tower. The dwarf slid down-ward, landing on one of the platforms. The goblins on the platform drew weapons.

The fight was a short one. Danielle turned away, remembering poor Diglet guarding the hedge into

Fairytown. It wasn't long before the bridge began to creak away from the tower.

"Looks like it's going to land one level below us," Talia said.

Metal squealed as if in pain, and then the bridge was swinging downward, fast enough to smash right through the walkway. But the Duchess' builders knew what they were doing. The walkway held, though Danielle could feel the impact in her legs even from one level away. Water splashed out of the grate below.

"Snow!" Talia shouted.

Stacia had used Snow's distraction with the bridge to launch another attack. Thorned vines now circled Snow's arms, dragging her down to the grate, where another reached for her neck. The dwarf of fire reached out to seize two of the vines. When he opened his hands a moment later, black ash sprinkled the water. He grabbed two more, and Snow was free once again.

Talia climbed over the railing. She lowered herself until she hung from the edge of the walkway. There, she swung her legs back and forth and jumped down to the bridge.

"You're next, Princess," Talia shouted.

Danielle moved toward Snow. "Are you sure you can stop her?"

Snow glanced back. Her eyes were bloodshot, and proximity to the flames had reddened her skin. She was crying, but her voice was hard as stone. "She's better prepared this time, and she knows what the dwarves can do, but I'm not leaving until she's destroyed. Go with Talia. I won't let her hurt you. I won't let her hurt anyone else."

She turned away, and the dwarves of darkness and light began to charge toward Stacia. At the same time, wind buffeted Stacia toward the edge of the bridge.

Snow's shoulders shook. "I'm sorry for what she did to you and Armand."

Danielle stepped back from the railing and grabbed Snow's arm. "Don't you dare do anything stupid. We'll be back soon with Armand, and I am not going home without you. Do you understand me?"

Snow knelt and used her knife to slice away a vine that had snagged her leg. "Go on. Before she destroys that bridge to stop you from crossing."

Danielle wanted to argue, but Snow was right. She turned back and climbed out over the railing, trying not to look at the rocky shore far below.

She landed hard, the weight of her son throwing off her balance. Talia caught her by the arm while she recovered.

"You're definitely heavier than you used to be," Talia said. Before Danielle could respond, a shadow dropped from the walkway overhead. For an instant, Danielle thought it was another darkling. But the figure grew, thinning as it stretched out to cover the bridge in darkness.

"Snow sent one of her dwarves to cover us," Talia said.

They were halfway across when the scream of twisting metal made them stop. Behind them, Stacia had changed tactics. The writhing vines had given up their assault on Snow. Instead, they twined around the walkway itself, tearing away the segment where Snow stood. A long section hung at an angle. Water spilled down to the cavern below.

Danielle pointed to where Snow lay flat, clinging to the broken walkway. Her hair flew as wind helped her to climb back up. Fire assailed the vines.

"She needs help." Talia took a step back.

Danielle wanted to follow. "We'll never get to her in time. Snow said she could beat Stacia and Rose. We have to trust her."

Talia shook her head. "Maybe you haven't noticed,

but Snow's not entirely clearheaded when it comes to her mother."

Snow pulled herself up, and a gust of wind helped her leap to the undamaged part of the walkway. Instantly, more vines shot from the water, dragging her to her knees and pinning her in place.

"I'm going," said Talia.

"Wait." Already Snow's dwarves had come to help her break free, while the dwarf of light flew at Stacia. Stacia cringed back, covering her eyes.

"She needs help!" Talia shouted.

"I know." Danielle looked up. This whole place was nothing but an enormous cave. She closed her eyes. *Please help my friend.*

"What are you calling?" Talia asked.

Danielle blinked. "How did you know—?"

"You bite your tongue when you do your silent summoning routine with the animals. Do you really think rats will be able to fight Stacia's magic?"

"Not rats." With a grim smile, Danielle pointed to the top of the cavern, where hundreds of black shapes fluttered toward Stacia. Soon a cloud of bats surrounded her, so thick Danielle could see nothing of Stacia herself.

"Come on," said Danielle. "Let's go raid the tower."

Snow's stone dwarf was waiting for them at the other side of the bridge. She stood on a broad platform of wood and metal that circled about a third of the tower. Huge sheets of thick oak had been worn smooth by decades of pacing guards. A lacework of silver metal threaded between the boards like the roots of a willow tree, securing it to the tower. The whole thing appeared delicate and flimsy, yet it supported the dwarf's weight with no sign of strain.

Two goblins cowered behind the dwarf. Well, two and a half, really. The dwarf hadn't been gentle.

The two survivors huddled together, their yellow eyes huge. A pile of cards sat forgotten between them. Neither one made any effort to raise the crossbows in their laps.

Talia smiled and scooped up both crossbows.

"We're here to see the Duchess and her guests," Danielle said, matching Talia's smile. "She should be expecting us."

Talia turned around. Stacia had managed to drive most of the bats back, but the delay had given Snow and her dwarves the upper hand. Stacia had already retreated halfway across the bridge. "Go," Talia said, nudging the stone statue. "Help her."

As the dwarf of stone ran to help Snow, Talia handed one crossbow to Danielle. She put her foot in the stirrup of the other, drawing back the heavy string, then raised it to her shoulder. Sighting carefully, she pulled the trigger.

The crossbow bolt rustled Stacia's gown as it flew past. Talia flung the crossbow over the edge of the platform in disgust. "Shoddy goblin garbage."

Talia yanked the other crossbow from Danielle's hand and turned to the goblins. "I'm pretty sure I can hit a closer target, though."

The goblins glanced at one another. Moving in unison, they stepped out of the way, clearing a path to the arched door behind.

Danielle drew her sword, eliciting panicked squeaks from both goblins. "Don't worry," she said. "Nobody's going to hurt you."

"That would be a first," muttered one. Their gazes never left her sword.

Talia studied the edge of the door, then dropped flat to peer beneath. "No lock, and no traps I can find." She glanced at the goblins. "The lack of traps is probably a good idea. No doubt they'd kill themselves trying to get back inside."

The door's handle was polished bronze, cast to re-semble a nude, very well-endowed elf. "Don't let Snow see this," Talia said. "She'll want to redecorate half the palace." Rolling her eyes, she grabbed the lever in the center and lifted.

The door opened easily, revealing a low, round room as wide as the entire tower. A blue fire flickered in the floor at the center. Smoke darkened the air, making Danielle cough. She kept one eye on the gob-lins, but they seemed content to cower in peace.

"You'd think the Duchess would have better guards," Danielle said as she stepped after Talia.

"Yes, you would." Talia stopped in mid-step. "Prin-cess, grab the door!"

Danielle tried, but she was too late. Untouched, the door slammed shut, plunging them into silence.

"The goblins are a ruse. There was no trap on the door because the whole room is the trap." Talia pointed through the blue-gray haze of smoke. Thirteen doors, evenly spaced, covered the walls. "Typical fairy mischief. I'm betting one of these doors will take us where we want to go."

"And the others?"

"The bottom of the sea, a dragon's mating pit, a goblin latrine . . . Fun places like that."

Danielle grabbed the handle of the door behind her. Thankfully, the handle on this side was shaped like a simple tree branch, so perfectly cast it appeared to be growing right out of the door. She gave it a quick tug. "I don't think it's latched," she said. "We can go back and ask the goblins which door—"

"No!" Talia seemed to fly across the room, slam-ming her shoulder into the door. "Nothing is that easy, Princess."

"There has to be a way," Danielle protested. "The goblins can't stay out on that ledge forever."

"What makes you think that door leads back to the

goblins?" asked Talia. She knelt, studying the base of the door. "The doors recognize the people, not the other way around. Snow would know how to find the right one."

Danielle moved to the next door. The hinges showed no sign of use. The metal was as clean as the day it was forged. The only difference was the handle. Tiny buds sprouted from the bronze.

Moving around the room, Danielle realized each successive handle took her further through the seasons. On the opposite side of the room, oak leaves bloomed from a handle so thin Danielle cut her finger on the edge. Acorns hung from later doors, and as she neared the end of the circle, she found withered leaves secured to the doors, as if they had been captured in mid-fall.

"I hate fairies," Talia muttered. She moved to one of the autumn doors and poked the falling leaves. "I hate riddles, too. It's early summer, so does that mean we pick one of the summer doors?"

"What about the fire?" Danielle hurried to the center of the room. A sunken circle, rimmed by an unbroken ring of white marble, contained the fire. Thick logs were arranged in a pyramid, though the wood didn't appear to burn. The smoke smelled of ginger and cinnamon.

"What are you going to do, burn down the doors?"

"I don't know." Danielle reached out, but the blue flames were far too hot. "Maybe the fire is a part of the riddle. The flames might change color when we touch the right one, or the smoke might flow toward the door we need, or—"

"I doubt it," said Talia. "More likely the Duchess uses the fire to spy on this room. We had a spy try that in the palace a year or so back. One of the candles in the throne room was burning with a peculiar pink tinge. We thought it was something in the wax. I

swapped it out and brought it to Snow. I wasn't thinking about anyone using the flames as scrying magic."
She glanced away. "Well, Snow likes pink. But the
first time she lit the wick, she told us there was an elf
watching on the other side of the flame."

"Why would the Duchess want to watch us?" Danielle asked.

"For her own amusement, probably," said Talia.
"I'm sure it's a great show, watching the poor humans
stumble around, arguing and trying one foolish plan
after another, until we finally open a door and unleash
our doom." She scowled at the fire. "Arrogant fairy
bi—"

"Wait," said Danielle. She stared down into the
flames. "Are you sure she's watching?"

"She has to know what's happening out there on
the bridge," said Talia. "She probably knows we made
it past her goblins. Yes, I'm sure."

Danielle straightened. Fairies had to play by the
rules, after all. "Duchess," she said, speaking as firmly
as she could. She tried to imitate the way Queen Beatrice spoke when she held court. "I am Princess Danielle Whiteshore, future queen of Lorindar. I have
been held in your home against my will, and I would
speak with you."

Taking Talia's arm, Danielle walked toward the
closest door.

"What are you doing?" Talia twisted free.

"Even the Duchess has to follow the treaty," Danielle said. "If I die, she will have knowingly murdered
a member of the royal family." She grabbed the handle of the door.

"Are you sure?" Talia asked.

Danielle forced a grin. "Trust me."

Talia rolled her eyes, but didn't try to pull Danielle away.

Danielle held her breath. She knew she was right.

She had to be right. The Duchess' role in this game was defined by her ignorance, her willing blindness to the identity of Danielle and Armand. She opened the door.

Nothing but blackness lay beyond. She heard Talia readying her crossbow. Putting a hand on her sword, Danielle stepped through the doorway.

Her foot touched stone. A feast of smells made her mouth water. Baked lamb, fresh bread, and some sort of sweet, fruity sauce or jam. Another step, and the darkness began to fade. A chandelier floated in the blackness ahead. Three rings of candles hung suspended by ropes of braided gold. Crystal teardrops dangled between the candles, capturing the light like tiny stars.

Danielle kept walking until she found herself in a long dining room. Marble staircases curved up the walls. Blue-and-white flowers bloomed from living railings. In the center of the room sat a table of polished black stone. At the far end of the table, beyond the platters and the goblets, a golden brazier burned with a warm blue flame.

Brahkop the troll was just rising from an oversized chair. To his left, sitting at the head of the table, sat a slender woman in a robe of white silk. The Duchess, presumably. She was a small woman, almost childlike. Golden threads in her robe wove images of birds which flew endless circles around her torso, twisting and diving to follow the contours of her body. Her hair was pure white, cut short and wild like a young boy's. A thin circlet of platinum sat on her brow, decorated with flakes of jade. Long, slender ears tapered to a point just above her crown. Her eyes were too large for her face, and they stared unblinking at Danielle and Talia.

Beside her, clasping the Duchess' hand in his own, sat Prince Armand.

He wore a black robe cut in the same style as the Duchess'. A serpentine dragon in silver thread undulated around his chest as he stood. His sword still hung from his hip. Danielle's chest tightened. There was no recognition in Armand's eyes.

"Duchess," snapped Brahkop. "This is a slave girl, a rebellious servant of my wife."

All true, Danielle noted. Incomplete, but true. Brahkop was being very careful not to lie to the Duchess.

Danielle opened her mouth, then froze. What was the proper form of address for a Duchess? My Lady? Your Grace? Were the titles different among fairykind? Her studies with *The Mortal's Guide to Faerie Courtesy* seemed a lifetime ago. The last thing she wanted to do was offend the Duchess.

She glanced back, but Talia appeared to be waiting for her. Was she actually following Danielle's lead?

Danielle swallowed and approached the table. "I've come for my husband . . . Your Grace." "Grace" seemed an appropriate word for one of fairy blood. The Duchess' expression didn't change. "Prince Armand was taken from me by my stepsisters, Charlotte and Stacia. That troll helped them use witchcraft to twist his affections."

The Duchess raised Armand's hand to her lips and planted a soft kiss on the knuckles. Danielle's chest tightened.

"I know nothing of witchcraft." Her voice was musical. "And your stepsister Stacia is host to a queen, which gives her higher standing than yourself, even if your claim is an honest one. She tells me Armand followed her of his own accord." Long fingers stroked the prince's arm. "Over time, Armand has come to appreciate my hospitality."

Danielle's hand was halfway to her sword before she caught herself. No doubt that was precisely what the Duchess wanted. If Danielle attacked, the Duchess would be within her rights to defend herself.

"Do you know this girl, Armand?" the Duchess asked.

Armand pursed his lips. His hair was longer than the last time Danielle had seen him, giving him a scruffy, wild look. His skin had paled, and his movements were listless. Danielle searched for any sign of recognition on that stubbled face.

Armand didn't have the keenest eyesight. Why else had he needed to bring along Danielle's forgotten slipper to confirm her identity, after the ball? But surely he had to know her now.

"I believe so," Armand said slowly. His next words crushed any hope Danielle might have felt. "Weren't you a servant at my palace, once?"

Brahkop chuckled. The Duchess turned back to Danielle.

Danielle pointed to Brahkop. "My stepsister may host a queen, but he is nothing but an exile, banished from both Fairytown and Lorindar. Demand the truth from him." She smiled at Brahkop. "You wouldn't dare lie to the Duchess, would you?"

Brahkop snarled and moved toward Danielle.

"Well, Brahkop?" The Duchess' soft words stopped the troll dead. A predatory grin played at her lips. She appeared to be enjoying this confrontation. "How do you answer?"

Brahkop said nothing. As Danielle had hoped, he seemed unable or unwilling to lie to the Duchess. But the contract he had made with Stacia and Charlotte bound him to silence.

Faint lines creased the Duchess' forehead. "Brahkop the exile, you are here as the husband of my guest, on my sufferance. I would be greatly displeased to find you have abused that hospitality."

"Never, Your Grace." Apparently Danielle had

guessed the right title after all. Brahkop turned to face the Duchess. "This woman assaulted me in my home and ordered my shop destroyed. She was born a commoner, and sought to gain the hand of the prince through magic and deceit."

The Duchess looked at Danielle. "Attacking one of our people is frowned upon, child. Even a casteless exile like him."

"Grant me one kiss," Danielle said. "Let me break the spell on Armand, and he will tell you himself."

"No!" Brahkop started to move toward her, then froze.

"Oops," whispered Talia.

"No?" The Duchess' voice was soft, but the unspoken threat in that single syllable made Danielle shiver. "You forget yourself, troll."

"Forgive me, Your Grace." Brahkop bowed low. "I meant—"

"Your stepsisters are human," the Duchess said, turning her back on Brahkop. "As is the prince. The treaty clearly prohibits me from interfering in human affairs." She glided toward the nearest staircase. "Therefore, I must leave you to settle matters among yourselves."

As she climbed the steps, a shadow broke away from the wall. A slender, taller version of the darklings moved to follow. An older darkling, perhaps? Where the children were wild and uncontrolled, this one moved with the easy grace of a snake. Had Danielle actually tried to attack the Duchess, he would have killed her before she knew he was there.

Talia's breath tickled her neck. "Brahkop won't move until the Duchess is gone. Once she's out of sight, get to the prince. You have to break the spell. I'll deal with the walking hairball."

Armand started to follow the Duchess. She glanced down at him and waved. "Stay there, darling." She plucked one of the blossoms from the railing and brought it to her nose. With a thin smile, she turned to Danielle. "If you've made it this far, I suppose that means your stepsister Stacia is dead."

She disappeared up the stairs before Danielle could answer.

"Stacia . . . dead?" Armand stepped away from the table, clearly shaken by the Duchess' words. "I loved her, once." His fingers brushed the hilt of his sword.

"Stacia's alive," Danielle said. At least, she had been the last time Danielle saw her. She moved toward Armand, keeping her hands away from her weapon. This was her husband. He loved her. No magic could destroy that. "Don't you remember me, Armand?"

Brahkop answered first. "What kind of love potion would it be if the subject kept his love for someone else? His past is nothing but a faint dream to him, girl. I could carve you up for a snack and he wouldn't stop me. He'd probably even pass the gravy when I asked."

"Don't you ever shut up?" Talia asked. She centered her crossbow on the troll's face and pulled the trigger.

The bolt sank into the troll's hair, then dropped to the ground. The thick troll hair was as good as armor. Brahkop laughed. "Is that goblin toy the best you can do, girl?"

Talia dropped the crossbow and bounded onto the table. Dropping low to avoid the tendrils of Brahkop's hair, she rolled to the end and grabbed the knife the Duchess had been using to carve her meat. The crystal handle shone as she tossed the knife from one hand to the other, testing its weight. "Small and poorly balanced, but it's still a fairy blade." She grabbed a fork in her other hand.

"Armand, they've come to take you from the Duchess!" Brahkop shouted.

Armand moved before Danielle could stop him. He crouched and drove his shoulder into her side, knocking her down. With Danielle out of the way, he drew his sword and lunged at Talia.

She sidestepped, jumping down on the opposite side of the table. That brought her within range of Brahkop. The troll's hair writhed like a hundred silver tentacles, all reaching for Talia.

The knife flashed, and several ropes of hair fell, separating into fine strands that blew across the floor. Talia grinned. "I like this knife."

Armand climbed onto the table, preparing to leap at Talia from behind.

"Armand, wait," Danielle said. "I'm carrying our son."

He turned so fast he stepped in Brahkop's plate. "My . . . my son?"

"*Our* son. The future king of Lorindar." She smiled and touched her belly. "Give me your hand. You might be able to feel him kicking." The baby wasn't moving at the moment, but she only needed to get close enough for one good kiss.

"How is that possible?"

"You mean you don't know?" Danielle tilted her head, trying to duplicate Snow's flirtatious smile. "You weren't this confused on our wedding night."

Armand flushed, but before he could respond, a thunderous crash made them both jump. Brahkop had hurled a chair at Talia. Fragments of that chair now littered the floor. Talia darted in, slicing away more of the troll's hair, but she couldn't get close enough to hit Brahkop himself.

"Please trust me," said Danielle. "You searched half the city to find me. My stepsisters tried to deceive you. My stepmother locked me away. But you still found me."

Armand looked toward the stairs the Duchess had taken, and the longing on his face hurt more than anything Danielle's stepsisters had ever done to her. But she kept herself calm, even managing a shaky smile. This wasn't his fault. He couldn't help himself. "You might not remember me, but you'll know your son." She reached for him.

"Don't believe her, Your Highness," shouted Brahkop. "Their companion is a witch who means to murder Stacia, and the Duchess as well."

"Liar!" said Danielle, but it was too late. Armand leaped away, raising his sword.

Talia snatched a broken chair leg and hurled it at Brahkop's face. He blocked, but Talia was already moving. She rolled along the ground, slicing a deep gash in Brahkop's leg, then scrambled aside before he could reach her.

And then Armand was attacking, and Danielle needed all of her concentration just to stay alive. She scrambled back, drawing her own sword as Armand lunged again. The glass blade rang like a bell as she knocked Armand's aside.

He thrust again, the tip of his blade ducking easily beneath Danielle's sword to jab her shoulder.

Pain ripped through her arm. She nearly dropped her sword. Armand hesitated, giving her the chance to back away. Blood darkened her sleeve, and a wave of dizziness made her stumble.

"Relax, Princess," Talia shouted. "Don't spill the wine."

Danielle nodded, trying to recall Talia's training. Blade raised, shoulders loose. Back straight, as though she was carrying a tray. Keep the knees bent, and—

Armand's next attack almost tore the sword from her hand. The wood inlaid in the handle grew rough, digging into her palm to help her keep her grip. She barely managed to swing the blade up to block a follow-up that would have slashed her throat.

There was too much to remember. She needed far more training before the movements would become automatic, the way Talia's were. Danielle staggered back, her parries growing wilder as she tried to keep up with Armand's attacks. Her own sword was sharper and lighter than any metal blade, but there were limits to what magic could do against a trained swordsman like Armand. Any moment now, he would get past her guard, and she would die upon her own husband's sword.

"Armand, please," she begged.

His blade beat hers aside, then sliced a bloody line across her thigh. "I won't let you hurt her," he said.

Danielle fell. Curse that flea-bitten mop of a troll, anyway. Brahkop had known precisely how to provoke Armand. She rolled beneath the table, barely avoiding another strike. Armand had always been so protective. Enchanted or not, he was still the same Armand, determined to defend those he loved.

He's still Armand. Danielle dropped her sword. Fear made her tremble as she crawled out, her hands raised.

"Danielle!" Talia spun and raised her knife, ready to throw.

"Talia, don't!" Danielle shouted. Talia didn't understand. She was going to kill Armand to save her.

Talia hesitated, and in that instant, Brahkop caught her. Ropes of hair snapped around her arm, and Danielle heard bone snap. Brahkop flung Talia across the room.

Danielle wrenched her attention back to Armand. "I yield," she said, kneeling. "You win."

Armand didn't speak.

"I know you," whispered Danielle. She held her

injured arm, trying to slow the blood. "I'm unarmed. Helpless. You won't kill me." She raised her chin. "I love you."

"I almost believe you when you say that." Armand grabbed Danielle's good arm and hauled her to her feet.

"Forgive me," whispered Danielle. She whimpered as she shifted her weight onto her wounded leg, then smashed her knee into Armand's groin. His sword clattered to the ground as he doubled over. Danielle grabbed the back of his robe and pulled him forward. Armand's forehead struck the floor, and he collapsed, moaning.

Pain flared in her arm as she struggled to roll him over. Blood dripped down to her elbow, but she didn't stop until he lay flat on his back. Sweat and tears stung her eyes. "I'm sorry," she said, straddling the prince. Before he could react, she leaned down and kissed him on the lips.

She wasn't sure what to expect. She imagined a rainbow of light bathing them both as the spell dissolved, and the sudden passion of Armand's return embrace. Or a newfound clarity in his eyes as her kiss drove the clouds from his mind.

Armand passed out.

"I almost think I should feel insulted." Danielle crawled away to retrieve her sword.

On the other side of the room, Talia had retreated halfway up the stairs. She had tucked the knife through her belt and held the Duchess' fork in her left hand. Her right arm hung limp at her side. Danielle could see bloody stripes where the troll's attack had torn the skin.

Brahkop pursued, his hair lashing over the railing to rip her apart.

Talia twisted to one side, then slammed the fork

down, pinning a lock of hair to the railing. She raced down the stairs.

She was almost fast enough. She would have been if not for the dark smear of troll blood at the base of the steps. Her foot slipped out from beneath her.

Brahkop's hand shot out, but his hair was still pinned, yanking him back before he could reach. His hair reared back to strike.

Quick as a cat, Talia drew her knife and threw. Danielle saw only a streak of silver, and then the ornately carved ivory hilt was protruding from Brahkop's throat.

The troll stumbled back, falling against the railing. He reached for the knife.

"Bad idea," said Talia.

Brahkop ripped the knife free. Before, blood had only trickled from the wound. But without the blade to staunch the flow, blood poured forth, darkening Brahkop's hair and dripping to the floor.

He struggled to speak. The gurgling sound was almost unintelligible. Almost.

Danielle averted her eyes as Brahkop whispered Stacia's name. And then his head slumped, and he was gone.

CHAPTER 15

❄

THE SILENCE THAT FOLLOWED Brahkop's death was, in many ways, more frightening than the previous clamor of battle. Danielle clutched her sword, peering up both staircases for any sign of the Duchess or her darkling servant.

Talia grabbed a round napkin of lace-rimmed satin from the table and pressed it to the wound in Danielle's arm. She worked one-handed, keeping her broken arm close to her body. "Hold this, and press hard. Is the prince—"

"He's alive," said Danielle. Their voices sounded so loud. She could hear nothing beyond the walls. Had Snow finished her battle with Stacia?

"Good." Talia used a second napkin to knot the first into place, then peered down at Armand. "How did you manage that?"

Danielle touched Armand's cheek. Blood matted his hair where his forehead had struck the floor, but his breathing was steady. His face was warm and still flushed from their fight.

"He passed out when I broke the spell," Danielle said, dodging the real question. She didn't think Armand would appreciate others knowing exactly how his wife had beaten him. "Do you know how to get out of here? We have to find Snow."

"Not yet." Talia checked Danielle's leg. "As soon as we get back, I'm teaching you to parry." More napkins soon covered Danielle's thigh. "Can you walk?"

"I think so."

Talia turned around. "No doors. You check that staircase. I'll check this one." She paused briefly by the table.

Danielle frowned when she saw what Talia was doing. "Tell me you're not stealing the Duchess' dinnerware."

Talia pointed to Brahkop. "We don't all have enchanted swords, Princess. I take what weapons I can get."

"You took the spoons, too."

Talia shrugged. "Old habits." She headed for the stairs.

Danielle did the same on the other side. As she reached the railing, a choked gasp made her whirl. Stacia stood beside Brahkop's body.

Danielle moved first, but Talia was faster, throwing one of her stolen knives at Stacia's head. An unseen force slapped the knife aside, sending it clattering to the ground.

Stacia barely noticed. All of her attention was on Brahkop. She reached for the troll, but her hand stopped before touching his face. She seemed frozen.

The battle outside the tower had taken its toll on Stacia. Her gown was torn, much of it burned away. Both sleeves were gone, and the skin of her right arm was red and blistered. A series of old scabs and scars marked her left arm where she had drawn blood for various spells. The most recent appeared red and inflamed. The poison on Stacia's knife might not have killed her, but it was clearly having an effect.

No matter how bad she looked, she was still alive.
Danielle tried not to think about what that meant.

"Where is Snow?" Talia jumped over the railing
and drew another knife.

Stacia didn't seem to hear. She wiped her eyes. "I'm
sorry, Brahkop," she whispered. "I heard your call. I
tried to come. . . ." She shuddered. "But Rose
wouldn't let me. She wanted me to keep fighting. I
came as soon as I regained control."

For a moment, Danielle felt pity. Stacia's grief
transformed her from a murderous witch to a young
child, ignored by her own mother, degraded by her
beautiful sister, taking out her pain on the only person
in the world lower than herself: Danielle.

Stacia brushed her sweaty hair back and turned to
Danielle. Tear streaks marked the soot and blood on
her face. "I loved him."

"I know." Danielle tilted her head toward Armand.
"And I love him. Stacia, tell me what happened to
Snow."

Stacia shook her head. "We were able to take control of one of her dwarves and turn it against your
witch friend. It threw her down into the lake. She
might have survived, I don't know. It was only when
she fell that Rose's anger broke enough for me to
answer Brahkop's call."

Talia threw her second knife. The spinning blade
slowed as it neared Stacia, stopping to hover in front
of her chest. A flick of Stacia's fingers sent the knife
spinning back toward Talia, faster than Danielle's eyes
could follow.

Talia was just as fast. Her hand swept up, and with
a muffled clink, the knife flew to one side. Talia adjusted her grip on the purloined spoon she had used
to block the knife. She shot a grim smile toward Danielle as she switched the spoon for her whip. "See?"

"So you found someone to restore your fairy gifts,"

said Stacia. "That must be how you killed my husband."

"Stacia, please don't do this." Danielle moved to the side, trying to put Stacia between herself and Talia. Before Danielle had taken more than a few steps, Stacia snapped her fingers.

The whip in Talia's hand uncoiled, lashing around Talia's throat.

Danielle raised her sword and moved closer. "Let her go!"

"I never should have trusted Charlotte to kill you," Stacia said. *"Give me your weapon."*

Danielle fought to hold on, but her fingers obeyed Stacia's will. She slowed to a walk, reversing her grip on the sword. Stacia reached out.

Stacia hadn't ordered her to surrender. As Stacia's hand closed over the hilt, Danielle punched her in the throat. She grabbed Stacia's wrist in both hands, trying to wrench the sword away.

Stacia pulled her knife with her free hand, cutting a shallow line across Danielle's stomach. Danielle backed away, collapsing as her wounded leg gave out.

"Idiot! I need that child." The voice was Stacia's, but the inflection was Rose's.

"Fight her, Stacia." Danielle started to crawl toward Talia. Talia's face was dark. She was using another knife to try to cut the whip. The handle lay on the floor, but the individual strands continued to strangle her.

"They killed Brahkop!" Stacia shouted.

"And they will be punished."

Danielle shivered. Both voices came from Stacia's mouth, one full of pain and grief, the other cold and hateful. She could see blood in Stacia's hand where she held Danielle's sword. As before, the weapon fought to escape Stacia's grasp. But this time, Stacia didn't seem to notice.

"Princess," Talia wheezed. She dropped to her knees. Her eyes flicked toward Stacia. She placed her knife on the floor and slid it toward Danielle.

"Stacia, you don't have to listen to her," said Danielle. She grabbed the knife. Stacia had never defied her own mother, and Rose was a far more terrifying master. But grief and anger had given Stacia strength. Danielle could see her fighting to throw off Rose's control.

To one side, Talia shook her head. *Use the knife*, she mouthed, and pantomimed stabbing Stacia.

Stacia smiled and walked toward Danielle. She raised Danielle's sword. Now it was Rose's turn to fight for control. "You can't. We need the child."

Stacia shook her head. "*You* need the child. I need to avenge my husband."

"Don't do this, Stacia." Danielle turned sideways, keeping the knife pointed at her stepsister. "I don't want to fight you."

"I loved him." Stacia swung.

Danielle tried to duck, but she wasn't fast enough. The blow felt like a heavy branch slamming into her neck. Danielle heard the unmistakable sound of breaking glass. She fell to the floor, grabbing her neck where the sword had struck. She felt bruised, but there was no blood.

Stacia backed away, staring at the broken sword. The glass blade had snapped close to the hilt. The broken blade had landed by Danielle's leg.

Crystalline splinters protruded from Stacia's forearm. Blood was already trickling down over her hand.

Stacia screamed and flung the hilt away. She clutched her knife in both hands and rushed at Danielle.

Danielle grabbed the broken blade and thrust the tip into her stepsister's stomach.

Behind her, Talia gasped for air as the strands of

the whip fell away. Stacia stumbled back. She grabbed the broken blade to pull it free, but only managed to cut her hands on the bloody glass.

"I'm sorry," Danielle said. Despite all of the torments Stacia and Charlotte had inflicted on her over the years, she felt only emptiness as she watched Stacia stumble. The cut on Danielle's stomach stung as she crawled toward her stepsister. She prayed Talia was right, that the poison on Stacia's knife wasn't enough to kill.

"Murderer," whispered Stacia. "Your mother would be so proud."

"Go on, then. Finish her." The words sounded distant and hollow, as if heard through a long corridor.

The ghost of Snow's mother stood behind her, shaking her head. Like the darklings, Rose seemed untouched by the light. But where the darklings absorbed the light, Rose simply ignored it. She was a woman always in shade, despite the bright flames from the chandelier overhead. Nor did she cast any shadow on the ground.

She was beautiful, with Snow's full lips and round cheeks, and dark eyes that shone like the sea at night. Slender and graceful, she circled Danielle and Stacia. A smell like burning meat wafted from her body, and Danielle wrinkled her nose.

Rose wore a simple gray gown, but the ragged hem was burned away. Flecks of orange danced along the bottom edge as she moved. Her feet were charred, looking more like burned firewood than anything human. Danielle remembered what Talia had said, how Snow's dwarves had tortured Rose before they killed her.

"Get back, Princess." Talia threw one of the Duchess' knives. It passed right through Rose's chest.

"I'm dead, remember?" Rose said, sounding annoyed. "You can't hurt me. Of course, you can't stop

me either." She strode toward Danielle, one hand
stretching toward her stomach.

Danielle crawled away. Talia moved to stand between her and the ghost, though there was nothing
she could do to protect Danielle.

"*I* can stop you." On the far side of the room, Snow
limped up the staircase, followed by the flaming dwarf.
A wash of heat preceded the dwarf's attack as he flew
across the room toward Rose.

The ghost clapped her hands. When she drew them
apart, a shadowy oval hovered between her palms. An
ebony frame inlaid with gold circled a dark mirror. As
the dwarf charged, his flaming reflection grew larger.
But the reflection was dimmer. The flames flickered
like a lantern whose wick had run dry. As the dwarf
sprang, Rose reached *through* the mirror. Her fingers
clamped around the dwarf's neck, and with no appar-
ent effort, drew him into the mirror. The mirror dissolved into smoke, taking the dwarf with it.

"That makes six of your seven dwarves." Rose
strode around the edge of the room, leaving ashen
prints that dissolved into smoke. "You've done quite
well, considering your lack of training. A mother could
be proud. But I've faced your demons before. Did you
really believe I wouldn't have prepared for them?"

Danielle and Talia exchanged glances. Without a
word, they moved to stand on either side of Snow.

"The dwarves can't touch her without crossing into
the realm of the dead," Snow whispered. "Without
Stacia, she's weaker, but—"

"What will you do with the last dwarf?" asked
Rose. "Your embodiment of magic. Will you send her
forth to fight me, or shall I rip her from you? I'll be
sure to put her power to good use." She smiled. "As
for you, Princess Danielle, it's a shame your son is
still so weak. If you'd given me and my darklings more
time, I might have been able to spare you. Instead,

I'm left with no choice but to take your body until he's ready."

Snow stiffened. "Don't believe her. She can't take an unwilling host."

Rose shook her head, an expression of mock-sadness on her shadowed face. "Not without your help, Daughter. When Stacia died, I thought I'd have to settle for Charlotte. But we've already seen that I can turn your dwarves to my use. That last dwarf, magic incarnate, should be more than strong enough to drive your friend from her own body." She smiled at Danielle. "If you're fortunate, the tattered remnants of your spirit might still live on in your body once I'm finished with it."

Danielle and Talia both looked at Snow. "Is that true?" Danielle whispered. "Can she possess me like she did Stacia?"

"Technically . . . yes." Snow's hand shook as she pointed at Rose. "Destroy her."

The room seemed to tilt and wobble. The air around Snow rippled, and a young girl surged from Snow's body. The final dwarf had the pale, round face of a child. Long black hair draped down her back like a cape. She could have been a younger incarnation of Snow.

The girl's bare feet slapped against the floor as she ran toward Rose. Plates and goblets shattered on the table as she passed. The flames in the chandelier flashed through every color of the rainbow while bits of crystal tore free and shot through the air to explode against the walls. One of the chairs began to smolder, while another sprouted leaves.

A sudden mania ran through Danielle's blood, bubbling up in her chest until she had to fight to keep from giggling or screaming. The room seemed to shift, as if the child was a vortex sucking her in.

Snow caught her arm. "I told you magic was the

most dangerous of the dwarves." She raised her chin.
"I promise I won't let my mother hurt you."

Danielle nodded. "I know."

The flames detached from the chandelier and
rushed toward Rose, tearing through her spectral
form. She stumbled back with each assault. The flames
returned again, fainter than before, but still enough to
drive Rose into the wall.

The third time, Rose managed to summon a small,
round mirror. The flames struck the mirror and disappeared. Then the mirror itself began to bubble, like
liquid boiling over a fire.

"Come to me, my child," Rose said, her voice tight
and strained. The girl stepped back. With the candles
extinguished, the only illumination came from the
burning chair at the table. The darkness made Rose
seem more solid.

The dwarf attacked again, leaping directly at the
mirror to wrest it from Rose's hands. Rose staggered
back, but didn't fall. Slowly, the darkness of the mirror
began to seep through the dwarf, drawing her into
that black pool.

Snow reached down and pulled out the knife at
her hip.

"Defiant to the last," said Rose. "Your father had
the same stubborn streak. Your last dwarf has failed,
and your mirrors are broken. You've lost, Daughter."

"I didn't expect her to defeat you, Mother," said
Snow. Her thumb moved across the delicate snowflake
engraving at the center of the knife's crossguard. She
flicked her thumb, and the snowflake swiveled aside,
revealing a small, perfectly polished mirror. "Only to
weaken and hold you."

Rose's mouth opened as she spied the tiny mirror.
She started to reach for Snow, but the mirror in her
hand lurched and buckled like a thing alive, forcing
her to grab it with both hands.

Snow held the knife flat against her heart, her hands clasped like she was praying. "Mirror, mirror, at my breast."

"Wait," Rose shouted. She wrestled the mirror around, trying to put it between herself and Snow. "Ermillina, *stop!*"

"Bring this ghost eternal rest." Snow threw her knife.

The mirror in the hilt flashed like sunlight as it left Snow's hand. The throw was weak, but the knife seemed to gain strength as it flew, moving faster and faster like an eagle diving for its prey. The blade hit Rose's dark mirror, which shattered, taking the final dwarf with it. The fragments dissipated before they hit the floor.

Rose grunted. Snow's knife protruded from the center of her chest.

"Good-bye, Mother," said Snow.

Moments later, Rose was gone. The knife clinked to the floor. Snow hurried to reclaim it, pushing the delicate snowflake back over the mirror. She drew a deep, slow breath, then turned back to Danielle and Talia. "I told you I wouldn't let her hurt you."

"What happened, Snow?" Talia asked, reaching out to touch Snow's hair. Strands of silver ran through Snow's glossy black locks. Danielle could see faint lines around the corners of Snow's eyes as well.

Snow pulled a lock of hair over her eyes, nearly cross-eyed as she studied it. "The dwarves took their price."

"They were supposed to take it from all three of us," Danielle said.

Snow shrugged. "I'm the one who summoned them."

"You knew." Talia's voice was cold.

"Of course I knew, silly." She gave Talia a quick hug. "Just like I knew you'd keep arguing with me,

trying to find another way, and we didn't have time.
But I love you both for offering." She stepped back
and waved at Armand. "We're alive. Armand is free.
Aren't you the one who's always saying we do what
we have to do? Now, can someone tell me why the
prince is asleep on the floor?"

"He tried to fight me," Danielle said. "I think I
broke the curse, but he hasn't woken up yet."

Snow placed her fingers over Armand's chest. "The
love spell is gone. There may be some side effects for
the next few days, though."

Danielle swallowed. "What do you mean?"

"That spell stifled his affection for you," Snow said.
She grinned. "Dam a river, and the pressure builds.
With the spell gone . . . let's just say I'll need some
extra strong thread to stitch your wounds, given what
you'll be doing."

"Oh." Despite everything, Danielle found herself
smiling in return. *"Oh."*

Snow cast several minor enchantments over Armand,
none of which roused him from his slumber. "He's
going to have to sleep it off," Snow decided. She approached Talia. "Let me see that arm."

While Snow used several pieces of a broken chair
to bind a makeshift splint around Talia's arm, Danielle
crossed the room and knelt in front of Stacia's body.
She had fallen beside Brahkop. Troll and human
blood pooled together, a gruesome, sticky mess of red
and black.

Stacia had truly loved him. "I'm glad you found
one another." The broken blade slid easily from her
stepsister's body. Danielle set it on the floor with the
hilt of her sword.

Movement in the shadows on the stairs made her
jump. The Duchess smiled as she followed her dark-

ling bodyguard down the steps. "Stacia played a dangerous game."

Both Talia and Snow started to cross the room. The Duchess waved her hand. "I wish to speak with Princess Danielle."

Princess. Danielle nodded to her friends. She was safe now.

"Great rewards require great risks," the Duchess went on. Danielle wondered if she was talking about Stacia or herself. "She was a strong, resourceful, intelligent, and determined young woman. More like you than her own sister, in truth."

Danielle shook her head. "They both tried to murder me. They used magic and deceit to take Armand. They—"

"Yes, yes, you're a nice girl and they were evil," said the Duchess, a touch of impatience in her voice. "They tried to steal your man. You simply slaughtered my servants, killed several of my guests in my own dining room, ripped one of my bridges from its mooring, terrorized my poor goblins, and interrupted my dinner."

On the other side of the table, Snow cleared her throat. "Actually, *I* did most of the slaughtering, Your Grace."

The Duchess ignored her. She glanced at the chandelier, and the candles flickered to life. A pair of darklings scurried out to begin clearing the debris from the floor. "You killed several of my children as well." This time, the threat in her voice was clear.

"Your children?" Danielle repeated, trying to hide her revulsion.

"Not in the same fashion as your own son. But the darklings are mine. That which I can create, I can also destroy. They know that, and they obey me." She waved a hand. "Fortunately, midsummer will be here soon, and I will be able to restore what you've taken from me."

"I had no choice," said Danielle. "I came to save my husband. I killed her to protect my son."

"And you took her husband in the process. There's an almost fairylike justice to it." She stepped over Armand and walked toward the table. "Once this mess is cleaned, would you care to join me for dinner, Princess? We were about to begin the main course when you and your companion . . . arrived. Griffin tongues roasted over dragon fire, glazed with honeysuckle sauce. My own recipe, and quite good."

"Stacia wasn't the only one playing a game, Your Grace," said Danielle.

"What are you doing?" Snow whispered. Danielle ignored her, all of her attention on the Duchess.

The Duchess turned around, spreading her fingers on the edge of the table. "Of course, Queen Rose played a role as well. A powerful witch, to postpone death for so long. I wish I'd known her while she lived."

"You came so close to usurping the fairy queen, years ago," said Danielle. "When the king took you as his slave, you escaped him as well. Yet I'm to believe such a master of deception was fooled by my stepsisters? By a pair of young, spoiled humans? How humiliating that must be for you."

If she hadn't been watching so closely, Danielle would have missed the slight stiffening of the Duchess' features. The Duchess straightened her robe, brushing away imaginary specks. "Fairies and humans have always played at such games, child. This time, your stepsisters and Queen Rose were the losers."

The terseness in her words told Danielle she had scored a point. Whether or not that was a good thing was impossible to say.

"Actually, Charlotte is still alive," said Danielle.

The Duchess blinked, the only sign of surprise. "I see."

"Once we're gone . . ." Danielle glanced at Talia. Charlotte had already tried to murder Danielle, as well as her unborn child. She had helped kidnap and enchant Armand. She and Stacia had destroyed the hazel tree which held her mother's spirit.

Talia nodded once. Danielle would be well within her rights to have her stepsister imprisoned, or even executed.

"Yes?" asked the Duchess.

"Please give her whatever she needs, then send her on her way," said Danielle.

Talia cleared her throat. "Princess, your stepsister is still a danger. You can't—"

"I can," Danielle said. "Charlotte is alone for the first time in her life. My birds killed her mother. I killed her sister." She turned to Snow. "When we get home, I want you to use your mirror. Charlotte is a poor witch. Without Rose and Stacia, I doubt she has the power to hide from you. You should have no trouble casting a spell to tell us if she ever comes within a hundred paces of the palace."

Snow nodded.

"That won't stop her from sending someone else to kill you," Talia muttered.

"No, it won't." Danielle smiled. "That's why I have you." She faced the Duchess. "Please tell my stepsister . . . tell her to leave Lorindar. If I ever see her again, I'll have her locked away for the rest of her days. Tell her she's free, and to find her own life."

The Duchess bowed her head. "As you wish, Your Highness. And for yourselves, I would be happy to provide an escort to guide you down to my borders. I'm afraid it wouldn't be prudent for my people to lead you all the way to the hedge, but—"

"Don't worry about it," said Snow. She had flipped

open the mirror in her knife, and was studying the
left side of her face. She tugged on a strand of gray
and pursed her lips. "Once we're outside, I can have
Arlorran summon us back."

"Thank you," said Danielle. She looked up into the
Duchess' cool eyes. "I'll be sure to remember everything you've done for me once I'm queen."

"Yes." The Duchess glanced at Stacia's body, then
back at Danielle. "So alike," she whispered.

Danielle ignored her, limping over to pick up the
broken pieces of her sword.

"When you wish to contact me, simply call me three
times," the Duchess said.

"Call you *what*?" Talia muttered.

Danielle brought her sword to Armand. She removed his sword belt and slid the blade into his scabbard. "I can't imagine that time will ever come."

"Oh, but it will." The amusement in the Duchess'
voice was enough to make Danielle turn around.

"What do you mean?"

"I'm talking about your son," said the Duchess with
mock-surprise. "Only a few months along, and already
he has been immersed in dark enchantments. Black
witchcraft, not to mention the fairy magic of my darkling children." She spread her hands. "Who knows
how that might affect a developing babe?"

Danielle spun. "How dare—"

Talia caught Danielle's arm. Strong fingers dug into
her elbow. "Act against her, in her own palace, and
she owns you," Talia whispered.

Danielle forced a stiff nod. "Thank you." She drew
a deep breath, then glanced at Talia, who loosened
her grip. "Which staircase will lead us from your
tower, Your Grace?"

"Either, if I so wish it," said the Duchess. "One last
thing, my dears, before you leave me. My people value

their privacy. I trust you'll keep my humble home a secret."

"Not from Beatrice," Danielle said. "And *I* trust you will treat my stepsister well until she leaves here, and that neither you nor any of your people will trouble us again."

The Duchess gave a grudging nod. " 'Trouble' is such a vague word, Princess. But you have my word that none of mine will harm you."

As promised, the Duchess' staircase brought them out at the base of the tower, where glowing waves lapped a beach of smooth black stones. The stagnant smell of salt water made her grimace, and she could hear the roar of the Duchess' waterfall behind her.

Talia and Snow had rigged a crude travois from a pair of goblin spears and one of Stacia's cloaks. With Stacia dead, the Duchess had offered her belongings to Danielle. It was a blatant attempt to earn her favor, one Danielle would have refused if there had been any other way to transport her husband out of the cavern. She would dispose of Stacia's things as soon as Armand was able to walk on his own.

Between Danielle's injuries and Talia's broken arm, Snow was the one stuck pulling Armand's weight along behind her. A pair of belts at the back of the travois allowed Talia to steady Armand's descent down the steps.

"You're sure he's going to recover?" Danielle asked. He was so pale. She knelt and held her palm above his mouth, needing to feel the warmth of his breath.

"As sure as I was the last four times you asked." Snow set the prince down and stretched. She drew her knife and uncovered the mirror, trying again to contact Queen Beatrice.

Danielle stepped away to rest against the damp stone of the tower wall. As short as the Duchess' staircase was, she had barely managed to keep up with the others. Between her wounded leg and the extra weight of pregnancy, she felt completely crippled. She couldn't even help with her husband, and the sight of the carved stone bridge leading out over the lake made her want to weep.

"Any luck?" asked Talia.

"Not yet." Snow slammed the knife back into its sheath. Something about the Duchess' cavern blocked her from reaching Beatrice. It made sense, really. If the Duchess wanted to keep this place a secret, she wouldn't allow people to use magic to peer into her domain.

"I'm sorry about your sword, Danielle," said Talia. "I can talk to the smith at the palace, see about having a new one forged for you. It won't be as light, but—"

"Thank you, but I'll keep this one." Danielle touched the pommel, smiling at the faint warmth that greeted her fingers. She had used Talia's whip to tie the hilt into place, as the broken blade wasn't long enough to hold it in the scabbard.

Talia frowned. "I don't understand. The sword broke when Stacia attacked you."

"I used the broken blade to stab Stacia." Danielle held up her hand, showing the unbroken skin of her palm. "If the magic had been destroyed, I would be short several fingers. Whatever power my mother wove into the glass is still there. I'll take the pieces to my father's workshop. I'll need new tools, but I'm sure I'll be able to repair it, with Snow's help."

"Good. Once you and the sword are both repaired, I'll see what I can do about teaching you to use it. I saw you fighting Armand. That was disgraceful, Princess." A faint smile belied the harshness of her words.

"I won, didn't I?"

Talia's smile grew. "Do you need more time to rest?"

Danielle craned her head to study the tower. On the walls, dwarves and darklings scurried about, repairing the damage Snow and her mother had caused. Already they had lowered chains to haul the broken segment of walkway back into place. "No. The sooner we're out of here, the happier I'll be."

Talia pointed toward a patch of darkness on the far side of the bridge. "That tunnel should lead us out to the water. Assuming the Duchess hasn't planned any surprises."

"The Duchess gave her word," Danielle said, limping toward the bridge. "She won't stop us from leaving." As an afterthought, she added, "Unless she decides she wants her silverware back."

"Her silverware?" Snow frowned. *"Talia?"*

Talia glared at Danielle. "Tattletale."

Danielle gave her a quick smile before turning her attention back to walking. The bridge had no railing, and it would be too easy to fall.

"I don't trust her," said Talia. Dark shapes darted through the water as they crossed the bridge. "Fairy plots have too many layers. What are we missing?"

"What do you mean?" asked Snow.

"No matter how things turned out, the Duchess stood to benefit." Talia tugged the back of Armand's travois closer to the bridge's center. "If Stacia had borne Armand's child, the Duchess would have earned the favor of the future king of Lorindar. Then they discovered Danielle was pregnant and brought her here. In addition, she knew they planned to give her Armand, so she would have a human prince as a prize, and the whole time, she made certain no blame would cling to her. According to fairy law, we can't prove her guilty of a single crime. Nobody who plans so thoroughly would let us walk away after everything that's happened with nothing to show for it."

They were finally approaching the far side of the

bridge. Danielle could see the bottom of the lake rising to meet them. Water lapped the foot of the bridge, and they waded through shallow water until they were out of the lake.

There, Danielle rubbed her sweaty hands on her shirt, then flexed her fingers. "Snow, was the Duchess telling the truth about my son? Could all of that magic have hurt him?"

Snow set the travois down again and touched Danielle's stomach. "I don't know. The curse Stacia cast on you is broken. I can't find any trace on you or within you." The baby squirmed, and delight suffused Snow's face. "Hey, I felt that!"

Danielle's smile faded as she looked up at the tower. "Fairies think in the long term, Talia. Remember? The Duchess won't stop us because she wants me to return of my own volition, to ask for her help. She wants me in her debt."

Neither Snow nor Talia spoke, which only solidified Danielle's suspicions. And Danielle would do it. She already knew that much. If there was truly something wrong with her son, and if Snow or Trittibar or Arlorran couldn't help, Danielle would call the Duchess.

"Come on," said Talia. "We're getting close. At least, I think we are. I was rat-sized the last time I came through here."

As they walked, the blue light of the cavern slowly faded to darkness behind them, replaced by the warmth of the fairy suns. Danielle squinted, and her eyes teared at the sight of golden light streaming through tattered vines at the mouth of the cave. She stepped carefully. Sparkles of glass still shone on the cave floor, remnants of Snow's mirrors.

"Do you think Charlotte will be all right?" she asked.

Talia snorted. "Should I care?"

Charlotte had never been alone. Danielle wanted to feel sorry for her, but every time she tried, she remembered Charlotte's face, her words spewing spit and rage as she tried to force poison down Danielle's throat.

Maybe being on her own would force her to grow, to learn to take care of herself, but deep inside, Danielle doubted it. Far more likely she would leap into a bad bargain here in Fairytown and end up a slave. If not to the Duchess, then to the dwarves or the pixies or whatever guide happened to find her first.

Danielle started walking. She needed rest, but she needed even more to be free of this place. She hesitated only briefly at the curtain of vines, remembering the last time. But the vines didn't react as she stepped into the blinding light.

Her eyes took a long time to adjust, after so long in the darkness. The scrape of wood on stone told her the others were following. She kept one hand on the cave wall, listening to the water and feeling the warmth on her skin.

A deep groan made her smile. The instant he passed into the sunlight, Prince Armand began to stir. He yawned and rubbed his eyes, then tried to sit up.

Snow hastily set the travois on the ground. Armand jerked his head around, his eyes widening. He stared at Talia and Snow, then turned to Danielle.

She sat down beside him, carefully stretching her leg off to the side. "Are you . . . do you remember me?"

Armand reached out, his fingers touching her cheek and pushing back her hair. His hand trembled. "You're really here."

And then she was kissing him. A part of her was tentative, afraid that if she held him too close or kissed him too hard, he might disappear again.

She risked it. Exhausted and wounded, she still found the strength to pin him against the ground, her lips seeking his until she had driven all of the fear and desperation and loneliness away.

Armand matched her passion, his hand sliding up the back of her neck to hold her close, until finally Snow cleared her throat and said, "You know, I helped rescue you, too."

Danielle pulled back slightly and tried to catch her breath. She could have shoved Snow into the water for interrupting. Though it was probably best that she had. They were still on the border of the Duchess' lands, after all. This was hardly the place for such . . . celebration.

Armand's face was close enough for her to feel his breath on her lips. Breath which was coming far more quickly than before, she was pleased to note.

"I missed you," she said.

"So I noticed."

She smiled and sat up. "Also, the next time you try to take a trip without me, I'm going to have Talia chain you to the bedpost."

"I can help, too," Snow piped up.

Armand blushed. "I'm sorry. That wasn't very princely of me, was it? I just . . ." He glanced down at himself. Danielle wouldn't have thought it possible for his face to grow more flushed, but he managed. "Can somebody please tell me what it is I'm wearing? How did I get here?"

"How much do you remember?" asked Snow.

He frowned. "Snow, isn't it? You're one of my mother's personal attendants. How did you—"

"Armand, please," said Danielle.

"I was in Emrildale. I remember taking a drink at the tavern, and everything else is like a dream." His face grew even redder. "Your stepsister, Stacia. I remember . . . I kissed her, didn't I? Oh, Danielle. Forgive me, I don't know how—"

"Stacia and Charlotte cast a spell," Danielle said. "It wasn't your fault."

"We're in Fairytown," Talia added, wading back to the shore. "The river's clear."

"Talia was afraid the Duchess would arrange some kind of ambush," Snow said. She leaned toward the prince as though she were sharing state secrets. "Talia's a little paranoid sometimes."

Talia splashed her.

"The Duchess?" Armand asked.

"The woman who's been holding you for the past month," Danielle explained.

He plucked at his robe. "Whoever she is, she has abominable taste in clothes. What kind of woman—" He blinked and turned away. "Oh, damn. I kissed her, too, didn't I?"

"You were enchanted," said Danielle.

"Enchanted or not, it doesn't matter. Married less than a year, and already I've strayed. I—"

Danielle punched him on the arm. "That's enough," she snapped. "I did *not* fight my way past goblins and living shadows, not to mention my stepsisters and a dead witch, just so you could mope around feeling guilty." With that, she twisted her hand into the front of his robe and pulled him up for another kiss.

"I see," said Armand a while later, somewhat breathlessly. He looked more closely at Danielle's companions. "The three of you rescued me? Alone?"

"Your mother didn't think it would be a good idea to invade Fairytown," Danielle said.

Armand squinted at Talia. "I've seen you around the palace as well. Talia. How did you—"

"They're my friends," Danielle said. She waited for him to ask more, but his attention had gone to the bandages on her leg and arm.

"We fought," Armand said slowly. "You and I. I tried to kill—"

"But you didn't," Danielle interrupted. "It wasn't you."

Snow rolled her eyes and turned to Talia. "*Men*. How much longer are we going to wait for him to notice?"

Talia shrugged. "If you hadn't stopped them, he probably would have figured it out while they were tearing one another's clothes off."

"Talia!" Danielle didn't know whether to laugh or throw something.

"What does she mean?" Armand's eyes widened. He looked ready to fall over. Danielle caught his arms. His expression changed from guilt and confusion to pure joy. "I remember. You told me you were carrying my son?"

"That's right."

He wrapped his arms around her and laughed.

As Danielle kissed her husband again, she heard Snow and Talia whispering behind them.

"Touching as this all is, I'd really like to get out of here," Talia said.

"I did warn her he'd be eager." Metal scraped as Snow uncovered the mirror in her knife. "I should be able to get in touch with Queen Bea while they indulge themselves."

Armand broke away from the kiss, though he kept his face close enough for his breath to tickle Danielle's ear. "Did she just call my mother 'Queen Bea'?"

Danielle laughed and kissed him again.

"Hey, Princess!" Snow waved her knife in the air. "She wants to talk to you and Armand."

Leaning on Armand for support, Danielle walked over to take the knife from Snow's hand. She couldn't make out much detail in the tiny mirror, but the relief on Beatrice's face was impossible to miss.

"I knew you'd save him, Danielle," Beatrice said. "Even Trittibar had given up hope. He came to me the other day, saying that after so long, it was likely the three of you had fallen prey to the dangers of Fairytown." She wiped her eyes. "I'm afraid I threat-

ened to stuff him through a keyhole if he said another word."

Armand leaned over the knife. "Hello, Mother."

"Armand." Beatrice reached out to touch the mirror. Her voice broke with a sound that blended laughter and tears. "What have you done to your hair?"

"Tilt the mirror," Snow called out. "Let her see
the robe!"

Armand's hand closed over Danielle's, keeping the
mirror oriented toward their faces.

"I'm all right, Mother," said Armand. "Though I
can't imagine what people will say when they learn
how Cinderella had to ride off to rescue her prince."

Danielle grinned. "Well, it *was* my turn."

The queen's image turned back to Danielle. "Well
done, Princess Whiteshore."

Those four words, spoken with such simple gratitude, made Danielle's eyes water. She managed a
quick "Thank you," then handed the mirror to Armand and stepped away before the queen could see
her cry.

"You were right, you know," said Talia, coming to
Danielle's side.

"Right about what?"

Talia waved her arm at the cave behind them. "I'm
the one who wanted you to stay behind, remember?
I was ready to lock you up to keep you from getting
in my way." She shook her head. "You're stronger
than I gave you credit for. Stronger than I was."

Danielle bowed her head. "I had no choice. I had
to protect my family."

"I suppose Armand is a good man, for a prince.
And your son—"

Danielle touched Talia's arm. "*All* of my family."

Talia's retort died on her lips, speared by Danielle's
unwavering gaze. "Oh," she said, her voice barely a
whisper.

"My father is sending men from Pine Bay to escort us home," said Armand. "They should reach the edge of Fairytown by nightfall."

Home. Her throat tightened. The word was like the first rays of sun after an ocean storm.

Snow brought her knife to her mouth, whispered a few words, and smiled. "Hi, Arlorran! Did you miss us?"

Danielle was amazed the mirror didn't crack from the volume of Arlorran's shout. "Snow! How in the name of Tirgoth's third nipple did you escape? Where are you? Are your friends with you? Does the Duchess know you've—"

"Arlorran, stop!" Laughing, Snow shook the knife until Arlorran sputtered. Fluttering her lashes, she asked, "Would you mind summoning the four of us back to your place?"

"Did you say four? Don't tell me you actually found the poor bastard!"

Talia coughed, and even Snow looked a little worried by Arlorran's bluntness, but Armand only laughed. "If he can get us away from here, he can call me whatever he'd like."

"Gather close," Snow said. "Everyone needs to be touching. But don't get carried away," she added, giving Danielle a mock scowl.

Danielle did her best to obey. Holding hands aggravated the wound in her arm, so Armand gently slid an arm around her waist instead.

"You realize we still need to make our way from Arlorran's place back to the hedge," Talia pointed out.

Armand studied each of them in turn. "Somehow, I find myself feeling sorry for the fairy who tries to stop you."

Danielle kissed him, then stepped forward, tightening their circle. "Let's go home."

Jim Hines

The **Jig the Goblin** series

"Clever satire… Reminiscent of Terry Pratchett
and Robert Asprin at their best."
—*Romantic Times*

"If you've always kinda rooted for the little guy,
even maybe had a bit of a place in your heart for
Gollum, rather than the Boromirs and Gandalfs
of the world, pick up *Goblin Quest*."
—*The SF Site*

"This exciting adult fairy tale is filled with
adventure and action, but the keys to the fantasy
are Jig and the belief that the mythological creatures are real in the realm of Jim C. Hines."
—*Midwest Book Review*

"A rollicking ride, enjoyable from beginning to
end… Jim Hines has just become one of my
must-read authors." -—Julie E. Czerneda

GOBLIN QUEST	978-07564-0400-0
GOBLIN HERO	978-07564-0442-0
GOBLIN WAR	978-07564-0493-2

To Order Call: 1-800-788-6262
www.dawbooks.com

DAW 100